THE BLOODHOUNDS
OF BROADWAY
AND OTHER STORIES
BY DAMON RUNYON

THE BLOODHOUNDS OF BROADWAY AND OTHER STORIES BY DAMON RUNYON

Introduction by Tom Clark,
Author of
The World of Damon Runyon

WILLIAM MORROW AND COMPANY, INC.
New York   *1981*

This book is dedicated to the memory of the late Damon Runyon, his son Damon Runyon, Jr., and their good friend the late Walter Winchell, and to all the beneficiaries of the Runyon-Winchell Cancer Fund. We wish to give special acknowledgment to the following persons whose cooperation, by way of research, permissions, interviews, and unswerving perseverance, made this book possible: Damon Runyon III and his sister D'Ann McKibben, the children of Damon Runyon, Jr.; David P. Faulkner, Esq., Guardian of the Person and Estate of Mary Runyon McCann, daughter of Damon Runyon, and his law associate, R. Edward Tepe, Esq.; Raoul Lionel Felder, Executor for Damon Runyon, Jr., who, along with the above-mentioned persons, devoted hundreds of hours of his time to help bring this volume to publication; Sheldon Abend, President of the American Play Company, Inc., New York City, the literary agent for the Guardian of Mary Runyon McCann and for the children of Damon Runyon, Jr., who "rode herd" on this entire project.

Copyright © 1981 by American Play Company, Inc.

Library of Congress Cataloging in Publication Data

Runyon, Damon, 1880-1946.
  The bloodhounds of Broadway and other stories.

  "Morrow quill paperbacks."

  Contents: A very honorable guy—Madame La Gimp—Dark Dolores—Social error—[etc.]
  I. Title.
PS3535.U52A6 1981   813'.52   81-4390
ISBN 0-688-00725-2   AACR2
ISBN 0-688-00625-6 (pbk.)

Printed in the United States of America

3 4 5 6 7 8 9 10

BOOK DESIGN BY MICHAEL MAUCERI

See page 336, which constitutes an extension of this copyright page, for further copyright information.

Contents

Introduction

Damon Runyon's Broadway tales are ironic mini-comedies based on the American outlaw code. It is the old Code of the West, transposed to Manhattan and the twentieth century. To live outside the law you must be honest, the saying used to go. Runyon rearranges it to read: To live outside the law you must be an interesting character, and anyway, no one is more honest than he has to be.

Runyon had outlaw roots. "My father was a product of the six-gun West," his son wrote in a memoir. "At one time somewhere in his prowls as a youth he actually packed a six-gun." That was in Denver at the turn of the century, where Runyon cut his writing teeth in the style of the Western pioneer reporter—on shot glasses and shotguns.

Referring to the family background, Runyon himself once confided to his son, "We come from a long line of Huguenot horse thieves who were run out of France by posses." Damon may have been stretching the tale a little, as he was accustomed to doing. But the spirit of his remark sums up the Runyon lineage accurately.

Damon's paternal grandfather, William Renoyan, an itinerant printer, led a band of gold-seeking adventurers in a cross-country boat expedition in 1852. His design was to discover an inland waterway to California, but the party wound up stranded on the dry Blue River of Kansas in August. There they founded the frontier village of Manhattan. Renoyan Americanized the family name to Runyan, and started a local newspaper. He taught the printer's trade to his son, Alfred. Alfred grew up to be a strong-minded character in his own right. Indian fighter, lover of the classics, gambler, drunkard, saloon orator, he was soon publishing and printing newspapers of his own—or, when his own papers collapsed, working for other people's.

Alfred's only son, Alfred Damon Runyan, was born in Manhattan in 1880. After a few more years of maverick newspapering around Kansas, Alfred, Sr., moved his wife, son and two daughters to Pueblo, Colorado. Elizabeth Damon Runyan was tubercular, a condition the high clear air of Colorado was expected to improve. It didn't, and she died before young Alfred Damon's eighth birthday. His sisters were sent back to live with their mother's family in Kansas.

The boy was thereafter a sort of newspaper and saloon orphan. ("He had the habit of silence, from the lonely early days when there was simply no one to listen to him," his son later observed.) According to most accounts, he left school in the fourth grade and spent his early years wandering barefoot on the streets of the steel-mill town of Pueblo, where there were plenty of bad habits to pick up. He was smoking cigarettes at age nine, drinking whiskey at fifteen, and not long afterward packing that six-gun his son mentions.

Young Al, as he was called, made his bed in his old man's flophouse room, learned about the world of high thought and letters from his old man's tavern monologues on Shakespeare, Buffalo Bill Cody and Billy the Kid, and soon, from the same source, was receiving an on-the-spot journalistic education in everything from how to handle hot type to how to handle a hot tip, whether it be on a news story or on the nose of a horse.

Apprenticed as printer's devil at the Pueblo *Evening News*, where his father worked at the time, young Al had his first reporting assignment at fourteen, to cover a lynching. This would be rough stuff for most boys of that tender age, but Al had already worked as a telegrapher's messenger in the red-light district of "Little Pittsburgh," as the wide-open town of Pueblo was known. He did the job.

The next year he was made a full-fledged news reporter. Two years after that, he'd moved over to the Pueblo *Evening Post*, where he received his first by-line. The printer misspelled his name, with an *o* instead of an *a*. Al became Alfred Damon Runyon on that day. (Later, in New York, an equally arbitrary journalistic "decision"—this time by an editor—resulted in the amputation of "Alfred" from Runyon's by-line.)

From his father, a philosophical individualist, young Al Runyon had already inherited a great respect for such independent types as gamblers and sportsmen and outlaws, together with a great curiosity about their exploits, both of which would remain with him for the rest of his life. So would his old man's cynicism about such institutions as religion, politics, high finance and so-called polite society, and also his old man's view of women as a deeply untrustworthy species. But perhaps the most important family legacy handed down from father to son was a great loyalty to the profession and life of newspapering.

Many years later, when "Damon Runyon" was a household name wherever newspapers were sold in this country, Damon's own son, Damon, Jr., wrote him a letter expressing discouragement over the possibilities of a journalistic career. "You say you don't know if you will ever be more than a better than average reporter," Runyon wrote back. "Well, my boy, I think that is better than being king."

From his early habit of long silences, young Al developed the skill of being a good listener. From the fate-enforced loneliness of being a half-abandoned motherless street-child he acquired the ability to make up his mind for himself. Attention, curiosity, detachment and a photographic memory—Runyon had all the reporter's tools from his teenage years on. Later, in New York, the most famous editors of his era (Arthur Brisbane of the *Journal* and Herbert Bayard Swope of the *World*) would call Runyon the greatest reporter in the business. That, to Damon, was the second highest form of praise, next to his paycheck. ("Get the Money" was always his slogan.)

When Runyon was seventeen, the battleship *Maine* was sunk in Havana harbor. Turned down because of his age by a Colorado cavalry enlistment office, Al headed north and talked his way into the Minnesota volunteers, with whom he quickly found himself fighting as an infantryman in the Philippines. Apparently he experienced combat against Moro insurgents, though the details are lost in legends, Runyon's own later mythologizing and the heroic sentimentalities of his Kiplingesque camp verse of the period.

By the beginning of the new century he was back in the States, free-riding the rails around Colorado between short-time newspaper jobs. His adventures as a railroad hobo gave him plenty of material he later used in newspaper vignettes and on such projects as ghostwriting a serialized autobiography for heavyweight champ Jack Dempsey, whose knockabout boyhood in the Rockies didn't differ too much from Runyon's own.

Denver became young Runyon's base. He staffed on the Denver *Post*, went west for a while and got a job with the San Francisco *Post*, then returned to the Mile-High City and landed on the payroll of the *Rocky Mountain News* in 1906. It was his four-year stint with the *News* that established him as a notable reporter, famed for his "stunt"-oriented feature writing, his personal handle on news stories and his unusual powers of observation. He also won a small local reputation as a poet, as well as a large one for his drinking—no mean feat in a ripsnorting community where, in the words of one pioneer of the period, "Them swinging doors never stopped twenty-four hours a day!"

Only when knocked off his feet by the pretty society reporter of the *News*, Ellen Egan, did Runyon reform his ways, and subdue the alcoholism that had often caused him to lose whole stretches of time and memory in wild drinking binges. In order to win Ellen's hand, and also because, as he later told his son, "I wanted to go places," he gave up the bottle for good.

To many who knew him in later years, when he smoked three packs of cigarettes and drank sixty cups of coffee every day, Runyon seemed to have a sharp and sour disposition much of the time—a fact that may be attributed to his decision to swear off alcohol around 1910. Thereafter, as he once joked, he "became positively famous for hanging out with drunks and never touching a drop."

Runyon was thirty when he went off to New York to find his fortune as a writer. His first Big Town job was in the sports department at the Hearst morning paper, the New York *American*. His colorful reporting of the New York Giants' spring baseball camp in 1911 won him enthusiastic readers and, shortly, a raise. Soon he had his own Manhattan apartment. Ellen Egan moved east from Denver to marry him. She gave Damon a daughter in 1914 and a son in 1918, both births occurring when he was off covering baseball games. This was a regularity chez Runyon: Father was never at home.

By the early twenties, Runyon was earning the princely salary of $25,000 a year as the star feature writer, news reporter and sports columnist in the Hearst empire. He was able to put Ellen up in the expensive fashion she fancied and also to develop refined tastes of his own in dining and dressing. But his schedule as a morning newspaper employee and his predilections for the nocturnal life of the town, with its entertaining characters, had already conjoined by this time to create a life style that was to keep Runyon permanently away from the family nest, on the move "around and about" (as he put it in his stories and in his expense account vouchers). The Upper West Side apartments where he kept his family were home to him in name only. He actually kept personal housekeeping in a series of bachelor scatters closer to the Broadway mainstream.

He usually rose late, and attended to a thorough first meal of the day at Lindy's restaurant (called "Mindy's" in the stories), where he mixed freely with a regular clientele made up not only of such big names as Arnold Rothstein—the famous "high shot" and free-lance bankroller—but also a miscellaneous crowd of show people, petty gamblers and hustlers. These were, in his view, highly innovative, inventive people, whose struggle to keep alive—by activities legal and illegal—made them worthy of interest. "What this fellow does," Runyon once said of such an acquaintance, "is the best he can, but the field, being slightly overcrowded, is none too well. It's a very crowded profession today."

More of the same types, particularly those of the betting persuasion, could be found of an afternoon, taking the sun on the pavement outside ticket agent Mike Jacobs's Broadway office—a stretch of concrete known locally as "Jacobs Beach." There Damon could be found rubbernecking, discussing odds on sporting events of the day or simply putting in time "on the Erie"—as he called the deliberate act of listening-in.

One of Runyon's most remarkable faculties was his gift for preserving (and often himself adopting) the speech patterns of others. Throughout the 1920s he was able to sit around in speakeasies and record in his head the syntax and vocabulary of Broadway night life and underworld characters, much of which made its way into that crowning reporting job of his career, the "guys and dolls" short stories. "He has caught with a high degree of insight the actual tone and phrase of the gangsters and racketeers of the town. Their talk is put down almost literally." So claimed one knowledgeable critic of the epoch, Heywood Broun. "To me the most impressive thing in *Guys and Dolls* is the sensitivity of the ear of Damon Runyon." That sensitive ear was the ear of a guy who was strictly asking for coffee at all times.

Some days in New York there was a ball game to cover, other days Runyon put in at the race track or doing the tour of the gyms, and evenings often found him alongside fight rings, pounding out his reports. There was always a story to file, and after that the night beat opened out into dining on the town and making the circuit of the card and dice games, then later, the drinking and dancing clubs. In the latter spots, Damon rubbed shoulders amiably with gangsters who were proven to have hearts by the fact that they kept losing them to the chorus dancers. These chorus "dolls" were outfitted, to quote one Runyon story, in barely enough costume "to make a pad for a crutch"—and were often in real life sophisticated gold diggers.

The association of sex and crime in the nightclub era was blatant enough. This was the period of the New Morality in America—a phenomenon that, many people suspected, was something the newspapers of the time invented in order to boost circulation. But in the nightclubs it was right there, out in the open. The half-naked dancing girls were wooed (and usually won) by men who had made their money in gambling, bootlegging and various rackets, including such "dodges" as banking and the stock market. From Runyon's highly educated and hardheaded viewpoint (he'd seen first-hand evidence of bank swindling and Wall Street "bucket shops"), these latter activities were, if anything, even *more* corrupt than the illicit operations of the bootleggers, gamblers, and such.

As for the New Morality, Damon Runyon had more opportunity to observe its violent fruits than most ordinary men, because of his position as the Hearst syndicate's number one trial reporter. No one could write a courtroom account with the swiftness, accuracy or descriptive color of Runyon, so every time some paramour or husband was bumped off in particularly sensational fashion, he was called into action. He became famous for his chilling portrait of Ruth Snyder, the "frosty blonde" who teamed up with a corset salesman to knock off her spouse. Reporting on this 1926 trial, Runyon compared the salesman's grip on the murder weapon—a sashweight—with the batting stance of Paul Waner, one of the most feared baseball hitters of the day. It was Runyon's somewhat cynical view that the public regarded murder as a very interesting kind of sport: "The Main Event," he called it.

Two years later Runyon's own marriage ended, not quite as violently. The much-neglected Ellen Runyon had taken up drinking, while Damon had for years been carrying torches for a series of chorus dancers. The Runyons divorced in 1928. Ellen died in sad circumstances in 1931, the year before Damon married Patrice Amati, an attractive Spanish dancer at the Silver Slipper nightclub.

Between marriages, Runyon moved into the Hotel Forrest at Forty-ninth and Broadway, where for three years his penthouse suite and the hotel lobby became the classrooms of a sort of semipermanent floating Broadway seminar. In attendance were students from such fields as liquor distilling, betting commissions, race track management, fight managing, wholesale clothing sales, boxing, acting and sportswriting. Professor Runyon, in residence, chaired the discussions. Between sessions, on his typewriter in the back room, he was working on a very important dissertation: a new kind of first-person narrative short story (five thousand words) with a classic twist ending, celebrating the guys and dolls of Broadway, describing their exploits in a purified present-tense tongue that was a very careful echo of their own, all to be carried off with a certain "half-boob air" (as the Professor called it) of humorous but knowing detachment.

"Madame La Gimp," one of the most popular and successful of Runyon's new dissertations, made playful use of his bride-to-be's Spanish background. "Miss Missouri Martin," in this story and others, represents "Texas" Guinan, the famous impresario and nightclub hostess who for a time had employed the second Mrs. Runyon. "The honorable Mayor James J. Walker," who is impersonated in this story by Good Time Charley Bernstein, was a special pal of Runyon's; he performed Damon and Patrice's wedding ceremony. ("Madame La Gimp" was the first of Runyon's tales of the Big Street to be purchased by the movies. Frank Capra bought it for Columbia at "a measly fifteen hundred dollars"—Capra's estimate; Runyon always claimed, perhaps out of embarrassment, to have received a few thousand more—and some twenty years later, after Capra had made a very successful film out of it, *Lady For A Day*, Columbia sold the rights for $225,000. The picture was later remade as *Pocketful of Miracles*.)

These were the early days of the Depression, when Runyon's free-lancing acquaintances were having to hustle harder than ever to keep alive. The repeal of Prohibition put thousands of underworld citizens out of work, and times were also hard even for legitimate citizens. From 1929 on, Runyon recorded the new surge of gangsterism created by what his narrator in "Breach of Promise" calls "the unemployment situation." He chronicles, with safely approximate veracity, the kidnapings, the shootings, the safe-crackings, the putting of people into sacks, the breaking and entering and the flinging of pineapples which explode. He tells, in "The Brain Goes Home," of the end of the regime of Rothstein, hints in "Dark Dolores" of the decline of Capone (Black Mike Marrio) and foretells in the same story the rise to preeminence of the principal New York gang boss of the 1930s, Francisco (Frank) Costello (Dave the Dude).

The illegal doings of his characters interest the narrator "more than somewhat," in Runyon's famous phrase; in fact, the author was probably expressing his own sentiments in the words of the slightly bemused narrator in "The Lemon Drop Kid": "It is only human nature to be deeply interested in larceny."

The thinly veiled facts behind these fables were known to most of Runyon's associates of the time. "I recognize the characters concerned as real people," Heywood Broun said. The gangsters of Runyon's tales are patterned on the great outlaw-individualists of his era—the Buffalo Bills and Billy the Kids of the Jazz Age.

Runyon soon began publishing his tales written in the Hotel Forrest. *Cosmopolitan* took one, then demanded more, and finally ran dozens, all at the previously unheard-of rate of a dollar a word. *Collier's* and *Saturday Evening Post* also ran many of the "guys and dolls" stories, at the same price. Runyon, already Hearst's best-paid reporter, now began to make some *real* money.

The stories were published in books, beginning in 1931 with the collection called *Guys and Dolls*, and then over and over again in paperback editions, some of which sold into the millions of copies. By the mid-thirties, Hollywood was buying up Runyon stories as fuel for popular gangster pictures. The studios bought sixteen tales in all, at increasingly higher prices, and soon Runyon was traveling back and forth regularly between New York and Hollywood, where he worked at $2,000 a week and up, contributing ideas and scripts. He maintained his column, which was now directed to subjects of general interest and syndicated across the country. He owned a stable of racehorses, a pack of hunting dogs and a handful of heavyweight fighters, all of which were famous for their expensive appetites. Runyon now dressed like a Broadway high shot, ate at the Colony and lived with his second wife at the Parc Vendome, when they weren't in California or Florida—where Runyon had built a $75,000 white villa across Miami Bay from the villa of his friend Al "Scarface" Capone.

Capone's Florida place was vacant much of the time after 1932, when the erstwhile gang boss went away to prison. When he left he gave Runyon his prize pair of whippets, as a keepsake. Capone knew Runyon liked dogs.

With the disappearance of Capone and many of the other underworld figures Runyon knew so well—theirs was a profession with a very high mortality rate—Runyon ceased to attempt more of his outlaw fictions. Nineteen of the twenty tales in this volume date from his period of greatest production, between 1929 and 1936. The exception is "The Lacework Kid," a patriotic sentimental tale from 1944 that memorializes Runyon's favorite card game (and the only one for which he claimed to have a gift), gin rummy.

Ironically, it was at the height of his success, in the early forties, when his column was at its peak and his work in greater demand than ever at the movie studios, that Runyon contracted cancer of the throat. His larynx and trachea were surgically removed, leaving him with metal pipes for eating and breathing. His wife divorced him and married a younger man. Controlling an agony of remorse, Runyon awarded her a generous divorce settlement and eventually a large place in his will. He took a bachelor apartment in New York, spent much of his time at the Stork Club with old friends (he communicated on note pads, having lost his voice) and, despite his encroaching illness, went out every dawn to follow police calls in his friend Walter Winchell's automobile. The two columnists, who'd been chums since the twenties (Winchell is "Waldo Winchester" in the stories), drove all over the city to turn up unusual and interesting crimes. Runyon used the sights and sounds on these trips as materials for his very moving final syndicated columns.

After a late and emotional reunion with his estranged son, Damon, Jr., Runyon grew gravely ill in late 1946. He died in December of that year. In his friend's memory, Winchell founded the Damon Runyon Cancer Fund, to which many notable mob figures immediately contributed (Frank Costello gave $25,000).

In accordance with Runyon's wish, his ashes were scattered over Broadway from an Eastern Airlines plane flown by Captain Eddie Rickenbacker, the World War I air ace, for whom, thirty years earlier, Runyon had ghostwritten some speeches. He'd also interviewed Rickenbacker a decade before *that*, when Eddie was in the race-car-driving game, and had written a sports page account of it. Those were only a few of the 60 million or so words that passed through the typewriter of reporter Runyon, who, to paraphrase one of his fellow Hearst columnists, Arthur J. "Bugs" Baer, would write you right out of the paper if you weren't careful.

For an earlier generation of readers, Runyon was an everyday experience. His newspaper columns and stories and his fictional tales were enjoyed by millions. One negative spin-off of this immense popularity was that it became a barrier to the acceptance of Runyon's fiction in "serious" literary circles, where in many cases the sheer success of a writer's work may be cited as an excuse for discriminating against it. At any rate, it would be no more fair to dismiss Runyon as a "popular writer" than it would be so to dismiss, say, Ring Lardner, who held an approximately equal position with Runyon in the public esteem, and who was an equally gifted writer—but who had for friends, not gangsters, but artistic people from Long Island like F. Scott Fitzgerald, Dorothy Parker and Edmund Wilson. You don't get your work taught in college courses and printed in anthologies (as Lardner's stories are, and Runyon's are not) by hanging around with Al Capone or Arnold Rothstein. That's always been half of Runyon's problem in academic circles.

The other half, I think, relates to the trick of "indirection," or the "half-boob air," which Runyon said he used to conceal the fact that he was always "a rebel at heart." The irony in the Broadway tales continues to waft like smoke over the heads of many of his academic readers. Runyon's trick of role-reversal, placing criminals and "legitimate" people on unfamiliar sides of the sympathy-meter in his stories, seems to bother many professors.

Jimmy Cannon, one of Runyon's chief sportswriting disciples, spoke interestingly on this subject in a recent book called *No Cheering in the Press Box*. "One of the odd things about Damon," Cannon said, "was that he was a very cultured man. He pretended he wasn't. He concealed his culture and much of his knowledge. I have no idea why—but I think Damon wanted to get as close to the people he wanted to write about as he could. He wrote about mugs because they were interesting people. Damon did things that were extraordinary for those times, and for these times. They talk about guys doing daring things. Well, Runyon's heroes were pimps and prostitutes and murderers. He treated them as human beings. That is now the style. He was one of the forerunners."

On certain urban-bred writers of our day, such as Jimmy Breslin, Peter Maas, Mike Royko, George V. Higgins, or Jim Murray, the Runyon style has had an obvious influence.

Runyon's own view on the subject of acceptance by the "academic mob" was one he stated simply and frequently. "My measure of success is money," he wrote. "I have no interest in artistic triumphs that are financial losers. I would like to have an artistic success that also made money, of course, but if I had to make a choice between the two, I would take the dough."

A notably hard-boiled attitude, to be sure. But then, as his cartoonist-sportswriter colleague of the 1920s, Tad Dorgan, often said, Damon was a "Ten Minute Egg"—as hard-boiled as they come. His tough demeanor, those who knew him best agreed, was calculated to conceal his feelings, which seemed to have been damaged beyond repair at some very early date, back in his half-mythological Wild West boyhood. Even his friends often complained that no one ever got to know Damon Runyon well. Runyon may or may not have preferred it that way. But no one who knew him disputes the fact that, as Bill Corum said, Runyon had "great character and the inner courage of a lion," and that, in the words of Runyon's own obit on the high-roller Rothstein, "he died game."

His reputation as a pioneering reporter is solid. His old columns can still be read for pleasure today. The *Dictionary of Slang* will tell you that Runyon, in his Broadway tales, nudged into the great common pool of spoken American a whole boatload of underworld expressions—the patois of Broadway. These expressions, to give only a token list, include such popular favorites as "cheaters" (for glasses), "cock-eyed" (for unconscious), "croak" (for die), "dukes" (for fists), "equalizer" (for gun), "hot spot" (for predicament), "kisser" (for mouth), "knock" (for criticism), "shill" (for pitch), "shiv" (for knife), "shoo-in" (for easy winner), "the shorts" (for lack of funds), and "monkey business" and "drop dead," which need no translation.

—TOM CLARK
Author of *The World of Damon Runyon*

A Very Honorable Guy

OFF AND ON I know Feet Samuels a matter of eight or ten years, up and down Broadway, and in and out, but I never have much truck with him because he is a guy I consider no dice. In fact, he does not mean a thing.

In the first place, Feet Samuels is generally broke, and there is no percentage in hanging around brokers. The way I look at it, you are not going to get anything off a guy who has not got anything. So while I am very sorry for brokers, and am always willing to hope that they get hold of something, I do not like to be around them. Long ago an old-timer who knows what he is talking about says to me:

"My boy," he says, "always try to rub up against money, for if you rub up against money long enough, some of it may rub off on you."

So in all the years I am around this town, I always try to keep in with the high shots and guys who carry these large coarse bank notes around with them, and I stay away from small operators and chiselers and brokers. And Feet Samuels is one of the worst brokers in this town, and has been such as long as I know him.

He is a big heavy guy with several chins and very funny feet, which is why he is called Feet. These feet are extra large feet, even for a big guy, and Dave the Dude says Feet wears violin cases for shoes. Of course this is not true, because Feet cannot get either of his feet in a violin case, unless it is a case for a very large violin, such as a cello.

I see Feet one night in the Hot Box, which is a night club, dancing with a doll by the name of Hortense Hathaway, who is in Georgie White's "Scandals," and what is she doing but standing on Feet's feet as if she is on sled runners, and Feet never knows it. He only thinks the old gondolas are a little extra heavy to shove around this night, because Hortense is no invalid. In fact, she is a good rangy welterweight.

She has blond hair and plenty to say, and her square monicker is Annie O'Brien, and not Hortense Hathaway at all. Furthermore, she comes from Newark, which is in New Jersey, and her papa is a taxi jockey by the name of Skush O'Brien, and a very rough guy, at that, if anybody asks you. But of course the daughter of a taxi jockey is as good as anybody else for Georgie White's "Scandals" as long as her shape is okay, and nobody ever hears any complaint from the customers about Hortense on this proposition.

She is what is called a show girl, and all she has to do is to walk around and about Georgie White's stage with only a few light bandages on and everybody considers her very beautiful, especially from the neck down, although personally I never care much for Hortense because she is very fresh to people. I often see her around the night clubs, and when she is in these deadfalls Hortense generally is wearing quite a number of diamond bracelets and fur wraps, and one thing and another, so I judge she is not doing bad for a doll from Newark, New Jersey.

Of course Feet Samuels never knows why so many other dolls besides Hortense are wishing to dance with him, but gets to thinking maybe it is because he has the old sex appeal and he is very sore indeed when Henri, the head waiter at the Hot Box, asks him to please stay off the floor except for every tenth dance, because Feet's feet take up so much room when he is on the floor that only two other dancers can work out at the same time, it being a very small floor.

I must tell you more about Feet's feet, because they are very remarkable feet indeed. They go off at different directions under him, very sharp, so if you see Feet standing on a corner it is very difficult to tell which way he is going, because one foot will be headed one way, and the other foot the other way. In fact, guys around Mindy's restaurant often make bets on the proposition as to which way Feet is headed when he is standing still.

What Feet Samuels does for a living is the best he can, which is the same thing many other guys in this town do for a living. He hustles some around the race tracks and crap games and prize fights, picking up a few bobs here and there as a runner for the bookmakers, or scalping bets, or steering suckers, but he is never really in the money in his whole life. He is always owing and always paying off, and I never see him but what he is troubled with the shorts as regards to dough.

The only good thing you can say about Feet Samuels is he is very honorable about his debts, and what he owes he pays when he can. Anybody will tell you this about Feet Samuels, although of course it is only what any hustler such as Feet must do if he wishes to protect his credit and keep in action. Still, you will be surprised how many guys forget to pay.

It is because Feet's word is considered good at all times that he is nearly always able to raise a little dough, even off The Brain, and The Brain is not an easy guy for anybody to raise dough off of. In fact, The Brain is very tough about letting people raise dough off of him.

If anybody gets any dough off of The Brain he wishes to know right away what time they are going to pay it back, with certain interest, and if they say at five-thirty Tuesday morning, they better not make it five-thirty-one Tuesday morning, or The Brain will consider them very unreliable and never let them have any money again. And when a guy loses his credit with The Brain he is in a very tough spot indeed in this town, for The Brain is the only man who always has dough.

Furthermore, some very unusual things often happen to guys who get money off of The Brain and fail to kick it back just when they promise, such as broken noses and sprained ankles and other injuries, for The Brain has people around him who seem to resent guys getting dough off of him and not kicking it back. Still, I know of The Brain letting some very surprising guys have dough, because he has a bug that he is a wonderful judge of guys' characters, and that he is never wrong on them, although I must say that no guy who gets dough off of The Brain is more surprising than Feet Samuels.

The Brain's right name is Armand Rosenthal, and he is called The Brain because he is so smart. He is well known to one and all in this town as a very large operator in gambling, and one thing and another, and nobody knows how much dough The Brain has, except that he must have plenty, because no matter how much dough is around, The Brain sooner or later gets hold of all of it. Some day I will tell you more about The Brain, but right now I wish to tell you about Feet Samuels.

It comes on a tough winter in New York, what with nearly all hands who have the price going to Miami and Havana and New Orleans, leaving the brokers behind. There is very little action of any kind in town with the high shots gone, and one night I run into Feet Samuels in Mindy's, and he is very sad indeed. He asks me if I happen to have a finnif on me, but of course I am not giving finnifs to guys like Feet Samuels, and finally he offers to compromise with me for a deuce, so I can see things must be very bad with Feet for him to come down from five dollars to two.

"My rent is away overdue for the shovel and broom," Feet says, "and I have a hard-hearted landlady who will not listen to reason. She says she will give me the wind if I do not lay something on the line at once. Things are never so bad with me," Feet says, "and I am thinking of doing something very desperate."

I cannot think of anything very desperate for Feet Samuels to do, except maybe go to work, and I know he is not going to do such a thing no matter what happens. In fact, in all the years I am around Broadway I never know any broker to get desperate enough to go to work.

I once hear Dave the Dude offer Feet Samuels a job riding rum between here and Philly at good wages, but Feet turns it down because he claims he cannot stand the open air, and anyway Feet says he hears riding rum is illegal and may land a guy in the pokey. So I know whatever Feet is going to do will be nothing difficult.

"The Brain is still in town," I say to Feet. "Why do you not put the lug on him? You stand okay with him."

"There is the big trouble," Feet says. "I owe The Brain a C note already, and I am supposed to pay him back by four o'clock Monday morning, and where I am going to get a hundred dollars I do not know, to say nothing of the other ten I must give him for interest."

"What are you figuring on doing?" I ask, for it is now a Thursday, and I can see Feet has very little time to get together such a sum.

"I am figuring on scragging myself," Feet says, very sad.

"What good am I to anybody? I have no family and no friends, and the world is packing enough weight without me. Yes, I think I will scrag myself."

"It is against the law to commit suicide in this man's town," I say, "although what the law can do to a guy who commits suicide I am never able to figure out."

"I do not care," Feet says. "I am sick and tired of it all. I am especially sick and tired of being broke. I never have more than a few quarters to rub together in my pants pocket. Everything I try turns out wrong. The only thing that keeps me from scragging myself at once is the C note I owe The Brain, because I do not wish to have him going around after I am dead and gone saying I am no good. And the toughest thing of all," Feet says, "is I am in love. I am in love with Hortense."

"Hortense?" I say, very much astonished indeed. "Why, Hortense is nothing but a big——"

"Stop!" Feet says. "Stop right here! I will not have her called a big boloney or whatever else big you are going to call her, because I love her. I cannot live without her. In fact," Feet says, "I do not wish to live without her."

"Well," I say, "what does Hortense think about you loving her?"

"She does not know it," Feet says. "I am ashamed to tell her, because naturally if I tell her I love her, Hortense will expect me to buy her some diamond bracelets, and naturally I cannot do this. But I think she likes me more than somewhat, because she looks at me in a certain way. But," Feet says, "there is some other guy who likes her also, and who is buying her diamond bracelets and what goes with them, which makes it very tough on me. I do not know who the guy is, and I do not think Hortense cares for him so much, but naturally any doll must give serious consideration to a guy who can buy her diamond bracelets. So I guess there is nothing for me to do but scrag myself."

Naturally I do not take Feet Samuels serious, and I forget about his troubles at once, because I figure he will wiggle out some way, but the next night he comes into Mindy's all pleasured up, and I figure he must make a scratch somewhere, for he is walking like a man with about sixty-five dollars on him.

But it seems Feet only has an idea, and very few ideas are worth sixty-five dollars.

"I am laying in bed thinking this afternoon," Feet says, "and I get to thinking how I can raise enough dough to pay off The Brain, and maybe a few other guys, and my landlady, and leave a few bobs over to help bury me. I am going to sell my body."

Well, naturally I am somewhat bewildered by this statement, so I ask Feet to explain, and here is his idea: He is going to find some doctor who wishes a dead body and sell his body to this doctor for as much as he can get, the body to be delivered after Feet scrags himself, which is to be within a certain time.

"I understand," Feet says, "that these croakers are always looking for bodies to practice on, and that good bodies are not easy to get nowadays."

"How much do you figure your body is worth?" I ask.

"Well," Feet says, "a body as big as mine ought to be worth at least a G."

"Feet," I say, "this all sounds most gruesome to me. Personally I do not know much about such a proposition, but I do not believe if doctors buy bodies at all that they buy them by the pound. And I do not believe you can get a thousand dollars for your body, especially while you are still alive, because how does a doctor know if you will deliver your body to him?"

"Why," Feet says, very indignant, "everybody knows I pay what I owe. I can give The Brain for reference, and he will okay me with anybody for keeping my word."

Well, it seems to me that there is very little sense to what Feet Samuels is talking about, and anyway I figure that maybe he blows his topper, which is what often happens to brokers, so I pay no more attention to him. But on Monday morning, just before four o'clock, I am in Mindy's, and what happens but in walks Feet with a handful of money, looking much pleased.

The Brain is also there at the table where he always sits facing the door so nobody can pop in on him without him seeing them first, because there are many people in this town that The Brain likes to see first if they are coming in where he is. Feet steps up to the table and lays a C note in front of The Brain and also a sawbuck, and The Brain looks up at the clock and smiles and says:

"Okay, Feet, you are on time."

It is very unusual for The Brain to smile about anything, but afterwards I hear he wins two C's off of Manny Mandelbaum, who bets him Feet will not pay off on time, so The Brain has a smile coming.

"By the way, Feet," The Brain says, "some doctor calls me up today and asks me if your word is good and you may be glad to know I tell him you are one hundred percent. I put the okay on you because I know you never fail to deliver on a promise. Are you sick, or something?"

"No," Feet says, "I am not sick. I just have a little business deal on with the guy. Thanks for the okay."

Then he comes over to the table where I am sitting, and I can see he still has money left in his duke. Naturally I am anxious to know where he makes the scratch, and by and by he tells me.

"I put over the proposition I am telling you about," Feet says. "I sell my body to a doctor over on Park Avenue by the name of Bodeeker, but I do not get a G for it as I expect. It seems bodies are not worth much right now because there are so many on the market, but Doc Bodeeker gives me four C's on thirty days' delivery.

"I never know it is so much trouble selling a body before," Feet says. "Three doctors call the cops on me when I proposition them, thinking I am daffy, but Doc Bodeeker is a nice old guy and is glad to do business with me, especially when I give The Brain as reference. Doc Bodeeker says he is looking for a head shaped just like mine for years, because it seems he is a shark on heads. But," Feet says, "I got to figure out some way of scragging myself besides jumping out a window, like I plan, because Doc Bodeeker does not wish my head mussed up."

"Well," I say, "this is certainly most ghastly to me and does not sound legitimate. Does The Brain know you sell your body?"

"No," Feet says, "Doc Bodeeker only asks him over the phone if my word is good and does not tell him why he wishes to know, but he is satisfied with The Brain's okay. Now I am going to pay my landlady, and take up a few other markers here and there, and feed myself up good until it is time to leave this bad old world behind."

But it seems Feet Samuels does not go to pay his landlady right away. Where he goes is to Johnny Crackow's crap game downtown, which is a crap game with a $500 limit where the high shots seldom go, but where there is always some action for a small operator. And as Feet walks into the joint it seems that Big Nig is trying to make four with the dice, and everybody knows that four is a hard point for Big Nig, or anybody else, to make.

So Feet Samuels looks on awhile watching Big Nig trying to make four, and a guy by the name of Whitey offers to take two to one for a C note that Big Nig makes this four, which is certainly more confidence than I will ever have in Big Nig. Naturally Feet hauls out a couple of his C notes at once, as anybody must do who has a couple of *C* notes, and bets Whitey two hundred to a hundred that Big Nig does not make the four. And right away Big Nig outs with a seven, so Feet wins the bet.

Well, to make a long story short, Feet stands there for some time betting guys that other guys will not make four, or whatever it is they are trying to make with the dice, and the first thing anybody knows Feet Samuels is six *G's* winner, and has the crap game all crippled up. I see him the next night up in the Hot Box, and this big first baseman, Hortense, is with him, sliding around on Feet's feet, and a blind man can see that she has on at least three more diamond bracelets than ever before.

A night or two later I hear of Feet beating Long George McCormack, a high shot from Los Angeles, out of eighteen *G's* playing a card game that is called low ball, and Feet Samuels has no more license to beat a guy like Long George playing low ball than I have to lick Jack Dempsey. But when a guy finally gets his rushes in gambling nothing can stop him for a while, and this is the way it is with Feet. Every night you hear of him winning plenty of dough at this or that.

He comes into Mindy's one morning, and naturally I move over to his table at once, because Feet is now in the money and is a guy anybody can associate with freely. I am just about to ask him how things are going with him, although I know they are going pretty good, when in pops a fierce-looking old guy with his face all covered with gray whiskers that stick out every which way, and whose eyes peek out of these whiskers very wild indeed. Feet turns pale as he sees the guy, but nods at him, and the guy nods back and goes out.

"Who is the Whiskers?" I ask Feet. "He is in here the other morning looking around, and he makes people very nervous because nobody can figure who he is or what his dodge may be."

"It is old Doc Bodeeker," Feet says. "He is around checking up on me to make sure I am still in town. Say, I am in a very hot spot one way and another."

"What are you worrying about?" I ask. "You got plenty of dough and about two weeks left to enjoy yourself before this Doc Bodeeker forecloses on you."

"I know," Feet says, very sad. "But now I get this dough things do not look as tough to me as formerly, and I am very sorry I make the deal with the doctor. Especially," Feet says, "on account of Hortense."

"What about Hortense?" I ask.

"I think she is commencing to love me since I am able to buy her more diamond bracelets than the other guy," Feet says. "If it is not for this thing hanging over me, I will ask her to marry me, and maybe she will do it, at that."

"Well, then," I say, "why do you not go to old Whiskers and pay him his dough back, and tell him you change your mind about selling your body, although of course if it is not for Whiskers' buying your body you will not have all this dough."

"I do go to him," Feet says, and I can see there are big tears in his eyes. "But he says he will not cancel the deal. He says he will not take the money back; what he wants is my body, because I have such a funny-shaped head. I offer him four times what he pays me, but he will not take it. He says my body must be delivered to him promptly on March first."

"Does Hortense know about this deal?" I ask.

"Oh, no, no!" Feet says. "And I will never tell her, because she will think I am crazy, and Hortense does not care for crazy guys. In fact, she is always complaining about the other guy who buys her the diamond bracelets, claiming he is a little crazy, and if she thinks I am the same way the chances are she will give me the breeze."

Now this is a situation, indeed, but what to do about it I do not know. I put the proposition up to a lawyer friend of mine the next day, and he says he does not believe the deal will hold good in court, but of course I know Feet Samuels does not wish to go to court, because the last time Feet goes to court he is held as a material witness and is in the Tombs ten days.

The lawyer says Feet can run away, but personally I consider this a very dishonorable idea after The Brain putting the okay on Feet with old Doc Bodeeker, and anyway I can see Feet is not going to do such a thing as long as Hortense is around. I can see that one hair of her head is stronger than the Atlantic cable with Feet Samuels.

A week slides by, and I do not see so much of Feet, but I hear of him murdering crap games and short card players, and winning plenty, and also going around the night clubs with Hortense who finally has so many bracelets there is no more room on her arms, and she puts a few of them on her ankles, which are not bad ankles to look at, at that, with or without bracelets.

Then goes another week, and it just happens I am standing in front of Mindy's about four-thirty one morning and thinking that Feet's time must be up and wondering how he makes out with old Doc Bodeeker, when all of a sudden I hear a ploppity-plop coming up Broadway, and what do I see but Feet Samuels running so fast he is passing taxis that are going thirty-five miles an hour like they are standing still. He is certainly stepping along.

There are no traffic lights and not much traffic at such an hour in the morning, and Feet passes me in a terrible hurry. And about twenty yards behind him comes an old guy with gray whiskers, and I can see it is nobody but Doc Bodeeker. What is more, he has a big long knife in one hand, and he seems to be reaching for Feet at every jump with the knife.

Well, this seems to me a most surprising spectacle, and I follow them to see what comes of it, because I can see at once that Doc Bodeeker is trying to collect Feet's body himself. But I am not much of a runner, and they are out of my sight in no time, and only that I am able to follow them by ear through Feet's feet going ploppity-plop I will never trail them.

They turn east into Fifty-fourth Street off Broadway, and when I finally reach the corner I see a crowd halfway down the block in front of the Hot Box, and I know this crowd has something to do with Feet and Doc Bodeeker even before I get to the door to find that Feet goes on in while Doc Bodeeker is arguing with Soldier Sweeney, the door man, because as Feet passes the Soldier he tells the Soldier not to let the guy who is chasing him in. And the Soldier, being a good friend of Feet's, is standing the doc off.

Well, it seems that Hortense is in the Hot Box waiting for Feet, and naturally she is much surprised to see him come in all out of breath, and so is everybody else in the joint, including Henri, the head waiter, who afterwards tells me what comes off there, because you see I am out in front.

"A crazy man is chasing me with a butcher knife," Feet says to Hortense. "If he gets inside I am a goner. He is down at the door trying to get in."

Now I will say one thing for Hortense, and this is she has plenty of nerve, but of course you will expect a daughter of Skush O'Brien to have plenty of nerve. Nobody ever has more moxie than Skush. Henri, the head waiter, tells me that Hortense does not get excited, but says she will just have a little peek at the guy who is chasing Feet.

The Hot Box is over a garage, and the kitchen windows look down into Fifty-fourth Street, and while Doc Bodeeker is arguing with Soldier Sweeney, I hear a window lift, and who looks out but Hortense. She takes one squint and yanks her head in quick, and Henri tells me afterwards she shrieks:

"My Lord, Feet! This is the same daffy old guy who sends me all the bracelets, and who wishes to marry me!"

"And he is the guy I sell my body to," Feet says, and then he tells Hortense the story of his deal with Doc Bodeeker.

"It is all for you, Horty," Feet says, although of course this is nothing but a big lie, because it is all for The Brain in the beginning. "I love you, and I only wish to get a little dough to show you a good time before I die. If it is not for this deal I will ask you to be my everloving wife."

Well, what happens but Hortense plunges right into Feet's arms, and gives him a big kiss on his ugly smush, and says to him like this:

"I love you too, Feet, because nobody ever makes such a sacrifice as to hock their body for me. Never mind the deal. I will marry you at once, only we must first get rid of this daffy old guy downstairs."

Then Hortense peeks out of the window again and hollers down at old Doc Bodeeker. "Go away," she says. "Go away, or I will chuck a moth in your whiskers, you old fool."

But the sight of her only seems to make old Doc Bodeeker a little wilder than somewhat, and he starts struggling with Soldier Sweeney very ferocious, so the Soldier takes the knife away from the doc and throws it away before somebody gets hurt with it.

Now it seems Hortense looks around the kitchen for something to chuck out the window at old Doc Bodeeker, and all she sees is a nice new ham which the chef just lays out on the table to slice up for ham sandwiches. This ham is a very large ham, such as will last the Hot Box a month, for they slice the ham in their ham sandwiches very, very thin up at the Hot Box. Anyway, Hortense grabs up the ham and runs to the window with it and gives it a heave without even stopping to take aim.

Well, this ham hits poor old Doc Bodeeker ker-bowie smack dab on the noggin. The doc does not fall down, but he commences staggering around with his legs bending under him like he is drunk.

I wish to help him because I feel sorry for a guy in such a spot as this, and what is more I consider it a dirty trick for a doll such as Hortense to slug anybody with a ham.

Well, I take charge of the old doc and lead him back down Broadway and into Mindy's, where I set him down and get him a cup of coffee and a Bismarck herring to revive him, while quite a number of citizens gather about him very sympathetic.

"My friends," the old doc says finally, looking around, "you see in me a broken-hearted man. I am not a crackpot, although of course my relatives may give you an argument on this proposition. I am in love with Hortense. I am in love with her from the night I first see her playing the part of a sunflower in 'Scandals.' I wish to marry her, as I am a widower of long standing, but somehow the idea of me marrying anybody never appeals to my sons and daughters.

"In fact," the doc says, dropping his voice to a whisper, "sometimes they even talk of locking me up when I wish to marry somebody. So naturally I never tell them about Hortense, because I fear they may try to discourage me. But I am deeply in love with her and send her many beautiful presents, although I am not able to see her often on account of my relatives. Then I find out Hortense is carrying on with this Feet Samuels.

"I am desperately jealous," the doc says, "but I do not know what to do. Finally Fate sends this Feet to me offering to sell his body. Of course I am not practicing for years, but I keep an office on Park Avenue just for old times' sake, and it is to this office he comes. At first I think he is crazy, but he refers me to Mr. Armand Rosenthal, the big sporting man, who assures me that Feet Samuels is all right.

"The idea strikes me that if I make a deal with Feet Samuels for his body as he proposes, he will wait until the time comes to pay his obligation and run away, and," the doc says, "I will never be troubled by his rivalry for the affections of Hortense again. But he does not depart. I do not reckon on the holding power of love.

"Finally in a jealous frenzy I take after him with a knife, figuring to scare him out of town. But it is too late. I can see now Hortense loves him in return, or she will not drop a scuttle of coal on me in his defense as she does.

"Yes, gentlemen," the old doc says, "I am broken-hearted. I also seem to have a large lump on my head. Besides, Hortense has all my presents, and Feet Samuels has my money, so I get the worst of it all around. I only hope and trust that my daughter Eloise, who is Mrs. Sidney Simmons Bragdon, does not hear of this or she may be as mad as she is the time I wish to marry the beautiful cigaret girl in Jimmy Kelley's."

Here Doc Bodeeker seems all busted up by his feelings and starts to shed tears, and everybody is feeling very sorry for him indeed, when up steps The Brain who is taking everything in.

"Do not worry about your presents and your dough," The Brain says. "I will make everything good, because I am the guy who okays Feet Samuels with you. I am wrong on a guy for the first time in my life, and I must pay, but Feet Samuels will be very, very sorry when I find him. Of course I do not figure on a doll in the case, and this always makes quite a difference, so I am really not a hundred percent wrong on the guy, at that.

"But," The Brain says, in a very loud voice so everybody can hear, "Feet Samuels is nothing but a dirty welsher for not turning in his body to you as per agreement, and as long as he lives he will never get another dollar or another okay off of me, or anybody I know. His credit is ruined forever on Broadway."

But I judge that Feet and Hortense do not care. The last time I hear of them they are away over in New Jersey where not even The Brain's guys dast to bother them on account of Skush O'Brien, and I understand they are raising chickens and children right and left, and that all of Hortense's bracelets are now in Newark municipal bonds, which I am told are not bad bonds, at that.

Madame La Gimp

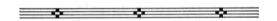

ONE NIGHT I am passing the corner of Fiftieth Street and Broadway, and what do I see but Dave the Dude standing in a doorway talking to a busted-down old Spanish doll by the name of Madame La Gimp. Or rather Madame La Gimp is talking to Dave the Dude, and what is more he is listening to her, because I can hear him say yes, yes, as he always does when he is really listening to anybody, which is very seldom.

Now this is a most surprising sight to me, because Madame La Gimp is not such an old doll as anybody will wish to listen to especially Dave the Dude. In fact, she is nothing but an old haybag, and generally somewhat ginned up. For fifteen years, or maybe sixteen, I see Madame La Gimp up and down Broadway, or sliding along through the Forties, sometimes selling newspapers, and sometimes selling flowers, and in all these years I seldom see her but what she seems to have about half a heat on from drinking gin.

Of course nobody ever takes the newspapers she sells, even after they buy them off of her, because they are generally yesterday's papers, and sometimes last week's, and nobody ever wants her flowers, even after they pay her for them, because they are flowers such as she gets off an undertaker over in Tenth Avenue, and they are very tired flowers, indeed.

Personally, I consider Madame La Gimp nothing but an old pest, but kind-hearted guys like Dave the Dude always stake her to a few pieces of silver when she comes shuffling along putting on the moan about her tough luck. She walks with a gimp in one leg, which is why she is called Madame La Gimp, and years ago I hear somebody say Madame La Gimp is once a Spanish dancer, and a big shot on Broadway, but that she meets up with an accident which puts her out of the dancing dodge, and that a busted romance makes her become a ginhead.

I remember somebody telling me once that Madame La Gimp is quite a beauty in her day, and has her own servants, and all this and that, but I always hear the same thing about every bum on Broadway, male and female, including some I know are bums, in spades, right from taw, so I do not pay any attention to these stories.

Still, I am willing to allow that maybe Madame La Gimp is once a fair looker, at that, and the chances are has a fair shape, because once or twice I see her when she is not ginned up, and has her hair combed, and she is not so bad-looking, although even then if you put her in a claiming race I do not think there is any danger of anybody claiming her out of it.

Mostly she is wearing raggedy clothes, and busted shoes, and her gray hair is generally hanging down her face, and when I say she is maybe fifty years old I am giving her plenty the best of it. Although she is Spanish, Madame La Gimp talks good English, and in fact she can cuss in English as good as anybody I ever hear, barring Dave the Dude.

Well, anyway, when Dave the Dude sees me as he is listening to Madame La Gimp, he motions me to wait, so I wait until she finally gets through gabbing to him and goes gimping away. Then Dave the Dude comes over to me looking much worried.

"This is quite a situation," Dave says. "The old doll is in a tough spot. It seems that she once has a baby which she calls by the name of Eulalie, being it is a girl baby, and she ships this baby off to her sister in a little town in Spain to raise up, because Madame La Gimp figures a baby is not apt to get much raising-up off of her as long as she is on Broadway. Well, this baby is on her way here. In fact," Dave says, "she will land next Saturday and here it is Wednesday already."

"Where is the baby's papa?" I ask Dave the Dude.

"Well," Dave says, "I do not ask Madame La Gimp this, because I do not consider it a fair question. A guy who goes around this town asking where babies' papas are, or even who they are, is apt to get the name of being nosey. Anyway, this has nothing whatever to do with the proposition, which is that Madame La Gimp's baby, Eulalie, is arriving here.

"Now," Dave says, "it seems that Madame La Gimp's baby, being now eighteen years old, is engaged to marry the son of a very proud old Spanish nobleman who lives in this little town in Spain, and it also seems that the very proud old Spanish nobleman, and his ever-loving wife, and the son, and Madame La Gimp's sister, are all with the baby. They are making a tour of the whole world, and will stop over here a couple of days just to see Madame La Gimp."

"It is commencing to sound to me like a movie such as a guy is apt to see at a midnight show," I say.

"Wait a minute," Dave says, getting impatient. "You are too gabby to suit me. Now it seems that the proud old Spanish nobleman does not wish his son to marry any lob, and one reason he is coming here is to look over Madame La Gimp, and see that she is okay. He thinks that Madame La Gimp's baby's own papa is dead, and that Madame La Gimp is now married to one of the richest and most aristocratic guys in America."

"How does the proud old Spanish nobleman get such an idea as this?" I ask. "It is a sure thing he never sees Madame La Gimp, or even a photograph of her as she is at present."

"I will tell you how," Dave the Dude says. "It seems Madame La Gimp gives her baby the idea that such is the case in her letters to her. It seems Madame La Gimp does a little scrubbing business around a swell apartment hotel in Park Avenue that is called the Marberry, and she cops stationery there and writes her baby in Spain on this stationery saying this is where she lives, and how rich and aristocratic her husband is. And what is more, Madame La Gimp has letters from her baby sent to her in care of the hotel and gets them out of the employees' mail."

"Why," I say, "Madame La Gimp is nothing but an old fraud to deceive people in this manner, especially a proud old Spanish nobleman. And," I say, "this proud old Spanish nobleman must be something of a chump to believe a mother will keep away from her baby all these years, especially if the mother has plenty of dough, although of course I do not know just how smart a proud old Spanish nobleman can be."

"Well," Dave says, "Madame La Gimp tells me the thing that makes the biggest hit of all with the proud old Spanish nobleman is that she keeps her baby in Spain all these years because she wishes her raised up a true Spanish baby in every respect until she is old enough to know what time it is. But I judge the proud old Spanish nobleman is none too bright, at that," Dave says, "because

Madame La Gimp tells me he always lives in this little town which does not even have running water in the bathrooms.

"But what I am getting at is this," Dave says. "We must have Madame La Gimp in a swell apartment in the Marberry with a rich and aristocratic guy for a husband by the time her baby gets here, because if the proud old Spanish nobleman finds out Madame La Gimp is nothing but a bum, it is a hundred to one he will cancel his son's engagement to Madame La Gimp's baby and break a lot of people's hearts, including his son's.

"Madame La Gimp tells me her baby is daffy about the young guy, and he is daffy about her, and there are enough broken hearts in this town as it is. I know how I will get the apartment, so you go and bring me Judge Henry G. Blake for a rich and aristocratic husband, or anyway for a husband."

Well, I know Dave the Dude to do many a daffy thing but never a thing as daffy as this. But I know there is no use arguing with him when he gets an idea, because if you argue with Dave the Dude too much he is apt to reach over and lay his Sunday punch on your snoot, and no argument is worth a punch on the snoot, especially from Dave the Dude.

So I go out looking for Judge Henry G. Blake to be Madame La Gimp's husband, although I am not so sure Judge Henry G. Blake will care to be anybody's husband, and especially Madame La Gimp's after he gets a load of her, for Judge Henry G. Blake is kind of a classy old guy.

To look at Judge Henry G. Blake, with his gray hair, and his nose glasses, and his stomach, you will think he is very important people, indeed. Of course Judge Henry G. Blake is not a judge, and never is a judge, but they call him Judge because he looks like a judge, and talks slow, and puts in many long words, which very few people understand.

They tell me Judge Blake once has plenty of dough, and is quite a guy in Wall Street, and a high shot along Broadway, but he misses a few guesses at the market, and winds up without much dough, as guys generally do who miss guesses at the market. What Judge Henry G. Blake does for a living at this time nobody knows, because he does nothing much whatever, and yet he seems to be a producer in a small way at all times.

Now and then he makes a trip across the ocean with such as Little Manuel, and other guys who ride the tubs, and sits in with them on games of bridge, and one thing and another, when they need him. Very often when he is riding the tubs, Little Manuel runs into some guy he cannot cheat, so he has to call in Judge Henry G. Blake to outplay the guy on the level, although of course Little Manuel will much rather get a guy's dough by cheating him than by outplaying him on the level. Why this is, I do not know, but this is the way Little Manuel is.

Anyway, you cannot say Judge Henry G. Blake is a bum, especially as he wears good clothes, with a wing collar, and a derby hat, and most people consider him a very nice old man. Personally I never catch the judge out of line on any proposition whatever, and he always says hello to me, very pleasant.

It takes me several hours to find Judge Henry G. Blake, but finally I locate him in Derle's billiard room playing a game of pool with a guy from Providence, Rhode Island. It seems the judge is playing the guy from Providence for five cents a ball, and the judge is about thirteen balls behind when I step into the joint, because naturally at five cents a ball the judge wishes the guy from Providence to win, so as to encourage him to play for maybe twenty-five cents a ball, the judge being very cute this way.

Well, when I step in I see the judge miss a shot anybody can make blindfolded, but as soon as I give him the office I wish to speak to him, the judge hauls off and belts in every ball on the table, bingity-bing, the last shot being a bank that will make Al de Oro stop and think, because when it comes to pool, the old judge is just naturally a curly wolf.

Afterwards he tells me he is very sorry I make him hurry up this way, because of course after the last shot he is never going to get the guy from Providence to play him pool even for fun, and the judge tells me the guy sizes up as a right good thing, at that.

Now Judge Henry G. Blake is not so excited when I tell him what Dave the Dude wishes to see him about, but naturally he is willing to do anything for Dave, because he knows that guys who are not willing to do things for Dave the Dude often have bad luck. The judge tells me that he is afraid he will not make much of a husband be-cause he tries it before several times on his own hook and is always a bust, but as long as this time it is not to be anything serious, he will tackle it. Anyway, Judge Henry G. Blake says, being aristocratic will come natural to him.

Well, when Dave the Dude starts out on any proposition, he is a wonder for fast working. The first thing he does is to turn Madame La Gimp over to Miss Billy Perry, who is now Dave's ever-loving wife which he takes out of tap-dancing in Miss Missouri Martin's Sixteen Hundred Club, and Miss Billy Perry calls in Miss Missouri Martin to help.

This is water on Miss Missouri Martin's wheel, because if there is anything she loves it is to stick her nose in other people's business, no matter what it is, but she is quite a help at that, although at first they have a tough time keeping her from telling Waldo Winchester, the scribe, about the whole cat-hop, so he will put a story in the *Morning Item* about it, with Miss Missouri Martin's name in it. Miss Missouri Martin does not believe in ever overlooking any publicity bets on the layout.

Anyway, it seems that between them Miss Billy Perry and Miss Missouri Martin get Madame La Gimp dolled up in a lot of new clothes, and run her through one of these beauty joints until she comes out very much changed, indeed. Afterwards I hear Miss Billy Perry and Miss Missouri Martin have quite a few words, because Miss Missouri Martin wishes to paint Madame La Gimp's hair the same color as her own, which is a high yellow, and buy her the same kind of dresses which Miss Missouri Martin wears herself, and Miss Missouri Martin gets much insulted when Miss Billy Perry says no, they are trying to dress Madame La Gimp to look like a lady.

They tell me Miss Missouri Martin thinks some of putting the slug on Miss Billy Perry for this crack, but happens to remember just in time that Miss Billy Perry is now Dave the Dude's ever-loving wife, and that nobody in this town can put the slug on Dave's ever-loving wife, except maybe Dave himself.

Now the next thing anybody knows, Madame La Gimp is in a swell eight- or nine-room apartment in the Marberry, and the way this comes about is as follows: It seems that one of Dave the Dude's most important champagne customers is a guy by the name of Rodney B. Emerson, who owns the apartment, but who is at his summer home in Newport, with his family, or anyway with his ever-loving wife.

This Rodney B. Emerson is quite a guy along Broadway, and a great hand for spending dough and looking for laughs, and he is very popular with the mob. Furthermore, he is obligated to Dave the Dude, because Dave sells him good champagne when most guys are trying to hand him the old phonus bolonus, and naturally Rodney B. Emerson appreciates this kind treatment.

He is a short, fat guy, with a round, red face, and a big laugh, and the kind of a guy Dave the Dude can call up at his home in Newport and explain the situation and ask for the loan of the apartment, which Dave does.

Well, it seems Rodney B. Emerson gets a big bang out of the idea, and he says to Dave the Dude like this:

"You not only can have the apartment, Dave, but I will come over and help you out. It will save a lot of explaining around the Marberry if I am there."

So he hops right over from Newport, and joins in with Dave the Dude, and I wish to say Rodney B. Emerson will always be kindly remembered by one and all for his cooperation, and nobody will ever again try to hand him the phonus bolonus when he is buying champagne, even if he is not buying it off of Dave the Dude.

Well, it is coming on Saturday and the boat from Spain is due, so Dave the Dude hires a big town car, and puts his own driver, Wop Sam, on it, as he does not wish any strange driver tipping off anybody that it is a hired car. Miss Missouri Martin is anxious to go to the boat with Madame La Gimp, and take her jazz band, the Hi Hi Boys, from her Sixteen Hundred Club with her to make it a real welcome, but nobody thinks much of this idea. Only Madame La Gimp and her husband, Judge Henry G. Blake, and Miss Billy Perry go, though the judge holds out for some time for Little Manuel, because Judge Blake says he wishes somebody around to tip him off in case there are any bad cracks made about him as a husband in Spanish, and Little Manuel is very Spanish.

The morning they go to meet the boat is the first time Judge Henry G. Blake gets a load of his ever-loving wife, Madame La Gimp, and by this time Miss Billy Perry and

Miss Missouri Martin give Madame La Gimp such a going-over that she is by no means the worst looker in the world. In fact, she looks first-rate, especially as she is off gin and says she is off it for good.

Judge Henry G. Blake is really quite surprised by her looks as he figures all along she will turn out to be a crow. In fact, Judge Blake hurls a couple of shots into himself to nerve himself for the ordeal, as he explains it, before he appears to go to the boat. Between these shots, and the nice clothes, and the good cleaning-up Miss Billy Perry and Miss Missouri Martin give Madame La Gimp, she is really a pleasant sight to the judge.

They tell me the meeting at the dock between Madame La Gimp and her baby is very affecting indeed, and when the proud old Spanish nobleman and his wife, and their son, and Madame La Gimp's sister, all go into action, too, there are enough tears around there to float all the battle-ships we once sink for Spain. Even Miss Billy Perry and Judge Henry G. Blake do some first-class crying, although the chances are the judge is worked up to the crying more by the shots he takes for his courage than by the meeting.

Still, I hear the old judge does himself proud, what with kissing Madame La Gimp's baby plenty, and duking the proud old Spanish nobleman, and his wife, and son, and giving Madame La Gimp's sister a good strong hug that squeezes her tongue out.

It turns out that the proud old Spanish nobleman has white sideburns, and is entitled Conde de Something, so his ever-loving wife is the Condesa, and the son is a very nice-looking quiet young guy any way you take him, who blushes every time anybody looks at him. As for Madame La Gimp's baby, she is as pretty as they come, and many guys are sorry they do not get Judge Henry G. Blake's job as stepfather, because he is able to take a kiss at Madame La Gimp's baby on what seems to be very small excuse. I never see a nicer-looking young couple, and anybody can see they are very fond of each other, indeed.

Madame La Gimp's sister is not such a doll as I will wish to have sawed off on me, and is up in the paints as regards to age, but she is also very quiet. None of the bunch talk any English, so Miss Billy Perry and Judge Henry G. Blake are pretty much outsiders on the way uptown. Anyway, the judge takes the wind as soon as they reach the Marberry, because the judge is now getting a little tired of being a husband. He says he has to take a trip out to Pittsburgh to buy four or five coal mines, but will be back the next day.

Well, it seems to me that everything is going perfect so far, and that it is good judgment to let it lay as it is, but nothing will do Dave the Dude but to have a reception the following night. I advise Dave the Dude against this idea, because I am afraid something will happen to spoil the whole cat-hop, but he will not listen to me, especially as Rodney B. Emerson is now in town and is a strong booster for the party, as he wishes to drink some of the good champagne he has planted in his apartment.

Furthermore, Miss Billy Perry and Miss Missouri Martin are very indignant at me when they hear about my advice, as it seems they both buy new dresses out of Dave the Dude's bank roll when they are dressing up Madame La Gimp, and they wish to spring these dresses somewhere where they can be seen. So the party is on.

I get to the Marberry around nine o'clock and who opens the door of Madame La Gimp's apartment for me but Moosh, the door man from Miss Missouri Martin's Sixteen Hundred Club. Furthermore, he is in his Sixteen Hundred Club uniform, except he has a clean shave. I wish Moosh a hello, and he never raps to me but only bows, and takes my hat.

The next guy I see is Rodney B. Emerson in evening clothes, and the minute he sees me he yells out, "Mister O. O. McIntyre." Well, of course I am not Mister O. O. McIntyre, and never put myself away as Mister O. O. McIntyre, and furthermore there is no resemblance whatever between Mister O. O. McIntyre and me, because I am a fairly good-looking guy, and I start to give Rodney B. Emerson an argument, when he whispers to me like this:

"Listen," he whispers, "we must have big names at this affair, so as to impress these people. The chances are they read the newspapers back there in Spain, and we must let them meet the folks they read about, so they will see Madame La Gimp is a real big shot to get such names to a party."

Then he takes me by the arm and leads me to a group of people in a corner of the room, which is about the size of the Grand Central waiting room.

"Mister O. O. McIntyre, the big writer!" Rodney B. Emerson says, and the next thing I know I am shaking hands with Mr. and Mrs. Conde, and their son, and with Madame La Gimp and her baby, and Madame La Gimp's sister, and finally with Judge Henry G. Blake, who has on a swallowtail coat, and does not give me much of a tumble. I figure the chances are Judge Henry G. Blake is getting a swelled head already, not to tumble up a guy who helps him get his job, but even at that I wish to say the old judge looks immense in his swallowtail coat, bowing and giving one and all the old castor oil smile.

Madame La Gimp is in a low-neck black dress and is wearing a lot of Miss Missouri Martin's diamonds, such as rings and bracelets, which Miss Missouri Martin insists on hanging on her, although I hear afterwards that Miss Missouri Martin has Johnny Brannigan, the plain clothes copper, watching these diamonds. I wonder at the time why Johnny is there but figure it is because he is a friend of Dave the Dude's. Miss Missouri Martin is no sucker, even if she is kind-hearted.

Anybody looking at Madame La Gimp will bet you all the coffee in Java that she never lives in a cellar over in Tenth Avenue, and drinks plenty of gin in her day. She has her gray hair piled up high on her head, with a big Spanish comb in it, and she reminds me of a picture I see somewhere, but I do not remember just where. And her baby, Eulalie, in a white dress is about as pretty a little doll as you will wish to see, and nobody can blame Judge Henry G. Blake for copping a kiss off of her now and then.

Well, pretty soon I hear Rodney B. Emerson bawling, "Mister Willie K. Vanderbilt," and in comes nobody but Big Nig, and Rodney B. Emerson leads him over to the group and introduces him.

Little Manuel is standing alongside Judge Henry G. Blake, and he explains in Spanish to Mr. and Mrs. Conde and the others that "Willie K. Vanderbilt" is a very large millionaire, and Mr. and Mrs. Conde seem much interested, anyway, though naturally Madame La Gimp and Judge Henry G. Blake are jerry to Big Nig, while Madame La Gimp's baby and the young guy are interested in nobody but each other.

Then I hear, "Mister Al Jolson," and in comes nobody but Tony Bertazzola, from the Chicken Club, who looks about as much like Al as I do like O. O. McIntyre, which is not at all. Next comes the "Very Reverend John Roach Straton," who seems to be Skeets Bolivar to me, then "the Honorable Mayor James J. Walker," and who is it but Good Time Charley Bernstein.

"Mister Otto H. Kahn" turns out to be Rochester Red, and "Mister Heywood Broun" is Nick the Greek, who asks me privately who Heywood Broun is, and gets very

sore at Rodney B. Emerson when I describe Heywood
Broun to him.

Finally there is quite a commotion at the door and
Rodney B. Emerson announces, "Mister Herbert Bayard
Swope" in an extra loud voice which makes everybody
look around, but it is nobody but the Pale Face Kid. He
gets me to one side, too, and wishes to know who Herbert
Bayard Swope is, and when I explain to him, the Pale
Face Kid gets so swelled up he will not speak to Death
House Donegan, who is only "Mister William Muldoon."

Well, it seems to me they are getting too strong when
they announce "Vice-President of the United States, the
Honorable Charles Curtis," and in pops Guinea Mike, and
I say as much to Dave the Dude, who is running around
every which way looking after things, but he only says,
"Well, if you do not know it is Guinea Mike, will you
know it is not Vice-President Curtis?"

But it seems to me all this is most disrespectful to our
leading citizens, especially when Rodney B. Emerson calls,
"The Honorable Police Commissioner, Mister Grover A.
Whalen," and in pops Wild William Wilkins, who is a
very hot man at this time, being wanted in several spots
for different raps. Dave the Dude takes personal charge
of Wild William and removes a rod from his pants pocket,
because none of the guests are supposed to come rodded
up, this being strictly a social matter.

I watch Mr. and Mrs. Conde, and I do not see that these
names are making any impression on them, and I afterwards
find out that they never get any newspapers in their town
in Spain except a little local bladder which only prints
the home news. In fact, Mr. and Mrs. Conde seem somewhat bored, although Mr. Conde cheers up no little and
looks interested when a lot of dolls drift in. They are
mainly dolls from Miss Missouri Martin's Sixteen Hundred
Club, and the Hot Box, but Rodney B. Emerson introduces

them as "Sophie Tucker," and "Theda Bara," and "Jeanne Eagels," and "Helen Morgan" and "Aunt Jemima," and one thing and another.

Well, pretty soon in comes Miss Missouri Martin's jazz band, the Hi Hi Boys, and the party commences getting up steam, especially when Dave the Dude gets Rodney B. Emerson to breaking out the old grape. By and by there is dancing going on, and a good time is being had by one and all, including Mr. and Mrs. Conde. In fact, after Mr. Conde gets a couple of jolts of the old grape, he turns out to be a pretty nice old skate, even if nobody can understand what he is talking about.

As for Judge Henry G. Blake, he is full of speed, indeed. By this time anybody can see that the judge is commencing to believe that all this is on the level and that he is really entertaining celebrities in his own home. You put a quart of good grape inside the old judge and he will believe anything. He soon dances himself plumb out of wind, and then I notice he is hanging around Madame La Gimp a lot.

Along about midnight, Dave the Dude has to go out into the kitchen and settle a battle there over a crap game, but otherwise everything is very peaceful. It seems that "Herbert Bayard Swope," "Vice-President Curtis" and "Grover Whalen" get a little game going, when "the Reverend John Roach Straton" steps up and cleans them in four passes, but it seems they soon discover that "the Reverend John Roach Straton" is using tops on them, which are very dishonest dice, and so they put the slug on "the Reverend John Roach Straton" and Dave the Dude has to split them out.

By and by I figure on taking the wind, and I look for Mr. and Mrs. Conde to tell them good night, but Mr. Conde and Miss Missouri Martin are still dancing, and

Miss Missouri Martin is pouring conversation into Mr. Conde's ear by the bucketful, and while Mr. Conde does not savvy a word she says, this makes no difference to Miss Missouri Martin. Let Miss Missouri Martin do all the talking, and she does not care a whoop if anybody understands her.

Mrs. Conde is over in a corner with "Herbert Bayard Swope," or the Pale Face Kid, who is trying to find out from her by using hog Latin and signs on her if there is any chance for a good twenty-one dealer in Spain, and of course Mrs. Conde is not able to make heads or tails of what he means, so I hunt up Madame La Gimp.

She is sitting in a darkish corner off by herself and I really do not see Judge Henry G. Blake leaning over her until I am almost on top of them, so I cannot help hearing what the judge is saying.

"I am wondering for two days," he says, "if by any chance you remember me. Do you know who I am?"

"I remember you," Madame La Gimp says. "I remember you—oh, so very well, Henry. How can I forget you? But I have no idea you recognize me after all these years."

"Twenty of them now," Judge Henry G. Blake says. "You are beautiful then. You are still beautiful."

Well, I can see the old grape is working first-class on Judge Henry G. Blake to make such remarks as this, although at that, in the half light, with the smile on her face, Madame La Gimp is not so bad. Still, give me them carrying a little less weight for age.

"Well, it is all your fault," Judge Henry G. Blake says. "You go and marry that chile con carne guy, and look what happens!"

I can see there is no sense in me horning in on Madame La Gimp and Judge Henry G. Blake while they are cutting up old touches in this manner, so I think I will just say good-by to the young people and let it go at that, but while I am looking for Madame La Gimp's baby, and her guy, I run into Dave the Dude.

"You will not find them here," Dave says. "By this time they are being married over at Saint Malachy's with my ever-loving wife and Big Nig standing up with them. We get the license for them yesterday afternoon. Can you imagine a couple of young saps wishing to wait until they go plumb around the world before getting married?"

Well, of course this elopement creates much excitement for a few minutes, but by Monday Mr. and Mrs. Conde and the young folks and Madame La Gimp's sister take a train for California to keep on going around the world, leaving us nothing to talk about but old Judge Henry G. Blake and Madame La Gimp getting themselves married too, and going to Detroit where Judge Henry G. Blake claims he has a brother in the plumbing business who will give him a job, although personally I think Judge Henry G. Blake figures to do a little booting on his own hook in and out of Canada. It is not like Judge Henry G. Blake to tie himself up to the plumbing business.

So there is nothing more to the story, except that Dave the Dude is around a few days later with a big sheet of paper in his duke and very, very indignant.

"If every single article listed here is not kicked back to the owners of the different joints in the Marberry that they are taken from by next Tuesday night, I will bust a lot of noses around this town," Dave says. "I am greatly mortified by such happenings at my social affairs, and everything must be returned at once. Especially," Dave says, "the baby grand piano that is removed from Apartment 9-D."

Dark Dolores

Waldo Winchester, the newspaper scribe, is saying to me the other night up in the Hot Box that it is a very great shame there are no dolls around such as in the old days to make good stories for the newspapers by knocking off guys right and left, because it seems that newspaper scribes consider a doll knocking off a guy very fine news indeed, especially if the doll or the guy belongs to the best people.

"Why," Waldo Winchester says, "if we only have a Cleopatra, or a Helen of Troy, or even a Queen Elizabeth around now guzzling guys every few minutes, think what a great thing it will be for the circulation of the newspapers, especially the tabloids. The best we get nowadays is some doll belting a guy with a sash weight, or maybe filling him full of slugs, and this is no longer exciting."

Then Waldo Winchester tells me about a doll by the name of Lorelei who hangs out in the Rhine River some time ago and stools sailors up to the rocks to get them wrecked, which I consider a dirty trick, although Waldo does not seem to make so much of it. Furthermore, he speaks of another doll by the name of Circe, who is quite a hand for luring guys to destruction, and by the time Waldo gets to Circe he is crying because there are no more dolls like her around to furnish news for the papers.

But of course the real reason Waldo is crying is not because he is so sorry about Circe. It is because he is full of the liquor they sell in the Hot Box, which is liquor that is apt to make anybody bust out crying on a very short notice. In fact, they sell the cryingest liquor in town up in the Hot Box.

Well, I get to thinking over these dolls Waldo Winchester speaks of, and thinks I, the chances are Dolores Dark connects up with one of them away back yonder, and maybe with all of them for all I know, Dolores Dark being the name of a doll I meet when I am in Atlantic City with Dave the Dude the time of the big peace conference.

Afterwards I hear she is called Dark Dolores in some spots on account of her complexion, but her name is really the other way around. But first I will explain how it is I am in Atlantic City with Dave the Dude at the time of the big peace conference as follows:

One afternoon I am walking along Broadway thinking of not much, when I come on Dave the Dude just getting in a taxicab with a suitcase in his duke, and the next thing I know Dave is jerking me into the cab and telling the jockey to go to the Penn Station. This is how I come to be in Atlantic City the time of the big peace conference, although of course I have nothing to do with the peace conference, and am only with Dave the Dude to keep him company.

I am a guy who is never too busy to keep people company, and Dave the Dude is a guy who just naturally loves company. In fact, he hates to go anywhere, or be anywhere, by himself, and the reason is because when he is by himself Dave the Dude has nobody to nod him yes, and if there is one thing Dave is very, very fond of, it is to have somebody to nod him yes. Why it is that Dave the Dude does not have Big Nig with him I do not know, for Big Nig is Dave's regular nod-guy.

But I am better than a raw hand myself at nodding. In fact, I am probably as good a nod-guy as there is in this town, where there must be three million nod-guys, and why not, because the way I look at it, it is no bother whatever to nod a guy. In fact, it saves a lot of conversation.

Anyway, there I am in Atlantic City the time of the big peace conference, although I wish to say right now that if I know in advance who is going to be at this peace conference, or that there is going to be any peace conference, I will never be anywhere near Atlantic City, because the parties mixed up in it are no kind of associates for a nervous guy like me.

It seems this peace conference is between certain citizens of St. Louis, such as Black Mike Marrio, Benny the Blond Jew and Scoodles Shea, who all have different mobs in St. Louis, and who are all ripping and tearing at each other for a couple of years over such propositions as to who shall have what in the way of business privileges of one kind and another, including alky, and liquor, and gambling.

From what I hear there is plenty of shooting going on between these mobs, and guys getting topped right and left. Also there is much heaving of bombs, and all this and that, until finally the only people making any dough in the town are the undertakers, and it seems there is no chance of anybody cutting in on the undertakers, though Scoodles Shea tries.

Well, Scoodles, who is a pretty smart guy, and who is

once in the war in France, finally remembers that when all the big nations get broke, and sick and tired of fighting, they hold a peace conference and straighten things out, so he sends word to Black Mike and Benny the Blond Jew that maybe it will be a good idea if they do the same thing, because half their guys are killed anyway, and trade is strictly on the bum.

It seems Black Mike and Benny think very well of this proposition, and are willing to meet Scoodles in a peace conference, but Scoodles, who is a very suspicious character, asks where they will hold this conference. He says he does not wish to hold any conference with Black Mike and Benny in St. Louis, except maybe in his own cellar, because he does not know of any other place in St. Louis where he will be safe from being guzzled by some of Black Mike's or Benny's guys, and he says he does not suppose Black Mike and Benny will care to go into his cellar with him.

Well, he supposes a hundred percent right, although I hear Black Mike's cellar is not a bad place, as he keeps his wine there, but still from what I see of him personally, Black Mike is not such a guy as I will care to chum up with in a cellar.

So Scoodles Shea finally asks how about Atlantic City, and it seems this is agreeable to Black Mike because he has a cousin in Atlantic City by the name of Pisano that he does not see since they leave the old country.

Benny the Blond Jew says any place is okay with him as long as it is not in the State of Missouri, because, he says, he does not care to be seen anywhere in the State of Missouri with Black Mike and Scoodles, as it will be a knock to his reputation. This seems to sound somewhat insulting, and almost busts up the peace conference before it starts, but finally Benny withdraws the bad crack, and says he does not mean the State of Missouri, but only

St. Louis, so the negotiations proceed, and they settle on Atlantic City as the spot.

Then Black Mike says some outside guy must sit in with them as a sort of umpire, and help them iron out their arguments, and Benny says he will take President Hoover, Colonel Lindberg, or Chief Justice Taft. Now of course this is great foolishness to think they can get any one of these parties, because the chances are President Hoover, Colonel Lindberg and Chief Justice Taft are too busy with other things to bother about ironing out a mob war in St. Louis.

So finally Scoodles Shea suggests Dave the Dude. Both Black Mike and Benny say Dave is okay, though Benny holds out for some time for at least Chief Justice Taft. So Dave the Dude is asked to act as umpire for the St. Louis guys, and he is glad to do same, for Dave often steps into towns where guys are battling and straightens them out, and sometimes they do not start battling again for several weeks after he leaves town.

You see, Dave the Dude is friendly with everybody everywhere, and is known to one and all as a right guy, and one who always gives everybody a square rattle in propositions of this kind. Furthermore, it is a pleasure for Dave to straighten guys out in other towns, because the battling tangles up his own business interests in spots such as St. Louis.

Now it seems that on their way to the station to catch a train for Atlantic City, Scoodles Shea and Black Mike and Benny decide to call on a young guy by the name of Frankie Farrone, who bobs up all of a sudden in St. Louis with plenty of nerve, and who is causing them no little bother one way and another.

In fact, it seems that this Frankie Farrone is as good a reason as any other why Scoodles and Black Mike and Benny are willing to hold a peace conference, because

Frankie Farrone is nobody's friend in particular and he is biting into all three wherever he can, showing no respect whatever to old-established guys.

It looks as if Frankie Farrone will sooner or later take the town away from them if they let him go far enough, and while each one of the three tries at different times to make a connection with him, it seems he is just naturally a lone wolf, and wishes no part of any of them. In fact, somebody hears Frankie Farrone say he expects to make Scoodles Shea and Black Mike and Benny jump out of a window before he is through with them, but whether he means one window, or three different windows, he does not say.

So there is really nothing to be done about Frankie Farrone but to call on him, especially as the three are now together, because the police pay no attention to his threats, and make no move to protect Scoodles and Black Mike and Benny, the law being very careless in St. Louis at this time.

Of course Frankie Farrone has no idea Scoodles and Black Mike and Benny are friendly with each other, and he is probably very much surprised when they drop in on him on their way to the station. In fact, I hear there is a surprised look still on his face when they pick him up later.

He is sitting in a speak-easy reading about the Cardinals losing another game to the Giants when Scoodles Shea comes in the front door, and Black Mike comes in the back door, and Benny the Blond Jew slides in through a side entrance, it being claimed afterwards that they know the owner of the joint and get him to fix it for them so they will have no bother about dropping in on Frankie Farrone sort of unexpected like.

Well, anyway, the next thing Frankie Farrone knows he has four slugs in him, one from Scoodles Shea, one from Benny, and two from Black Mike, who seems to be more liberal than the others. The chances are they will put more slugs in him, only they leave their taxi a block away with the engine running, and they know the St. Louis taxi jockeys are terrible for jumping the meter on guys who keep them waiting.

So they go on to catch their train, and they are all at the Ritz Hotel in Atlantic City when Dave the Dude and I get there, and they have a nice layout of rooms looking out over the ocean, for these are highclass guys in every respect, and very good spenders.

They are sitting around a table with their coats off playing pinochle and drinking liquor when Dave and I show up, and right away Black Mike says: "Hello, Dave; where do we find the tomatoes?"

I can see at once that this Black Mike is a guy who has little bringing-up, or he will not speak of dolls as tomatoes, although of course different guys have different names for dolls, such as broads, and pancakes, and cookies, and tomatoes, which I claim are not respectful.

This Black Mike is a Guinea, and not a bad-looking Guinea, at that, except for a big scar on one cheek which I suppose is done by somebody trying to give him a laughing mouth. Some Guins, especially Sicilians, can swing a shiv so as to give a guy a slash that leaves him looking as if he is always laughing out of his mouth, although generally this is only for dolls who are not on the level with their everloving guys.

Benny the Blond Jew is a tall pale guy, with soft light-colored hair and blue eyes, and if I do not happen to know that he personally knocks off about nine guys I will consider him as harmless a looking guy as I ever see. Scoodles Shea is a big red-headed muzzler with a lot of freckles and a big grin all over his kisser.

They are all maybe thirty-odd, and wear colored silk shirts, with soft collars fastened with gold pins, and Black

Mike and Scoodles Shea are wearing diamond rings and wrist watches. Unless you know who they are you will never figure them to be gorills, even from St. Louis, although at the same time the chances are you will not figure them to be altar boys, unless you are very simple indeed.

They seem to be getting along first-rate together, which is not surprising, because it will be considered very bad taste indeed for guys such as these from one town to go into another town and start up any heat. It will be regarded as showing no respect whatever for the local citizens. Anyway, Atlantic City is never considered a spot for anything but pleasure, and even guys from Philly who may be mad at each other, and who meet up in Atlantic City, generally wait until they get outside the city limits before taking up any arguments. Many a guy gets the old business on the roads outside Atlantic City who can be much more handily settled right in town if it will not be considered disrespectful to the local citizens.

Well, it seems that not only Black Mike wishes to meet up with some dolls, but Scoodles Shea and Benny are also thinking of such, because the first two things guys away from home think of are liquor and dolls, although personally I never give these matters much of a tumble. I am a nervous guy, and liquor and dolls are by no means good for the nerves, especially dolls.

Furthermore, I can see that Dave the Dude is not so anxious about them as you will expect, because Dave is now married to Miss Billy Perry, and if Miss Billy Perry hears that Dave is having any truck with liquor and dolls, especially dolls, it is apt to cause gossip around his house.

But Dave figures he is a sort of host in this territory, because the others are strangers to Atlantic City, and important people where they come from, so we go down to Joe Goss' joint, which is a big cabaret just off the Boardwalk, and in no time there are half a dozen dolls of different shapes and sizes from Joe Goss' chorus, and also several of Joe Goss' hostesses, for Joe Goss gets many tired business men from New York among his customers, and there is nothing a tired business man from New York appreciates more than a lively hostess. Furthermore, Joe Goss himself is sitting with us as a mark of respect to Dave the Dude.

Black Mike and Scoodles and Benny are talking with the dolls and dancing with them now and then, and a good time is being had by one and all, as far as I can see, including Dave the Dude after he gets a couple of slams of Joe Goss' liquor in him and commences to forget about Miss Billy Perry. In fact, Dave so far forgets about Miss Billy Perry that he gets out on the floor with one of the dolls, and dances some, which shows you what a couple of slams of Joe Goss' liquor will do to a guy.

Most of the dolls are just such dolls as you will find in a cabaret but there is one among them who seems to be a hostess, and whose name seems to be Dolores, and who is a lily for looks. It is afterwards that I find out her other name is Dark, and it is Dave the Dude who afterwards finds out that she is called Dark Dolores in spots.

She is about as good a looker as a guy will wish to clap an eye on. She is tall and limber, like a buggy whip, and she has hair as black as the ace of spades, and maybe blacker, and all smooth and shiny. Her eyes are black and as big as doughnuts, and she has a look in them that somehow makes me think she may know more than she lets on, which I afterwards find out is very true, indeed.

She does not have much to say, and I notice she does not drink, and does not seem to be so friendly with the other dolls, so I figure her a fresh-laid one around there, especially as Joe Goss himself does not act as familiar towards her as he does towards most of his dolls, although I can see him give her many a nasty look on account of her passing up drinks.

In fact, nobody gives her much of a tumble at all at first, because guys generally like gabby dolls in situations such as this. But finally I notice that Benny the Blond Jew is taking his peeks at her, and I figure it is because he has better judgment than the others, although I do not understand how Dave the Dude can overlook such a bet, because no better judge of dolls ever lives than Dave the Dude.

But even Benny does not talk to Dolores or offer to dance with her and at one time when Joe Goss is in another part of the joint chilling a beef from some customer about a check, or maybe about the liquor, which calls for at least a mild beef, and the others are out on the floor dancing, Dolores and I are left all alone at the table. We sit there quite a spell with plenty of silence between us, because I am never much of a hand to chew the fat with dolls, but finally, not because I wish to know or care a whoop but just to make small talk, I ask her how long she is in Atlantic City.

"I get here this afternoon, and go to work for Mr. Goss just this very night," she says. "I am from Detroit."

Now I do not ask her where she is from, and her sticking in this information makes me commence to think that maybe she is a gabby doll after all, but she dries up and does not say anything else until the others come back to the table.

Now Benny the Blond Jew moves into a chair alongside Dolores, and I hear him say:

"Are you ever in St. Louis? Your face is very familiar to me."

"No," she says. "I am from Cleveland. I am never in St. Louis in my life."

"Well," Benny says, "you look like somebody I see before in St. Louis. It is very strange, because I cannot believe it possible for there to be more than one wonderful beautiful doll like you."

I can see Benny is there with the old stuff when it comes to carrying on a social conversation, but I am wondering how it comes this Dolores is from Detroit with me and from Cleveland with him. Still, I know a thousand dolls who cannot remember offhand where they are from if you ask them quick.

By and by Scoodles Shea and Black Mike notice Benny is all tangled in conversation with Dolores, which makes them take a second peek at her, and by this time they are peeking through plenty of Joe Goss' liquor, which probably makes her look ten times more beautiful than she really is. And I wish to say that any doll ten times more beautiful than Dolores is nothing but a dream.

Anyway, before long Dolores is getting much attention from Black Mike and Scoodles, as well as Benny, and the rest of the dolls finally take the wind, because nobody is giving them a tumble any more. And even Dave the Dude begins taking dead aim at Dolores until I remind him that he must call up Miss Billy Perry, so he spends the next half-hour in a phone booth explaining to Miss Billy Perry that he is in his hotel in the hay, and that he loves her very dearly.

Well, we are in Joe Goss' joint until five o'clock A.M., with Black Mike and Scoodles and Benny talking to Dolores and taking turns dancing with her, and Dave the Dude is plumb wore out, especially as Miss Billy Perry tells him she knows he is a liar and a bum as she can hear an orchestra playing "I Get So Blue When It Rains" and for him to just wait until she sees him. Then we take Dolores and go to Childs' restaurant on the Boardwalk and have some coffee, and finally all hands escort her to a little flea-bag in North Carolina Avenue where she says she is stopping.

"What are you doing this afternoon, beautiful one?" asks Benny the Blond Jew as we are telling her good night, even though it is morning, and at this crack Black Mike and Scoodles Shea look at Benny very, very cross.

"I am going bathing in front of the Ritz," she says. "Do some of you boys wish to come along with me?"

Well, it seems that Black Mike and Scoodles and Benny all think this is a wonderful idea, but it does not go so big with Dave the Dude or me. In fact, by this time Dave the Dude and me are pretty sick of Dolores, and only wishing to get back to the hotel and give the old Ostermoor a strong play.

"Anyway," Dave says, "we must start our conference this afternoon and get through with it, because my ever-loving doll is already steaming, and I have plenty of business to look after in New York."

But the conference does not start this afternoon, or the next night, or the next day, or the next day following, because in the afternoons Black Mike and Scoodles and Benny are in the ocean with Dolores and at night they are in Joe Goss' joint, and in between they are taking her riding in rolling chairs on the Boardwalk, or feeding her around the different hotels. No one guy is ever alone with her as far I can see, except when she is dancing with one in Joe Goss' joint, and about the third night they are so jealous of each other they all try to dance with her at once.

Well, naturally even Joe Goss complains about this because it makes confusion on his dance floor, and looks unusual, so Dolores settles the proposition by not dancing with anybody, and I figure this is a good break for her, as no doll's dogs can stand all the dancing Black Mike and Scoodles and Benny wish to do.

The biggest rolling chair on the Boardwalk only takes in three guys, or two guys and one doll, or what is much better, one guy and two dolls, so when Dolores is in a rolling chair with a guy sitting on each side of her, the other walks alongside the chair, which is a peculiar sight, indeed. How they decide the guy who walks I never know, but I suppose Dolores fixes it. When she is in bathing in the ocean, Black

Mike and Scoodles and Benny all stick so close to her that she is really quite crowded at times.

I doubt if even Waldo Winchester, the scribe, who hears of a lot of things, ever hears of such a situation as this with three guys all daffy over the same doll, and guys who do not think any too well of each other to begin with. I can see they are getting more and more hostile toward each other over her, but when they are not with Dolores, they stick close to each other for fear one will cop a sneak, and get her to himself.

I am very much puzzled because Black Mike and Scoodles and Benny do not get their rods out and start a shooting match among themselves over her, but I find that Dave the Dude makes them turn in their rods to him the second day because he does not care to have them doing any target practice around Atlantic City. So they cannot start a shooting match among themselves if they wish, and the reason they do not put the slug on each other is because Dolores tells them she hates tough guys who go around putting the slug on people. So they are being gentlemen, bar a few bad cracks passing among them now and then.

Well, it comes on a Friday, and there we are in Atlantic City since a Monday and nothing stirring on the peace conference as yet, and Dave the Dude is very much disgusted indeed, especially as Miss Billy Perry is laying the blast on him plenty every night over the telephone until Dave is sorry that he ever thinks of marrying Miss Billy Perry.

All night Friday and into Saturday morning we are in Joe Goss', and personally I can think of many other places I will rather be. To begin with, I never care to be around gorills when they are drinking, and when you take gorills who are drinking and get them all crazy about the same doll, they are apt to turn out to be no gentlemen any minute. The only reason I stick around is because Dave the Dude sticks, and the only reason Dave the Dude sticks is to keep these guys from giving Atlantic City a bad name.

I do not know who it is who suggests a daybreak swimming party, because I am half asleep, and so is Dave the Dude, but I hear afterwards it is Dolores. Anyway, the next thing anybody knows we are out on the beach and Dolores and Black Mike and Scoodles Shea and Benny the Blond Jew are in their bathing suits and the dawn is touching up the old ocean very beautiful.

Of course Dave the Dude and me are not in bathing suits, because in the first place neither of us is any hand for going in bathing, and in the second place, if we are going in bathing we will not go in bathing at such an hour. Furthermore, as far as I am personally concerned, I hope I am never in a bathing suit if I will look no better in it than Black Mike, while Scoodles Shea is no Gene Tunney in regards to shape. Benny the Blond Jew is the only one who looks human, and I do not give even him more than sixty-five points.

Dave the Dude and me stand around watching them, and mostly we are watching Dolores. She is in a red bathing suit, with a red rubber cap over her black hair, and while most dolls in bathing suits hurt my eyes, she is still beautiful. I will always claim she is the most beautiful thing I ever see, bar Blue Larkspur, and of course Blue Larkspur is a race horse and not a doll. I am very glad that Miss Billy Perry is not present to see the look in Dave the Dude's eyes as he watches Dolores in her bathing suit, for Miss Billy Perry is quick to take offense.

When she is in the water, Dolores slides around like a big beautiful red fish. You can see she loves it. The chances are I can swim better on my back than Black Mike or Scoodles Shea can on their stomachs and Benny the Blond Jew is no Gertrude Ederle, but of course I am allowing for them being well loaded with Joe Goss' liquor, and a load of Joe Goss' liquor is not apt to float well anywhere.

Well, after they paddle around in the ocean a while,

Dolores and her three Romeos lay out on the sand, and Dave the Dude and me are just figuring on going to bed, when all of a sudden we see Dolores jump up and start running for the ocean with Black Mike and Benny head-and-head just behind her, and Scoodles Shea half a length back.

She tears into the water, kicking it every which way until she gets to where it is deep, when she starts to swim, heading for the open sea. Black Mike and Scoodles Shea and Benny the Blond Jew are paddling after her like blazes. We can see it is some kind of a chase, and we stand watching it. We can see Dolores' little red cap bouncing along over the water like a rubber ball on a sidewalk, with Black Mike and Scoodles and Benny staggering along behind her, for Joe Goss' liquor will make a guy stagger on land or sea.

She is away ahead of them at first, but then she seems to pull up and let them get closer to her. When Black Mike, who is leading the other two, gets within maybe fifty yards of her, her red cap bounces away again, always going farther out. It strikes me that Dolores is sort of swimming in wide circles, now half turning as if coming back to the beach, and then taking a swing that carries her seaward again. When I come to think it over afterwards, I can see that when you are watching her it does not look as if she is swimming away from the beach and yet all the time she is getting away from it.

One of her circles takes her almost back to Benny, who is a bad last to Black Mike and Scoodles Shea, and in fact she gets so close to Benny that he is lunging for her, when she slides away again, and is off faster than any fish I ever see afloat. Then she does the same to Black Mike and Scoodles. I figure they are playing tag in the water, or some such, and while this may be all right for guys who are full of liquor, and a light-headed doll, I do not consider it a proper amusement at such an hour for guys in their right senses, like Dave the Dude and me.

So I am pleased when he says we better go to bed, because by this time Dolores and Black Mike and Scoodles Shea and Benny seem to be very far out in the water indeed. As we are strolling along the Boardwalk, I look back again and there they are, no bigger than pin points on the water, and it seems to me that I can see only three pin points, at that, but I figure Dolores is so far out I cannot see her through the haze.

"They will be good and tuckered out by the time they get back," I say to Dave the Dude.

"I hope they drown," Dave says, but a few days later he apologizes for this crack, and explains he makes it only because he is tired and disgusted.

Well, I often think now that it is strange neither Dave the Dude or me see anything unnatural in the whole play, but we do not even mention Dolores or Black Mike or Scoodles Shea or Benny the Blond Jew until late in the afternoon when we are putting on the old grapefruit and ham and eggs in Dave's room and Dave is looking out over the ocean.

"Say," he says, as if he just happens to remember it, "do you know those guys are away out yonder the last we see of them? I wonder if they get back okay?"

And as if answering his question there is a knock on the door, and who walks in but Dolores. She looks all fagged out, but she is so beautiful I will say she seems to light up the room, only I do not wish anybody to think I am getting romantic. Anyway, she is beautiful, but her voice is very tired as she says to Dave the Dude:

"Your friends from St. Louis will not return, Mister Dave the Dude. They do not swim so well, but better than I thought. The one that is called Black Mike and Scoodles Shea turn back when we are about three miles out, but they never reach the shore. I see them both go down for the last time. I make sure of this, Mister Dave the Dude. The pale one, Benny, lasts a little farther although he is the worst swimmer of them all, and he never turns back. He is still trying to follow me when a cramp gets him and he sinks. I guess he loves me the most, at that, as he always claims."

Well, naturally, I am greatly horrified by this news, especially as she tells it without batting one of her beautiful eyes.

"Do you mean to tell us you let these poor guys drown out there in all this salt water?" I say, very indignant. "Why, you are nothing but a cad."

But Dave the Dude makes a sign for me to shut up, and Dolores says:

"I come within a quarter of a mile of swimming the English Channel in 1927, as you will see by looking up the records," she says, "and I can swim the Mississippi one-handed, but I cannot pack three big guys such as these on my back. Even," she says, "if I care to, which I do not. Benny is the only one who speaks to me before he goes. The last time I circle back to him he waves his hand and says, 'I know all along I see you somewhere before. I remember now. You are Frankie Farrone's doll.'"

"And you are?" asks Dave the Dude.

"His widow," says Dolores. "I promise him as he lays in his coffin that these men will die, and they are dead. I spend my last dollar getting to this town by airplane, but I get here, and I get them. Only it is more the hand of Providence," she says. "Now I will not need this."

And she tosses out on the table among our breakfast dishes a little bottle that we find out afterwards is full of enough cyanide to kill forty mules, which always makes me think that this Dolores is a doll who means business.

"There is only one thing I wish to know," Dave the Dude says. "Only one thing. How do you coax these fat-heads to follow you out in the water?"

"This is the easiest thing of all," Dolores says. "It is an

inspiration to me as we lay out on the beach. I tell them I will marry the first one who reaches me in the water. I do not wish to seem hard-hearted, but it is a relief to me when I see Black Mike sink. Can you imagine being married to such a bum?"

It is not until we are going home that Dave the Dude has anything to say about the proposition, and then he speaks to me as follows:

"You know," Dave says, "I will always consider I get a very lucky break that Dolores does not include me in her offer, or the chances are I will be swimming yet."

Social Error

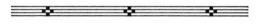

WHEN MR. ZIEGFELD picks a doll she is apt to be above the average when it comes to looks, for Mr. Ziegfeld is by no means a chump at picking dolls. But when Mr. Ziegfeld picks Miss Midgie Muldoon, he beats his own best record, or anyway ties it. I never see a better-looking doll in my life, although she is somewhat smaller than I like them. I like my dolls big enough to take a good hold on, and Miss Midgie Muldoon is only about knee-high to a Pomeranian. But she is very cute, and I do not blame Handsome Jack Maddigan for going daffy about her.

Now most any doll on Broadway will be very glad indeed to have Handsome Jack Maddigan give her a tumble, so it is very surprising to one and all when Miss Midgie Muldoon plays the chill for Handsome Jack, especially when you figure that Miss Midgie Muldoon is nothing but a chorus doll, while Handsome Jack is quite a high shot in this town. But one night in the Hot Box when Handsome Jack sends word to Miss Midgie Muldoon by Miss Billy

Perry, who is Dave the Dude's wife, that he will like to
meet up with her, Miss Midgie Muldoon sends word back
to Handsome Jack that she is not meeting up with tough
guys.

Well, naturally this crack burns Handsome Jack up quite
some. But Dave the Dude says never mind, and furthermore
Dave says Miss Midgie Muldoon's crack serves Handsome
Jack right for sitting around shooting off his mouth, and
putting himself away as a tough guy, because if there is
anything Dave hates it is a guy letting on he is tough, no
matter how tough he really is, and Handsome Jack is certainly such a guy.

He is a big tall blond guy who comes up out of what they
call Hell's Kitchen over on the West Side, and if he has a
little more sense the chances are he will be as important a
guy as Dave the Dude himself in time, instead of generally
working for Dave, but Handsome Jack likes to wear very
good clothes, and drink, and sit around a lot, and also do
plenty of talking, and no matter how much dough he makes
he never seems able to hold much of anything.

Personally, I never care to have any truck with Handsome Jack because he always strikes me as a guy who is a
little too quick on the trigger to suit me, and I always figure
the best you are going to get out of being around guys who
are quick on the trigger is the worst of it, and so any time I
see Handsome Jack I give him the back of my neck. But
there are many people in this world such as Basil Valentine
who love to be around these characters.

This Basil Valentine is a little guy who wears horn cheaters and writes articles for the magazines, and is personally a
very nice little guy, and as harmless as a water snake, but he
cannot have a whole lot of sense, or he will not be hanging
out with Handsome Jack and other such characters.

If a guy hangs out with tough guys long enough he is apt
to get to thinking maybe he is tough himself, and by and by

other people may get the idea he is tough, and the first thing you know along comes some copper in plain clothes, such as Johnny Brannigan, of the strongarm squad, and biffs him on the noggin with a blackjack just to see how tough he is. As I say, Basil Valentine is a very harmless guy, but after he is hanging out with Handsome Jack a while, I hear Basil talking very tough to a bus boy, and the chances are he is building himself up to talk tough to a waiter, and then maybe to a head waiter, and finally he may consider himself tough enough to talk tough to anybody.

I can show you many a guy who is supposed to be strictly legitimate sitting around with guys who are figured as tough guys, and why this is I do not know, but I am speaking to Waldo Winchester, the newspaper scribe, about the proposition one night, and Waldo Winchester, who is a half-smart guy in many respects, says it is what is called an underworld complex. Waldo Winchester says many legitimate people are much interested in the doings of tough guys, and consider them very romantic, and he says if I do not believe it look at all the junk the newspapers print making heroes out of tough guys.

Waldo Winchester says the underworld complex is a very common complex and that Basil Valentine has it, and so has Miss Harriet Mackyle, or she will not be all the time sticking her snoot into joints where tough guys hang out. This Miss Harriet Mackyle is one of these rich dolls who wears snaky-looking evening clothes, and has her hair cut like a boy's, with her ears sticking out, and is always around the night traps, generally with some guy with a little mustache, and a way of talking like an Englishman, and come to think of it I do see her in tough joints more than somewhat, saying hello to different parties such as nobody in their right minds will say hello to, including such as Red Henry, who is just back from Dannemora, after being away for quite a spell for taking things out of somebody's safe and blowing the safe open to take these things.

In fact, I see Miss Harriet Mackyle dancing one night in the Hearts and Flowers club, which is a very tough joint, indeed, and who is she dancing with but Red Henry, and when I ask Waldo Winchester what he makes of this proposition, he says it is part of the underworld complex he is talking about. He says Miss Harriet Mackyle probably thinks it smart to tell her swell friends she dances with a safe blower, although personally if I am going to dance with a safe blower at all, which does not seem likely, I will pick me out a nicer safe blower than Red Henry, because he is such a guy as does not take a bath since he leaves Dannemora, and he is back from Dannemora for several months.

One party who does not seem to have much of Waldo Winchester's underworld complex as far as I can see is Miss Midgie Muldoon, because I never see her around any night traps except such as the Hot Box and the Sixteen Hundred club, which are considered very nice places, and reasonably safe for anybody who does not get too far out of line, and Miss Midgie Muldoon is always with very legitimate guys such as Buddy Donaldson, the song writer, or Walter Gumble, who plays the trombone in Paul Whiteman's band, or maybe sometimes with Paul Hawley, the actor.

Furthermore, when she is around such places, Miss Midgie Muldoon minds her own business quite a bit, and always looks right past Handsome Jack Maddigan, which burns Jack up all the more. It is the first time Handsome Jack ever runs into a doll who does not seem excited about him, and he does not know what to make of such a situation.

Well, what happens but Dave the Dude comes to me one day and says to me like this: "Listen," Dave says, "this doll Miss Harriet Mackyle is one of my best customers for highgrade merchandise, and is as good as wheat in the bin, and she is asking a favor of me. She is giving a party Sunday night in her joint over on Park Avenue, and she wishes me to invite some of the mob, so go around and tell about a dozen guys to be there all dressed, and not get too fresh, because a big order of Scotch and champagne goes with the favor."

Now such a party is by no means unusual, although generally it is some swell guy who gives it rather than a doll, and he gets Broadway guys to be there to show his pals what a mixer he is. Waldo Winchester says it is to give color to things, though where the color comes in I do not know, for Broadway guys, such as will go to a party like this, are apt to just sit around and say nothing, and act very gentlemanly, because they figure they are on exhibition like freaks, and the only way you can get them to such parties in the first place is through some such connection as Miss Harriet Mackyle has with Dave the Dude.

Anyway, I go around and about and tell a lot of guys what Dave the Dude wishes them to do, and among others I tell Handsome Jack, who is tickled to death by the invitation, because if there is anything Jack loves more than anything else it is to be in a spot where he can show off some. Furthermore, Handsome Jack has a sneaking idea Miss Harriet Mackyle is red hot for him because she sometimes gives him the old eye when she sees him around the Sixteen Hundred club, and other spots, but then she does the same thing to Big Nig, and a lot of other guys I can mention, because that is just naturally the way Miss Harriet Mackyle is. But of course I do not speak of this to Handsome Jack. Basil Valentine is with Jack when I invite him, so I tell Basil to come along, too, because I do not wish him to think I am a snob.

It turns out that Basil is one of the very first guys to show up Sunday night at Miss Harriet Mackyle's apartment, where I am already on hand to help get in the Scotch and champagne, and to make Miss Harriet Mackyle acquainted with such of the mob as I invite, although I find we are about lost in the shuffle of guys with little mustaches, and dolls in evening clothes that leave plenty of them sticking out here and there. It seems everybody on Broadway is there, as well as a lot of Park Avenue, and Mr. Ziegfeld is especially well represented and among his people I see Miss Midgie Muldoon, although I have to stand on tiptoe to see her on account of the guys with little mustaches around her, and their interest in Miss Midgie Muldoon proves that they are not such saps as they look, even if they do wear little mustaches.

It is a very large apartment, and the first thing I notice is a big green parrot swinging in a ring hung from the ceiling in a corner of what seems to be the main room, and the reason I notice this parrot is because it is letting out a squawk now and then, and yelling different words, such as Polly wants a cracker. They are also a lot of canary birds hung around the joint, so I judge Miss Harriet Mackyle loves animals, as well as peculiar people, such as she has for guests.

I am somewhat surprised to see Red Henry all dressed up in evening clothes moving around among the guests. I do not invite Red Henry, so I suppose Miss Harriet Mackyle invites him, or he hears rumors of the party, and just crashes in, but personally I consider it very bad taste on Red Henry's part to show himself in such a spot, and so does everybody else that knows him, although he seems to be minding his own business pretty well.

Finally when the serious drinking is under way, and a good time is being had by one and all, Miss Harriet Mackyle comes over to me and says to me like this: "Now tell me about your different friends, so I can tell my other guests. They will be thrilled to death meeting these bad characters."

"Well," I say, "you see the little guy over there staring at you as if you are a ghost, or some such? Well, he is nobody but Bad Basil Valentine, who will kill you quicker than you can say scat, and maybe quicker. He is undoubtedly the toughest guy here tonight, or anywhere else in this man's town for that matter. Yes, ma'am, Bad Basil Valentine is one dead tough mug," I say, "although he is harmless looking at this time. Bad Basil kills many a guy in his day. In fact, Miss Mackyle," I say, "Bad Basil can scarcely sleep good any night he does not kill some guy."

"My goodness!" Miss Harriet Mackyle says, looking Basil over very carefully. "He does not look so bad at first glance, although now that I examine him closely I believe I do detect a sinister gleam in his eye."

Well, Miss Harriet Mackyle can hardly wait until she gets away from me, and the next I see of her she has Basil Valentine surrounded and is almost chewing his ear off as she gabs to him, and anybody can see that Basil is all pleasured up by this attention. In fact, Basil is snagged if ever I see a guy snagged, and personally I do not blame him because Miss Harriet Mackyle may not look a million, but she has a couple, and you can see enough of her in her evening clothes to know that nothing about her is phony.

The party is going big along toward one o'clock when all of a sudden in comes Handsome Jack Maddigan with half a heat on, and in five minutes he is all over the joint, drinking everything that is offered him, and making a fast play for all the dolls, and talking very loud. He is sored up more than somewhat when he finds Miss Harriet Mackyle does not give him much of a tumble, because he figures she will be calling him on top the minute he blows in, but Miss Harriet Mackyle is too busy with Basil Valentine finding out from Basil how he knocks off six of Al Capone's mob out in Chicago one time when he is out there on a pleasure trip.

Well, while feeling sored up about Miss Harriet Mackyle passing him up for Basil Valentine, and not knowing how

it comes Basil is in so stout with her, Handsome Jack bumps
into Red Henry, and Red Henry makes some fresh crack to
Jack about Basil moving in on him, which causes Handsome Jack to hit Red Henry on the chin, and knock him
half into the lap of Miss Midgie Muldoon, who is sitting in
a chair with a lot of little mustaches around her.

Naturally this incident causes some excitement for a moment. But the way Miss Midgie Muldoon takes it is very
surprising. She just sort of dusts Red Henry off her, and
stands up no bigger than a demi-tasse, and looks Handsome
Jack right in the eye very cool, and says, "Ah, a parlor
tough guy." Then she walks away, leaving Handsome Jack
with his mouth open, because he does not know up to this
moment that Miss Midgie Muldoon is present.

Well, somebody heaves Red Henry out of the joint, and
the party continues, but I see Handsome Jack wandering
around looking very lonesome, and with not much speed
left compared to what he brings in. Somehow I figure
Handsome Jack is looking for Miss Midgie Muldoon, but
she keeps off among the little mustaches, and finally Handsome Jack takes to belting the old grape right freely to get
his zing back. He gets himself pretty well organized, and
when he suddenly comes upon Miss Midgie Muldoon standing by herself for a moment, he is feeling very brisk indeed,
and he says to her like this: "Hello, Beautiful, are you playing the hard-to-get for me?" But Miss Midgie Muldoon only
looks him in the eye again and says: "Ah, the parlor tough
guy! Go away, tough guy. I do not like tough guys."

Well, this is not so encouraging when you come to think
of it, but Handsome Jack is a guy who will never be ruled
off for not trying with the dolls, and he is just about to begin giving her a little more work, when all of a sudden a
voice goes "Ha-ha-ha," and then it says: "Hello, you fool!"

Now of course it is nothing but the parrot talking, and it
says, again, "Ha-ha-ha. Hello, you fool!" Of course the

parrot, whose name turns out to be Polly, does not mean Handsome Jack, but of course Handsome Jack does not know the parrot does not mean him, and naturally he feels very much insulted. Furthermore, he has plenty of champagne inside him. So all of a sudden he outs with the old equalizer and lets go at Polly, and the next minute there are green feathers flying all over the joint, and poor old Mister, or maybe Missus, Polly is stretched out as dead as a doornail, and maybe deader.

Well, I never see a doll carry on like Miss Harriet Mackyle does when she finds out her Polly is a goner, and what she says to Handsome Jack is really very cutting, and quite extensive, and the chances are Handsome Jack will finally haul off and smack Miss Harriet Mackyle in the snoot, only he realizes he is already guilty of a very grave social error in shooting the parrot, and he does not wish to make it any worse.

Anyway, Miss Midgie Muldoon is standing looking at Handsome Jack out of her great big round beautiful eyes with what Waldo Winchester, the scribe, afterward tells me is plenty of scorn, and it looks to me as if Handsome Jack feels worse about Miss Midgie Muldoon's looks than he does about what Miss Harriet Mackyle is saying to him. But Miss Midgie Muldoon never opens her mouth. She just keeps looking at him for quite a spell, and then finally walks away, and it looks to me as if she is ready to bust out crying any minute, maybe because she feels sorry for Polly.

Well, naturally Handsome Jack's error busts up the party because Miss Harriet Mackyle does not wish to take any chances on Handsome Jack starting in to pot her canaries, so we all go away leaving Miss Harriet Mackyle weeping over what she can find of Polly, and Basil Valentine crying with her, which I consider very chummy of Basil, at that.

A couple of nights later Basil comes into Mindy's restaurant, where I happen to be sitting with Handsome Jack, and anybody can tell that Basil is much worried about something.

"Jack," he says, "Miss Harriet Mackyle is very, very, very angry about you shooting Polly. In fact, she hates you, because Polly is a family heirloom."

"Well," Jack says, "tell her I apologize, and will get her a new parrot as soon as I get the price. You know I am broke now. Tell her I am very sorry, although," Jack says, "her parrot has no right to call me a fool, and I leave this to anybody."

"Miss Harriet Mackyle is after me every day to shoot you, Jack," Basil says. "She thinks I am a very tough guy, and that I will shoot anybody on short notice, and she wishes me to shoot you. In fact, she is somewhat displeased because I do not shoot you when you shoot poor Polly, but of course I explain to her I do not have a gun at the moment. Now Miss Harriet Mackyle says if I do not shoot you she will not love me, and I greatly wish to have Miss Harriet Mackyle love me, because I am practically daffy about her. So," Basil says, "I am wondering how much you will take to hold still and let me shoot you, Jack?"

"Why," Handsome Jack says, very much astonished, "you must be screwy."

"Of course I do not mean to really shoot you, Jack," Basil says. "I mean to maybe shoot you with a blank cartridge, so Miss Harriet Mackyle will think I am shooting you sure enough, which will make her very grateful to me. I am thinking that maybe I can pay you $1,500 for such a job although this sum represents nearly my life savings."

"Why," Handsome Jack says, "your proposition sounds very reasonable, at that. I am just wondering where I can get hold of a few bobs to send Miss Midgie Muldoon a bar pin, or some such, and see if I cannot round myself up with her. She is still playing plenty of chill for me. You better make it two grand while you are about it."

Well, Basil Valentine finally agrees to pay the two grand. Furthermore, Basil promises to put the dough up in advance with Dave the Dude, or some other reliable party, as this is rather an unusual business deal, and naturally Handsome Jack wishes to have his interests fully protected.

Well, the thing comes off a few nights later in the Hot Box, and it is all pretty well laid out in advance. It is understood that Basil is to bring Miss Harriet Mackyle into the Hot Box after regular hours when there are not apt to be any too many people around, and to find Handsome Jack there. Basil is to out with a gun and take a crack at Handsome Jack, and Handsome Jack is to let on he is hit, and Basil is to get Miss Harriet Mackyle out of the joint in the confusion.

Handsome Jack promises to lay low a few weeks afterwards so it will look as if he is dead, and Basil figures that in the meantime Miss Harriet Mackyle will be so grateful to him that she will love him very much indeed, and maybe marry him, which is really the big idea with Basil.

It is pretty generally known to one and all what is coming off, and quite a number of guys drift into the Hot Box during the night, including Dave the Dude, who seems to be getting quite a bang out of the situation. But who also bobs up very unexpectedly but Miss Midgie Muldoon with Buddy Donaldson, the song writer.

Handsome Jack is all upset by Miss Midgie Muldoon being there, but she never as much as looks at him. So Handsome Jack takes to drinking Scotch more than somewhat, and everybody commences to worry about whether he will hold still for Basil Valentine to shoot him, even with a blank cartridge. The Hot Box closes at 3 o'clock in the morning, and everybody is always turned out except the regulars. So by 3:30 there are only about a dozen guys and dolls in the joint when in comes Basil Valentine and Miss Harriet Mackyle.

Handsome Jack happens to be standing with his back to the door and not far from the table where Miss Midgie Muldoon and this Buddy Donaldson are sitting when Basil and Miss Harriet Mackyle come in, and right away Basil sings out, his voice wobbling no little: "Handsome Jack Maddigan, your time has come!" At this Handsome Jack turns around, and there is Basil Valentine tugging a big rod out of the hind pocket of his pants.

The next thing anybody knows, there is a scream, and a doll's voice cries: "Jack! Look out, Jack!" and out of her seat and over to Handsome Jack Maddigan bounces Miss Midgie Muldoon, and just as Basil finally raises the rod and turns it on, Miss Midgie Muldoon plants herself right in front of Jack and stretches out her arms on either side of her as if to shield him.

Well, the gun goes bingo in Basil's hand, but instead of falling like he is supposed to do, Handsome Jack stands there with his mouth open looking at Miss Midgie Muldoon, not knowing what to make of her jumping between him and the gun, and it is a good thing he does not fall, at that, because he is able to catch Miss Midgie Muldoon as she starts to keel over. At first we think maybe it is only a faint, but she has on a low-neck dress, and across her left shoulder there slowly spreads a red smear, and what is this red smear but blood, and as Handsome Jack grabs her she says to him like this: "Hold me, dear, I am hurt."

Now this is most unexpected, indeed, and is by no means a part of the play. Basil Valentine is standing by the door with the rod in his duke looking quite astonished, and making no move to get Miss Harriet Mackyle out of the joint as he is supposed to the minute he fires, and Miss Harriet Mackyle is letting out a few offhand screams which are very piercing, and saying she never thinks that Basil will take her seriously and really plug anybody for

her, although she also says she appreciates his thoughtful-
ness, at that.

You can see Basil is standing there wondering what goes
wrong, when Dave the Dude, who is a fast thinker under
all circumstances, takes a quick peek at Miss Midgie Muldoon, and then jumps across the room and nails Basil.
"Why," Dave says to Basil, "you are nothing but a rascal.
You mean to kill him after all. You do not shoot a blank,
you throw a slug, and you get Miss Midgie Muldoon with
it in the shoulder."

Well, Basil is a pretty sick-looking toad as Dave the
Dude takes hold of him, and Miss Harriet Mackyle is putting on a few extra yips when Basil says: "My goodness,
Dave," he says. "I never know this gun is really loaded.
In fact, I forget all about getting a gun of my own until
the last minute, and am looking around for one when Red
Henry comes along and says he will lend me his. I explain
to him how the whole proposition is a joke, and tell him I
must have blanks, and he kindly takes the lead out of the
cartridges in front of my own eyes and makes them blank."

"The chances are Red Henry works a quick change on
you," Dave the Dude says. "Red Henry is very angry at
Jack for hitting him on the chin."

Then Dave takes the rod out of Basil's hand and breaks
it open, and sure enough there are enough real slugs in it
to sink a rowboat and no blanks whatever, which surprises
Basil Valentine no little.

"Now," Dave says, "get away from here before Jack
realizes what happens, and keep out of sight until you hear
from me, because if Miss Midgie Muldoon croaks it may
cause some gossip. Furthermore," Dave says, "take this
squawking doll with you."

Well, you can see that Dave the Dude is pretty much
steamed up, and he remains steamed up until it comes out

that Miss Midgie Muldoon is only a little bit shot, and is by no means in danger of dying. We take her over to the Polyclinic Hospital, and a guy there digs the bullet out of her shoulder, and we leave her there with Handsome Jack holding her tight in his arms, and swearing he will never be tough again, but will get her a nice little home on Basil Valentine's two grand, and find himself a job, and take no more part in his old life, all of which seems to sound fair enough.

It is a couple of years before we hear of Miss Harriet Mackyle again, and then she is Mrs. Basil Valentine, and is living in Naples over in Italy, and the people there are very much surprised because Mrs. Basil Valentine never lets Mr. Basil Valentine associate with guys over ten years old, and never lets him handle anything more dangerous than a niblick.

So this is about all there is to the story, except that when Handsome Jack Maddigan and Miss Midgie Muldoon stand up to be married by Father Leonard, Dave the Dude sizes them up a minute, and then turns to me and says like this:

"Look," Dave says, "and tell me where does Miss Midgie Muldoon's shoulder come up to on Jack's left side."

"Well," I say, "her shoulder comes just up to Jack's heart."

"So you see," Dave says, "it is just as well for Jack she stops Basil's bullet, at that."

Blood Pressure

It is maybe eleven-thirty of a Wednesday night, and I am standing at the corner of Forty-eighth Street and Seventh Avenue, thinking about my blood pressure, which is a proposition I never before think much about.

In fact, I never hear of my blood pressure before this Wednesday afternoon when I go around to see Doc Brennan about my stomach, and he puts a gag on my arm and tells me that my blood pressure is higher than a cat's back, and the idea is for me to be careful about what I eat, and to avoid excitement, or I may pop off all of a sudden when I am least expecting it.

"A nervous man such as you with a blood pressure away up in the paint cards must live quietly," Doc Brennan says. "Ten bucks, please," he says.

Well, I am standing there thinking it is not going to be so tough to avoid excitement the way things are around this town right now, and wishing I have my ten bucks back to bet it on Sun Beau in the fourth race at Pimlico the next day, when all of a sudden I look up, and who is in front of me but Rusty Charley.

Now if I have any idea Rusty Charley is coming my way, you can go and bet all the coffee in Java I will be somewhere else at once, for Rusty Charley is not a guy I wish to have any truck with whatever. In fact, I wish no part of him. Furthermore, nobody else in this town wishes to have any part of Rusty Charley, for he is a hard guy indeed. In fact, there is no harder guy anywhere in the world. He is a big wide guy with two large hard hands and a great deal of very bad disposition, and he thinks nothing of knocking people down and stepping on their kissers if he feels like it.

In fact, this Rusty Charley is what is called a gorill, because he is known to often carry a gun in his pants pocket, and sometimes to shoot people down as dead as door nails with it if he does not like the way they wear their hats—and Rusty Charley is very critical of hats. The chances are Rusty Charley shoots many a guy in this man's town, and those he does not shoot he sticks with his shiv—which is a knife—and the only reason he is not in jail is because he just gets out of it, and the law does not have time to think up something to put him back in again for.

Anyway, the first thing I know about Rusty Charley being in my neighborhood is when I hear him saying: "Well, well, well, here we are!"

Then he grabs me by the collar, so it is no use of me thinking of taking it on the lam away from there, although I greatly wish to do so.

"Hello, Rusty," I say, very pleasant. "What is the score?"

"Everything is about even," Rusty says. "I am glad to see you, because I am looking for company. I am over in Philadelphia for three days on business."

"I hope and trust that you do all right for yourself in

Philly, Rusty," I say; but his news makes me very nervous, because I am a great hand for reading the papers and I have a pretty good idea what Rusty's business in Philly is. It is only the day before that I see a little item from Philly in the papers about how Gloomy Gus Smallwood, who is a very large operator in the alcohol business there, is guzzled right at his front door.

Of course I do not know that Rusty Charley is the party who guzzles Gloomy Gus Smallwood, but Rusty Charley is in Philly when Gus is guzzled, and I can put two and two together as well as anybody. It is the same thing as if there is a bank robbery in Cleveland, Ohio, and Rusty Charley is in Cleveland, Ohio, or near there. So I am very nervous, and I figure it is a sure thing my blood pressure is going up every second.

"How much dough do you have on you?" Rusty says. "I am plumb broke."

"I do not have more than a couple of bobs, Rusty," I say. "I pay a doctor ten bucks today to find out my blood pressure is very bad. But of course you are welcome to what I have."

"Well, a couple of bobs is no good to high-class guys like you and me," Rusty says. "Let us go to Nathan Detroit's crap game and win some money."

Now, of course, I do not wish to go to Nathan Detroit's crap game; and if I do wish to go there I do not wish to go with Rusty Charley, because a guy is sometimes judged by the company he keeps, especially around crap games, and Rusty Charley is apt to be considered bad company. Anyway, I do not have any dough to shoot craps with, and if I do have dough to shoot craps with, I will not shoot craps with it at all, but will bet it on Sun Beau, or maybe take it home and pay off some of the overhead around my joint, such as rent.

Furthermore, I remember what Doc Brennan tells me

about avoiding excitement, and I know there is apt to be excitement around Nathan Detroit's crap game if Rusty Charley goes there, and maybe run my blood pressure up and cause me to pop off very unexpected. In fact, I already feel my blood jumping more than somewhat inside me, but naturally I am not going to give Rusty Charley any argument, so we go to Nathan Detroit's crap game.

This crap game is over a garage in Fifty-second Street this particular night, though sometimes it is over a restaurant in Forty-seventh Street, or in back of a cigar store in Forty-fourth Street. In fact, Nathan Detroit's crap game is apt to be anywhere, because it moves around every night, as there is no sense in a crap game staying in one spot until the coppers find out where it is.

So Nathan Detroit moves his crap game from spot to spot, and citizens wishing to do business with him have to ask where he is every night; and of course almost everybody on Broadway knows this, as Nathan Detroit has guys walking up and down, and around and about, telling the public his address, and giving out the password for the evening.

Well, Jack the Beefer is sitting in an automobile outside the garage in Fifty-second Street when Rusty Charley and I come along, and he says "Kansas City," very low, as we pass, this being the password for the evening; but we do not have to use any password whatever when we climb the stairs over the garage, because the minute Solid John, the doorman, peeks out through his peephole when we knock, and sees Rusty Charley with me, he opens up very quick indeed, and gives us a big castor-oil smile, for nobody in this town is keeping doors shut on Rusty Charley very long.

It is a very dirty room over the garage, and full of smoke, and the crap game is on an old pool table; and around the table and packed in so close you cannot get a knitting needle between any two guys with a mawl, are all the high shots in town, for there is plenty of money around at this time, and many citizens are very prosperous. Furthermore, I wish to say there are some very tough guys around the table, too, including guys who will shoot you in the head, or maybe the stomach, and think nothing whatever about the matter.

In fact, when I see such guys as Harry the Horse, from Brooklyn, and Sleepout Sam Levinsky, and Lone Louie, from Harlem, I know this is a bad place for my blood pressure, for these are very tough guys indeed, and are known as such to one and all in this town.

But there they are wedged up against the table with Nick the Greek, Big Nig, Gray John, Okay Okun, and many other high shots, and they all have big coarse G notes in their hands which they are tossing around back and forth as if these G notes are nothing but pieces of waste paper.

On the outside of the mob at the table are a lot of small operators who are trying to cram their fists in between the high shots now and then to get down a bet, and there are also guys present who are called Shylocks, because they will lend you dough when you go broke at the table, on watches or rings, or maybe cuff links, at very good interest.

Well, as I say, there is no room at the table for as many as one more very thin guy when we walk into the joint, but Rusty Charley lets out a big hello as we enter, and the guys all look around, and the next minute there is space at the table big enough not only for Rusty Charley but for me too. It really is quite magical the way there is suddenly room for us when there is no room whatever for anybody when we come in.

"Who is the gunner?" Rusty Charley asks, looking all around.

"Why, you are, Charley," Big Nig, the stick man in the game, says very quick, handing Charley a pair of dice, although afterward I hear that his pal is right in the middle of a roll trying to make nine when we step up to the table. Everybody is very quiet, just looking at Charley. Nobody pays any attention to me, because I am known to one and all as a guy who is just around, and nobody figures me in on any part of Charley, although Harry the Horse looks at me once in a way that I know is no good for my blood pressure, or for anybody else's blood pressure as far as this goes.

Well, Charley takes the dice and turns to a little guy in a derby hat who is standing next to him scrooching back so Charley will not notice him, and Charley lifts the derby hat off the little guy's head, and rattles the dice in his hand, and chucks them into the hat and goes "Hah!" like crap shooters always do when they are rolling the dice. Then Charley peeks into the hat and says "Ten," although he does not let anybody else look in the hat, not even me, so nobody knows if Charley throws a ten, or what.

But, of course, nobody around is going to up and doubt that Rusty Charley throws a ten, because Charley may figure it is the same thing as calling him a liar, and Charley is such a guy as is apt to hate being called a liar.

Now Nathan Detroit's crap game is what is called a head-and-head game, although some guys call it a fading game, because the guys bet against each other rather than against the bank, or house. It is just the same kind of game as when two guys get together and start shooting craps against each other, and Nathan Detroit does not have to bother with a regular crap table and a layout such as they have in gambling houses. In fact, about all Nathan Detroit has to do with the game is to find a spot, furnish the dice and take his percentage which is by no means bad.

In such a game as this there is no real action until a guy is out on a point, and then the guys around commence to bet he makes this point, or that he does not make this point, and the odds in any country in the world that a guy does not make a ten with a pair of dice before he rolls seven, is two to one.

Well, when Charley says he rolls ten in the derby hat nobody opens their trap, and Charley looks all around the table, and all of a sudden he sees Jew Louie at one end, although Jew Louie seems to be trying to shrink himself up when Charley's eyes light on him.

"I will take the odds for five C's," Charley says, "and Louie, you get it"—meaning he is letting Louie bet him $1000 to $500 that he does not make his ten.

Now Jew Louie is a small operator at all times and more of a Shylock than he is a player, and the only reason he is up there against the table at all at this moment is because he moves up to lend Nick the Greek some dough; and ordinarily there is no more chance of Jew Louie betting a thousand to five hundred on any proposition whatever than there is of him giving his dough to the Salvation Army, which is no chance at all. It is a sure thing he will never think of betting a thousand to five hundred a guy will not make ten with the dice, and when Rusty Charley tells Louie he has such a bet, Louie starts trembling all over.

The others around the table do not say a word, and so Charley rattles the dice again in his duke, blows on them, and chucks them into the derby hat and says "Hah!" But, of course, nobody can see in the derby hat except Charley, and he peeks in at the dice and says "Five." He rattles the dice once more and chucks them into the derby and says "Hah!" and then after peeking into the hat at the dice he says "Eight." I am commencing to sweat for fear he may heave a seven in the hat and blow his bet, and I know

Charley has no five C's to pay off with, although, of course, I also know Charley has no idea of paying off, no matter what he heaves.

On the next chuck, Charley yells "Money!"—meaning he finally makes his ten, although nobody sees it but him; and he reaches out his hand to Jew Louie, and Jew Louie hands him a big fat G note, very, very slow. In all my life I never see a sadder-looking guy than Louie when he is parting with his dough. If Louie has any idea of asking Charley to let him see the dice in the hat to make sure about the ten, he does not speak about the matter, and as Charley does not seem to wish to show the ten around, nobody else says anything either, probably figuring Rusty Charley is not a guy who is apt to let anybody question his word especially over such a small matter as a ten.

"Well," Charley says, putting Louie's G note in his pocket, "I think this is enough for me tonight," and he hands the derby hat back to the little guy who owns it and motions me to come on, which I am glad to do, as the silence in the joint is making my stomach go up and down inside me, and I know this is bad for my blood pressure. Nobody as much as opens his face from the time we go in until we start out, and you will be surprised how nervous it makes you to be in a big crowd with everybody dead still, especially when you figure it a spot that is liable to get hot any minute. It is only just as we get to the door that anybody speaks, and who is it but Jew Louie, who pipes up and says to Rusty Charley like this:

"Charley," he says, "do you make it the hard way?"

Well, everybody laughs, and we go on out, but I never hear myself whether Charley makes his ten with a six and a four, or with two fives—which is the hard way to make a ten with the dice—although I often wonder about the matter afterward.

I am hoping that I can now get away from Rusty

Charley and go on home, because I can see he is the last guy in the world to have around a blood pressure, and, furthermore, that people may get the wrong idea of me if I stick around with him, but when I suggest going to Charley, he seems to be hurt.

"Why," Charley says, "you are a fine guy to be talking of quitting a pal just as we are starting out. You will certainly stay with me because I like company, and we will go down to Ikey the Pig's and play stuss. Ikey is an old friend of mine, and I owe him a complimentary play."

Now, of course, I do not wish to go to Ikey the Pig's, because it is a place away downtown, and I do not wish to play stuss, because this is a game which I am never able to figure out myself, and, furthermore, I remember Doc Brennan says I ought to get a little sleep now and then; but I see no use in hurting Charley's feelings, especially as he is apt to do something drastic to me if I do not go.

So he calls a taxi, and we start downtown for Ikey the Pig's, and the jockey who is driving the short goes so fast that it makes my blood pressure go up a foot to a foot and a half from the way I feel inside, although Rusty Charley pays no attention to the speed. Finally I stick my head out the window and ask the jockey to please take it a little easy, as I wish to get where I am going all in one piece, but the guy only keeps busting along.

We are at the corner of Nineteenth and Broadway when all of a sudden Rusty Charley yells at the jockey to pull up a minute, which the guy does. Then Charley steps out of the cab and says to the jockey like this:

"When a customer asks you to take it easy, why do you not be nice and take it easy? Now see what you get."

And Rusty Charley hauls off and clips the jockey a punch on the chin that knocks the poor guy right off the seat into the street, and then Charley climbs into the seat himself and away we go with Charley driving, leaving the guy stretched out as stiff as a board. Now Rusty Charley once drives a short for a living himself, until the coppers get an idea that he is not always delivering his customers to the right address, especially such as may happen to be drunk when he gets them, and he is a pretty fair driver, but he only looks one way, which is straight ahead.

Personally, I never wish to ride with Charley in a taxicab under any circumstances, especially if he is driving, because he certainly drives very fast. He pulls up a block from Ikey the Pig's, and says we will leave the short there until somebody finds it and turns it in, but just as we are walking away from the short up steps a copper in uniform and claims we cannot park the short in this spot without a driver.

Well, Rusty Charley just naturally hates to have coppers give him any advice, so what does he do but peek up and down the street to see if anybody is looking, and then haul off and clout the copper on the chin, knocking him bow-legged. I wish to say I never see a more accurate puncher than Rusty Charley, because he always connects with that old button. As the copper tumbles, Rusty Charley grabs me by the arm and starts me running up a side street, and after we go about a block we dodge into Ikey the Pig's.

It is what is called a stuss house, and many prominent citizens of the neighborhood are present playing stuss. Nobody seems any too glad to see Rusty Charley, although Ikey the Pig lets on he is tickled half to death. This Ikey the Pig is a short fat-necked guy who will look very natural at New Year's, undressed, and with an apple in his mouth, but it seems he and Rusty Charley are really old-time friends, and think fairly well of each other in spots.

But I can see that Ikey the Pig is not so tickled when he finds Charley is there to gamble, although Charley flashes his G note at once, and says he does not mind losing a little dough to Ikey just for old time's sake. But I judge Ikey the Pig knows he is never going to handle Charley's G note, because Charley puts it back in his pocket and it never comes out again even though Charley gets off loser playing stuss right away.

Well, at five o'clock in the morning, Charley is stuck one hundred and thirty G's, which is plenty of money even when a guy is playing on his muscle, and of course Ikey the Pig knows there is no chance of getting one hundred and thirty cents off of Rusty Charley, let alone that many thousands. Everybody else is gone by this time and Ikey wishes to close up. He is willing to take Charley's marker for a million if necessary to get Charley out, but the trouble is in stuss a guy is entitled to get back a percentage of what he loses, and Ikey figures Charley is sure to wish this percentage even if he gives a marker, and the percentage will wreck Ikey's joint.

Furthermore, Rusty Charley says he will not quit loser under such circumstances because Ikey is his friend, so what happens Ikey finally sends out and hires a cheater by the name of Dopey Goldberg, who takes to dealing the game and in no time he has Rusty Charley even by cheating in Rusty Charley's favor.

Personally, I do not pay much attention to the play but grab myself a few winks of sleep in a chair in a corner, and the rest seems to help my blood pressure no little. In fact, I am not noticing my blood pressure at all when Rusty Charley and I get out of Ikey the Pig's, because I figure Charley will let me go home and I can go to bed. But although it is six o'clock, and coming on broad daylight when we leave Ikey's, Charley is still full of zing, and nothing will do him but we must go to a joint that is called the Bohemian Club.

Well, this idea starts my blood pressure going again,

because the Bohemian Club is nothing but a deadfall where guys and dolls go when there is positively no other place in town open, and it is run by a guy by the name of Knife O'Halloran, who comes from down around Greenwich Village and is considered a very bad character. It is well known to one and all that a guy is apt to lose his life in Knife O'Halloran's any night, even if he does nothing more than drink Knife O'Halloran's liquor.

But Rusty Charley insists on going there, so naturally I go with him; and at first everything is very quiet and peaceful, except that a lot of guys and dolls in evening clothes, who wind up there after being in the night clubs all night, are yelling in one corner of the joint. Rusty Charley and Knife O'Halloran are having a drink together out of a bottle which Knife carries in his pocket, so as not to get it mixed up with the liquor he sells his customers, and are cutting up old touches of the time when they run with the Hudson Dusters together, when all of a sudden in comes four coppers in plain clothes.

Now these coppers are off duty and are meaning no harm to anybody, and are only wishing to have a dram or two before going home, and the chances are they will pay no attention to Rusty Charley if he minds his own business, although of course they know who he is very well indeed and will take great pleasure in putting the old sleeve on him if they only have a few charges against him, which they do not. So they do not give him a tumble. But if there is one thing Rusty Charley hates it is a copper, and he starts eying them from the minute they sit down at a table, and by and by I hear him say to Knife O'Halloran like this:

"Knife," Charley says, "what is the most beautiful sight in the world?"

"I do not know, Charley," Knife says. "What is the most beautiful sight in the world?"

"Four dead coppers in a row," Charley says.

Well, at this I personally ease myself over toward the door, because I never wish to have any trouble with coppers, and especially with four coppers, so I do not see everything that comes off. All I see is Rusty Charley grabbing at the big foot which one of the coppers kicks at him, and then everybody seems to go into a huddle, and the guys and dolls in evening dress start squawking, and my blood pressure goes up to maybe a million.

I get outside the door, but I do not go away at once as anybody with any sense will do, but stand there listening to what is going on inside, which seems to be nothing more than a loud noise like ker-bump, ker-bump, ker-bump. I am not afraid there will be any shooting, because as far as Rusty Charley is concerned he is too smart to shoot any coppers, which is the worst thing a guy can do in this town, and the coppers are not likely to start any blasting because they will not wish it to come out that they are in a joint such as the Bohemian Club off duty. So I figure they will all just take it out in pulling and hauling.

Finally the noise inside dies down, and by and by the door opens and out comes Rusty Charley, dusting himself off here and there with his hands and looking very much pleased, indeed, and through the door before it flies shut again I catch a glimpse of a lot of guys stretched out on the floor. Furthermore, I can still hear guys and dolls hollering.

"Well, well," Rusty Charley says, "I am commencing to think you take the wind on me, and am just about to get mad at you, but here you are. Let us go away from this joint, because they are making so much noise inside you cannot hear yourself think. Let us go to my joint and make my old woman cook us up some breakfast, and then we can catch some sleep. A little ham and eggs will not be bad to take right now."

Well, naturally ham and eggs are appealing to me no little at this time, but I do not care to go to Rusty Charley's joint. As far as I am personally concerned, I have enough of Rusty Charley to do me a long, long time, and I do not care to enter into his home life to any extent whatever, although to tell the truth I am somewhat surprised to learn he has any such life. I believe I do once hear that Rusty Charley marries one of the neighbors' children, and that he lives somewhere over on Tenth Avenue in the Forties, but nobody really knows much about this, and everybody figures if it is true his wife must lead a terrible dog's life.

But while I do not wish to go to Charley's joint I cannot very well refuse a civil invitation to eat ham and eggs, especially as Charley is looking at me in a very much surprised way because I do not seem so glad and I can see that it is not everyone that he invites to his joint. So I thank him, and say there is nothing I will enjoy more than ham and eggs such as his old woman will cook for us, and by and by we are walking along Tenth Avenue up around Forty-fifth Street.

It is still fairly early in the morning, and business guys are opening up their joints for the day, and little children are skipping along the sidewalks going to school and laughing tee-hee, and old dolls are shaking bedclothes and one thing and another out of the windows of the tenement houses, but when they spot Rusty Charley and me everybody becomes very quiet, indeed, and I can see that Charley is greatly respected in his own neighborhood. The business guys hurry into their joints, and the little children stop skipping and tee-heeing and go tip-toeing along, and the old dolls yank in their noodles, and a great quiet comes to the street. In fact, about all you can hear is the heels of Rusty Charley and me hitting on the sidewalk.

There is an ice wagon with a couple of horses hitched to it standing in front of a store, and when he sees the horses Rusty Charley seems to get a big idea. He stops and looks the horses over very carefully, although as far as I can see they are nothing but horses, and big and fat, and sleepy-looking horses, at that. Finally Rusty Charley says to me like this:

"When I am a young guy," he says, "I am a very good puncher with my right hand, and often I hit a horse on the skull with my fist and knock it down. I wonder," he says, "if I lose my punch. The last copper I hit back there gets up twice on me."

Then he steps up to one of the ice-wagon horses and hauls off and biffs it right between the eyes with a right-hand smack that does not travel more than four inches, and down goes old Mister Horse to his knees looking very much surprised, indeed. I see many a hard puncher in my day, including Dempsey when he really can punch, but I never see a harder punch than Rusty Charley gives this horse.

Well, the ice-wagon driver comes busting out of the store all heated up over what happens to his horse, but he cools out the minute he sees Rusty Charley, and goes on back into the store leaving the horse still taking a count, while Rusty Charley and I keep walking. Finally we come to the entrance of a tenement house that Rusty Charley says is where he lives, and in front of this house is a wop with a push cart loaded with fruit and vegetables and one thing and another, which Rusty Charley tips over as we go into the house, leaving the wop yelling very loud, and maybe cussing us in wop for all I know. I am very glad, personally, we finally get somewhere, because I can feel that my blood pressure is getting worse every minute I am with Rusty Charley.

We climb two flights of stairs, and then Charley opens

a door and we step into a room where there is a pretty little red-headed doll about knee high to a flivver, who looks as if she may just get out of the hay, because her red hair is flying around every which way on her head, and her eyes seem still gummed up with sleep. At first I think she is a very cute sight, indeed, and then I see something in her eyes that tells me this doll, whoever she is, is feeling very hostile to one and all.

"Hello, tootsie," Rusty Charley says. "How about some ham and eggs for me and my pal here? We are all tired out going around and about."

Well, the little red-headed doll just looks at him without saying a word. She is standing in the middle of the floor with one hand behind her, and all of a sudden she brings this hand around, and what does she have in it but a young baseball bat, such as kids play ball with, and which cost maybe two bits; and the next thing I know I hear something go ker-bap, and I can see she smacks Rusty Charley on the side of the noggin with the bat.

Naturally I am greatly horrified at this business, and figure Rusty Charley will kill her at once, and then I will be in a jam for witnessing the murder and will be held in jail several years like all witnesses to anything in this man's town; but Rusty Charley only falls into a big rocking-chair in a corner of the room and sits there with one hand to his head, saying, "Now hold on, tootsie," and "Wait a minute there, honey." I recollect hearing him say, "We have company for breakfast," and then the little red-headed doll turns on me and gives me a look such as I will always remember, although I smile at her very pleasant and mention it is a nice morning.

Finally she says to me like this:

"So you are the trambo who keeps my husband out all night, are you, you trambo?" she says, and with this she starts for me, and I start for the door; and by this time my blood pressure is all out of whack, because I can see that Mrs. Rusty Charley is excited more than somewhat. I get my hand on the knob and just then something hits me alongside the noggin, which I afterward figure must be the baseball bat, although I remember having a sneaking idea the roof caves in on me.

How I get the door open I do not know, because I am very dizzy in the head and my legs are wobbling, but when I think back over the situation I remember going down a lot of steps very fast, and by and by the fresh air strikes me, and I figure I am in the clear. But all of a sudden I feel another strange sensation back of my head and something goes plop against my noggin, and I figure at first that maybe my blood pressure runs up so high that it squirts out the top of my bean. Then I peek around over my shoulder just once to see that Mrs. Rusty Charley is standing beside the wop peddler's cart snatching fruit and vegetables of one kind and another off the cart and chucking them at me.

But what she hits me with back of the head is not an apple, or a peach, or a rutabaga, or a cabbage, or even a casaba melon, but a brickbat that the wop has on his cart to weight down the paper sacks in which he sells his goods. It is this brickbat which makes a lump on the back of my head so big that Doc Brennan thinks it is a tumor when I go to him the next day about my stomach, and I never tell him any different.

"But," Doc Brennan says, when he takes my blood pressure again, "your pressure is down below normal now, and as far as it is concerned you are in no danger whatever. It only goes to show what just a little bit of quiet living will do for a guy," Doc Brennan says. "Ten bucks, please," he says.

"Gentlemen, The King!"

ON TUESDAY EVENINGS I always go to Bobby's Chop House to get myself a beef stew, the beef stews in Bobby's being very nourishing, indeed, and quite reasonable. In fact, the beef stews in Bobby's are considered a most fashionable dish by one and all on Broadway on Tuesday evenings.

So on this Tuesday evening I am talking about, I am in Bobby's wrapping myself around a beef stew and reading the race results in the *Journal*, when who comes into the joint but two old friends of mine from Philly, and a third guy I never see before in my life, but who seems to be an old sort of guy, and very fierce looking.

One of these old friends of mine from Philly is a guy by the name of Izzy Cheesecake, who is called Izzy Cheesecake because he is all the time eating cheesecake around delicatessen joints, although of course this is nothing against him, as cheesecake is very popular in some circles, and goes very good with java. Anyway, this Izzy Cheesecake has another name, which is Morris something, and he is slightly Jewish, and has a large beezer, and is considered a handy man in many respects.

The other old friend of mine from Philly is a guy by the name of Kitty Quick, who is maybe thirty-two or three years old, and who is a lively guy in every way. He is a great hand for wearing good clothes, and he is mobbed up with some very good people in Philly in his day, and at one time has plenty of dough, although I hear that lately things are not going so good for Kitty Quick, or for anybody else in Philly, as far as that is concerned.

Now of course I do not rap to these old friends of mine from Philly at once, and in fact I put the *Journal* up in front of my face, because it is never good policy to rap to visitors in this town, especially visitors from Philly, until you know why they are visiting. But it seems that Kitty Quick spies me before I can get the *Journal* up high enough, and he comes over to my table at once, bringing Izzy Cheesecake and the other guy with him, so naturally I give them a big hello, very cordial, and ask them to sit down and have a few beef stews with me, and as they pull up chairs, Kitty Quick says to me like this:

"Do you know Jo-jo from Chicago?" he says, pointing his thumb at the third guy.

Well, of course I know Jo-jo by his reputation, which is very alarming, but I never meet up with him before, and if it is left to me, I will never meet up with him at all, because Jo-jo is considered a very uncouth character, even in Chicago.

He is an Italian, and a short wide guy, very heavy set, and slow moving, and with jowls you can cut steaks off of, and sleepy eyes, and he somehow reminds me of an old lion I once see in a cage in Ringling's circus. He has a black moustache, and he is an old timer out in Chicago, and is pointed out to visitors to the city as a very remarkable guy because he lives as long as he does, which is maybe forty years.

His right name is Antonio something, and why he is called Jo-jo I never hear, but I suppose it is because Jo-jo is handier than Antonio. He shakes hands with me, and says he is pleased to meet me, and then he sits down and begins taking on beef stew very rapidly while Kitty Quick says to me as follows:

"Listen," he says, "do you know anybody in Europe?"

Well, this is a most unexpected question, and naturally I am not going to reply to unexpected questions by guys from Philly without thinking them over very carefully, so to gain time while I think, I say to Kitty Quick:

"Which Europe do you mean?"

"Why," Kitty says, greatly surprised, "is there more than one Europe? I mean the big Europe on the Atlantic Ocean. This is the Europe where we are going, and if you know anybody there we will be glad to go around and say hello to them for you. We are going to Europe on the biggest proposition anybody ever hears of," he says. "In fact," he says, "it is a proposition which will make us all rich. We are sailing tonight."

Well, offhand I cannot think of anybody I know in Europe, and if I do know anybody there I will certainly not wish such parties as Kitty Quick, and Izzy Cheesecake, and Jo-jo going around saying hello to them, but of course I do not mention such a thought out loud. I only say I hope and trust that they have a very good bon voyage and do not suffer too much from seasickness. Naturally I do not ask what their proposition is, because if I ask such a question they may think I wish to find out, and will consider me a very nosey guy, but I figure the chances are they are going over to look after some commercial matter, such as Scotch, or maybe cordials.

Anyway, Kitty Quick, and Izzy Cheesecake and Jo-jo

eat up quite a few beef stews, and leave me to pay the check, and this is the last I see or hear of any of them for several months. Then one day I am in Philly to see a prize fight, and I run into Kitty Quick on Broad Street, looking pretty much the same as usual, and I ask him how he comes out in Europe.

"It is no good," Kitty says. "The trip is something of a bust, although we see many interesting sights, and have quite a few experiences. Maybe," Kitty says, "you will like to hear why we go to Europe? It is a very unusual story, indeed, and is by no means a lie, and I will be pleased to tell it to someone I think will believe it."

So we go into Walter's restaurant, and sit down in a corner, and order up a little java, and Kitty Quick tells me the story as follows:

It all begins (Kitty says) with a certain big lawyer coming to me here in Philly, and wishing to know if I care to take up a proposition which will make me rich, and naturally I say I can think of nothing that will please me more, because at this time things are very bad indeed in Philly, what with investigations going on here and there, and plenty of heat around and about, and I do not have more than a few bobs in my pants pocket, and can think of no way to get any more.

So this lawyer takes me to the Ritz-Carlton hotel, and there he introduces me to a guy by the name of Count Saro, and the lawyer says he will okay anything Saro has to say to me 100 percent, and then he immediately takes the wind as if he does not care to hear what Saro has to say. But I know this mouthpiece is not putting any proposition away as okay unless he knows it is pretty much okay, because he is a smart guy at his own dodge, and everything else, and has plenty of coconuts.

Now this Count Saro is a little guy with an eyebrow moustache, and he wears striped pants, and white spats, and a cutaway coat, and a monocle in one eye, and he seems to be a foreign nobleman, although he talks English first rate. I do not care much for Count Saro's looks, but I will say one thing for him, he is very businesslike, and gets down to cases at once.

He tells me that he is the representative of a political party in his home country in Europe which has a King, and this country wishes to get rid of the King, because Count Saro says Kings are out of style in Europe, and that no country can get anywhere with a King these days. His proposition is for me to take any assistants I figure I may need and go over and get rid of this King, and Count Saro says he will pay two hundred G's for the job in good old American scratch, and will lay twenty-five G's on the line at once, leaving the balance with the lawyer to be paid to me when everything is finished.

Well, this is a most astonishing proposition, indeed, because while I often hear of propositions to get rid of other guys, I never before hear of a proposition to get rid of a King. Furthermore, it does not sound reasonable to me, as getting rid of a King is apt to attract plenty of attention, and criticism, but Count Saro explains to me that his country is a small, out-of-the-way country, and that his political party will take control of the telegraph wires and everything else as soon as I get rid of the King, so nobody will give the news much of a tumble outside the country.

"Everything will be done very quietly, and in good order," Count Saro says, "and there will be no danger to you whatever."

Well, naturally I wish to know from Count Saro why he does not get somebody in his own country to do such a job, especially if he can pay so well for it, and he says to me like this:

"Well," he says, "in the first place there is no one in our country with enough experience in such matters to be trusted, and in the second place we do not wish anyone in our country to seem to be tangled up with getting rid of the King. It will cause internal complications," he says. "An outsider is more logical," he says, "because it is quite well known that in the palace of the King there are many valuable jewels, and it will seem a natural play for outsiders, especially Americans, to break into the palace to get these jewels, and if they happen to get rid of the King while getting the jewels, no one will think it is anything more than an accident, such as often occurs in your country."

Furthermore, Count Saro tells me that everything will be laid out for me in advance by his people, so I will have no great bother getting into the palace to get rid of the King, but he says of course I must not really take the valuable jewels, because his political party wishes to keep them for itself.

Well, I do not care much for the general idea at all, but Count Saro whips out a bundle of scratch, and weeds off twenty-five large coarse notes of a G apiece, and there it is in front of me, and looking at all this dough, and thinking how tough times are, what with banks busting here and there, I am very much tempted indeed, especially as I am commencing to think this Count Saro is some kind of a nut, and is only speaking through his hat about getting rid of a King.

"Listen," I say to Count Saro, as he sits there watching me, "how do you know I will not take this dough off of you and then never do anything whatever for it?"

"Why," he says, much surprised, "you are recommended to me as an honest man, and I accept your references. Anyway," he says, "if you do not carry out your agreement with me, you will only hurt yourself, because you will lose a hundred and seventy-five G's more, and the lawyer will make you very hard to catch."

Well, the upshot of it is I shake hands with Count Saro, and then go out to find Izzy Cheesecake, although I am still thinking Count Saro is a little daffy, and while I am looking for Izzy, who do I see but Jo-jo, and Jo-jo tells me that he is on a vacation from Chicago, for a while, because it seems somebody out there claims he is a public enemy, which Jo-jo says is nothing but a big lie, as he is really very fond of the public at all times.

Naturally I am glad to come across a guy such as Jo-jo, because he is most trustworthy, and naturally Jo-jo is very glad to hear of a proposition that will turn him an honest dollar while he is on his vacation. So Jo-jo and Izzy and I have a meeting, and we agree that I am to have a hundred G's for finding the plant, while Izzy and Jo-jo are to get fifty G's apiece, and this is how we come to go to Europe.

Well, we land at a certain spot in Europe, and who is there to meet us but another guy with a monocle, who states that his name is Baron von Terp, or some such, and who says he is representing Count Saro, and I am commencing to wonder if Count Saro's country is filled with one-eyed guys. Anyway, this Baron von Terp takes us traveling by trains and automobiles for several days, until finally after an extra long hop in an automobile we come to the outskirts of a nice looking little burg, which seems to be the place we are headed for.

Now Baron von Terp drops us in a little hotel on the outskirts of the town, and says he must leave us because he cannot afford to be seen with us, although he explains he does not mean this as a knock to us. In fact, Baron von Terp says he finds us very nice traveling companions, indeed, except for Jo-jo wishing to engage in target practice along the route with his automatic roscoe, and using such animals as stray dogs, and chickens for his targets. He says he does not even mind Izzy Cheesecake's singing, although personally I will always consider this one of the big drawbacks to the journey.

Before he goes, Baron von Terp draws me a rough diagram of the inside of the palace where we are to get rid of the King, giving me a layout of all the rooms and doors. He says usually there are guards in and about this palace, but that his people arrange it so these guards will not be present around nine o'clock this night, except one guy who may be on guard at the door of the King's bedroom, and Baron von Terp says if we guzzle this guy it will be all right with him, because he does not like the guy, anyway.

But the general idea, he says, is for us to work fast and quietly, so as to be in and out of there inside of an hour or so, leaving no trail behind us, and I say this will suit me and Izzy Cheesecake and Jo-jo very well, indeed, as we are getting tired of traveling, and wish to go somewhere and take a long rest.

Well, after explaining all this, Baron von Terp takes the wind, leaving us a big fast car with an ugly looking guy driving it who does not talk much English, but is supposed to know all the routes, and it is in this car that we leave the little hotel just before nine o'clock as per instructions, and head for the palace, which turns out to be nothing but a large square old building in the middle of a sort of park, with the town around and about, but some distance off.

Ugly-face drives right into this park and up to what seems to be the front door of the building, and the three of us get out of the car, and Ugly-face pulls the car off into the shadow of some trees to wait for us.

Personally, I am looking for plenty of heat when we start to go into the palace, and I have the old equalizer where I can get at it without too much trouble, while Jo-jo and Izzy Cheesecake also have their rods handy. But just as Baron von Terp tells us there are no guards around, and in fact there is not a soul in sight as we walk into the palace door, and find ourselves in a big hall with paintings, and armor, and old swords, and one thing and another hanging around and about, and I can see that this is a perfect plant, indeed.

I out with my diagram and see where the King's bedroom is located on the second floor, and when we get there, walking very easy, and ready to start blasting away if necessary, who is at the door but a big tall guy in a uniform, who is very much surprised at seeing us, and who starts to holler something or other, but what it is nobody will ever know, because just as he opens his mouth, Izzy Cheesecake taps him on the noggin with the butt of a forty-five, and knocks him cock-eyed.

Then Jo-jo grabs some cord off a heavy silk curtain which is hanging across the door, and ties the guy up good and tight, and wads a handkerchief into his kisser in case the guy comes to, and wishes to start hollering again, and when all this is done, I quietly turn the knob of the door to the King's bedroom, and we step into a room that looks more like a young convention hall than it does a bedroom, except that it is hung around and about with silk drapes, and there is much gilt furniture here and there.

Well, who is in this room but a nice looking doll, and a little kid of maybe eight or nine years old, and the kid is in a big bed with a canopy over it like the entrance to a night club, only silk, and the doll is sitting alongside the bed reading to the kid out of a book. It is a very homelike scene, indeed, and causes us to stop and look around in great surprise, for we are certainly not expecting such a scene at all.

As we stand there in the middle of the room somewhat confused the doll turns and looks at us, and the little kid sits up in bed. He is a fat little guy with a chubby face, and a lot of curly hair, and eyes as big as pancakes, and maybe bigger. The doll turns very pale when she sees us, and shakes so the book she is reading falls to the floor, but the kid does not seem scared, and he says to us in very good English like this:

"Who are you?" he says.

Well, this is a fair question, at that, but naturally we do not wish to state who we are at this time, so I say:

"Never mind who we are, where is the King?"

"The King?" the kid says, sitting up straight in the bed, "why, I am the King."

Now of course this seems a very nonsensical crack to us, because we have brains enough to know that Kings do not come as small as this little squirt, and anyway we are in no mood to dicker with him, so I say to the doll as follows:

"Listen," I say, "we do not care for any kidding at this time, because we are in a great hurry. Where is the King?"

"Why," she says, her voice trembling quite some, "this is indeed the King, and I am his governess. Who are you, and what do you want? How do you get in here?" she says. "Where are the guards?"

"Lady," I say, and I am greatly surprised at myself for being so patient with her, "this kid may be a King, but we want the big King. We want the head King himself," I say.

"There is no other," she says, and the little kid chips in like this:

"My father dies two years ago, and I am the King in his place," he says. "Are you English, like Miss Peabody here?" he says. "Who is the funny looking old man back there?"

Well, of course Jo-jo is funny looking, at that, but no one ever before is impolite enough to speak of it to his face, and Jo-jo begins growling quite some, while Izzy Cheese-cake speaks as follows:

"Why," Izzy says, "this is a very great outrage. We are

sent to get rid of a King, and here the King is nothing but a little punk. Personally," Izzy says, "I am not in favor of getting rid of punks, male or female."

"Well," Jo-jo says, "I am against it myself as a rule, but this is a pretty fresh punk."

"Now," I say, "there seems to be some mistake around here, at that. Let us sit down and talk things over quietly, and see if we cannot get this matter straightened out. It looks to me," I say, "as if this Count Saro is nothing but a swindler."

"Count Saro," the doll says, getting up and coming over to me, and looking very much alarmed. "Count Saro, do you say? Oh, sir, Count Saro is a very bad man. He is the tool of the Grand Duke Gino of this country, who is this little boy's uncle. The Grand Duke will be king himself if it is not for this boy, and we suspect many plots against the little chap's safety. Oh, gentlemen," she says, "you surely do not mean any harm to this poor orphan child?"

Well, this is about the first time in their lives that Jo-jo and Izzy Cheesecake are ever mentioned by anybody as gentlemen, and I can see that it softens them up quite some, especially as the little kid is grinning at them very cheerful, although of course he will not be so cheerful if he knows who he is grinning at.

"Why," Jo-jo says, "the Grand Duke is nothing but a rascal for wishing harm to such a little guy as this, although of course," Jo-jo says, "if he is a grown-up King it will be a different matter."

"Who are you?" the little kid says again.

"We are Americans," I say, very proud to mention my home country. "We are from Philly and Chicago, two very good towns, at that."

Well, the little kid's eyes get bigger than ever, and he climbs right out of bed and walks over to us looking very cute in his blue silk pajamas, and his bare feet.

"Chicago?" he says. "Do you know Mr. Capone?"

"Al?" says Jo-jo. "Do I know Al? Why, Al and me are just like this," he says, although personally I do not believe Al Capone will know Jo-jo if he meets him in broad daylight. "Where do you know Al from?" he asks.

"Oh, I do not know him," the kid says. "But I read about him in the magazines, and about the machine guns, and the pineapples. Do you know about the pineapples?" he says.

"Do I know about pineapples?" Jo-jo says, as if his feelings are hurt by the question. "He asks me do I know about the pineapples. Why," he says, "look here."

And what does this Jo-jo do but out with a little round gadget which I recognize at once as a bomb such as these Guineas like to chuck at people they do not like, especially Guineas from Chicago. Of course I never know Jo-jo is packing this article around and about with him, and Jo-jo can see I am much astonished, and by no means pleased, because he says to me like this:

"I bring this along in case of a bear fight," he says. "They are very handy in a bear fight."

Well, the next thing anybody knows we are all talking about this and that very pleasant, especially the little kid and Jo-jo, who is telling lies faster than a horse can trot about Chicago and Mr. Capone, and I hope and trust that Al never hears some of the lies Jo-jo tells, or he may hold it against me for being with Jo-jo when these lies come off.

I am talking to the doll, whose name seems to be Miss Peabody, and who is not so hard to take, at that, and at the same time I am keeping an eye on Izzy Cheesecake, who is wandering around the room looking things over. The chances are Izzy is trying to find a few of the valuable jewels such as I mention to him when telling him about the proposition of getting rid of the King, and in fact I am taking a stray peek here and there myself, but I do not see anything worth while.

This Miss Peabody is explaining to me about the politics of the country, and it seems the reason the Grand Duke wishes to get rid of the little kid King and be King himself is because he has a business deal on with a big nation near by which wishes to control the kid King's country. I judge from what Miss Peabody tells me that this country is no bigger than Delaware county, Pa., and it seems to me a lot of bother about no more country than this, but Miss Peabody says it is a very nice little country, at that.

She says it will be very lovely indeed if it is not for the Grand Duke Gino, because the little kid King stands okay with the people, but it seems the old Grand Duke is pretty much boss of everything, and Miss Peabody says she is personally long afraid that he will finally try to do something very drastic indeed to get rid of the kid King on account of the kid seeming so healthy. Well, naturally I do not state to her that our middle name is drastic, because I do not wish Miss Peabody to have a bad opinion of us.

Now nothing will do but Jo-jo must show the kid his automatic, which is as long as your arm, and maybe longer, and the kid is greatly delighted, and takes the rod and starts pointing it here and there and saying boom-boom, as kids will do. But what happens he pulls the trigger, and it seems that Jo-jo does not have the safety on, so the roscoe really goes boom-boom twice before the kid can take his finger off the trigger.

Well, the first shot smashes a big jar over in one corner of the room, which Miss Peabody afterwards tells me is worth fifteen G's if it is worth a dime, and the second slug knocks off Izzy Cheesecake's derby hat, which serves Izzy right, at that, as he is keeping his hat on in the presence of a lady. Naturally these shots are very disturbing to me at the moment, but afterwards I learn they are a very good thing, indeed, because it seems a lot of guys who are hanging around outside, including Baron von Terp, and several prominent politicians of the country, watching and listening to see what comes off, hurry right home and go to bed, figuring the King is rid of per contract, and wishing to be found in bed if anybody comes around asking questions.

Well, Jo-jo is finally out of lies about Chicago and Mr. Capone, when the little kid seems to get a new idea and goes rummaging around the room looking for something, and just as I am hoping he is about to donate the valuable jewels to us he comes up with a box, and what is in this box but a baseball bat, and a catcher's mitt, and a baseball, and it is very strange indeed to find such homelike articles so far away from home, especially as Babe Ruth's name is on the bat.

"Do you know about these things?" the little kid asks Jo-jo. "They are from America, and they are sent to me by one of our people when he is visiting there, but nobody here seems to know what they are for?"

"Do I know about them?" Jo-jo says, fondling them very tenderly, indeed. "He asks me do I know about them. Why," he says, "in my time I am the greatest hitter on the West Side Blues back in dear old Chi."

Well, now nothing will do the kid but we must show him how these baseball articles work, so Izzy Cheesecake, who claims he is once a star backstopper with the Vine Streets back in Philly puts on a pad and mask, and Jo-jo takes the bat and lays a small sofa pillow down on the floor for a home plate, and insists that I pitch to him. Now it is years since I handle a baseball, although I wish to say that in my day I am as good an amateur pitcher as there is around Gray's Ferry in Philly, and the chances are I will be with the A's if I do not have other things to do.

So I take off my coat, and get down to the far end of the

room, while Jo-jo squares away at the plate, with Izzy Cheesecake behind it. I can see by the way he stands that Jo-jo is bound to be a sucker for a curve, so I take a good windup, and cut loose with the old fadeaway, but of course my arm is not what it used to be, and the ball does not break as I expect, so what happens but Jo-jo belts the old apple right through a high window in what will be right field if the room is laid off like Shibe Park.

Well, Jo-jo starts running as if he is going to first, but of course there is no place in particular for him to run, and he almost knocks his brains out against a wall, and the ball is lost, and the game winds up right there, but the little kid is tickled silly over this business, and even Miss Peabody laughs, and she does not look to me like a doll who gets many laughs out of life, at that.

It is now nearly ten o'clock, and Miss Peabody says if she can find anybody around she will get us something to eat, and this sounds very reasonable, indeed, so I step out-side the door and bring in the guy we tie up there, who seems to be wide awake by now, and very much surprised, and quite indignant, and Miss Peabody says something to him in a language which I do not understand. When I come to think it all over afterwards, I am greatly astonished at the way I trust Miss Peabody, because there is no reason why she shall not tell the guy to get the law, but I suppose I trust her because she seems to have an honest face.

Anyway, the guy in the uniform goes away rubbing his noggin, and pretty soon in comes another guy who seems to be a butler, or some such, and who is also greatly sur-prised at seeing us, and Miss Peabody rattles off something to him and he starts hustling in tables, and dishes, and sand-wiches, and coffee, and one thing and another in no time at all.

Well, there we are, the five of us sitting around the table

eating and drinking, because what does the butler do but bring in a couple of bottles of good old pre-war champagne, which is very pleasant to the taste, although Izzy Cheesecake embarrasses me no little by telling Miss Peabody that if she can dig up any considerable quantity of this stuff he will make her plenty of bobs by peddling it in our country, and will also cut the King in.

When the butler fills the wine glasses the first time, Miss Peabody picks hers up, and looks at us, and naturally we have sense enough to pick ours up, too, and then she stands up on her feet and raises her glass high above her head, and says like this:

"Gentlemen, The King!"

Well, I stand up at this, and Jo-jo and Izzy Cheesecake stand up with me, and we say, all together:

"The King!"

And then we swig our champagne, and sit down again and the little kid laughs all over and claps his hands and seems to think it is plenty of fun, which it is, at that, although Miss Peabody does not let him have any wine, and is somewhat indignant when she catches Jo-jo trying to slip him a snort under the table.

Well, finally the kid does not wish us to leave him at all, especially Jo-jo, but Miss Peabody says he must get some sleep, so we tell him we will be back some day, and we take our hats and say good-by, and leave him standing in the bedroom door with Miss Peabody at his side, and the little kid's arm is around her waist, and I find myself wishing it is my arm, at that.

Of course we never go back again, and in fact we get out of the country this very night, and take the first boat out of the first seaport we hit and return to the United States of America, and the gladdest guy in all the world to see us go is Ugly-face, because he has to drive us about a thousand miles with the muzzle of a rod digging into his ribs.

So (Kitty Quick says) now you know why we go to Europe.

Well, naturally, I am greatly interested in his story, and especially in what Kitty says about the pre-war champagne, because I can see that there may be great business opportunities in such a place if a guy can get in with the right people, but one thing Kitty will never tell me is where the country is located, except that it is located in Europe.

"You see," Kitty says, "we are all strong Republicans here in Philly, and I will not get the Republican administration of this country tangled up in any international squabble for the world. You see," he says, "when we land back home I find a little item of cable news in a paper which says the Grand Duke Gino dies as a result of injuries received in an accident in his home some weeks before.

"And," Kitty says, "I am never sure but what these injuries may be caused by Jo-jo insisting on Ugly-face driving us around to the Grand Duke's house the night we leave and popping his pineapple into the Grand Duke's bedroom window."

The Brain Goes Home

ONE NIGHT The Brain is walking me up and down Broadway in front of Mindy's Restaurant, and speaking of this and that, when along comes a red-headed raggedy doll selling apples at five cents per copy, and The Brain, being very fond of apples, grabs one out of her basket and hands her a five-dollar bill.

The red-headed raggedy doll, who is maybe thirty-odd and is nothing but a crow as far as looks are concerned, squints at the finnif, and says to The Brain like this:

"I do not have change for so much money," she says, "but I will go and get it in a minute."

"You keep the change," The Brain says, biting a big hunk out of the apple and taking my arm to start me walking again.

Well, the raggedy doll looks at The Brain again, and it seems to me that all of a sudden there are large tears in her eyes as she says:

"Oh, thank you, sir! Thank you, thank you, and God bless you, sir!"

And then she goes on up the street in a hurry, with her hands over her eyes and her shoulders shaking, and The Brain turns around very much astonished, and watches her until she is out of sight.

"Why, my goodness!" The Brain says. "I give Doris Clare ten G's last night, and she does not make half as much fuss over it as this doll does over a pound note."

"Well," I say, "maybe the apple doll needs a pound note more than Doris needs ten G's."

"Maybe so," The Brain says. "And of course, Doris gives me much more in return than just an apple and a God bless me. Doris gives me her love. I guess," The Brain says, "that love costs me about as much dough as any guy that ever lives."

"I guess it does," I say, and the chances are we both guess right, because offhand I figure that if The Brain gets out on three hundred G's per year for love he is running his love business very economically indeed, because it is well known to one and all that The Brain has three different dolls, besides an ever-loving wife.

In fact, The Brain is sometimes spoken of by many citizens as the "Love King," but only behind his back, because The Brain likes to think his love affairs are a great secret to all but maybe a few, although the only guy I ever see in this town who does not know all about them is a guy who is deaf, dumb and blind.

I once read a story about a guy by the name of King Solomon who lives a long time ago and who has a thousand dolls all at once, which is going in for dolls on a very large scale indeed, but I guarantee that all of King Solomon's dolls put together are not as expensive as any one of The Brain's dolls. The overhead on Doris Clare alone will drive an ordinary guy daffy, and Doris is practically frugal compared to Cynthia Harris and Bobby Baker.

Then there is Charlotte, who is The Brain's ever-loving

wife and who has a society bug and needs plenty of coconuts at all times to keep her a going concern. I once hear
The Brain tell Bobby Baker that his ever-loving wife is a
bit of an invalid, but as a matter of fact there is never anything the matter with Charlotte that a few bobs will not
cure, although of course this goes for nearly every doll in
this world who is an invalid.

When a guy is knocking around Broadway as long as
The Brain, he is bound to accumulate dolls here and there,
but most guys accumulate one at a time, and when this one
runs out on him, as Broadway dolls will do, he accumulates
another, and so on, and so on, until he is too old to care
about such matters as dolls, which is when he is maybe a
hundred and four years old, although I hear of several guys
who beat even this record.

But when The Brain accumulates a doll he seems to keep
her accumulated, and none of them ever run out on him,
and while this will be a very great nuisance to the average
guy, it pleases The Brain no little because it makes him think
he has a very great power over dolls.

"They are not to blame if they fall in love with me," The
Brain says to me one night. "I will not cause one of them
any sorrow for all the world."

Well, of course it is most astonishing to me to hear a guy
as smart as The Brain using such language, but I figure he
may really believe it, because The Brain thinks very good of
himself at all times. However, some guys claim that the real
reason The Brain keeps all his dolls is because he is too selfish
to give them away, although personally I will not take any
of them if The Brain throws in a cash bonus, except maybe
Bobby Baker.

Anyway, The Brain keeps his dolls accumulated, and
furthermore he spends plenty of dough on them, what with
buying them automobiles and furs and diamonds and swell
places to live in—especially swell places to live in. One time

I tell The Brain he will save himself plenty if he hires a house and bunches his dolls together in one big happy family, instead of having them scattered all over town, but The Brain says this idea is no good.

"In the first place," he says, "they do not know about each other, except Doris and Cynthia and Bobby know about Charlotte, although she does not know about them. They each think they are the only one with me. So if I corral them all together they will be jealous of each other over my love. Anyway," The Brain says, "such an arrangement will be very immoral and against the law. No," he says, "it is better to have them in different spots, because think of the many homes it gives me to go to in case I wish to go home. In fact," The Brain says, "I guess I have more homes to go to than any other guy on Broadway."

Well, this may be true, but what The Brain wants with a lot of different homes is a very great mystery on Broadway, because he seldom goes home, anyway, his idea in not going home being that something may happen in this town while he is at home that he is not in on. The Brain seldom goes anywhere in particular. He never goes out in public with any one of his dolls, except maybe once or twice a year with Charlotte, his ever-loving wife, and finally he even stops going with her because Doris Clare says it does not look good to Doris' personal friends.

The Brain marries Charlotte long before he becomes the biggest guy in gambling operations in the East, and a millionaire two or three times over, but he is never much of a hand to sit around home and chew the fat with his ever-loving wife, as husbands often do. Furthermore, when he is poor he has to live in a neighborhood which is too far away for it to be convenient for him to go home, so finally he gets out of the habit of going there.

But Charlotte is not such a doll as cares to spend more than one or two years looking at the pictures on the wall, because it seems the pictures on her wall are nothing but pictures of cows in the meadow and houses covered with snow, so she does not go home any more than necessary, either, and has her own friends and is very happy indeed, especially after The Brain gets so he can send in right along.

I will say one thing about The Brain and his dolls: he never picks a crow. He has a very good eye for faces and shapes, and even Charlotte, his ever-loving wife, is not a crow, although she is not as young as she used to be. As for Doris Clare, she is one of the great beauties on the Ziegfeld roof in her day, and while her day is by no means yesterday, or even the day before, Doris holds on pretty well in the matter of looks. Giving her a shade the best of it, I will say that Doris is thirty-two or -three, but she has plenty of zing left in her, at that, and her hair remains very blond, no matter what.

In fact, The Brain does not care much if his dolls are blond or brunette, because Cynthia Harris' hair is as black as the inside of a wolf, while Bobby Baker is betwixt and between, her hair being a light brown. Cynthia Harris is more of a Johnny-come-lately than Doris, being out of Mr. Earl Carroll's "Vanities," and I hear she first comes to New York as Miss Somebody in one of these beauty contests which she will win hands down if one of the judges does not get a big wink from a Miss Somebody Else.

Of course Cynthia is doing some winking herself at this time, but it seems that she picks a guy to wink at thinking he is one of the judges, when he is nothing but a newspaperman and has no say whatever about the decision.

Well, Mr. Earl Carroll feels sorry for Cynthia, so he puts her in the "Vanities" and lets her walk around raw, and The Brain sees her, and the next thing anybody knows she is riding in a big foreign automobile the size of a rum chaser, and is chucking a terrible swell.

Personally, I always consider Bobby Baker the smartest of all The Brain's dolls, because she is just middling as to looks and she does not have any of the advantages of life like Doris Clare and Cynthia Harris, such as jobs on the stage where they can walk around showing off their shapes to guys such as The Brain. Bobby Baker starts off as nothing but a private secretary to a guy in Wall Street, and naturally she is always wearing clothes, or anyway, as many clothes as an ordinary doll wears nowadays, which is not so many, at that.

It seems that The Brain once has some business with the guy Bobby works for and happens to get talking to Bobby, and she tells him how she always wishes to meet him, what with hearing and reading about him, and how he is just as handsome and romantic-looking as she always pictures him to herself.

Now I wish to say I will never call any doll a liar, being at all times a gentleman, and for all I know, Bobby Baker may really think The Brain is handsome and romantic-looking, but personally I figure if she is not lying to him, she is at least a little excited when she makes such a statement to The Brain. The best you can give The Brain at this time is that he is very well dressed.

He is maybe forty years old, give or take a couple of years, and he is commencing to get a little bunchy about the middle, what with sitting down at card tables so much and never taking any exercise outside of walking guys such as me up and down in front of Mindy's for a few hours every night. He has a clean-looking face, always very white around the gills, and he has nice teeth and a nice smile when he wishes to smile, which is never at guys who owe him dough.

And I will say for The Brain he has what is called personality. He tells a story well, although he is always the hero of any story he tells, and he knows how to make himself agreeable to dolls in many ways. He has a pretty fair sort of education, and while dolls such as Cynthia and Doris, and maybe Charlotte, too, will rather have a charge account at Cartier's than all the education in Yale and Harvard put together, it seems that Bobby Baker likes highbrow gab, so naturally she gets plenty of same from The Brain.

Well, pretty soon Bobby is riding around in a car bigger than Cynthia's, though neither is as big as Doris' car, and all the neighbors' children over in Flatbush, which is where Bobby hails from, are very jealous of her and running around spreading gossip about her, but keeping their eyes open for big cars themselves. Personally, I always figure The Brain lowers himself socially by taking up with a doll from Flatbush, especially as Bobby Baker soon goes in for literary guys, such as newspaper scribes and similar characters around Greenwich Village.

But there is no denying Bobby Baker is a very smart little doll, and in the four or five years she is one of The Brain's dolls, she gets more dough out of him than all the others put together, because she is always telling him how much she loves him, and saying she cannot do without him, while Doris Clare and Cynthia Harris sometimes forget to mention this more than once or twice a month.

Now what happens early one morning but a guy by the name of Daffy Jack hauls off and sticks a shiv in The Brain's left side. It seems that this is done at the request of a certain party by the name of Homer Swing, who owes The Brain plenty of dough in a gambling transaction, and who becomes very indignant when The Brain presses him somewhat for payment. It seems that Daffy Jack, who is considered a very good shiv artist, aims at The Brain's heart, but misses it by a couple of inches, leaving The Brain with a very bad cut in his side which calls for some stitching.

Big Nig, the crap shooter, and I are standing at Fifty-second Street and Seventh Avenue along about two A.M., speaking of not much, when The Brain comes stumbling out of Fifty-second Street, and falls in Big Nig's arms, practically ruining a brand-new topcoat which Big Nig pays sixty bucks for a few days back with the blood that is coming out of the cut. Naturally, Big Nig is indignant about this, but we can see that it is no time to be speaking to The Brain about such matters. We can see that The Brain is carved up quite some, and is in a bad way.

Of course we are not greatly surprised at seeing The Brain in this condition, because for years he is practically no price around this town, what with this guy and that being anxious to do something or other to him, but we are never expecting to see him carved up like a turkey. We are expecting to see him with a few slugs in him, and both Big Nig and me are very angry to think that there are guys around who will use such instruments as a knife on anybody.

But while we are thinking it over, The Brain says to me like this:

"Call Hymie Weissberger, and Doc Frisch," he says, "and take me home."

Naturally, a guy such as The Brain wishes his lawyer before he wishes his doctor, and Hymie Weissberger is The Brain's mouthpiece, and a very sure-footed guy, at that.

"Well," I say, "we better take you to a hospital where you can get good attention at once."

"No," The Brain says. "I wish to keep this secret. It will be a bad thing for me right now to have this get out, and if you take me to a hospital they must report it to the coppers. Take me home."

Naturally, I say which home, being somewhat confused about The Brain's homes, and he seems to study a minute as if this is a question to be well thought out.

"Park Avenue," The Brain says finally, so Big Nig stops a taxicab, and we help The Brain into the cab and tell the jockey to take us to the apartment house on Park Avenue near Sixty-fourth where The Brain's ever-loving wife Charlotte lives.

When we get there, I figure it is best for me to go up first and break the news gently to Charlotte, because I can see what a shock it is bound to be to any ever-loving wife to have her husband brought home in the early hours of the morning all shived up.

Well, the door man and the elevator guy in the apartment house give me an argument about going up to The Brain's apartment, saying a blow out of some kind is going on there, but after I explain to them that The Brain is sick, they let me go. A big fat butler comes to the door of the apartment when I ring, and I can see there are many dolls and guys in evening clothes in the apartment, and somebody is singing very loud.

The butler tries to tell me I cannot see Charlotte, but I finally convince him it is best, so by and by she comes to the door, and a very pleasant sight she is, at that, with jewelry all over her. I stall around awhile, so as not to alarm her too much, and then I tell her The Brain meets with an accident and that we have him outside in a cab, and ask her where shall we put him.

"Why," she says, "put him in a hospital, of course. I am entertaining some very important people tonight, and I cannot have them disturbed by bringing in a hospital patient. Take him to a hospital, and tell him I will come and see him tomorrow and bring him some broth."

I try to explain to her that The Brain does not need

any broth, but a nice place to lie down in, but finally she gets very testy with me and shuts the door in my face, saying as follows:

"Take him to a hospital, I tell you. This is a ridiculous hour for him to be coming home, anyway. It is twenty years since he comes home so early."

Then as I am waiting for the elevator, she opens the door again just a little bit and says:

"By the way, is he hurt bad?"

I say we do not know how bad he is hurt, and she shuts the door again, and I go back to the cab again, thinking what a heartless doll she is, although I can see where it will be very inconvenient for her to bust up her party, at that.

The Brain is lying back in the corner of the cab, his eyes half closed, and by this time it seems that Big Nig stops the blood somewhat with a handkerchief, but The Brain acts somewhat weak to me. He sort of rouses himself when I climb in the cab, and when I tell him his ever-loving wife is not home he smiles a bit and whispers:

"Take me to Doris."

Now Doris lives in a big apartment house away over on West Seventy-second Street near the Drive, and I tell the taxi jockey to go there while The Brain seems to slide off into a doze. Then Big Nig leans over to me and says to me like this:

"No use taking him there," Big Nig says. "I see Doris going out tonight all dressed up in her ermine coat with this actor guy, Jack Walen, she is stuck on. It is a very great scandal around and about the way they carry on. Let us take him to Cynthia," Nig says. "She is a very large-hearted doll who will be very glad to take him in."

Now Cynthia Harris has a big suite of rooms that cost fifteen G's a year in a big hotel just off Fifth Avenue, Cynthia being a doll who likes to be downtown so if she hears of anything coming off anywhere she can get there very rapidly. When we arrive at the hotel I call her on the house phone and tell her I must see her about something very important, so Cynthia says for me to come up.

It is now maybe three-fifteen, and I am somewhat surprised to find Cynthia home, at that, but there she is, and looking very beautiful indeed in a negligee with her hair hanging down, and I can see that The Brain is no chump when it comes to picking them. She gives me a hello pleasant enough, but as soon as I explain what I am there for, her kisser gets very stern and she says to me like this:

"Listen," she says, "I got trouble enough around this joint, what with two guys getting in a fight over me at a little gathering I have here last night and the house copper coming in to split them out, and I do not care to have any more. Suppose it gets out that The Brain is here? What will the newspapers print about me? Think of my reputation!"

Well, in about ten minutes I can see there is no use arguing with her, because she can talk faster than I can, and mostly she talks about what a knock it will be to her reputation if she takes The Brain in, so I leave her standing at the door in her negligee, still looking very beautiful, at that.

There is now nothing for us to do but take The Brain to Bobby Baker, who lives in a duplex apartment in Sutton Place over by the East River, where the swells set up a colony of nice apartments in the heart of an old tenement-house neighborhood, and as we are on our way there with The Brain lying back in the cab just barely breathing, I say to Big Nig like this:

"Nig," I say, "when we get to Bobby's, we will carry The Brain in without asking her first and just dump him on her so she cannot refuse to take him in, although," I say, "Bobby Baker is a nice little doll, and I am pretty sure she will do anything she can for him, especially," I say, "since he pays fifty *G's* for this apartment we are going to."

So when the taxicab stops in front of Bobby's house, Nig and I take The Brain out of the cab and lug him between us up to the door of Bobby's apartment, where I ring the bell. Bobby opens the door herself, and I happen to see a guy's legs zip into a room in the apartment behind her, although of course there is nothing wrong in such a sight, even though the guy's legs are in pink pajamas.

Naturally, Bobby is greatly astonished to see us with The Brain dangling between us, but she does not invite us in as I explain to her that The Brain is stabbed and that his last words are for us to take him to his Bobby. Furthermore, she does not let me finish my story which will be very sad indeed, if she keeps on listening.

"If you do not take him away from here at once," Bobby says, before I am down to the pathetic part, "I will call the cops and you guys will be arrested on suspicion that you know something about how he gets hurt."

Then she slams the door on us, and we lug The Brain back down the stairs into the street, because all of a sudden it strikes us that Bobby is right, and if The Brain is found in our possession all stabbed up, and he happens to croak, we are in a very tough spot, because the cops just naturally love to refuse to believe guys like Big Nig and me, no matter what we say.

Furthermore, the same idea must hit the taxicab jockey after we lift The Brain out of the cab, because he is nowhere to be seen, and there we are away over by the East River in the early morning, with no other taxis in sight, and a cop liable to happen along any minute.

Well, there is nothing for us to do but get away from there, so Big Nig and I start moving, with me carrying

The Brain's feet, and Big Nig his head. We get several blocks away from Sutton Place, going very slow and hiding in dark doorways when we hear anybody coming, and now we are in a section of tenement houses, when all of a sudden up out of the basement of one of these tenements pops a doll.

She sees us before we can get in a dark place, and she seems to have plenty of nerve for a doll, because she comes right over to us and looks at Big Nig and me, and then looks at The Brain, who loses his hat somewhere along the line, so his pale face is plain to be seen by even the dim street light.

"Why," the doll says, "it is the kind gentleman who gives me the five dollars for the apple—the money that buys the medicine that saves my Joey's life. What is the matter?"

"Well," I say to the doll, who is still raggedy and still red-headed, "there is nothing much the matter except if we do not get him somewhere soon, this guy will up and croak on us."

"Bring him into my house," she says, pointing to the joint she just comes out of. "It is not much of a place, but you can let him rest there until you get help. I am just going over here to a drug store to get some more medicine for Joey, although he is out of danger now, thanks to this gentleman."

So we lug The Brain down the basement steps with the doll leading the way, and we follow her into a room that smells like a Chinese laundry and seems to be full of kids sleeping on the floor. There is only one bed in the room, and it is not much of a bed any way you take it, and there seems to be a kid in this bed, too, but the red-headed doll rolls this kid over to one side of the bed and motions us to lay The Brain alongside of the kid. Then she gets a wet rag and starts bathing The Brain's noggin.

He finally opens his eyes and looks at the red-headed raggedy doll, and she grins at him very pleasant. When I think things over afterwards, I figure The Brain is conscious of much of what is going on when we are packing him around, although he does not say anything, maybe because he is too weak. Anyway, he turns his head to Big Nig, and says to him like this:

"Bring Weissberger and Frisch as quick as you can," he says. "Anyway, get Weissberger. I do not know how bad I am hurt, and I must tell him some things."

Well, The Brain is hurt pretty bad, as it turns out, and in fact he never gets well, but he stays in the basement dump until he dies three days later, with the red-headed raggedy doll nursing him alongside her sick kid Joey, because the croaker, old Doc Frisch, says it is no good moving The Brain, and may only make him pop off sooner. In fact, Doc Frisch is much astonished that The Brain lives at all, considering the way we lug him around.

I am present at The Brain's funeral at Wiggins' Funeral Parlors, like everybody else on Broadway, and I wish to say I never see more flowers in all my life. They are all over the casket and knee-deep on the floor, and some of the pieces must cost plenty, the price of flowers being what they are in this town nowadays. In fact, I judge it is the size and cost of the different pieces that makes me notice a little bundle of faded red carnations not much bigger than your fist that is laying alongside a pillow of violets the size of a horse blanket.

There is a small card tied to the carnations, and it says on this card, as follows: "To a kind gentleman," and it comes to my mind that out of all the thousands of dollars' worth of flowers there, these faded carnations represent the only true sincerity. I mention this to Big Nig, and he says the chances are I am right, but that even true sincerity is not going to do The Brain any good where he is going.

Anybody will tell you that for offhand weeping at a funeral The Brain's ever-loving wife Charlotte does herself very proud indeed, but she is not one-two-seven with Doris Clare, Cynthia Harris and Bobby Baker. In fact, Bobby Baker weeps so loud that there is some talk of heaving her out of the funeral altogether.

However, I afterwards hear that loud as they are at the funeral it is nothing to the weep they all put on when it comes out that The Brain has Hymie Weissberger draw up a new will while he is dying and leaves all his dough to the red-headed raggedy doll, whose name seems to be O'Halloran, and who is the widow of a bricklayer and has five kids.

Well, at first all the citizens along Broadway say it is a wonderful thing for The Brain to do, and serves his ever-loving wife and Doris and Cynthia and Bobby just right; and from the way one and all speaks you will think they are going to build a monument to The Brain for his generosity to the red-headed raggedy doll.

But about two weeks after he is dead, I hear citizens saying the chances are the red-headed raggedy doll is nothing but one of The Brain's old-time dolls, and that maybe the kids are his and that he leaves them the dough because his conscience hurts him at the finish, for this is the way Broadway is. But personally I know it cannot be true, for if there is one thing The Brain never has it is a conscience.

✿ ✿ ✿

The Bloodhounds of Broadway

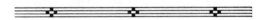

ONE MORNING along about four bells, I am standing in front of Mindy's restaurant on Broadway with a guy by the name of Regret, who has this name because it seems he wins a very large bet the year the Whitney filly, Regret, grabs the Kentucky Derby, and can never forget it, which is maybe because it is the only very large bet he ever wins in his life.

What this guy's real name is I never hear, and anyway names make no difference to me, especially on Broadway, because the chances are that no matter what name a guy has, it is not his square name. So, as far as I am concerned, Regret is as good a name as any other for this guy I am talking about, who is a fat guy, and very gabby, though generally he is talking about nothing but horses, and how he gets beat three dirty noses the day before at Belmont, or wherever the horses are running.

In all the years I know Regret he must get beat ten thousand noses, and always they are dirty noses, to hear him tell it. In fact, I never once hear him say he is beat a clean nose, but of course this is only the way horse racing guys talk. What Regret does for a living besides betting on horses I do not know, but he seems to do pretty well at it, because he is always around and about, and generally well dressed, and with a lot of big cigars sticking up out of his vest pocket.

It is generally pretty quiet on Broadway along about four bells in the morning, because at such an hour the citizens are mostly in speak-easies, and night clubs, and on this morning I am talking about it is very quiet, indeed, except for a guy by the name of Marvin Clay hollering at a young doll because she will not get into a taxicab with him to go to his apartment. But of course Regret and I do not pay much attention to such a scene, except that Regret remarks that the young doll seems to have more sense than you will expect to see in a doll loose on Broadway at four bells in the morning, because it is well known to one and all that any doll who goes to Marvin Clay's apartment, either has no brains whatever, or wishes to go there.

This Marvin Clay is a very prominent society guy, who is a great hand for hanging out in night clubs, and he has plenty of scratch which comes down to him from his old man, who makes it out of railroads and one thing and another. But Marvin Clay is a most obnoxious character, being loud and ungentlemanly at all times, on account of having all this scratch, and being always very rough and abusive with young dolls such as work in night clubs, and who have to stand for such treatment from Marvin Clay because he is a very good customer.

He is generally in evening clothes, as he is seldom around and about except in the evening, and he is maybe fifty years old, and has a very ugly mugg, which is covered with blotches, and pimples, but of course a guy who has as much scratch as Marvin Clay does not have to be so very handsome, at that, and he is very welcome indeed wherever he goes on Broadway. Personally, I wish no part of such a guy as Marvin Clay, although I suppose in my time on Broadway I must see a thousand guys like him, and there will always be guys like Marvin Clay on Broadway as long as they have old men to make plenty of scratch out of railroads to keep them going.

Well, by and by Marvin Clay gets the doll in the taxicab, and away they go, and it is all quiet again on Broadway, and Regret and I stand there speaking of this and that, and one thing and another, when along comes a very strange looking guy leading two very strange looking dogs. The guy is so thin I figure he must be about two pounds lighter than a stack of wheats. He has a long nose, and a sad face, and he is wearing a floppy old black felt hat, and he has on a flannel shirt, and baggy corduroy pants, and a see-more coat, which is a coat that lets you see more hip pockets than coat.

Personally, I never see a stranger looking guy on Broadway, and I wish to say I see some very strange looking guys on Broadway in my day. But if the guy is strange looking, the dogs are even stranger looking, because they have big heads, and jowls that hang down like an old-time faro bank dealer's, and long ears the size of bed sheets. Furthermore, they have wrinkled faces, and big, round eyes that seem so sad I half expect to see them bust out crying.

The dogs are a sort of black and yellow in color, and have long tails, and they are so thin you can see their ribs sticking out of their hides. I can see at once that the dogs and the guy leading them can use a few Hamburgers very nicely, but then so can a lot of other guys on Broadway at this time, leaving out the dogs.

Well, Regret is much interested in the dogs right away,

because he is a guy who is very fond of animals of all kinds, and nothing will do but he must stop the guy and start asking questions about what sort of dogs they are, and in fact I am also anxious to hear myself, because while I see many a pooch in my time I never see anything like these.

"They is bloodhounds," the sad looking guy says in a very sad voice, and with one of these accents such as Southern guys always have. "They is man-tracking bloodhounds from Georgia."

Now of course both Regret and me know what bloodhounds are because we see such animals chasing Eliza across the ice in Uncle Tom's Cabin when we are young squirts, but this is the first time either of us meet up with any bloodhounds personally, especially on Broadway. So we get to talking quite a bit to the guy, and his story is as sad as his face, and makes us both feel very sorry for him.

In fact, the first thing we know we have him and the bloodhounds in Mindy's and are feeding one and all big steaks, although Mindy puts up an awful squawk about us bringing the dogs in, and asks us what we think he is running, anyway. When Regret starts to tell him, Mindy says never mind, but not to bring any more Shetland ponies into his joint again as long as we live.

Well, it seems that the sad looking guy's name is John Wangle, and he comes from a town down in Georgia where his uncle is the high sheriff, and one of the bloodhounds' name is Nip, and the other is Tuck, and they are both trained from infancy to track down guys such as lags who escape from the county pokey, and bad niggers, and one thing and another, and after John Wangle gets the kinks out of his belly on Mindy's steaks, and starts talking good, you must either figure him a high class liar, or the hounds the greatest man-trackers the world ever sees.

Now, looking at the dogs after they swallow six big sirloins apiece, and a lot of matzoths, which Mindy has left over from the Jewish holidays, and a joblot of goulash from the dinner bill, and some other odds and ends, the best I can figure them is hearty eaters, because they are now lying down on the floor with their faces hidden behind their ears, and are snoring so loud you can scarcely hear yourself think.

How John Wangle comes to be in New York with these bloodhounds is quite a story, indeed. It seems that a New York guy drifts into John's old home town in Georgia when the bloodhounds are tracking down a bad nigger, and this guy figures it will be a wonderful idea to take John Wangle and the dogs to New York and hire them out to the movies to track down the villains in the pictures. But when they get to New York, it seems the movies have other arrangements for tracking down their villains, and the guy runs out of scratch and blows away, leaving John Wangle and the bloodhounds stranded.

So here John Wangle is with Nip and Tuck in New York, and they are all living together in one room in a tenement house over in West Forty-ninth Street, and things are pretty tough with them, because John does not know how to get back to Georgia unless he walks, and he hears the walking is no good south of Roanoke. When I ask him why he does not write to his uncle, the high sheriff down there in Georgia, John Wangle says there are two reasons, one being that he cannot write, and the other that his uncle cannot read.

Then I ask him why he does not sell the bloodhounds, and he says it is because the market for bloodhounds is very quiet in New York, and furthermore if he goes back to Georgia without the bloodhounds, his uncle is apt to knock his ears down. Anyway, John Wangle says he personally loves Nip and Tuck very dearly, and in fact he says it is only his great love for them that keeps him from eating one or the other, and maybe both, the past week, when his hunger is very great indeed.

Well, I never before see Regret so much interested in any situation as he is in John Wangle and the bloodhounds, but personally I am getting very tired of them, because the one that is called Nip finally wakes up and starts chewing on my leg, thinking it is maybe more steak, and when I kick him in the snoot, John Wangle scowls at me, and Regret says only very mean guys are unkind to dumb animals.

But to show you that John Wangle and his bloodhounds are not so dumb, they come moseying along past Mindy's every morning after this at about the same time, and Regret is always there ready to feed them, although he now has to take the grub out on the sidewalk, as Mindy will not allow the hounds in the joint again. Naturally Nip and Tuck become very fond of Regret, but they are by no means as fond of him as John Wangle, because John is commencing to fat up very nicely, and the bloodhounds are also taking on weight.

Now what happens but Regret does not show up in front of Mindy's for several mornings hand running, because it seems that Regret makes a very nice score for himself one day against the horses, and buys himself a brand new Tuxedo, and starts stepping out around the night clubs, and especially around Miss Missouri Martin's Three Hundred Club, where there are many beautiful young dolls who dance around with no more clothes on them than will make a pad for a crutch, and it is well known that Regret dearly loves such scenes.

Furthermore, I hear reports around and about of Regret becoming very fond of a doll by the name of Miss Lovey Lou, who works in Miss Missouri Martin's Three Hundred Club, and of him getting in some kind of a jam

with Marvin Clay over this doll, and smacking Marvin
Clay in the kisser, so I figure Regret is getting a little
simple, as guys who hang around Broadway long enough
are bound to do. Now, when John Wangle and Nip and
Tuck come around looking for a handout, there is nothing
much doing for them, as nobody else around Mindy's feels
any great interest in bloodhounds, especially such interest
as will cause them to buy steaks, and soon Nip and Tuck
are commencing to look very sad again, and John Wangle
is downcast more than somewhat.

It is early morning again, and warm, and a number of
citizens are out in front of Mindy's as usual, breathing the
fresh air, when along comes a police inspector by the name
of McNamara, who is a friend of mine, with a bunch of
plain clothes coppers with him, and Inspector McNamara
tells me he is on his way to investigate a situation in an
apartment house over in West Fifty-fourth Street, about
three blocks away, where it seems a guy is shot, and not
having anything else to do, I go with them, although as a
rule I do not care to associate with coppers, because it
arouses criticism from other citizens.

Well, who is the guy who is shot but Marvin Clay, and
he is stretched out on the floor in the living room of his
apartment in evening clothes, with his shirt front covered
with blood, and after Inspector McNamara takes a close
peek at him, he sees that Marvin Clay is plugged smack
dab in the chest, and that he seems to be fairly dead.
Furthermore, there seems to be no clue whatever to who
does the shooting, and Inspector McNamara says it is undoubtedly a very great mystery, and will be duck soup for
the newspapers, especially as they do not have a good
shooting mystery for several days.

Well, of course all this is none of my business, but all of
a sudden I happen to think of John Wangle and his bloodhounds, and it seems to me it will be a great opportunity

for them, so I say to the Inspector as follows:

"Listen, Mac," I say, "there is a guy here with a pair of man-tracking bloodhounds from Georgia who are very expert in tracking down matters such as this, and," I say, "maybe they can track down the rascal who shoots Marvin Clay, because the trail must be hotter than mustard right now."

Well, afterwards I hear there is much indignation over my suggestion, because many citizens feel that the party who shoots Marvin Clay is entitled to more consideration than being tracked with bloodhounds. In fact, some think the party is entitled to a medal, but this discussion does not come up until later.

Anyway, at first the Inspector does not think much of my idea, and the other coppers are very skeptical, and claim that the best way to do under the circumstances is to arrest everybody in sight and hold them as material witnesses for a month or so, but the trouble is there is nobody in sight to arrest at this time, except maybe me, and the Inspector is a broad-minded guy, and finally he says all right, bring on the bloodhounds.

So I hasten back to Mindy's, and sure enough John Wangle and Nip and Tuck are out on the sidewalk peering at every passing face in the hope that maybe one of these faces will belong to Regret. It is a very pathetic sight, indeed, but John Wangle cheers up when I explain about Marvin Clay to him, and hurries back to the apartment house with me so fast that he stretches Nip's neck a foot, and is pulling Tuck along on his stomach half the time.

Well, when we get back to the apartment, John Wangle leads Nip and Tuck up to Marvin Clay, and they snuffle him all over, because it seems bloodhounds are quite accustomed to dead guys. Then John Wangle unhooks their leashes, and yells something at them, and the hounds begin snuffling all around and about the joint, with Inspector

McNamara and the other coppers watching with great interest. All of a sudden Nip and Tuck go busting out of the apartment and into the street, with John Wangle after them, and all the rest of us after John Wangle. They head across Fifty-fourth Street back to Broadway, and the next thing anybody knows they are doing plenty of snuffling around in front of Mindy's.

By and by they take off up Broadway with their snozzles to the sidewalk, and we follow them very excited, because even the coppers now admit that it seems to be a sure thing they are red hot on the trail of the party who shoots Marvin Clay. At first Nip and Tuck are walking, but pretty soon they break into a lope, and there we are loping after them, John Wangle, the Inspector, and me, and the coppers.

Naturally, such a sight as this attracts quite some attention as we go along from any citizens stirring at this hour, and by and by milkmen are climbing down off their wagons, and scavenger guys are leaving their trucks standing where they are, and newsboys are dropping everything, and one and all joining in the chase, so by the time we hit Broadway and Fifty-sixth there is quite a delegation following the hounds with John Wangle in front, just behind Nip and Tuck, and yelling at them now and then as follows:

"Hold to it, boys!"

At Fifty-sixth the hounds turn east off Broadway and stop at the door of what seems to be an old garage, this door being closed very tight, and Nip and Tuck seem to wish to get through this door, so the Inspector and the coppers kick the door open, and who is in the garage having a big crap game but many prominent citizens of Broadway. Naturally, these citizens are greatly astonished at seeing the bloodhounds, and the rest of us, especially the coppers, and they start running every which way trying to get out of the joint, because crap shooting is quite illegal in these parts.

But the Inspector only says Ah-ha, and starts jotting down names in a note book as if it is something he will refer to later, and Nip and Tuck are out of the joint almost as soon as they get in and are snuffling on down Fifty-sixth. They stop at four more doors in Fifty-sixth Street along, and when the coppers kick open these doors they find they are nothing but speakeasies, although one is a hop joint, and the citizens in these places are greatly put out by the excitement, especially as Inspector McNamara keeps jotting down things in his note book.

Finally the Inspector starts glaring very fiercely at the coppers with us, and anybody can see that he is much displeased to find so much illegality going on in this district, and the coppers are starting in to hate Nip and Tuck quite freely, and one copper says to me like this:

"Why," he says, "these mutts are nothing but stool pigeons."

Well, naturally, the noise of John Wangle's yelling, and the gabble of the mob following the hounds makes quite a disturbance, and arouses many of the neighbors in the apartment houses and hotels in the side streets, especially as this is summer, and most everybody has their windows open.

In fact, we see many touseled heads poked out of windows, and hear guys and dolls inquiring as follows:

"What is going on?"

It seems that when word gets about that bloodhounds are tracking down a wrongdoer it causes great uneasiness all through the Fifties, and in fact I afterwards hear that three guys are taken to the Polyclinic suffering with broken ankles and severe bruises from hopping out of windows in the hotels we pass in the chase, or from falling off of fire escapes.

Well, all of a sudden Nip and Tuck swing back into Seventh Avenue, and pop into the entrance of a small apartment house, and go tearing up the stairs to the first floor, and when we get there these bloodhounds are scratching vigorously at the door of Apartment B-2, and going woofle-woofle, and we are all greatly excited, indeed, but the door opens, and who is standing there but a doll by the name of Maud Milligan, who is well known to one and all as the ever-loving doll of Big Nig, the crap shooter, who is down in Hot Springs at this time taking the waters, or whatever it is guys take in Hot Springs.

Now, Maud Milligan is not such a doll as I will care to have any part of, being red-headed, and very stern, and I am glad Nip and Tuck do not waste any more time in her apartment than it takes for them to run through her living room and across her bed, because Maud is commencing to put the old eye on such of us present as she happens to know. But Nip and Tuck are in and out of the joint before you can say scat, because it is only a two-room apartment, at that, and we on our way down the stairs and back into Seventh Avenue again while Inspector McNamara is still jotting down something in his note book.

Finally where do these hounds wind up, with about four hundred citizens behind them, and everybody perspiring quite freely indeed from the exercise, but at the door of Miss Missouri Martin's Three Hundred Club, and the doorman, who is a guy by the name of Soldier Sweeney, tries to shoo them away, but Nip runs between the Soldier's legs and upsets him, and Tuck steps in the Soldier's eye in trotting over him, and most of the crowd behind the hounds tread on him in passing, so the old Soldier is pretty well flattened out at the finish.

Nip and Tuck are now more excited than somewhat, and are going zoople-zoople in loud voices as they bust into the Three Hundred Club with John Wangle and the law, and all these citizens behind them. There is a very large crowd present and Miss Missouri Martin is squatted on the back of a chair in the middle of the dance floor when we enter, and is about to start her show when she sees the mob surge in, and at first she is greatly pleased because she thinks new business arrives, and if there is anything Miss Missouri Martin dearly loves, it is new business.

But before she can say hello, sucker, or anything else whatever, Nip runs under her chair, thinking maybe he is a dachshund, and dumps Miss Missouri Martin on the dance floor, and she lays there squawking no little, while the next thing anybody knows, Nip and Tuck are over in one corner of the joint, and are eagerly crawling up and down a fat guy who is sitting there with a doll alongside of him, and who is the fat guy but Regret!

Well, as Nip and Tuck rush at Regret he naturally gets up to defend himself, but they both hit him at the same time, and over he goes on top of the doll who is with him, and who seems to be nobody but Miss Lovey Lou. She is getting quite a squashing with Regret's heft spread out over her, and she is screaming quite some, especially when Nip lets out a foot of tongue and washes her make-up off her face, reaching for Regret. In fact, Miss Lovey Lou seems to be more afraid of the bloodhounds than she does of being squashed to death, for when John Wangle and I hasten to her rescue and pull her out from under Regret she is moaning as follows:

"Oh, do not let them devour me—I will confess."

Well, as nobody but me and John Wangle seem to hear this crack, because everybody else is busy trying to split out Regret and the bloodhounds, and as John Wangle does not seem to understand what Miss Lovey Lou is mumbling about, I shove her off into the crowd, and on back into the kitchen, which is now quite deserted, what with all the help being out watching the muss in the corner, and I say to her like this:

"What is it you confess?" I say. "Is it about Marvin Clay?"

"Yes," she says. "It is about him. He is a pig," she says. "I shoot him, and I am glad of it. He is not satisfied with what he does to me two years ago, but he tries his deviltry on my baby sister. He has her in his apartment and when I find it out and go to get her, he says he will not let her go. So I shoot him. With my brother's pistol," she says, "and I take my baby sister home with me, and I hope he is dead, and gone where he belongs."

"Well, now," I say, "I am not going to give you any argument as to where Marvin Clay belongs, but," I say, "you skip out of here and go on home, and wait until we can do something about this situation, while I go back and help Regret, who seems to be in a tough spot."

"Oh, do not let these terrible dogs eat him up," she says, and with this she takes the breeze and I return to the other room to find there is much confusion, indeed, because it seems that Regret is now very indignant at Nip and Tuck, especially when he discovers that one of them plants his big old paw right on the front of Regret's shirt bosom, leaving a dirty mark. So when he struggles to his feet, Regret starts letting go with both hands, and he is by no means a bad puncher for a guy who does not do much punching as a rule. In fact, he flattens Nip with a right hand to the jaw, and knocks Tuck plumb across the room with a left hook.

Well, poor Tuck slides over the slick dance floor into Miss Missouri Martin just as she is getting to her feet again, and bowls her over once more, but Miss Missouri Martin is also indignant by this time, and she gets up and kicks Tuck in a most unladylike manner. Of course, Tuck does not know so much about Miss Martin, but he is pretty sure his old friend Regret is only playing with him, so back he goes to Regret with his tongue out, and his tail wagging, and there is no telling how long this may go on if John Wangle does not step in and grab both hounds, while Inspector McNamara puts the arm on Regret and tells him he is under arrest for shooting Marvin Clay.

Well, of course everybody can see at once that Regret must be the guilty party all right, especially when it is remembered that he once has trouble with Marvin Clay, and one and all present are looking at Regret in great disgust, and saying you can see by his face that he is nothing but a degenerate type.

Furthermore, Inspector McNamara makes a speech to Miss Missouri Martin's customers in which he congratulates John Wangle and Nip and Tuck on their wonderful work in tracking down this terrible criminal, and at the same time putting in a few boosts for the police department, while Regret stands there paying very little attention to what the Inspector is saying, but trying to edge himself over close enough to Nip and Tuck to give them the old foot.

Well, the customers applaud what Inspector McNamara says, and Miss Missouri Martin gets up a collection of over two C's for John Wangle and his hounds, not counting what she holds out for herself. Also the chef comes forward and takes John Wangle and Nip and Tuck back into the kitchen, and stuffs them full of food, although personally I will just as soon not have any of the food they serve in the Three Hundred Club.

They take Regret to the jail house, and he does not seem to understand why he is under arrest, but he knows it has something to do with Nip and Tuck and he tries to bribe one of the coppers to put the bloodhounds in the same cell with him for awhile, though naturally the copper will not consider such a proposition. While Regret is being booked at the jail house, word comes around that Marvin Clay is not only not dead, but the chances are he will get well, which he finally does, at that.

Moreover, he finally bails Regret out, and not only refuses to prosecute him but skips the country as soon as he is able to move, although Regret lays in the sneezer for several weeks, at that, never letting on after he learns the real situation that he is not the party who plugs Marvin Clay. Naturally, Miss Lovey Lou is very grateful to Regret for his wonderful sacrifice, and will no doubt become his ever-loving wife in a minute, if Regret thinks to ask her, but it seems Regret finds himself brooding so much over the idea of an ever-loving wife who is so handy with a roscoe that he never really asks.

In the meantime, John Wangle and Nip and Tuck go back to Georgia on the dough collected by Miss Missouri Martin, and with a big reputation as man-trackers. So this is all there is to the story, except that one night I run into Regret with a suit case in his hand, and he is perspiring very freely, although it is not so hot, at that, and when I ask him if he is going away, he says this is indeed his general idea. Moreover, he says he is going very far away. Naturally, I ask him why this is, and Regret says to me as follows:

"Well," he says, "ever since Big Nig, the crap shooter, comes back from Hot Springs, and hears how the bloodhounds track the shooter of Marvin Clay, he is walking up and down looking at me out of the corner of his eye. In fact," Regret says, "I can see that Big Nig is studying something over in his mind, and while Big Nig is a guy who is not such a fast thinker as others, I am afraid he may finally think himself to a bad conclusion.

"I am afraid," Regret says, "that Big Nig will think himself to the conclusion that Nip and Tuck are tracking me instead of the shooter, as many evil-minded guys are already whispering around and about, and that he may get the wrong idea about the trail leading to Maud Milligan's door."

Broadway Financier

OF ALL THE SCORES made by dolls on Broadway the past twenty-five years, there is no doubt but what the very largest score is made by a doll who is called Silk, when she knocks off a banker by the name of Israel Ib, for the size of Silk's score is three million one hundred bobs and a few odd cents.

It is admitted by one and all who know about these matters that the record up to this time is held by a doll by the name of Irma Teak, who knocks off a Russian duke back in 1911 when Russian dukes are considered very useful by dolls, although of course in these days Russian dukes are about as useful as dandruff. Anyway, Irma Teak's score off this Russian duke is up around a million, and she moves to London with her duke and chucks quite a swell around there for a time. But finally Irma Teak goes blind, which is a tough break for her as she can no longer see how jealous she is making other dolls with her diamonds and sables and one thing and another, so what good are they to her, after all?

I know Irma Teak when she is a show doll at the old Winter Garden, and I also know the doll by the name of Mazie Mitz, who is in a Florodora revival, and who makes a score of maybe three hundred G's off a guy who has a string of ten-cent stores, and three hundred G's is by no means hay. But Mazie Mitz finally hauls off and runs away with a saxophone player she is in love with and so winds up back of the fifteen ball.

Furthermore, I know Clara Simmons, the model from Rickson's, who gets a five-story town house and a country place on Long Island off a guy in Wall Street for birthday presents, and while I never meet this guy personally, I always figure he must be very dumb because anybody who knows Clara Simmons knows she will be just as well satisfied with a bottle of perfume for a birthday present. For all I know, Clara Simmons may still own the town house and the country place, but she must be shoving on toward forty now, so naturally nobody on Broadway cares what becomes of her.

I know a hundred other dolls who run up different scores, and some of them are very fair scores, indeed, but none of these scores are anything much alongside Silk's score off Israel Ib, and this score is all the more surprising because Silk starts out being greatly prejudiced against bankers. I am no booster for bankers myself, as I consider them very stony-hearted guys, but I am not prejudiced against them. In fact, I consider bankers very necessary, because if we do not have bankers many citizens will not be able to think of anybody to give a check on.

It is quite a while before she meets Israel Ib that Silk explains to me why she is prejudiced against bankers. It is when she is nothing but a chorus doll in Johnny Oakley's joint on Fifty-third Street, and comes into Mindy's after she gets through work, which is generally along about four o'clock in the morning.

At such an hour many citizens are sitting around Mindy's resting from the crap games and one thing and another, and dolls from the different joints around and about, including chorus dolls and hostesses, drop in for something to eat before going home, and generally these dolls are still in their make-up and very tired.

Naturally they come to know the citizens who are sitting around, and say hello, and maybe accept the hospitality of these citizens, such as java and Danish pastry, or maybe a few scrambled eggs, and it is all very pleasant and harmless, because a citizen who is all tuckered out from shooting craps is not going to get any high blood pressure over a tired chorus doll or a hostess, and especially a hostess.

Well, one morning Silk is sitting at my table guzzling a cup of java and a piece of apple pie, when in comes The Greek looking very weary, The Greek being a high shot who is well known far and wide. He drops into a chair alongside me and orders a Bismarck herring with sliced onions to come along, which is a dish that is considered most invigorating, and then The Greek mentions that he is playing the bank for twenty-four hours hand running, so right away Silk speaks up as follows:

"I hate banks," she says. "Furthermore," she says, "I hate bankers. If it is not for a banker maybe I will not be slaving in Johnny Oakley's dirty little drum for thirty bobs per week. Maybe my mamma will still be alive, and I will be living at home with her instead of in a flea bag in Forty-seventh Street.

"My mamma once saves up three hundred bobs from scrubbing floors in an office building to send me to school," Silk says, "and a banker in one of the buildings where she does this scrubbing tells her to put her dough in his bank, and what happens but the bank busts and it is such a terrible blow to my mamma that she ups and dies. I am very small at the time," Silk says, "but I can remember standing in front of the busted bank with my mamma, and my mamma crying her eyes out."

Well, personally, I consider Silk's crack about Johnny Oakley's joint uncalled for, as it is by no means little, but I explain to her that what The Greek is talking about is a faro bank, and not a bank you put money in, as such a bank is called a jug, and not a bank at all, while faro bank is a gambling game, and the reason I explain this to Silk is because everybody always explains things to her.

The idea is everybody wishes Silk to be well smartened up, especially everybody who hangs out around Mindy's, because she is an orphan and never has a chance to go to school, and we do not wish her to grow up dumb like the average doll, as one and all are very fond of Silk from the first minute she bobs up around Mindy's.

Now at this time Silk is maybe seventeen years old and weighs maybe ninety pounds, sopping wet, and she is straight up and down like a boy. She has soft brown hair and brown eyes that seem too big for her face, and she looks right at you when she talks to you and she talks to you like one guy to another guy. In fact, I always claim there is more guy in Silk than there is doll, as she finally gets so she thinks like a guy, which is maybe because she associates more with guys than she does with other dolls and gets a guy's slant on things in general.

She loves to sit around Mindy's in the early morning gabbing with different citizens, although she does more listening than gabbing herself, and she loves to listen to gab about horse-racing and baseball and fights and crap-shooting and to guys cutting up old touches and whatever else is worth gabbing about, and she seldom sticks in her oar, except maybe to ask a question. Naturally a doll who is willing to listen instead of wishing to gab herself is bound to be popular because if there is anything most citizens hate and despise it is a gabby doll.

So then many citizens take a real interest in Silk's education, including Regret, the horse-player, who explains to her how to build up a sucker to betting on a hot horse, although personally I do not consider such knowledge of any more value to a young doll just starting out in the world than the lesson Big Nig, the crap-shooter, gives her one night on how to switch in a pair of tops on a craps game.

Then there is Doc Daro, who is considered one of the highest-class operators that ever rides the tubs in his day, being a great hand for traveling back and forth across the ocean and out-playing other passengers at bridge and poker and one thing and another, but who finally gets rheumatism in his hands so bad he can no longer shuffle the cards. And of course if Doc Daro cannot shuffle the cards there is no sense whatever in him trying to play games of skill any more.

Doc Daro is always telling Silk what rascals guys are and explaining to her the different kinds of business they will try to give her, this being the same kind of business the Doc gives dolls himself in his time. The Doc has an idea that a young doll who is battling Broadway needs plenty of education along such lines, but Silk tells me privately that she is jerry to the stuff Doc is telling her when she is five years old.

The guy I figure does Silk the most good is an old pappy guy by the name of Professor D, who is always reading books when he is not busy doping the horses. In fact, Professor D is considered somewhat daffy on the subject of reading books, but it seems he gets the habit from being a teacher in a college out in Ohio before he becomes a horse-player. Anyway, Professor D takes to giving Silk books to read, and what is more she reads them and talks them over afterward with the professor, who is greatly pleased by this.

"She is a bright little doll," Professor D says to me one day. "Furthermore," the professor says, "she has soul."

"Well," I say, "Big Nig claims she can palm a pair of dice as good as anybody he ever sees."

But the professor only says heigh-ho, and goes along, and I can see he does not consider me a character worth having much truck with, even though I am as much interested in Silk's education as anybody else.

Well, what happens one night but the regular singer in Johnny Oakley's joint, a doll by the name of Myrtle Marigold, hauls off and catches the measles from her twelve-year-old son, and as Johnny has enough trouble getting customers into his joint without giving them the measles after getting them there, he gives Myrtle Marigold plenty of wind at once.

But there he is without anybody to sing Stacker Lee to his customers, Stacker Lee being a ditty with which Myrtle Marigold panics the customers, so Johnny looks his chorus over and finally asks Silk if she can sing. And Silk says she can sing all right, but that she will not sing Stacker Lee, because she considers it a low-down lullaby, at best. She says she will sing something classical and, being desperate for singing, Johnny Oakley says go ahead. So what does Silk do but sing a very old song called Annie Laurie, which she learns from her mamma, and she sings this song so loud that sobs are heard all over the joint.

Of course if anybody investigates they will learn that the sobbing is being done by Professor D and Big Nig and The Greek, who happen to be in the joint at the time, and what they are sobbing about is the idea of Silk singing at all, but Johnny Oakley considers her a big hit and keeps her singing Annie Laurie right along, and one night Harry

Fitz, the booking agent, drops in and hears her singing and tells Ziegfeld he discovers a doll with a brand-new style.

Naturally Ziggie signs her up at once for the Follies, because he has great faith in Harry Fitz's judgment but after Ziggie hears Silk sing he asks her if she can do anything else, and is greatly relieved when he learns she can dance.

So Silk becomes a Ziegfeld dancer, and she is quite a sensation with the dramatic critics on the night she opens because she dances with all her clothes on, which is considered a very great novelty indeed. The citizens around Mindy's chip in and send Silk a taxicab full of orchids, and a floral pillow, and Professor D contributes a book called The Outline of History, and Silk is the happiest doll in town.

A year goes by, and what a year in the Follies does for Silk is most astonishing. Personally, I never see a lot of change in her looks, except her figure fills out so it has bumps here and there where a doll is entitled to have bumps, and her face grows to fit her eyes more, but everybody else claims she becomes beautiful, and her picture is always in the papers and dozens of guys are always hanging around after her and sending her flowers and one thing and another.

One guy in particular starts sending her jewelry, which Silk always brings around to Mindy's for Jewelry Joe to look at, this Jewelry Joe being a guy who peddles jewelry along Broadway for years, and who can tell you in a second what a piece of jewelry is worth.

Jewelry Joe finds that the jewelry Silk brings around is nothing much but slum, and naturally he advises her to have no further truck with any party who cannot send in anything better than this, but one morning she shows up in Mindy's with an emerald ring the size of a cake of soap, and the minute Jewelry Joe sees the emerald he tells Silk that whoever donates this is worthy of very careful consideration.

Now it seems that the party who sends the emerald is nobody but Israel Ib, the banker who owns the jug down on the lower East Side that is called the Bank of the Bridges, and the way Silk comes to connect with him is most unusual. It is through a young guy by the name of Simeon Slotsky, who is a teller in Israel Ib's jug, and who sees Silk dancing one night in the Follies and goes right off his ka-zip about her.

It is this Simeon Slotsky who is sending the jewelry that Silk first brings around, and the way he is buying this jewelry is by copping a little dough out of the jug now and then which does not belong to him. Naturally this is a most dishonest action, and by and by they catch up with Simeon Slotsky in the jug, and Israel Ib is going to place him in the pokey.

Well, Simeon Slotsky does not wish to be placed in the pokey and not knowing what else to do, what does he do but go to Silk and tell her his story, explaining that he commits this dishonest business only because he is daffy about her, even though Silk never gives him a tumble, and in fact never says as much as two words to him before.

He tells her that he comes of respectable old parents down on the lower East Side, who will be very sad if he is placed in the pokey, especially his mamma, but Israel Ib is bound and determined to put him away, because Israel Ib is greatly opposed to anybody copping dough out of his jug. Simeon Slotsky says his mamma cries all over Israel Ib's vest trying to cry him out of the idea of placing her son in the pokey, but that Israel Ib is a very hard-hearted guy and will not give in no matter what, and furthermore he is very indignant because Simeon's mamma's tears spot up his vest. So Simeon says it looks as if he must go to the pokey unless Silk can think of something.

Now Silk is very young herself and very tenderhearted and she is sorry for Simeon Slotsky, because she can see he is nothing but a hundred-per-cent chump, so she sits down and writes a letter to Israel Ib asking him to call on her backstage at the Follies on a matter of great importance. Of course Silk does not know that it is not the proper caper to be writing a banker such a letter, and ordinarily it is a thousand to one, according to the way The Greek figures the odds, that a banker will pay no attention to such a letter except maybe to notify his lawyer.

But it seems that the letter tickles Israel Ib, as he always secretly wishes to get a peek backstage at the Follies to see if the dolls back there wear as few clothes as he hears, so he shows up the very same night, and in five minutes Silk has him all rounded up as far as Simeon Slotsky is concerned. Israel Ib says he will straighten out everything and send Simeon to a job in a jug out West.

So the next day Simeon Slotsky comes around and thanks Silk for all she does for him, and bawls quite some, and gets a photograph off her with her name signed to it which he says he will give to his mamma so she can stick it up on her wall on the East Side to always remember the doll who saves her son, and then Simeon Slotsky goes on about his business, and for all I know becomes a very honest and useful citizen. And forty-eight hours later, Silk is wearing the emerald from Israel Ib.

Now this Israel Ib is by no means a Broadway character, and in fact few ever hear of him before he bobs up sending Silk an emerald ring. In fact, it seems that Israel Ib is a quiet, industrious guy, who has nothing on his mind but running his jug and making plenty of scratch until the night he goes to see Silk.

He is a little short fat guy of maybe forty-odd at this time with a little round stomach sticking out in front of him and he always wears a white vest on his stomach, with a pair of gold-rimmed cheaters hanging on a black ribbon across the vest. He has a large snozzle and is as homely as a mud fence, any way you take him, but it is well known to one and all that he is a coming guy in the banking dodge.

Silk is always making jokes about Israel Ib, because naturally she cannot see much to such a looking guy, but every morning she comes into Mindy's with all kinds of swag, such as bracelets and rings and brooches, and Jewelry Joe finally speaks to her very severely and tells her that a guy who can send her such merchandise is no joking matter.

There is no doubt that Israel Ib is dizzy about her, and personally I consider it very sad that a guy as smart as he must be lets himself get tangled up in such a situation. But then I remember that guys ten thousand times smarter than Israel Ib let themselves get tangled up the same way, so it is all even.

The upshot of the whole business is that Silk begins to pay a little serious attention to Israel Ib, and the next thing anybody knows she quits the Follies and takes to living in a large apartment on Park Avenue and riding around in a big car with a guy in uniform driving her, and she has enough fur coats for a tribe of Eskimos, including a chinchilla flogger that moves Israel back thirty G's.

Furthermore, it comes out that the apartment house she is living in is in her own name, and some citizens are greatly surprised, as they do not figure a doll just off Broadway smart enough to get anything in her own name, except maybe a traffic summons. But Professor D says he is not surprised because he once makes Silk read a book entitled The Importance of Property.

We do not see much of Silk any more these days, but every now and then we hear rumors of her getting more apartment houses and business buildings in her own name, and the citizens around Mindy's are greatly pleased because they figure it proves that the trouble they take educating

Silk is by no means wasted. Finally we hear Silk goes to Europe, and for nearly two years she is living in Paris and other spots, and some say the reason she sticks around Europe is because she finds out all of a sudden that Israel Ib is a married guy, although personally I figure Silk must know this all along, because it certainly is no mystery. In fact, Israel Ib is very much married, indeed, and his ever-loving wife is a big fat old doll whose family has plenty of potatoes.

The chances are Silk is sick and tired of looking at Israel Ib, and stays abroad so she will not have to look at his ugly kisser more than two or three times a year, which is about as often as Israel Ib can think up excuses to go over and see her. Then one winter we hear that Silk is coming home to stay, and it is the winter of 1930 when things are very tough, indeed.

It is close to Christmas when Silk lands one morning around eleven o'clock from the steamship, and it seems she is expecting Israel Ib to meet her at the dock, but Israel Ib is not present, and nobody else is there to tell her why Israel Ib is absent.

It seems that some of Silk's luggage is being held up by the customs guys, as she brings over enough merchandise of one kind and another to stock a department store, and she wishes to see Israel Ib to get this matter straightened out, so she hires a taxi and tells the jockey to take her to Israel Ib's jug, figuring to stop in a minute and give Israel Ib his instructions, and maybe a good rousting around for not meeting her.

Now Silk never before goes to Israel Ib's jug, which is deep down on the lower East Side where many citizens wear long whiskers and do not speak much English, and where there always seems to be a smell of herring around and about, and she is greatly surprised and much disgusted by her surroundings as she approaches the corner where Israel Ib's jug stands.

Furthermore, she is much surprised to find a big crowd in front of the jug, and this crowd is made up of many whiskers and old dolls wearing shawls over their heads, and kids of all sizes and shapes, and everybody in the crowd seems much excited, and there is plenty of moaning and groaning from one and all, and especially from an old doll who is standing in the doorway of a little store a couple of doors from the jug.

In fact, this old doll is making more racket than all the rest of the crowd put together, and at times is raising her voice to a scream and crying out in a strange language words that sound quite hostile.

Silk's taxi cannot get through the mob and a copper steps up and tells the driver he better make a detour, so Silk asks the copper why these people are raising such a rumpus in the street, instead of being home keeping warm, for it is colder than a blonde's heart, and there is plenty of ice around about.

"Why," the copper says, "do you not hear? This jug busts this morning and the guy who runs it, Israel Ib, is over in the Tombs, and the people are nervous because many of them have their potatoes in the jug. In fact," the copper says, "some of them, including the old doll over there in front of the store who is doing all the screeching, have their lifetime savings in this jug, and it looks as if they are ruined. It is very sad," he says, "because they are very, very poor people."

And then tears come to his eyes, and he boffs an old guy with whiskers over the skull with his club because the old guy is moaning so loud the copper can scarcely make himself heard.

Now naturally all this is most surprising news to Silk, and

while she is pretty much sored up because she cannot see Israel Ib to get her merchandise out of the customs, she has the taxi jockey take her away from these scenes right away, and up to her apartment in Park Avenue, which she has ready for her coming home. Then she sends out for the early editions of the evening papers and reads all about what a rapscallion Israel Ib is for letting his jug bust right in the poor people's faces.

It seems that Israel Ib is placed in the Tombs because somebody suspects something illegal about the busting, but of course nobody figures Israel Ib will be kept in the Tombs long on account of being a banker, and in fact there is already some talk that the parties who placed him there in the first place may find themselves in plenty of heat later on, because it is considered most discourteous to a banker to place him in the Tombs where the accommodations are by no means first class.

One of the papers has a story about Israel Ib's everloving wife taking it on the lam as soon as the news gets out about the jug busting and Israel Ib being in the Tombs, and about her saying he can get out of this predicament the best way he can, but that she will never help with as much as a thin dime of her dough and hinting pretty strong that Israel Ib's trouble is on account of him squandering the jug's scratch on a doll.

The story says she is going back to her people, and from the way the story reads it sounds as if the scribe who writes it figures this is one good break, at least, for Israel Ib.

Now these hints let out by Israel Ib's ever-loving wife about him squandering the jug's scratch on a doll are printed as facts in the morning papers the next morning, and maybe if Silk bothers to read these morning sheets she will think better of going down to Israel Ib's jug again, because her name is mentioned right out, and there are big pictures of her in the papers from her old days in the Follies.

But there Silk is in a taxi in front of the Bank of the

Bridges at nine o'clock the next morning, and it seems her brain is buzzing with quite a large idea, although this idea does not come out until later.

There is already quite a crowd around the jug again, as it is always very difficult to make people who live on the lower East Side and wear whiskers and shawls understand about such matters as busted jugs. They are apt to hang around a busted jug for days at a time with their bank books in their hands, and sometimes it takes as much as a week to convince such people that their potatoes are gone for good, and make them disperse to their homes and start saving more.

There is still much moaning and groaning, though not as much as the day before, and every now and then the old doll pops out of the little store and stands in the doorway and shakes her fist at the busted jug and hollers in a strange language. A short, greasy-looking guy with bristly whiskers and an old black derby hat jammed down over his ears is standing with a morning paper spread out in his hands, and a bunch of other guys are around him listening to him read what the paper has to say about the situation.

Just one copper is walking up and down now, and it is the copper who speaks to Silk the day before, and he seems to remember her as she gets out of the taxi and he walks over to her, while a lot of people stop moaning and groaning to take a gander at her, for it is by no means a common sight to see such a looking doll in this neighborhood.

The copper no more than says good morning to Silk when the guy who is reading the paper stops reading and takes a peek at her, and then at her picture which is on the page in front of him. Then he points at the picture and points at Silk, and begins jabbering a blue streak to the guys around him. About this time the old doll peeps out of the store to shake her fist at Israel Ib's jug again and, hearing the jabbering, she joins the bunch around the guy with the paper.

She listens to the jabbering a while, peeking over the guy's shoulder at the picture, and then taking a good long look at

Silk, and then all of a sudden the old doll turns and pops back into the store.

Now all the shawls and whiskers start gathering around Silk and the copper, and anybody can tell from the way they are looking that they are all sored up, and what they are sored up at is Silk, because naturally they figure out that she is the doll whose picture is in the morning paper and is therefore the doll who is responsible for Israel Ib's jug busting.

But of course the copper does not know that they are sored up at Silk, and figures they are gathering around just out of curiosity, as people will do when they see a copper talking to anybody. He is a young copper and naturally he does not wish to have an audience when he is speaking to such a looking doll as Silk, even if most of the audience cannot understand English, so as the crowd nudges closer he gets his club ready to boff a few skulls.

Just about then half a brickbat hits him under the right ear, and he begins wobbling about very loose at the hinges, and at the same minute all the shawls and whiskers take to pulling and hauling at Silk. There are about a hundred of the shawls and whiskers to begin with and more are coming up from every-which direction, and they are all yelling and screaming and punching and scratching at Silk.

She is knocked down two or three times, and many shawls and whiskers are walking up and down her person while she is on the ground, and she is bleeding here and there, and the chances are they will kill her as dead as a doornail in their excitement if the old doll from the little store near the jug does not bob up all of a sudden with a mop handle in her duke and starts boffing the shawls and whiskers on their noggins.

In fact, the old doll plays a regular tune on these noggins with the mop handle, sometimes knocking a shawl or whiskers quite bowlegged, and soon clearing a path through the crowd to Silk and taking hold of Silk and dragging her off into the store just as the reserves and an ambulance arrive.

The young copper is still wobbling about from the brick-bat and speaking of how he hears the birdies singing in the trees, although of course there are no birdies in this neighborhood at such a time of year, and no trees either, and there are maybe half a dozen shawls and whiskers sitting on the pavement rubbing their noggins, and others are diving into doorways here and there, and there is much confusion generally.

So the ambulance takes Silk and some of the shawls and whiskers to a hospital and Professor D and Doc Daro visit her there a couple of hours later, finding her in bed somewhat plastered up in spots but in no danger, and naturally Professor D and Doc Daro wish to know what she is doing around Israel Ib's jug, anyway.

"Why," Silk says, "I am not able to sleep a wink all last night thinking of these poor people suffering on account of me taking Israel Ib's dough, although," Silk says, "of course I do not know it is wrong dough when I receive it. I do not know Israel Ib is clipping these poor people. But seeing them around the jug yesterday morning, I remember what happens to my poor mamma when the jug busts on her. I see her standing in front of the busted jug with me beside her, crying her eyes out, and my heart is very heavy," Silk says. "So I get to thinking," she says, "that it will be a very nice thing, indeed, if I am first to tell the poor souls who have their dough in Israel Ib's jug that they are going to get it back."

"Wait a minute," Doc Daro says. "What do you mean—they are going to get their dough back?"

"Why," Silk says, "I consult with Judge Goldstein, who is my tongue, and a very good guy, at that, and fairly honest, last night, and Judge Goldstein tells me that I am worth in negotiable securities and real estate and jewelry, and one thing and another about three million, one hundred bobs, and a few odd cents.

"Judge Goldstein tells me," Silk says, "that such a sum

will more than pay off all the depositors in Israel Ib's jug. In fact, Judge Goldstein tells me that what I have probably represents most of the deposits in the jug, and," she says, "I sign everything I own in this world over to Judge Goldstein to do this, although Judge Goldstein says there is no doubt I can beat any attempt to take my dough away from me if I wish to keep it.

"So," Silk says, "I am so happy to think these poor people will get their dough back that I cannot wait for Judge Goldstein to let it out. I wish to break the news to them myself, but," Silk says, "before I can say a word they hop on me and start giving me a pasting, and if it is not for the old doll with the mop handle maybe you will have to chip in to bury me, because I certainly do not have enough dough left to bury myself."

Well, this is about all there is to the story, except that the Bank of the Bridges pays off one hundred per cent on the dollar, and what is more Israel Ib is running it again, and doing very well, indeed, and his ever-loving wife returns to him, and everything is hotsy-totsy between them.

As for Silk, she is back on Broadway, and the last time I see her she is in love with a very legitimate guy who is in the hotel business, and while he does not strike me as having much brains, he has plenty of youth running for him, and Silk says it is the best break she ever gets in her life when Israel Ib's jug busts.

But anybody will tell you that the best break Silk ever gets is when the old doll on the lower East Side recognizes her from the photograph she has stuck up on the wall in the little store near Israel Ib's jug as the doll who once saves her son, Simeon Slotsky, from being placed in the pokey.

Dancing Dan's Christmas

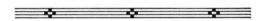

Now ONE TIME it comes on Christmas, and in fact it is the evening before Christmas, and I am in Good Time Charley Bernstein's little speakeasy in West Forty-seventh Street, wishing Charley a Merry Christmas and having a few hot Tom and Jerrys with him.

This hot Tom and Jerry is an old-time drink that is once used by one and all in this country to celebrate Christmas with, and in fact it is once so popular that many people think Christmas is invented only to furnish an excuse for hot Tom and Jerry, although of course this is by no means true.

But anybody will tell you that there is nothing that brings out the true holiday spirit like hot Tom and Jerry, and I hear that since Tom and Jerry goes out of style in the United States, the holiday spirit is never quite the same.

The reason hot Tom and Jerry goes out of style is because it is necessary to use rum and one thing and another in making Tom and Jerry, and naturally when rum becomes illegal in this country Tom and Jerry is also against the law, because rum is something that is very hard to get around town these days.

For a while some people try making hot Tom and Jerry without putting rum in it, but somehow it never has the same old holiday spirit, so nearly everybody finally gives up in disgust, and this is not surprising, as making Tom and Jerry is by no means child's play. In fact, it takes quite an expert to make good Tom and Jerry, and in the days when it is not illegal a good hot Tom and Jerry maker commands good wages and many friends.

Now of course Good Time Charley and I are not using rum in the Tom and Jerry we are making, as we do not wish to do anything illegal. What we are using is rye whiskey that Good Time Charley gets on a doctor's prescription from a drug store, as we are personally drinking this hot Tom and Jerry and naturally we are not foolish enough to use any of Good Time Charley's own rye in it.

The prescription for the rye whisky comes from old Doc Moggs, who prescribes it for Good Time Charley's rheumatism in case Charley happens to get any rheumatism, as Doc Moggs says there is nothing better for rheumatism than rye whisky, especially if it is made up in a hot Tom and Jerry. In fact, old Doc Moggs comes around and has a few seidels of hot Tom and Jerry with us for his own rheumatism.

He comes around during the afternoon, for Good Time Charley and I start making this Tom and Jerry early in the day, so as to be sure to have enough to last us over Christmas, and it is now along toward six o'clock, and our holiday spirit is practically one hundred per cent.

Well, as Good Time Charley and I are expressing our holiday sentiments to each other over our hot Tom and

Jerry, and I am trying to think up the poem about the night before Christmas and all through the house, which I know will interest Charley no little, all of a sudden there is a big knock at the front door, and when Charley opens the door who comes in carrying a large package under one arm but a guy by the name of Dancing Dan.

This Dancing Dan is a good-looking young guy, who always seems well-dressed, and he is called by the name of Dancing Dan because he is a great hand for dancing around and about with dolls in night clubs, and other spots where there is any dancing. In fact, Dan never seems to be doing anything else, although I hear rumors that when he is not dancing he is carrying on in a most illegal manner at one thing and another. But of course you can always hear rumors in this town about anybody, and personally I am rather fond of Dancing Dan as he always seems to be getting a great belt out of life.

Anybody in town will tell you that Dancing Dan is a guy with no Barnaby whatever in him, and in fact he has about as much gizzard as anybody around, although I wish to say I always question his judgment in dancing so much with Miss Muriel O'Neill, who works in the Half Moon night club. And the reason I question his judgment in this respect is because everybody knows that Miss Muriel O'Neill is a doll who is very well thought of by Heine Schmitz, and Heine Schmitz is not such a guy as will take kindly to anybody dancing more than once and a half with a doll that he thinks well of.

This Heine Schmitz is a very influential citizen of Harlem, where he has large interests in beer, and other business enterprises, and it is by no means violating any confidence to tell you that Heine Schmitz will just as soon blow your brains out as look at you. In fact, I hear sooner. Anyway, he is not a guy to monkey with and many citizens take the trouble to advise Dancing Dan that he is not only away out of line in dancing with Miss Muriel O'Neill, but that he is knocking his own price down to where he is no price at all.

But Dancing Dan only laughs ha-ha, and goes on dancing with Miss Muriel O'Neill any time he gets a chance, and Good Time Charley says he does not blame him, at that, as Miss Muriel O'Neill is so beautiful that he will be dancing with her himself no matter what, if he is five years younger and can get a Roscoe out as fast as in the days when he runs with Paddy the Link and other fast guys.

Well, anyway, as Dancing Dan comes in he weighs up the joint in one quick peek, and then he tosses the package he is carrying into a corner where it goes plunk, as if there is something very heavy in it, and then he steps up to the bar alongside of Charley and me and wishes to know what we are drinking.

Naturally we start boosting hot Tom and Jerry to Dancing Dan, and he says he will take a crack at it with us, and after one crack, Dancing Dan says he will have another crack, and Merry Christmas to us with it, and the first thing anybody knows it is a couple of hours later and we are still having cracks at the hot Tom and Jerry with Dancing Dan, and Dan says he never drinks anything so soothing in his life. In fact, Dancing Dan says he will recommend Tom and Jerry to everybody he knows, only he does not know anybody good enough for Tom and Jerry, except maybe Miss Muriel O'Neill, and she does not drink anything with drugstore rye in it.

Well, several times while we are drinking this Tom and Jerry, customers come to the door of Good Time Charley's little speakeasy and knock, but by now Charley is commencing to be afraid they will wish Tom and Jerry, too, and he does not feel we will have enough for ourselves, so he hangs out a sign which says "Closed on

Account of Christmas," and the only one he will let in is a guy by the name of Ooky, who is nothing but an old rum-dum, and who is going around all week dressed like Santa Claus and carrying a sign advertising Moe Lewinsky's clothing joint around in Sixth Avenue.

This Ooky is still wearing his Santa Claus outfit when Charley lets him in, and the reason Charley permits such a character as Ooky in his joint is because Ooky does the porter work for Charley when he is not Santa Claus for Moe Lewinsky, such as sweeping out, and washing the glasses, and one thing and another.

Well, it is about nine-thirty when Ooky comes in, and his puppies are aching, and he is all petered out generally from walking up and down and here and there with his sign, for any time a guy is Santa Claus for Moe Lewinsky he must earn his dough. In fact, Ooky is so fatigued, and his puppies hurt him so much that Dancing Dan and Good Time Charley and I all feel very sorry for him, and invite him to have a few mugs of hot Tom and Jerry with us, and wish him plenty of Merry Christmas.

But old Ooky is not accustomed to Tom and Jerry and after about the fifth mug he folds up in a chair, and goes right to sleep on us. He is wearing a pretty good Santa Claus make-up, what with a nice red suit trimmed with white cotton, and a wig, and false nose, and long white whiskers, and a big sack stuffed with excelsior on his back and if I do not know Santa Claus is not apt to be such a guy as will snore loud enough to rattle the windows, I will think Ooky is Santa Claus sure enough.

Well, we forget Ooky and let him sleep, and go on with our hot Tom and Jerry, and in the meantime we try to think up a few songs appropriate to Christmas, and Dancing Dan finally renders My Dad's Dinner Pail in a nice baritone and very loud, while I do first rate with Will You Love Me in December As You Do in May?

But personally I always think Good Time Charley Bernstein is a little out of line trying to sing a hymn in Jewish
on such an occasion, and it causes words between us.

While we are singing many customers come to the
door and knock, and then they read Charley's sign, and
this seems to cause some unrest among them, and some
of them stand outside saying it is a great outrage, until
Charley sticks his noggin out the door and threatens to
bust somebody's beezer if they do not go on about their
business and stop disturbing peaceful citizens.

Naturally the customers go away, as they do not wish
their beezers busted, and Dancing Dan and Charley and
I continue drinking our hot Tom and Jerry, and with each
Tom and Jerry we are wishing one another a very Merry
Christmas, and sometimes a very Happy New Year, al-
though of course this does not go for Good Time Charley
as yet, because Charley has his New Year separate from
Dancing Dan and me.

By and by we take to waking Ooky up in his Santa
Claus outfit and offering him more hot Tom and Jerry,
and wishing him Merry Christmas, but Ooky only gets
sore and calls us names, so we can see he does not have
the right holiday spirit in him, and let him alone until
along about midnight when Dancing Dan wishes to see
how he looks as Santa Claus.

So Good Time Charley and I help Dancing Dan pull
off Ooky's outfit and put it on Dan, and this is easy as
Ooky only has this Santa Claus outfit on over his ordinary
clothes, and he does not even wake up when we are un-
dressing him of the Santa Claus uniform.

Well, I wish to say I see many a Santa Claus in my time,
but I never see a better looking Santa Claus than Dancing
Dan, especially after he gets the wig and white whiskers
fixed just right, and we put a sofa pillow that Good Time

Charley happens to have around the joint for the cat to sleep on down his pants to give Dancing Dan a nice fat stomach such as Santa Claus is bound to have.

In fact, after Dancing Dan looks at himself in a mirror awhile he is greatly pleased with his appearance, while Good Time Charley is practically hysterical, although personally I am commencing to resent Charley's interest in Santa Claus, and Christmas generally, as he by no means has any claim on these matters. But then I remember Charley furnishes the hot Tom and Jerry, so I am more tolerant toward him.

"Well," Charley finally says, "it is a great pity we do not know where there are some stockings hung up somewhere, because then," he says, "you can go around and stuff things in these stockings, as I always hear this is the main idea of a Santa Claus. But," Charley says, "I do not suppose anybody in this section has any stockings hung up, or if they have," he says, "the chances are they are so full of holes they will not hold anything. Anyway," Charley says, "even if there are any stockings hung up we do not have anything to stuff in them, although personally," he says, "I will gladly donate a few pints of Scotch."

Well, I am pointing out that we have no reindeer and that a Santa Claus is bound to look like a terrible sap if he goes around without any reindeer, but Charley's remarks seem to give Dancing Dan an idea, for all of a sudden he speaks as follows:

"Why," Dancing Dan says, "I know where a stocking is hung up. It is hung up at Miss Muriel O'Neill's flat over here in West Forty-ninth Street. This stocking is hung up by nobody but a party by the name of Gammer O'Neill, who is Miss Muriel O'Neill's grandmamma," Dancing Dan says. "Gammer O'Neill is going on ninety-odd," he says "and Miss Muriel O'Neill tells me she cannot hold out much longer, what with one thing and another, including being a little childish in spots.

"Now," Dancing Dan says, "I remember Miss Muriel O'Neill is telling me just the other night how Gammer O'Neill hangs up her stocking on Christmas Eve all her life, and," he says, "I judge from what Miss Muriel O'Neill says that the old doll always believes Santa Claus will come along some Christmas and fill the stocking full of beautiful gifts. But," Dancing Dan says, "Miss Muriel O'Neill tells me Santa Claus never does this, although Miss Muriel O'Neill personally always takes a few gifts home and pops them into the stocking to make Gammer O'Neill feel better.

"But, of course," Dancing Dan says, "these gifts are nothing much because Miss Muriel O'Neill is very poor, and proud, and also good, and will not take a dime off of anybody and I can lick the guy who says she will, although," Dancing Dan says, "between me, and Heine Schmitz, and a raft of other guys I can mention, Miss Muriel O'Neill can take plenty."

Well, I know that what Dancing Dan states about Miss Muriel O'Neill is quite true, and in fact it is a matter that is often discussed on Broadway, because Miss Muriel O'Neill cannot get more than twenty bobs per week working in the Half Moon, and it is well known to one and all that this is no kind of dough for a doll as beautiful as Miss Muriel O'Neill.

"Now," Dancing Dan goes on, "it seems that while Gammer O'Neill is very happy to get whatever she finds in her stocking on Christmas morning, she does not understand why Santa Claus is not more liberal, and," he says, "Miss Muriel O'Neill is saying to me that she only wishes she can give Gammer O'Neill one real big Christmas before the old doll puts her checks back in the rack.

"So," Dancing Dan states, "here is a job for us. Miss Muriel O'Neill and her grandmamma live all alone in this flat over in West Forty-ninth Street, and," he says, "at such an hour as this Miss Muriel O'Neill is bound to be working, and the chances are Gammer O'Neill is sound asleep, and we will just hop over there and Santa Claus will fill up her stocking with beautiful gifts."

Well, I say, I do not see where we are going to get any beautiful gifts at this time of night, what with all the stores being closed, unless we dash into an all-night drug store and buy a few bottles of perfume and a bum toilet set as guys always do when they forget about their ever-loving wives until after store hours on Christmas Eve, but Dancing Dan says never mind about this, but let us have a few more Tom and Jerrys first.

So we have a few more Tom and Jerrys, and then Dancing Dan picks up the package he heaves into the corner, and dumps most of the excelsior out of Ooky's Santa Claus sack, and puts the bundle in, and Good Time Charley turns out all the lights but one, and leaves a bottle of Scotch on the table in front of Ooky for a Christmas gift, and away we go.

Personally, I regret very much leaving the hot Tom and Jerry, but then I am also very enthusiastic about going along to help Dancing Dan play Santa Claus, while Good Time Charley is practically overjoyed, as it is the first time in his life Charley is ever mixed up in so much holiday spirit. In fact, nothing will do Charley but that we stop in a couple of spots and have a few drinks to Santa Claus' health, and these visits are a big success, although everybody is much surprised to see Charley and me with Santa Claus, especially Charley, although nobody recognizes Dancing Dan.

But of course there are no hot Tom and Jerrys in these spots we visit, and we have to drink whatever is on hand,

and personally I will always believe that the noggin I have on me afterwards comes of mixing the drinks we get in these spots with my Tom and Jerry.

As we go up Broadway, headed for Forty-ninth Street, Charley and I see many citizens we know and give them a large hello, and wish them Merry Christmas, and some of these citizens shake hands with Santa Claus, not knowing he is nobody but Dancing Dan, although later I understand there is some gossip among these citizens because they claim a Santa Claus with such a breath on him as our Santa Claus has is a little out of line.

And once we are somewhat embarrassed when a lot of little kids going home with their parents from a late Christmas party somewhere gather about Santa Claus with shouts of childish glee, and some of them wish to climb up Santa Claus' legs. Naturally, Santa Claus gets a little peevish, and calls them a few names, and one of the parents comes up and wishes to know what is the idea of Santa Claus using such language, and Santa Claus takes a punch at the parent, all of which is no doubt most astonishing to the little kids who have an idea of Santa Claus as a very kindly old guy. But of course they do not know about Dancing Dan mixing the liquor we get in the spots we visit with his Tom and Jerry, or they will understand how even Santa Claus can lose his temper.

Well, finally we arrive in front of the place where Dancing Dan says Miss Muriel O'Neill and her grandmamma live, and it is nothing but a tenement house not far back of Madison Square Garden, and furthermore it is a walk-up, and at this time there are no lights burning in the joint except a gas jet in the main hall, and by the light of this jet we look at the names on the letter boxes, such as you always find in the hall of these joints, and we see that Miss Muriel O'Neill and her grandmamma live on the fifth floor.

This is the top floor, and personally I do not like the idea of walking up five flights of stairs, and I am willing to let Dancing Dan and Good Time Charley go, but Dancing Dan insists we must all go, and finally I agree because Charley is commencing to argue that the right way for us to do is to get on the roof and let Santa Claus go down a chimney, and is making so much noise I am afraid he will wake somebody up.

So up the stairs we climb and finally we come to a door on the top floor that has a little card in a slot that says O'Neill, so we know we reach our destination. Dancing Dan first tries the knob, and right away the door opens, and we are in a little two- or three-room flat, with not much furniture in it, and what furniture there is is very poor. One single gas jet is burning near a bed in a room just off the one the door opens into, and by this light we see a very old doll is sleeping on the bed, so we judge this is nobody but Gammer O'Neill.

On her face is a large smile, as if she is dreaming of something very pleasant. On a chair at the head of the bed is hung a long black stocking, and it seems to be such a stocking as is often patched and mended, so I can see that what Miss Muriel O'Neill tells Dancing Dan about her grandmamma hanging up her stocking is really true, although up to this time I have my doubts.

Well, I am willing to pack in after one gander at the old doll, especially as Good Time Charley is commencing to prowl around the flat to see if there is a chimney where Santa Claus can come down, and is knocking things over, but Dancing Dan stands looking down at Gammer O'Neill for a long time.

Finally he unslings the sack on his back, and takes out his package, and unties this package, and all of a sudden out pops a raft of big diamond bracelets, and diamond rings, and diamond brooches, and diamond necklaces, and

I do not know what all else in the way of diamonds, and Dancing Dan and I begin stuffing these diamonds into the stocking and Good Time Charley pitches in and helps us.

There are enough diamonds to fill the stocking to the muzzle, and it is no small stocking, at that, and I judge that Gammer O'Neill has a pretty fair set of bunting sticks when she is young. In fact, there are so many diamonds that we have enough left over to make a nice little pile on the chair after we fill the stocking plumb up, leaving a nice diamond-studded vanity case sticking out the top where we figure it will hit Gammer O'Neill's eye when she wakes up.

And it is not until I get out in the fresh air again that all of a sudden I remember seeing large headlines in the afternoon papers about a five-hundred-G's stick-up in the afternoon of one of the biggest diamond merchants in Maiden Lane while he is sitting in his office, and I also recall once hearing rumors that Dancing Dan is one of the best lone-hand git-'em-up guys in the world.

Naturally, I commence to wonder if I am in the proper company when I am with Dancing Dan, even if he is Santa Claus. So I leave him on the next corner arguing with Good Time Charley about whether they ought to go and find some more presents somewhere, and look for other stockings to stuff, and I hasten on home, and go to bed.

The next day I find I have such a noggin that I do not care to stir around, and in fact I do not stir around much for a couple of weeks.

Then one night I drop around to Good Time Charley's little speakeasy, and ask Charley what is doing.

"Well," Charley says, "many things are doing, and personally," he says, "I am greatly surprised I do not see you at Gammer O'Neill's wake. You know Gammer O'Neill leaves this wicked old world a couple of days after Christmas," Good Time Charley says, "and," he says, "Miss Muriel O'Neill states that Doc Moggs claims it is at least a day after she is entitled to go, but she is sustained," Charley says, "by great happiness on finding her stocking filled with beautiful gifts on Christmas morning.

"According to Miss Muriel O'Neill," Charley says, "Gammer O'Neill dies practically convinced that there is a Santa Claus, although of course," he says, "Miss Muriel O'Neill does not tell her the real owner of the gifts, an all-right guy by the name of Shapiro leaves the gifts with her after Miss Muriel O'Neill notifies him of the finding of same.

"It seems," Charley says, "this Shapiro is a tenderhearted guy, who is willing to help keep Gammer O'Neill with us a little longer when Doc Moggs says leaving the gifts with her will do it.

"So," Charley says, "everything is quite all right, as the coppers cannot figure anything except that maybe the rascal who takes the gifts from Shapiro gets conscience stricken, and leaves them the first place he can, and Miss Muriel O'Neill receives a ten-G's reward for finding the gifts and returning them. And," Charley says, "I hear Dancing Dan is in San Francisco and is figuring on reforming and becoming a dancing teacher, so he can marry Miss Muriel O'Neill, and of course," he says, "we all hope and trust she never learns any details of Dancing Dan's career."

Well, it is Christmas Eve a year later that I run into a guy by the name of Shotgun Sam, who is mobbed up with Heine Schmitz in Harlem, and who is a very, very obnoxious character indeed.

"Well, well, well," Shotgun says, "the last time I see

you is another Christmas Eve like this, and you are coming out of Good Time Charley's joint, and," he says, "you certainly have your pots on."

"Well, Shotgun," I say, "I am sorry you get such a wrong impression of me, but the truth is," I say, "on the occasion you speak of, I am suffering from a dizzy feeling in my head."

"It is all right with me," Shotgun says. "I have a tip this guy Dancing Dan is in Good Time Charley's the night I see you, and Mockie Morgan, and Gunner Jack and me are casing the joint, because," he says, "Heine Schmitz is all sored up at Dan over some doll, although of course," Shotgun says, "it is all right now, as Heine has another doll.

"Anyway," he says, "we never get to see Dancing Dan. We watch the joint from six-thirty in the evening until daylight Christmas morning, and nobody goes in all night but old Ooky the Santa Claus guy in his Santa Claus make-up, and," Shotgun says, "nobody comes out except you and Good Time Charley and Ooky.

"Well," Shotgun says, "it is a great break for Dancing Dan he never goes in or comes out of Good Time Charley's, at that, because," he says, "we are waiting for him on the second-floor front of the building across the way with some nice little sawed-offs, and are under orders from Heine not to miss."

"Well, Shotgun," I say, "Merry Christmas."

"Well, all right," Shotgun says, "Merry Christmas."

🏵 🏵 🏵

It Comes Up Mud

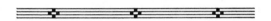

PERSONALLY, I never criticize Miss Beulah Beauregard for breaking her engagement to Little Alfie, because from what she tells me she becomes engaged to him under false pretenses, and I do not approve of guys using false pretenses on dolls, except, of course, when nothing else will do.

It seems that Little Alfie promises to show Miss Beulah Beauregard the life of Riley following the races with him when he gets her to give up a first-class job displaying her shape to the customers in the 900 Club, although Miss Beulah Beauregard frankly admits that Little Alfie does not say what Riley, and afterwards Little Alfie states that he must be thinking of Four-eyes Riley when he makes the promise, and everybody knows that Four-eyes Riley is nothing but a bum, in spades.

Anyway, the life Little Alfie shows Miss Beulah Beauregard after they become engaged is by no means exciting, according to what she tells me, as Little Alfie is always going

around the race tracks with one or two crocodiles that he
calls race horses, trying to win a few bobs for himself, and
generally Little Alfie is broke and struggling, and Miss
Beulah Beauregard says this is no existence for a member of
a proud old Southern family such as the Beauregards.

In fact, Miss Beulah Beauregard often tells me that she
has half a mind to leave Little Alfie and return to her
ancestral home in Georgia, only she can never think of any
way of getting there without walking, and Miss Beulah
Beauregard says it always makes her feet sore to walk very
far, although the only time anybody ever hears of Miss
Beulah Beauregard doing much walking is the time she is
shell-roaded on the Pelham Parkway by some Yale guys
when she gets cross with them.

It seems that when Little Alfie is first canvassing Miss
Beulah Beauregard to be his fiancée he builds her up to expect diamonds and furs and limousines and one thing and
another, but the only diamond she ever sees is in an engagement hoop that Little Alfie gives her as the old convincer
when he happens to be in the money for a moment, and
it is a very small diamond, at that, and needs a high north
light when you look at it.

But Miss Beulah Beauregard treasures this diamond very
highly just the same, and one reason she finally breaks off
her engagement to Little Alfie is because he borrows the
diamond one day during the Hialeah meeting at Miami without mentioning the matter to her, and hocks it for five bobs
which he bets on an old caterpillar of his by the name of
Governor Hicks to show.

Well, the chances are Miss Beulah Beauregard will not
mind Little Alfie's borrowing the diamond so much if he
does not take the twenty-five bobs he wins when Governor
Hicks drops in there in the third hole and sends it to Colonel Matt Winn in Louisville to enter a three-year-old of
his by the name of Last Hope in the Kentucky Derby, this

Last Hope being the only other horse Little Alfie owns at this time.

Such an action makes Miss Beulah Beauregard very indignant indeed, because she says a babe in arms will know Last Hope cannot walk a mile and a quarter, which is the Derby distance, let alone run so far, and that even if Last Hope can run a mile and a quarter, he cannot run it fast enough to get up a sweat.

In fact, Miss Beulah Beauregard and Little Alfie have words over this proposition, because Little Alfie is very high on Last Hope and will not stand for anybody insulting this particular horse, not even his fiancée, although he never seems to mind what anybody says about Governor Hicks, and, in fact, he often says it himself.

Personally, I do not understand what Little Alfie sees in Last Hope, because the horse never starts more than once or twice since it is born, and then has a tough time finishing last, but Little Alfie says the fifty G's that Colonel Winn gives to the winner of the Kentucky Derby is just the same as in the jug in his name, especially if it comes up mud on Derby Day, for Little Alfie claims that Last Hope is bred to just naturally eat mud.

Well, Miss Beulah Beauregard says there is no doubt Little Alfie blows his topper, and that there is no percentage in her remaining engaged to a crack-pot, and many citizens put in with her on her statement because they consider entering Last Hope in the Derby very great foolishness, no matter if it comes up mud or what, and right away Tom Shaw offers 1,000 to 1 against the horse in the future book, and everybody says Tom is underlaying the price at that.

Miss Beulah Beauregard states that she is very discouraged by the way things turn out, and that she scarcely knows what to do, because she fears her shape changes so much in the four or five years she is engaged to Little Alfie that the customers at the 900 Club may not care to look at it any more, especially if they have to pay for this privilege, although personally I will pay any reasonable cover charge to look at Miss Beulah Beauregard's shape any time, if it is all I suspect. As far as I can see it is still a very nice shape indeed, if you care for shapes.

Miss Beulah Beauregard is at this time maybe twenty-five or twenty-six, and is built like a first baseman, being tall and rangy. She has hay-colored hair, and blue eyes, and lots of health, and a very good appetite. In fact, I once see Miss Beulah Beauregard putting on the fried chicken in the Seven Seas restaurant in a way that greatly astonishes me, because I never know before that members of proud old Southern families are such hearty eaters. Furthermore, Miss Beulah Beauregard has a very Southern accent, which makes her sound quite cute, except maybe when she is a little excited and is putting the zing on somebody, such as Little Alfie.

Well, Little Alfie says he regrets exceedingly that Miss Beulah Beauregard sees fit to break their engagement, and will not be with him when he cuts up the Derby dough, as he is planning a swell wedding for her at French Lick after the race, and even has a list all made out of the presents he is going to buy her, including another diamond, and now he has all this bother of writing out the list for nothing.

Furthermore, Little Alfie says he is so accustomed to having Miss Beulah Beauregard as his fiancée that he scarcely knows what to do without her, and he goes around with a very sad puss, and is generally quite low in his mind, because there is no doubt that Little Alfie loves Miss Beulah Beauregard more than somewhat.

But other citizens are around stating that the real reason Miss Beulah Beauregard breaks her engagement to Little Alfie is because a guy by the name of Mr. Paul D. Veere

is making a powerful play for her, and she does not wish
him to know that she has any truck with a character such
as Little Alfie, for of course Little Alfie is by no means
anything much to look at, and, furthermore, what with
hanging out with his horses most of the time, he never
smells like any rose geranium.

It seems that this Mr. Paul D. Veere is a New York
banker, and he has a little mustache, and plenty of coconuts, and Miss Beulah Beauregard meets up with him one
morning when she is displaying her shape on the beach
at the Roney Plaza for nothing, and it also seems that there
is enough of her shape left to interest Mr. Paul D. Veere
no little.

In fact, the next thing anybody knows, Mr. Paul D.
Veere is taking Miss Beulah Beauregard here and there,
and around and about, although at this time Miss Beulah
Beauregard is still engaged to Little Alfie, and the only
reason Little Alfie does not notice Mr. Paul D. Veere at
first is because he is busy training Last Hope to win the
Kentucky Derby, and hustling around trying to get a few
bobs together every day to stand off the overhead, including Miss Beulah Beauregard, because naturally Miss Beulah
Beauregard cannot bear the idea of living in a fleabag, such
as the place where Little Alfie resides, but has to have a
nice room at the Roney Plaza.

Well, personally, I have nothing against bankers as a
class, and in fact I never meet up with many bankers in my
life, but somehow I do not care for Mr. Paul D. Veere's
looks. He looks to me like a stony-hearted guy, although
of course nobody ever sees any banker who does not look
stony-hearted, because it seems that being bankers just
naturally makes them look this way.

But Mr. Paul D. Veere is by no means an old guy, and
the chances are he speaks of something else besides horses
to Miss Beulah Beauregard, and furthermore he probably

does not smell like horses all the time, so nobody can blame Miss Beulah Beauregard for going around and about with him, although many citizens claim she is a little out of line in accepting Mr. Paul D. Veere's play while she is still engaged to Little Alfie. In fact, there is great indignation in some circles about this, as many citizens feel that Miss Beulah Beauregard is setting a bad example to other fiancées.

But after Miss Beulah Beauregard formally announces that their engagement is off, it is agreed by one and all that she has a right to do as she pleases, and that Little Alfie himself gets out of line in what happens at Hialeah a few days later when he finally notices that Miss Beulah Beauregard seems to be with Mr. Paul D. Veere, and on very friendly terms with him, at that. In fact, Little Alfie comes upon Mr. Paul D. Veere in the act of kissing Miss Beulah Beauregard behind a hibiscus bush out near the paddock, and this scene is most revolting to Little Alfie as he never cares for hibiscus, anyway.

He forgets that Miss Beulah Beauregard is no longer his fiancée, and tries to take a punch at Mr. Paul D. Veere, but he is stopped by a number of detectives, who are greatly horrified at the idea of anybody taking a punch at a guy who has as many coconuts as Mr. Paul D. Veere, and while they are expostulating with Little Alfie, Miss Beulah Beauregard disappears from the scene and is observed no more in Miami. Furthermore, Mr. Paul D. Veere also disappears, but of course nobody minds this very much, and, in fact, his disappearance is a great relief to all citizens who have fiancées in Miami at this time.

But it seems that before he disappears Mr. Paul D. Veere calls on certain officials of the Jockey Club and weighs in the sacks on Little Alfie, stating that he is a most dangerous character to have loose around a race track, and naturally the officials are bound to listen to a guy who has as many coconuts as Mr. Paul D. Veere.

So a day or two later old Cap Duhaine, the head detective around the race track, sends for Little Alfie and asks him what he thinks will become of all the prominent citizens such as bankers if guys go around taking punches at them and scaring them half to death, and Little Alfie cannot think of any answer to this conundrum offhand, especially as Cap Duhaine then asks Little Alfie if it will be convenient for him to take his two horses elsewhere.

Well, Little Alfie can see that Cap Duhaine is hinting in a polite way that he is not wanted around Hialeah any more, and Little Alfie is a guy who can take a hint as well as the next guy, especially when Cap Duhaine tells him in confidence that the racing stewards do not seem able to get over the idea that some scalawag slips a firecracker into Governor Hicks the day old Governor Hicks runs third, because it seems from what Cap Duhaine says that the stewards consider it practically supernatural for Governor Hicks to run third anywhere, any time.

So there Little Alfie is in Miami, as clean as a jaybird, with two horses on his hands, and no way to ship them to any place where horses are of any account, and it is quite a predicament indeed, and causes Little Alfie to ponder quite some. And the upshot of his pondering is that Little Alfie scrapes up a few bobs here and there, and a few oats, and climbs on Governor Hicks one day and boots him in the slats and tells him to giddyup, and away he goes out of Miami, headed north, riding Governor Hicks and leading Last Hope behind him on a rope.

Naturally, this is considered a most unusual spectacle by one and all who witness it and, in fact, it is the first time anybody can remember a horse owner such as Little Alfie riding one of his own horses off in this way, and Gloomy Gus is offering to lay plenty of 5 to 1 that Governor Hicks never makes Palm Beach with Little Alfie up, as it is well known that the old Governor has bum legs and is half out of wind and is apt to pig it any time.

But it seems that Governor Hicks makes Palm Beach all right with Little Alfie up and going so easy that many citizens are around asking Gloomy for a price against Jacksonville. Furthermore, many citizens are now saying that Little Alfie is a pretty smart guy at that, to think of such an economical idea, and numerous other horse owners are looking their stock over to see if they have anything to ride up north themselves.

Many citizens are also saying that Little Alfie gets a great break when Miss Beulah Beauregard runs out on him, because it takes plenty of weight off him in the way of railroad fare and one thing and another; but it seems Little Alfie does not feel this way about the matter at all.

It seems that Little Alfie often thinks about Miss Beulah Beauregard as he goes jogging along to the north, and sometimes he talks to Governor Hicks and Last Hope about her, and especially to Last Hope, as Little Alfie always considers Governor Hicks somewhat dumb. Also Little Alfie sometimes sings sad love songs right out loud as he is riding along, although the first time he starts to sing he frightens Last Hope and causes him to break loose from the lead rope and run away, and Little Alfie is an hour catching him. But after this Last Hope gets so he does not mind Little Alfie's voice so much, except when Little Alfie tries to hit high C.

Well, Little Alfie has a very nice ride, at that, because the weather is fine and the farmers along the road feed him and his horses, and he has nothing whatever to worry about except a few saddle galls, and about getting to Kentucky for the Derby in May, and here it is only late in February, and anyway Little Alfie does not figure to ride any farther than maybe Maryland where he is bound to make a scratch so he can ship from there.

Now, one day Little Alfie is riding along a road through a stretch of piney woods, a matter of maybe ninety-odd miles north of Jacksonville, which puts him in the State of Georgia, when he passes a half-plowed field on one side of the road near a ramshackly old house and beholds a most unusual scene:

A large white mule hitched to a plow is sitting down in the field and a tall doll in a sunbonnet and a gingham dress is standing beside the mule crying very heartily.

Naturally, the spectacle of a doll in distress, or even a doll who is not in distress, is bound to attract Little Alfie's attention, so he tells Governor Hicks and Last Hope to whoa, and then he asks the doll what is eating her, and the doll looks up at him out of her sunbonnet, and who is this doll but Miss Beulah Beauregard.

Of course Little Alfie is somewhat surprised to see Miss Beulah Beauregard crying over a mule, and especially in a sunbonnet, so he climbs down off of Governor Hicks to inquire into this situation, and right away Miss Beulah Beauregard rushes up to Little Alfie and chucks herself into his arms and speaks as follows:

"Oh, Alfie," Miss Beulah Beauregard says, "I am so glad you find me. I am thinking of you day and night, and wondering if you forgive me. Oh, Alfie, I love you," she says. "I am very sorry I go away with Mr. Paul D. Veere. He is nothing but a great rapscallion," she says. "He promises to make me his ever-loving wife when he gets me to accompany him from Miami to his shooting lodge on the Altamaha River, twenty-five miles from here, although," she says, "I never know before he has such a lodge in these parts.

"And," Miss Beulah Beauregard says, "the very first day I have to pop him with a pot of cold cream and render him half unconscious to escape his advances. Oh, Alfie," she says, "Mr. Paul D. Veere's intentions towards me are by no means honorable. Furthermore," she says, "I learn he already has an ever-loving wife and three children in New York."

Well, of course Little Alfie is slightly perplexed by this matter and can scarcely think of anything much to say, but finally he says to Miss Beulah Beauregard like this:

"Well," he says, "but what about the mule?"

"Oh," Miss Beulah Beauregard says, "his name is Abimelech, and I am plowing with him when he hauls off and sits down and refuses to budge. He is the only mule we own," she says, "and he is old and ornery, and nobody can do anything whatever with him when he wishes to sit down. But," she says, "my papa will be very angry because he expects me to get this field all plowed up by suppertime. In fact," Miss Beulah Beauregard says, "I am afraid my papa will be so angry he will give me a whopping, because he by no means forgives me as yet for coming home, and this is why I am shedding tears when you come along."

Then Miss Beulah Beauregard begins crying again as if her heart will break, and if there is one thing Little Alfie hates and despises it is to see a doll crying, and especially Miss Beulah Beauregard, for Miss Beulah Beauregard can cry in a way to wake the dead when she is going good, so Little Alfie holds her so close to his chest he ruins four cigars in his vest pocket, and speaks to her as follows:

"Tut, tut," Little Alfie says. "Tut, tut, tut, tut, tut," he says. "Dry your eyes and we will just hitch old Governor Hicks here to the plow and get this field plowed quicker than you can say scat, because," Little Alfie says, "when I am a young squirt, I am the best plower in Columbia County, New York."

Well, this idea cheers Miss Beulah Beauregard up no little, and so Little Alfie ties Last Hope to a tree and takes the harness off Abimelech, the mule, who keeps right on sitting down as if he does not care what happens, and puts the harness on Governor Hicks and hitches Governor Hicks to the plow, and the way the old Governor carries on when he finds out they wish him to pull a plow is really most surprising. In fact, Little Alfie has to get a club and reason with Governor Hicks before he will settle down and start pulling the plow.

It turns out that Little Alfie is a first-class plower, at that, and while he is plowing, Miss Beulah Beauregard walks along with him and talks a blue streak, and Little Alfie learns more things from her in half an hour than he ever before suspects in some years, and especially about Miss Beulah Beauregard herself.

It seems that the ramshackly old house is Miss Beulah Beauregard's ancestral home, and that her people are very poor, and live in these piney woods for generations, and that their name is Benson and not Beauregard at all, this being nothing but a name that Miss Beulah Beauregard herself thinks up out of her own head when she goes to New York to display her shape.

Furthermore, when they go to the house it comes out that Miss Beulah Beauregard's papa is a tall, skinny old guy with a goatee, who can lie faster than Little Alfie claims Last Hope can run. But it seems that the old skeezicks takes quite an interest in Last Hope when Little Alfie begins telling him what a great horse this horse is, especially in the mud, and how he is going to win the Kentucky Derby.

In fact, Miss Beulah Beauregard's papa seems to believe everything Little Alfie tells him, and as he is the first guy Little Alfie ever meets up with who believes anything he tells about anything whatever, it is a privilege and a pleasure for Little Alfie to talk to him. Miss Beulah Beauregard also has a mamma who turns out to be very fat, and full of Southern hospitality, and quite handy with a skillet.

Then there is a grown brother by the name of Jeff, who is practically a genius, as he knows how to disguise skimmin's so it makes a person only a little sick when they drink it, this skimmin's being a drink which is made from skimmings that come to the top on boiling sugar cane, and generally it tastes like gasoline, and is very fatal indeed.

Now, the consequences are Little Alfie finds this place very pleasant, and he decides to spend a few weeks there, paying for his keep with the services of Governor Hicks as a plow horse, especially as he is now practically engaged to Miss Beulah Beauregard all over again and she will not listen to him leaving without her. But they have no money for her railroad fare, and Little Alfie becomes very indignant when she suggests she can ride Last Hope on north while he is riding Governor Hicks, and wishes to know if she thinks a Derby candidate can be used for a truck horse.

Well, this almost causes Miss Beulah Beauregard to start breaking the engagement all over again, as she figures it is a dirty crack about her heft, but her papa steps in and says they must remain until Governor Hicks gets through with the plowing anyway, or he will know the reason why. So Little Alfie stays, and he puts in all his spare time training Last Hope and wondering who he can write to for enough dough to send Miss Beulah Beauregard north when the time comes.

He trains Last Hope by walking him and galloping him along the country roads in person, and taking care of him as if he is a baby, and what with this work, and the jog up from Miami, Last Hope fills out very strong and hearty, and anybody must admit that he is not a bad-looking beetle, though maybe a little more leggy than some like to see.

Now, it comes a Sunday, and all day long there is a very large storm with rain and wind that takes to knocking over big trees, and one thing and another, and no one is able to go outdoors much. So late in the evening Little Alfie and Miss Beulah Beauregard and all the Bensons are gathered about the stove in the kitchen drinking skimmin's, and Little Alfie is telling them all over again about how Last Hope will win the Kentucky Derby, especially if it comes up mud, when they hear a hammering at the door.

When the door is opened, who comes in but Mr. Paul D. Veere, sopping wet from head to foot, including his little mustache, and limping so he can scarcely walk, and naturally his appearance nonplusses Miss Beulah Beauregard and Little Alfie, who can never forget that Mr. Paul D. Veere is largely responsible for the saddle galls he gets riding up from Miami.

In fact, several times since he stops at Miss Beulah Beauregard's ancestral home, Little Alfie thinks of Mr. Paul D. Veere, and every time he thinks of him he is in favor of going over to Mr. Paul D. Veere's shooting lodge on the Altamaha and speaking to him severely.

But Miss Beulah Beauregard always stops him, stating that the proud old Southern families in this vicinity are somewhat partial to the bankers and other rich guys from the North who have shooting lodges around and about in the piney woods, and especially on the Altamaha, because these guys furnish a market to the local citizens for hunting guides, and corn liquor, and one thing and another.

Miss Beulah Beauregard says if a guest of the Bensons speaks to Mr. Paul D. Veere severely, it may be held against the family, and it seems that the Benson family cannot stand any more beefs against it just at this particular time. So Little Alfie never goes, and here all of a sudden is Mr. Paul D. Veere right in his lap.

Naturally, Little Alfie steps forward and starts winding up a large right hand with the idea of parking it on Mr.

Paul D. Veere's chin, but Mr. Paul D. Veere seems to see that there is hostility afoot, and he backs up against the wall, and raises his hand, and speaks as follows:

"Folks," Mr. Paul D. Veere says, "I just go into a ditch in my automobile half a mile up the road. My car is a wreck," he says, "and my right leg seems so badly hurt I am just barely able to drag myself here. Now, folks," he says, "it is almost a matter of life or death with me to get to the station at Tillinghast in time to flag the Orange Blossom Special. It is the last train tonight to Jacksonville, and I must be in Jacksonville before midnight so I can hire an airplane and get to New York by the time my bank opens at ten o'clock in the morning. It is about ten hours by plane from Jacksonville to New York," Mr. Paul D. Veere says, "so if I can catch the Orange Blossom, I will be able to just about make it!"

Then he goes on speaking in a low voice and states that he receives a telephone message from New York an hour or so before at his lodge telling him he must hurry home, and right away afterwards, while he is trying to telephone the station at Tillinghast to make sure they will hold the Orange Blossom until he gets there, no matter what, all the telephone and telegraph wires around and about go down in the storm.

So he starts for the station in his car, and just as it looks as if he may make it, his car runs smack-dab into a ditch and Mr. Paul D. Veere's leg is hurt so there is no chance he can walk the rest of the way to the station, and there Mr. Paul D. Veere is.

"It is a very desperate case, folks," Mr. Paul D. Veere says. "Let me take your automobile, and I will reward you liberally."

Well, at this Miss Beulah Beauregard's papa looks at a clock on the kitchen wall and states as follows:

"We do not keep an automobile, neighbor," he says,

"and anyway," he says, "it is quite a piece from here to Tillinghast and the Orange Blossom is due in ten minutes, so I do not see how you can possibly make it. Rest your hat, neighbor," Miss Beulah Beauregard's papa says, "and have some skimmin's, and take things easy, and I will look at your leg and see how bad you are bunged up."

Well, Mr. Paul D. Veere seems to turn as pale as a pillow as he hears this about the time, and then he says:

"Lend me a horse and buggy," he says. "I must be in New York in person in the morning. No one else will do but me," he says and as he speaks these words he looks at Miss Beulah Beauregard, and then at Little Alfie as if he is speaking to them personally, although up to this time he does not look at either of them after he comes into the kitchen.

"Why, neighbor," Miss Beulah Beauregard's papa says, "we do not keep a buggy, and even if we do keep a buggy we do not have time to hitch up anything to a buggy. Neighbor," he says, "you are certainly on a bust if you think you can catch the Orange Blossom now."

"Well, then," Mr. Paul D. Veere says, very sorrowful, "I will have to go to jail."

Then he flops himself down in a chair and covers his face with his hands, and he is a spectacle such as is bound to touch almost any heart, and when she sees him in this state, Miss Beulah Beauregard begins crying because she hates to see anybody as sorrowed up as Mr. Paul D. Veere, and between sobs she asks Little Alfie to think of something to do about the situation.

"Let Mr. Paul D. Veere ride Governor Hicks to the station," Miss Beulah Beauregard says. "After all," she says, "I cannot forget his courtesy in sending me halfway here in his car from his shooting lodge after I pop him with the pot of cold cream, instead of making me walk as those Yale guys do the time they redlight me."

"Why," Little Alfie says, "it is a mile and a quarter from the gate out here to the station. I know," he says, "because I get a guy in an automobile to clock it on his meter one day last week, figuring to give Last Hope a work-out over the full Derby route pretty soon. The road must be fetlock deep in mud at this time, and," Little Alfie says, "Governor Hicks cannot as much as stand up in the mud. The only horse in the world that can run fast enough through this mud to make the Orange Blossom is Last Hope, but," Little Alfie says, "of course I'm not letting anybody ride a horse as valuable as Last Hope to catch trains."

Well, at this Mr. Paul D. Veere lifts his head and looks at Little Alfie with great interest and speaks as follows:

"How much is this valuable horse worth?" Mr. Paul D. Veere says.

"Why," Little Alfie says, "he is worth anyway fifty G's to me, because," he says, "this is the sum Colonel Winn is giving to the winner of the Kentucky Derby, and there is no doubt whatever that Last Hope will be this winner, especially," Little Alfie says, "if it comes up mud."

"I do not carry any such large sum of money as you mention on my person," Mr. Paul D. Veere says, "but," he says, "if you are willing to trust me, I will give you my I O U for same, just to let me ride your horse to the station. I am once the best amateur steeplechase rider in the Hunts Club," Mr. Paul D. Veere says, "and if your horse can run at all there is still a chance for me to keep out of jail."

Well, the chances are Little Alfie will by no means consider extending a line of credit for fifty G's to Mr. Paul D. Veere or any other banker, and especially a banker who is once an amateur steeplechase jock, because if there is one thing Little Alfie does not trust it is an amateur steeplechase jock, and furthermore Little Alfie is somewhat offended because Mr. Paul D. Veere seems to think he is running a livery stable.

But Miss Beulah Beauregard is now crying so loud nobody can scarcely hear themselves think, and Little Alfie gets to figuring what she may say to him if he does not rent Last Hope to Mr. Paul D. Veere at this time and it comes out later that Last Hope does not happen to win the Kentucky Derby after all. So he finally says all right, and Mr. Paul D. Veere at once outs with a little gold pencil and a notebook, and scribbles off a marker for fifty G's to Little Alfie.

And the next thing anybody knows, Little Alfie is leading Last Hope out of the barn and up to the gate with nothing on him but a bridle as Little Alfie does not wish to waste time saddling, and as he is boosting Mr. Paul D. Veere onto Last Hope Little Alfie speaks as follows:

"You have three minutes left," Little Alfie says. "It is almost a straight course, except for a long turn going into the last quarter. Let this fellow run," he says. "You will find plenty of mud all the way, but," Little Alfie says, "this is a mud-running fool. In fact," Little Alfie says, "you are pretty lucky it comes up mud."

Then he gives Last Hope a smack on the hip and away goes Last Hope lickity-split through the mud and anybody can see from the way Mr. Paul D. Veere is sitting on him that Mr. Paul D. Veere knows what time it is when it comes to riding. In fact, Little Alfie himself says he never sees a better seat anywhere in his life, especially for a guy who is riding bareback.

Well, Little Alfie watches them go down the road in a gob of mud, and it will always be one of the large regrets of Little Alfie's life that he leaves his split-second super in hock in Miami, because he says he is sure Last Hope runs the first quarter through the mud faster than any quarter is ever run before in this world. But of course Little Alfie is more excited than somewhat at this moment, and the chances are he exaggerates Last Hope's speed.

However, there is no doubt that Last Hope goes over the road very rapidly, indeed, as a colored party who is out squirrel hunting comes along a few minutes afterwards and tells Little Alfie that something goes past him on the road so fast he cannot tell exactly what it is, but he states that he is pretty sure it is old Henry Devil himself, because he smells smoke as it passes him, and hears a voice yelling hi-yah. But of course the chances are this voice is nothing but the voice of Mr. Paul D. Veere yelling words of encouragement to Last Hope.

It is not until the station master at Tillinghast, a guy by the name of Asbury Potts, drives over to Miss Beulah Beauregard's ancestral home an hour later that Little Alfie hears that as Last Hope pulls up at the station and Mr. Paul D. Veere dismounts with so much mud on him that nobody can tell if he is a plaster cast or what, the horse is gimping as bad as Mr. Paul D. Veere himself, and Asbury Potts says there is no doubt Last Hope bows a tendon, or some such, and that if they are able to get him to the races again he will eat his old wool hat.

"But, personally," Asbury Potts says as he mentions this sad news, "I do not see what Mr. Paul D. Veere's hurry is, at that, to be pushing a horse so hard. He has fifty-seven seconds left by my watch when the Orange Blossom pulls in right on time to the dot," Asbury Potts says.

Well, at this Little Alfie sits down and starts figuring, and finally he figures that Last Hope runs the mile and a quarter in around 2.03 in the mud, with maybe 160 pounds up, for Mr. Paul D. Veere is no feather duster, and no horse ever runs a mile and a quarter in the mud in the Kentucky Derby as fast as this, or anywhere else as far as anybody knows, so Little Alfie claims that this is practically flying.

But of course few citizens ever accept Little Alfie's figures as strictly official, because they do not know if Asbury
Potts' watch is properly regulated for timing race horses,
even though Asbury Potts is one hundred per cent right
when he says they will never be able to get Last Hope to
the races again.

Well, I meet up with Little Alfie one night this summer
in Mindy's restaurant on Broadway, and it is the first time
he is observed in these parts in some time, and he seems
to be looking very prosperous, indeed, and after we get
to cutting up old touches, he tells me the reason for this
prosperity.

It seems that after Mr. Paul D. Veere returns to New
York and puts back in his bank whatever it is that it is
advisable for him to put back, or takes out whatever it
is that seems best to take out, and gets himself all rounded
up so there is no chance of his going to jail, he remembers
that there is a slight difference between him and Little
Alfie, so what does Mr. Paul D. Veere do but sit down
and write out a check for fifty G's to Little Alfie to take
up his I O U, so Little Alfie is nothing out on account
of losing the Kentucky Derby, and, in fact, he is stone
rich, and I am glad to hear of it, because I always sym-
pathize deeply with him in his bereavement over the loss
of Last Hope. Then I ask Little Alfie what he is doing
in New York at this time, and he states to me as follows:

"Well," Little Alfie says, "I will tell you. The other
day," he says, "I get to thinking things over, and among
other things I get to thinking that after Last Hope wins the
Kentucky Derby, he is a sure thing to go on and also
win the Maryland Preakness, because," Little Alfie says,
"the Preakness is a sixteenth of a mile shorter than the
Derby, and a horse that can run a mile and a quarter in the
mud in around 2.03 with a brick house on his back is
bound to make anything that wears hair look silly at a

mile and three-sixteenths, especially," Little Alfie says, "if it comes up mud.

"So," Little Alfie says, "I am going to call on Mr. Paul D. Veere and see if he does not wish to pay me the Preakness stake, too, because," he says, "I am building the finest house in South Georgia at Last Hope, which is my stock farm where Last Hope himself is on public exhibition, and I can always use a few bobs here and there."

"Well, Alfie," I says, "this seems to me to be a very fair proposition, indeed, and," I says, "I am sure Mr. Paul D. Veere will take care of it as soon as it is called to his attention, as there is no doubt you and Last Hope are of great service to Mr. Paul D. Veere. By the way, Alfie," I say, "what ever becomes of Governor Hicks?"

"Why," Little Alfie says, "do you know Governor Hicks turns out to be a terrible disappointment to me as a plow horse? He learns how to sit down from Abimelech, the mule, and nothing will make him stir, not even the same encouragement I give him the day he drops down there third at Hialeah.

"But," Little Alfie says, "my ever-loving wife is figuring on using the old Governor as a saddle horse for our twins, Beulah and Little Alfie, Junior, when they get old enough, although," he says, "I tell her the Governor will never be worth a dime in such a way, especially," Little Alfie says, "if it comes up mud."

Broadway Complex

It is along toward four o'clock one morning, and I am sitting in Mindy's restaurant on Broadway with Ambrose Hammer, the newspaper scribe, enjoying a sturgeon sandwich, which is wonderful brain food, and listening to Ambrose tell me what is wrong with the world, and I am somewhat discouraged by what he tells me, for Ambrose is such a guy as is always very pessimistic about everything.

He is especially very pessimistic about the show business, as Ambrose is what is called a dramatic critic, and he has to go around nearly every night and look at the new plays that people are always putting in the theaters, and I judge from what Ambrose says that this is a very great hardship, and that he seldom gets much pleasure out of life.

Furthermore, I judge from what Ambrose tells me that there is no little danger in being a dramatic critic, because it seems that only a short time before this he goes to a play that is called Never-Never, and Ambrose says it is a very bad play, indeed, and he so states in his newspaper, and in fact Ambrose states in his newspaper that the play smells in nine different keys, and that so does the acting of the leading man, a guy by the name of Fergus Appleton.

Well, the next day Ambrose runs into this Fergus Appleton in front of the Hotel Astor, and what does Fergus Appleton do but haul off and belt Ambrose over the noggin with a cane, and ruin a nice new fall derby for Ambrose, and when Ambrose puts in an expense account to his newspaper for this kady they refuse to pay it, so Ambrose is out four bobs.

And anyway, Ambrose says, the theatergoing public never appreciates what a dramatic critic does for it, because it seems that even though he tips the public off that Never-Never is strictly a turkey, it is a great succes, and, moreover, Fergus Appleton is now going around with a doll who is nobody but Miss Florentine Fayette, the daughter of old Hannibal Fayette.

And anybody will tell you that old Hannibal Fayette is very, very, very rich, and has a piece of many different propositions, including the newspaper that Ambrose Hammer works for, although of course at the time Ambrose speaks of Fergus Appleton's acting, he has no idea Fergus is going to wind up going around with Miss Florentine Fayette.

So Ambrose says the chances are his newspaper will give him the heave-o as soon as Fergus Appleton gets the opportunity to drop the zing in on him, but Ambrose says he does not care a cuss as he is writing a play himself that will show the theatergoing public what a real play is.

Well, Ambrose is writing this play ever since I know him, which is a matter of several years, and he tells me about it so often that I can play any part in it myself with a little practice, and he is just getting around to going over his first act with me again when in comes a guy by the name of Cecil Earl, who is what is called a master of ceremonies at the Golden Slipper night club.

Personally, I never see Cecil Earl but once or twice before in my life, and he always strikes me as a very quiet and modest young guy, for a master of ceremonies, and I am greatly surprised at the way he comes in, as he is acting very bold and aggressive toward one and all, and is speaking out loud in a harsh, disagreeable tone of voice, and in general is acting like a guy who is looking for trouble, which is certainly no way for a master of ceremonies to act.

But of course if a guy is looking for trouble on Broadway along toward four o'clock in the morning, anybody will tell you that the right address is nowhere else but Mindy's, because at such an hour many citizens are gathered there, and are commencing to get a little cross wondering where they are going to make a scratch for the morrow's operations, such as playing the horses.

It is a sure thing that any citizen who makes his scratch before four o'clock in the morning is at home getting his rest, so he will arise fully refreshed for whatever the day may bring forth, and also to avoid the bite he is apt to encounter in Mindy's from citizens who do not make a scratch.

However, the citizens who are present the morning I am speaking of do not pay much attention to Cecil Earl when he comes in, as he is nothing but a tall, skinny young guy, with slick black hair, such as you are apt to see anywhere along Broadway at any time, especially standing in front of theatrical booking offices. In fact, to look at Cecil you will bet he is maybe a saxophone player, as there is something about him that makes you think of a saxophone player right away and, to tell the truth, Cecil can tootle a pretty fair sax, at that, if the play happens to come up.

Well, Cecil sits down at a table where several influential citizens are sitting, including Nathan Detroit, who runs the crap game, and Big Nig, the crap shooter, and Regret, the horse player, and Upstate Red, who is one of the best faro bank players in the world whenever he can find a faro bank and something to play it with, and these citizens are discussing some very serious matters, when out of a clear sky Cecil ups and speaks to them as follows:

"Listen," Cecil says, "if youse guys do not stop making so much noise, I may cool you all off."

Well, naturally, this is most repulsive language to use to such influential citizens, and furthermore it is very illiterate to say youse, so without changing the subject Nathan Detroit reaches out and picks up an order of ham and eggs, Southern style, that Charley, the waiter, just puts in front of Upstate Red, and taps Cecil on the onion with same.

It is unfortunate for Cecil that Nathan Detroit does not remove the ham and eggs, Southern style, from the platter before tapping Cecil with the order, because it is a very hard platter, and Cecil is knocked as stiff as a plank, and maybe stiffer, and it becomes necessary to summon old Doctor Moggs to bring him back to life.

Well, of course none of us know that Cecil is at the moment Jack Legs Diamond, or Mad Dog Coll, or some other very tough gorill, and in fact this does not come out until Ambrose Hammer later starts in investigating the strange actions of Cecil Earl, and then Nathan Detroit apologizes to Cecil, and also to the chef in Mindy's for treating an order of ham and eggs, Southern style, so disrespectfully.

It comes out that Cecil is subject to spells of being somebody else besides Cecil Earl, and Ambrose Hammer gives us a very long explanation of this situation, only Ambrose finally becomes so scientific that nobody can keep cases on him. But we gather in a general way from what Ambrose says that Cecil Earl is very susceptible to suggestion from anything he reads, or is told.

In fact, Ambrose says he is the most susceptible guy of this kind he ever meets up with in his life, and it seems that when he is going to Harvard College, which is before he starts in being a dramatic critic, Ambrose makes quite a study of these matters.

Personally, I always claim that Cecil Earl is a little screwy, or if he is not screwy that he will do very well as a pinch-hitter until a screwy guy comes to bat, but Ambrose Hammer says no. Ambrose says it is true that Cecil may be bobbing a trifle, but that he is by no means entirely off his nut. Ambrose says that Cecil only has delusions of grandeur, and complexes, and I do not know what all else, but Ambrose says it is 9 to 10 and take your pick whether Cecil is a genius or a daffydill.

Ambrose says that Cecil is like an actor playing a different part every now and then, only Cecil tries to live every part he plays, and Ambrose claims that if we have actors with as much sense as Cecil in playing parts, the show business will be a lot better off. But of course Ambrose cares very little for actors since Fergus Appleton ruins his kady.

Well, the next time I see Cecil he comes in Mindy's again, and this time it seems he is Jack Dempsey, and while ordinarily nobody will mind him being Jack Dempsey, or even Gene Tunney, although he is not the type for Gene Tunney, Cecil takes to throwing left hooks at citizens' chins, so finally Sam the Singer gets up and lets a right hand go inside a left hook, and once more Cecil folds up like an old accordion.

When I speak of this to Ambrose Hammer, he says that being Jack Dempsey is entirely a false complex for Cecil, brought on mainly by Cecil taking a few belts at the Golden Slipper liquor during the evening. In fact, Ambrose says this particular complex does not count. But I notice that after this Cecil is never anybody very brash when he is around Mindy's.

Sometimes he is somebody else besides Cecil Earl for as long as a week at a stretch, and in fact once he is Napoleon for two whole weeks, but Ambrose Hammer says this is nothing. Ambrose says he personally knows guys who are Napoleon all their lives. But of course Ambrose means that these guys are only Napoleon in their own minds. He says that the only difference between Cecil and them is that Cecil's complex breaks out on him in public, while the other guys are Napoleons only in their own bedrooms.

Personally, I think such guys are entitled to be locked up in spots with high walls around and about, but Ambrose seems to make nothing much of it, and anyway this Cecil Earl is as harmless as a bag of marshmallows, no matter who he is being.

One thing I must say for Cecil Earl, he is nearly always an interesting guy to talk to, because he nearly always has a different personality, and in fact the only time he is uninteresting is when he is being nobody but Cecil Earl. Then he is a very quiet guy with a sad face and he is so bashful and retiring that you will scarcely believe he is the same guy who goes around all one week being Mussolini in his own mind.

Now I wish to say that Cecil Earl does not often go around making any public display of these spells of his, except when the character calls for a display, such as the time he is George Bernard Shaw, and in fact unless you know him personally you may sometimes figure him just a guy sitting back in a corner somewhere with nothing whatever on his mind, and you will never even suspect that you are in the presence of J. Pierpont Morgan studying out a way to make us all rich.

It gets so that nobody resents Cecil being anything he pleases, except once when he is Senator Huey Long, and once when he is Hitler, and makes the mistake of wandering down on the lower East Side and saying so. In fact, it gets so everybody along Broadway puts in with him and helps him be whoever he is, as much as possible, although I always claim he has a bad influence on some citizens, for instance Regret, the horse player.

It seems that Regret catches a complex off of Cecil Earl one day, and for twenty-four hours he is Pittsburgh Phil, the race track plunger, and goes overboard with every bookie down at Belmont Park and has to hide out for some time before he can get himself straightened out.

Now Cecil Earl is a good master of ceremonies in a night club, if you care for masters of ceremonies, a master of ceremonies in a night club being a guy who is supposed to make cute cracks, and to introduce any celebrities who happen to be sitting around the joint, such as actors and prominent merchants, so the other customers can give them a big hand, and this is by no means an easy job, as sometimes a master of ceremonies may overlook a celebrity, and the celebrity becomes terribly insulted.

But it seems that Cecil Earl is smart enough to introduce all the people in the Golden Slipper every night and call for a big hand for them, no matter who they are, so nobody can get insulted, although one night he introduces a new head waiter, thinking he is nothing but a customer, and the head waiter is somewhat insulted, at that, and threatens to quit, because he claims being introduced in a night club is no boost for him.

Anyway, Cecil gets a nice piece of money for being master of ceremonies at the Golden Slipper, and when he is working there his complexes do not seem to bother him very much, and he is never anybody more serious than Harry Richman or Mort Downey. And it is at the Golden

Slipper that he meets this guy, Fergus Appleton, and Miss Florentine Fayette.

Now Miss Florentine Fayette is a tall, slim, black-haired doll, and so beautiful she is practically untrue, but she has a kisser that never seems to relax, and furthermore she never seems much interested in anything whatever. In fact, if Miss Florentine Fayette's papa does not have so many cucumbers, I will say she is slightly dumb, but for all I know it may be against the law to say a doll whose papa has all these cucumbers is dumb. So I will only say that she does not strike me as right bright.

She is a great hand for going around night clubs and sitting there practically unconscious for hours at a time, and always this Fergus Appleton is with her, and before long it gets around that Fergus Appleton wishes to make Miss Florentine Fayette his ever-loving wife, and everybody admits that it will be a very nice score, indeed, for an actor.

Personally, I see nothing wrong with this situation because, to tell you the truth, I will just naturally love to make Miss Florentine Fayette my own ever-loving wife if her papa's cucumbers go with it, but of course Ambrose Hammer does not approve of the idea of her becoming Fergus Appleton's wife, because Ambrose can see how it may work out to his disadvantage.

This Fergus Appleton is a fine-looking guy of maybe forty, with iron-gray hair that makes him appear very romantic, and he is always well dressed in spats and one thing and another, and he smokes cigarettes in a holder nearly a foot long, and wears a watch on one wrist and a slave bracelet on the other, and a big ring on each hand, and sometimes a monocle in one eye, although Ambrose Hammer claims that this is strictly the old ackamarackuss.

There is no doubt that Fergus Appleton is a very chesty guy, and likes to pose around in public places, but I see maybe a million guys like him in my time on Broadway, and not all of them are actors, so I do not hate him for his posing, or for his slave bracelet, or the monocle either, although naturally I consider him out of line in busting my friend Ambrose Hammer's new derby, and I promise Ambrose that the first time Fergus Appleton shows up in a new derby, or even an old one, I will see that somebody busts it, if I have to do it myself.

The only thing wrong I see about Fergus Appleton is that he is a smart-Alecky guy, and when he first finds out about Cecil Earl's complexes he starts working on them to amuse the guys and dolls who hang out around the Golden Slipper with him and Miss Florentine Fayette.

Moreover, it seems that somehow Cecil Earl is very susceptible, indeed, to Fergus Appleton's suggestions, and for a while Fergus Appleton makes quite a sucker of Cecil Earl.

Then all of a sudden Fergus Appleton stops making a sucker of Cecil, and the next thing anybody knows Fergus Appleton is becoming quite pally with Cecil, and I see them around Mindy's, and other late spots after the Golden Slipper closes, and sometimes Miss Florentine Fayette is with them, although Cecil Earl is such a guy as does not care much for the society of dolls, and in fact is very much embarrassed when they are around, which is most surprising conduct for a master of ceremonies in a night club, as such characters are usually pretty fresh with dolls.

But of course even the freshest master of ceremonies is apt to be a little bashful when such a doll as Miss Florentine Fayette is around, on account of her papa having so many cucumbers, and when she is present Cecil Earl seldom opens his trap, but just sits looking at her and letting Fergus Appleton do all the gabbing, which suits Fergus Appleton fine, as he does not mind hearing himself gab, and in fact loves it.

Sometimes I run into just Cecil Earl and Fergus Appleton, and generally they have their heads close together, and are talking low and serious, like two business guys with a large deal coming up between them.

Furthermore, I can see that Cecil Earl is looking very mysterious and solemn himself, so I figure that maybe they are doping out a new play together and that Cecil is acting one of the parts, and whatever it is they are doing I consider it quite big-hearted of Fergus Appleton to take such a friendly interest in Cecil.

But somehow Ambrose Hammer does not like it. In fact, Ambrose Hammer speaks of the matter at some length to me, and says to me like this:

"It is unnatural," he says. "It is unnatural for a guy like Fergus Appleton, who is such a guy as never has a thought in the world for anybody but himself, to be playing the warm for a guy like Cecil Earl. There is something wrong in this business, and," Ambrose says, "I am going to find out what it is."

Well, personally I do not see where it is any of Ambrose Hammer's put-in even if there is something wrong, but Ambrose is always poking his beezer into other people's business, and he starts watching Cecil and Fergus Appleton with great interest whenever he happens to run into them.

Finally it comes an early Sunday morning, and Ambrose Hammer and I are in Mindy's as usual, when in comes Cecil Earl all alone, with a book under one arm. He sits down at a table in a corner booth all by himself and orders a western sandwich and starts in to read his book, and nothing will do Ambrose Hammer but for us to go over and talk to Cecil.

When he sees us coming, he closes his book and drops it in his lap and gives us a very weak hello. It is the first time we see him alone in quite a spell, and finally Ambrose

Hammer asks where is Fergus Appleton, although Ambrose really does not care where he is, unless it happens to turn out that he is in a pesthouse suffering from small-pox.

Cecil says Fergus Appleton has to go over to Philadelphia on business over the week-end, and then Ambrose asks Cecil where Miss Florentine Fayette is, and Cecil says he does not know but supposes she is home.

"Well," Ambrose Hammer says, "Miss Florentine Fayette is certainly a beautiful doll, even if she does look a little bit colder than I like them, but," he says, "what she sees in such a pish-tush as Fergus Appleton I do not know."

Now at this Cecil Earl busts right out crying, and naturally Ambrose Hammer and I are greatly astonished at such an exhibition, because we do not see any occasion for tears, and personally I am figuring on taking it on the Dan O'Leary away from there before somebody gets to thinking we do Cecil some great wrong, when Cecil speaks as follows:

"I love her," Cecil says. "I love her with all my heart and soul. But she belongs to my best friend. For two cents I will take this dagger that Fergus gives me and end it all, because life is not worth living without Miss Florentine Fayette."

And with this Cecil Earl outs with a big long stabber, which is a spectacle that is most disquieting to me as I know such articles are against the law in this man's town. So I make Cecil put it right back in his pocket and while I am doing this Ambrose Hammer reaches down beside Cecil and grabs the book Cecil is reading, and while Cecil is still sobbing Ambrose looks this volume over.

It turns out to be a book called The Hundred-Per-Cent-Perfect Crime, but what interests Ambrose Hammer more than anything else is a lead-pencil drawing on one of the blank pages in the front part of the book. Afterwards

Ambrose sketches this drawing out for me as near as he can remember it on the back of one of Mindy's menu cards, and it looks to me like the drawing of the ground floor of a small house, with a line on one side on which is written the word Menahan, and Ambrose says he figures this means a street.

But in the meantime Ambrose tries to soothe Cecil Earl and to get him to stop crying, and when Cecil finally does dry up he sees Ambrose has his book, and he makes a grab for it and creates quite a scene until he gets it back.

Personally, I cannot make head or tail of the sketch that Ambrose draws for me, and I cannot see that there is anything to it anyway, but Ambrose seems to regard it as of some importance.

Well, I do not see Ambrose Hammer for several days, but I am hearing strange stories of him being seen with Cecil Earl in the afternoons when Fergus Appleton is playing matinees in Never-Never, and early in the evenings when Fergus Appleton is doing his night performances, and I also hear that Ambrose always seems to be talking very earnestly to Cecil Earl, and sometimes throwing his arms about in a most excited manner.

Then one morning Ambrose Hammer looks me up again in Mindy's, and he is smiling a very large smile, as if he is greatly pleased with something, which is quite surprising as Ambrose Hammer is seldom pleased with anything. Finally he says to me like this:

"Well," Ambrose says, "I learn the meaning of the drawing in Cecil Earl's book. It is the plan of a house on Menahan Street, away over in Brooklyn. And the way I learn this is very, very clever, indeed," Ambrose says. "I stake a chambermaid to let me into Fergus Appleton's joint in the Dazzy apartments, and what do I find there just as I expect but a letter from a certain number on this street?"

"Why," I say to Ambrose Hammer, "I am greatly horrified by your statement. You are nothing but a burglar, and if Fergus Appleton finds this out he will turn you over to the officers of the law, and you will lose your job and everything else."

"No," Ambrose says, "I will not lose my job, because old Hannibal Fayette is around the office yesterday raising an awful row about his daughter wishing to marry an actor, and saying he will give he does not know what if anybody can bust this romance up. The chances are," Ambrose says, "he will make me editor in chief of the paper, and then I will can a lot of guys I do not like. Fergus Appleton is to meet Cecil Earl here this morning, and in the meantime I will relate the story to you."

But before Ambrose can tell me the story, in comes Fergus Appleton, and Miss Florentine Fayette is with him, and they sit down at a table not far from us, and Fergus Appleton looks around and sees Ambrose and gives him a terrible scowl. Furthermore, he says something to Miss Florentine Fayette, and she looks at Ambrose, too, but she does not scowl or anything else, but only looks very dead-pan.

Fergus Appleton is in evening clothes and has on his monocle, and Miss Florentine Fayette is wearing such a gown that anybody can see how beautiful she is, no matter if her face does not have much expression. They are sitting there without much conversation passing between them, when all of a sudden in walks Cecil Earl, full of speed and much excited.

He comes in with such a rush that he almost flattens Regret, the horse player, who is on his way out, and Regret is about to call him a dirty name when he sees a spectacle that will always be remembered in Mindy's, for Cecil Earl walks right over to Miss Florentine Fayette as she is sitting there beside Fergus Appleton, and without saying as much as boo to Fergus Appleton, Cecil grabs Miss Florentine Fayette up in his arms with surprising strength and gives her a big sizzling kiss, and says to her like this:

"Florentine," he says, "I love you."

Then he squeezes her to his bosom so tight that it looks as if he is about to squeeze her right out through the top of her gown like squeezing toothpaste out of a tube, and says to her again, as follows:

"I love you. Oh, how I love you."

Well, at first Fergus Appleton is so astonished at this proposition that he can scarcely stir, and the chances are he cannot believe his eyes. Furthermore, many other citizens who are present partaking of their Bismarck herring, and one thing and another, are also astonished, and they are commencing to think that maybe Cecil Earl is having a complex about being King Kong, when Fergus Appleton finally gets to his feet and speaks in a loud tone of voice as follows:

"Why," Fergus Appleton says, "you are nothing but a scurvy fellow, and unless you unhand my fiancée, the chances are I will annihilate you."

Naturally, Fergus Appleton is somewhat excited, and in fact he is so excited that he drops his monocle to the floor, and it breaks into several pieces. At first he seems to have some idea of dropping a big right hand on Cecil Earl somewhere, but Cecil is pretty well covered by Miss Florentine Fayette, so Fergus Appleton can see that if he lets a right hand go he is bound to strike Miss Florentine Fayette right where she lives.

So he only grabs hold of Miss Florentine Fayette, and tries to pull her loose from Cecil Earl, and Cecil Earl not only holds her tighter, but Miss Florentine Fayette seems to be doing some holding to Cecil herself, so Fergus Appleton cannot peel her off, although he gets one stocking and a piece of elastic strap from somewhere. Then one and all are greatly surprised to hear Miss Florentine Fayette speak to Fergus Appleton like this:

"Go away, you old porous plaster," Miss Florentine Fayette says. "I love only my Cecil. Hold me tighter, Cecil, you great big bear," Miss Florentine Fayette says, although of course Cecil looks about as much like a bear as Ambrose Hammer looks like a porcupine.

Well, of course, there is great commotion in Mindy's, because Cecil Earl is putting on a love scene such as makes many citizens very homesick, and Fergus Appleton does not seem to know what to do, when Ambrose Hammer gets to him and whispers a few words in his ear, and all of a sudden Fergus Appleton turns and walks out of Mindy's and disappears, and furthermore nobody ever sees him in these parts again.

By and by Mindy himself comes up and tells Cecil Earl and Miss Florentine Fayette that the chef is complaining because he cannot seem to make ice in his refrigerator while they are in the joint, and will they please go away. So Cecil Earl and Miss Florentine Fayette go, and then Ambrose Hammer comes back to me and finishes his story.

"Well," Ambrose says, "I go over to the certain number on Menahan Street, and what do I find there but a crippled-up middle-aged doll who is nobody but Fergus Appleton's ever-loving wife, and furthermore she is such for over twenty years. She tells me that Fergus is the meanest guy that ever breathes the breath of life, and that he is persecuting her for a long time in every way he can think of because she will not give him a divorce.

"And," Ambrose says, "the reason she will not give him a divorce is because he knocks her downstairs a long time ago, and makes her a cripple for life, and leaves her to the care of her own people. But of course I do not tell her," Ambrose says, "that she narrowly escapes being murdered through him, for the meaning of the floor plan of the house in Cecil's book, and the meaning of the book itself, and of the dagger, is that Fergus Appleton is working on Cecil Earl until he has him believing that he can be the super-murderer of the age."

"Why," I say to Ambrose Hammer, "I am greatly shocked by these revelations. Why, Fergus Appleton is nothing but a fellow."

"Well," Ambrose says, "he is pretty cute, at that. He has Cecil thinking that it will be a wonderful thing to be the guy who commits the hundred-per-cent-perfect crime, and furthermore Fergus promises to make Cecil rich after he marries Miss Florentine Fayette."

"But," I say, "what I do not understand is what makes Cecil become such a violent lover all of a sudden."

"Why," Ambrose Hammer says, "when Cecil lets it out that he loves Miss Florentine Fayette, it gives me a nice clue to the whole situation. I take Cecil in hand and give him a little coaching and, furthermore, I make him a present of a book myself. He finds it more interesting than anything Fergus Appleton gives him. In fact," Ambrose says, "I recommend it to you. When Cecil comes in here this morning, he is not Cecil Earl, the potential Perfect Murderer. He is nobody but the world's champion heavy lover, old Don Juan."

Well, Ambrose does not get to be editor in chief of his newspaper. In fact, he just misses getting the outdoors, because Cecil Earl and Miss Florentine Fayette elope, and get married, and go out to Hollywood on a honeymoon, and never return, and old Hannibal Fayette claims it is just as bad for his daughter to marry a movie actor as a guy on the stage, even though Cecil turns out to be the greatest drawing card on the screen because he can heat up love scenes so good.

But I always say that Cecil Earl is quite an ingrate, because he refuses a part in Ambrose Hammer's play when Ambrose finally gets it written, and makes his biggest hit in a screen version of Never-Never.

The Three Wise Guys

One cold winter afternoon I am standing at the bar in Good Time Charley's little drum in West 49th Street, partaking of a mixture of rock candy and rye whisky, and this is a most surprising thing for me to be doing, as I am by no means a rumpot, and very seldom indulge in alcoholic beverages in any way, shape, manner, or form.

But when I step into Good Time Charley's on the afternoon in question, I am feeling as if maybe I have a touch of grippe coming on, and Good Time Charley tells me that there is nothing in this world as good for a touch of grippe as rock candy and rye whisky, as it assassinates the germs at once.

It seems that Good Time Charley always keeps a stock of rock candy and rye whisky on hand for touches of the grippe, and he gives me a few doses immediately, and in fact Charley takes a few doses with me, as he says there is no telling but what I am scattering germs of my touch of the grippe all around the joint, and he must safeguard his health. We are both commencing to feel much better when the door opens, and who comes in but a guy by the name of Blondy Swanson.

This Blondy Swanson is a big, six-foot-two guy, with straw-colored hair, and pink cheeks, and he is originally out of Harlem, and it is well known to one and all that in his day he is the largest puller on the Atlantic seaboard. In fact, for upwards of ten years, Blondy is bringing wet goods into New York from Canada, and one place and another, and in all this time he never gets a fall, which is considered a phenomenal record for an operator as extensive as Blondy.

Well, Blondy steps up alongside me at the bar, and I ask him if he cares to have a few doses of rock candy and rye whisky with me and Good Time Charley, and Blondy says he will consider it a privilege and a pleasure, because, he says, he always has something of a sweet tooth. So we have these few doses, and I say to Blondy Swanson that I hope and trust that business is thriving with him.

"I have no business," Blondy Swanson says, "I retire from business."

Well, if J. Pierpont Morgan, or John D. Rockefeller, or Henry Ford step up and tell me they retire from business, I will not be more astonished than I am by this statement from Blondy Swanson, and in fact not as much. I consider Blondy's statement the most important commercial announcement I hear in many years, and naturally I ask him why he makes such a decision, and what is to become of thousands of citizens who are dependent on him for merchandise.

"Well," Blondy says, "I retire from business because I am one hundred per cent American citizen. In fact," he says, "I am a patriot. I serve my country in the late war. I am cited at Château-Thierry. I always vote the straight Democratic ticket, except," he says, "when we figure it better to elect some Republican. I always stand up when the band plays the Star Spangled Banner. One year I even pay an income tax," Blondy says.

And of course I know that many of these things are true, although I remember hearing rumors that if the draft officer is along half an hour later than he is, he will not see Blondy for heel dust, and that what Blondy is cited for at Château-Thierry is for not robbing the dead.

But of course I do not speak of these matters to Blondy Swanson, because Blondy is not such a guy as will care to listen to rumors, and may become indignant, and when Blondy is indignant he is very difficult to get along with.

"Now," Blondy says, "I am a bootie for a long time, and supply very fine merchandise to my trade, as everybody knows, and it is a respectable business, because one and all in this country are in favor of it, except the prohibitionists. But," he says, "I can see into the future, and I can see that one of these days they are going to repeal the prohibition law, and then it will be most unpatriotic to be bringing in wet goods from foreign parts in competition with home industry. So I retire," Blondy says.

"Well, Blondy," I say, "your sentiments certainly do you credit, and if we have more citizens as high minded as you are, this will be a better country."

"Furthermore," Blondy says, "there is no money in booting any more. All the booties in this country are broke. I am broke myself," he says. "I just lose the last piece of property I own in the world, which is the twenty-five-G home I build in Atlantic City, figuring to spend the rest of my days there with Miss Clarabelle Cobb, before she takes a runout powder on me. Well," Blondy says, "if I only listen to Miss Clarabelle Cobb, I will now be an honest clerk in a gents' furnishing store, with maybe a cute little apartment up around 110th Street, and children running all around and about."

And with this, Blondy sighs heavily, and I sigh with him, because the romance of Blondy Swanson and Miss Clarabelle Cobb is well known to one and all on Broadway.

It goes back a matter of anyway six years when Blondy Swanson is making money so fast he can scarcely stop to count it, and at this time Miss Clarabelle Cobb is the most beautiful doll in this town, and many citizens almost lose their minds just gazing at her when she is a member of Mr. Georgie White's Scandals, including Blondy Swanson.

In fact, after Blondy Swanson sees Miss Clarabelle Cobb in just one performance of Mr. Georgie White's Scandals, he is never quite the same guy again. He goes to a lot of bother meeting up with Miss Clarabelle Cobb, and then he takes to hanging out around Mr. Georgie White's stage door, and sending Miss Clarabelle Cobb ten-pound boxes of candy, and floral horseshoes, and wreaths, and also packages of trinkets, including such articles as diamond bracelets, and brooches, and vanity cases, for there is no denying that Blondy is a fast guy with a dollar.

But it seems that Miss Clarabelle Cobb will not accept any of these offerings, except the candy and the flowers, and she goes so far as to return a sable coat that Blondy sends her one very cold day, and she is openly criticized for this action by some of the other dolls in Mr. Georgie White's Scandals, for they say that after all there is a limit even to eccentricity.

But Miss Clarabelle Cobb states that she is not accepting valuable offerings from any guy, and especially a guy who is engaged in trafficking in the demon rum, because she says that his money is nothing but blood money that comes from breaking the law of the land, although, as a matter of fact, this is a dead wrong rap against Blondy Swason, as he never handles a drop of rum in his life, but only Scotch, and furthermore he keeps himself pretty well straightened out with the law.

The idea is, Miss Clarabelle Cobb comes of very religious people back in Akron, Ohio, and she is taught from childhood that rum is a terrible thing, and personally I think it is myself, except in cocktails, and furthermore, the last thing her mamma tells her when she leaves for New York is to beware of any guys who come around offering her diamond bracelets and fur coats, because her mamma says such guys are undoubtedly snakes in the grass, and probably on the make.

But while she will not accept his offerings, Miss Clarabelle Cobb does not object to going out with Blondy Swanson now and then, and putting on the chicken Mexicaine, and the lobster Newburg, and other items of this nature, and any time you put a good-looking young guy and a beautiful doll together over the chicken Mexicaine and the lobster Newburg often enough, you are apt to have a case of love on your hands.

And this is what happens to Blondy Swanson and Miss Clarabelle Cobb, and in fact they become in love more than somewhat, and Blondy Swanson is wishing to marry Miss Clarabelle Cobb, but one night over a batch of lobster Newburg, she says to him like this:

"Blondy," she says, "I love you, and," she says, "I will marry you in a minute if you get out of trafficking in rum. I will marry you if you are out of the rum business, and do not have a dime, but I will never marry you as long as you are dealing in rum, no matter if you have a hundred million."

Well, Blondy says he will get out of the racket at once, and he keeps saying this every now and then for a year or so, and the chances are that several times he means it, but when a guy is in this business in those days as strong as Blondy Swanson it is not so easy for him to get out, even if he wishes to do so. And then one day Miss Clarabelle Cobb has a talk with Blondy, and says to him as follows:

"Blondy," she says, "I still love you, but you care more for your business than you do for me. So I am going back to Ohio," she says. "I am sick and tired of Broadway, anyhow. Some day when you are really through with the terrible traffic you are now engaged in, come to me."

And with this, Miss Clarabelle Cobb takes plenty of outdoors on Blondy Swanson, and is seen no more in these parts. At first Blondy thinks she is only trying to put a little pressure on him, and will be back, but as the weeks become months, and the months finally count up into years, Blondy can see that she is by no means clowning with him. Furthermore, he never hears from her, and all he knows is she is back in Akron, Ohio.

Well, Blondy is always promising himself that he will soon pack in on hauling wet goods, and go look up Miss Clarabelle Cobb and marry her, but he keeps putting it off, and putting it off, until finally one day he hears that Miss Clarabelle Cobb marries some legitimate guy in Akron, and this is a terrible blow to Blondy, indeed, and from this day he never looks at another doll again, or anyway not much.

Naturally, I express my deep sympathy to Blondy about being broke, and I also mention that my heart bleeds for him in his loss of Miss Clarabelle Cobb, and we have a few doses of rock candy and rye whisky on both propositions, and by this time Good Time Charley runs out of rock candy, and anyway it is a lot of bother for him to be mixing it up with the rye whisky, so we have the rye whisky without the rock candy, and personally I do not notice much difference.

Well, while we are standing there at the bar having our rye whisky without the rock candy, who comes in but an old guy by the name of The Dutchman, who is known to one and all as a most illegal character in every respect. In fact, The Dutchman has no standing whatever in the community, and I am somewhat surprised to see him appear in Good Time Charley's, because The Dutchman is generally a lammie from some place, and the gendarmes everywhere are always anxious to have a chat with him. The last I hear of The Dutchman he is in college somewhere out West for highway robbery, although afterwards he tells me it is a case of mistaken identity. It seems he mistakes a copper in plain clothes for a groceryman.

The Dutchman is an old-fashioned looking guy of maybe fifty-odd, and he has gray hair, and a stubby gray beard, and he is short, and thickset, and always good-natured, even when there is no call for it, and to look at him you will think there is no more harm in him than there is in a preacher, and maybe not as much.

As The Dutchman comes in, he takes a peek all around and about as if he is looking for somebody in particular, and when he sees Blondy Swanson he moves up alongside Blondy and begins whispering to Blondy until Blondy pulls away and tells him to speak freely.

Now The Dutchman has a very interesting story, and it goes like this: It seems that about eight or nine months back The Dutchman is mobbed up with a party of three very classy heavy guys who make quite a good thing of going around knocking off safes in small-town jugs, and post offices, and stores in small towns, and taking the money, or whatever else is valuable in these safes. This is once quite a popular custom in this country, although it dies out to some extent of late years because they improve the brand of safes so much it is a lot of bother knocking them off, but it comes back during the depression when there is no other way of making money, until it is a very prosperous business again. And of course this is very nice for old-time heavy guys, such as The Dutchman, because it gives them something to do in their old age.

Anyway, it seems that this party The Dutchman is with goes over into Pennsylvania one night on a tip from a friend and knocks off a safe in a factory office, and gets a pay roll amounting to maybe fifty G's. But it seems that while they are making their getaway in an automobile, the gendarmes take out after them, and there is a chase, during which there is considerable blasting back and forth.

Well, finally in this blasting, the three guys with The Dutchman get cooled off, and The Dutchman also gets shot up quite some, and he abandons the automobile out on an open road, taking the money, which is in a gripsack, with him, and he somehow manages to escape the gendarmes by going across country, and hiding here and there.

But The Dutchman gets pretty well petered out, what with his wounds, and trying to lug the gripsack, and one night he comes to an old deserted barn, and he decides to stash the gripsack in this barn, because there is no chance he can keep lugging it around much longer. So he takes up a few boards in the floor of the barn, and digs a nice hole in the ground underneath and plants the gripsack there, figuring to come back some day and pick it up.

Well, The Dutchman gets over into New Jersey one way and another, and lays up in a town by the name of New Brunswick until his wounds are healed, which requires considerable time as The Dutchman cannot take it nowadays as good as he can when he is younger.

Furthermore, even after The Dutchman recovers and gets to thinking of going after the stashed gripsack, he finds he is about half out of confidence, which is what happens to all guys when they commence getting old, and he figures that it may be a good idea to declare somebody else in to help him, and the first guy he thinks of is Blondy

Swanson, because he knows Blondy Swanson is a very able citizen in every respect.

"Now, Blondy," The Dutchman says, "if you like my proposition, I am willing to cut you in for fifty per cent, and fifty per cent of fifty G's is by no means pretzels in these times."

"Well, Dutchman," Blondy says, "I will gladly assist you in this enterprise on the terms you state. It appeals to me as a legitimate proposition, because there is no doubt this dough is coming to you, and from now on I am strictly legit. But in the meantime, let us have some more rock candy and rye whisky, without the rock candy, while we discuss the matter further."

But it seems that The Dutchman does not care for rock candy and rye whisky, even without the rock candy, so Blondy Swanson and me and Good Time Charley continue taking our doses, and Blondy keeps getting more enthusiastic about The Dutchman's proposition until finally I become enthusiastic myself, and I say I think I will go along as it is an opportunity to see new sections of the country, while Good Time Charley states that it will always be the great regret of his life that his business keeps him from going, but that he will provide us with an ample store of rock candy and rye whisky, without the rock candy, in case we run into any touches of the grippe.

Well, anyway, this is how I come to be riding around in an old can belonging to The Dutchman on a very cold Christmas Eve with The Dutchman and Blondy Swanson, although none of us happen to think of it being Christmas Eve until we notice that there seems to be holly wreaths in windows here and there as we go bouncing along the roads, and finally we pass a little church that is all lit up, and somebody opens the door as we are passing, and we see a big Christmas tree inside the church, and it

is a very pleasant sight, indeed, and in fact it makes me
a little homesick, although of course the chances are I will
not be seeing any Christmas trees even if I am home.

We leave Good Time Charley's along mid-afternoon,
with The Dutchman driving this old can of his, and all I
seem to remember about the trip is going through a lot of
little towns so fast they seem strung together, because most
of the time I am dozing in the back seat.

Blondy Swanson is riding in the front seat with The
Dutchman and Blondy also cops a little snooze now and
then as we are going along, but whenever he happens to
wake up he pokes me awake, too, so we can take a dose
of rock candy and rye whisky, without the rock candy.
So in many respects it is quite an enjoyable journey.

I recollect the little church because we pass it right after
we go busting through a pretty fair-sized town, and I hear
The Dutchman say the old barn is now only a short distance away, and by this time it is dark, and colder than a
deputy sheriff's heart, and there is snow on the ground,
although it is clear overhead, and I am wishing I am back
in Mindy's restaurant wrapping myself around a nice
T-bone steak, when I hear Blondy Swanson ask The
Dutchman if he is sure he knows where he is going, as
this seems to be an untraveled road, and The Dutchman
states as follows:

"Why," he says, "I know I am on the right road. I am
following the big star you see up ahead of us, because I
remember seeing this star always in front of me when I am
going along this road before."

So we keep following the star, but it turns out that it is
not a star at all, but a light shining from the window of a
ramshackle old frame building pretty well off to one side
of the road and on a rise of ground, and when The Dutchman sees this light, he is greatly nonplussed, indeed, and
speaks as follows:

"Well," he says, "this looks very much like my barn, but my barn does not call for a light in it. Let us investigate this matter before we go any farther."

So The Dutchman gets out of the old can, and slips up to one side of the building and peeks through the window, and then he comes back and motions for Blondy and me to also take a peek through this window, which is nothing but a square hole cut in the side of the building with wooden bars across it, but no window panes, and what we behold inside by the dim light of a lantern hung on a nail on a post is really most surprising.

There is no doubt whatever that we are looking at the inside of a very old barn, for there are several stalls for horses, or maybe cows, here and there, but somebody seems to be living in the barn, as we can see a table, and a couple of chairs, and a tin stove, in which there is a little fire, and on the floor in one corner is what seems to be a sort of a bed.

Furthermore, there seems to be somebody lying on the bed and making quite a fuss in the way of groaning and crying and carrying on generally in a loud tone of voice, and there is no doubt that it is the voice of a doll, and anybody can tell that this doll is in some distress.

Well, here is a situation, indeed, and we move away from the barn to talk it over.

The Dutchman is greatly discouraged, because he gets to thinking that if this doll is living in the barn for any length of time, his plant may be discovered. He is willing to go away and wait awhile, but Blondy Swanson seems to be doing quite some thinking, and finally Blondy says like this:

"Why," Blondy says, "the doll in this barn seems to be sick, and only a bounder and a cad will walk away from a sick doll, especially," Blondy says, "a sick doll who is a total stranger to him. In fact, it will take a very large heel to do such a thing. The idea is for us to go inside and see if we can do anything for this sick doll," Blondy says.

Well, I say to Blondy Swanson that the chances are the doll's ever-loving husband, or somebody, is in town, or maybe over to the nearest neighbors digging up assistance, and will be back in a jiffy, and that this is no place for us to be found.

"No," Blondy says, "it cannot be as you state. The snow on the ground is anyway a day old. There are no tracks around the door of this old joint, going or coming, and it is a cinch if anybody knows there is a sick doll here, they will have plenty of time to get help before this. I am going inside and look things over," Blondy says.

Naturally, The Dutchman and I go too, because we do not wish to be left alone outside, and it is no trouble whatever to get into the barn, as the door is unlocked, and all we have to do is walk in. And when we walk in with Blondy Swanson leading the way, the doll on the bed on the floor half raises up to look at us, and although the light of the lantern is none too good, anybody can see that this doll is nobody but Miss Clarabelle Cobb, although personally I see some change in her since she is in Mr. Georgie White's Scandals.

She stays half raised up on the bed looking at Blondy Swanson for as long as you can count ten, if you count fast, then she falls back and starts crying and carrying on again, and at this The Dutchman kneels down on the floor beside her to find out what is eating her.

All of a sudden The Dutchman jumps up and speaks to us as follows:

"Why," he says, "this is quite a delicate situation, to be sure. In fact," he says, "I must request you guys to step outside. What we really need for this case is a doctor, but it is too late to send for one. However, I will endeavor to do the best I can under the circumstances."

Then The Dutchman starts taking off his overcoat, and Blondy Swanson stands looking at him with such a strange expression on his kisser that The Dutchman laughs out loud, and says like this:

"Do not worry about anything, Blondy," The Dutchman says. "I am maybe a little out of practice since my old lady put her checks back in the rack, but she leaves eight kids alive and kicking, and I bring them all in except one, because we are seldom able to afford a croaker."

So Blondy Swanson and I step out of the barn and after a while The Dutchman calls us and we go back into the barn to find he has a big fire going in the stove, and the place nice and warm.

Miss Clarabelle Cobb is now all quieted down, and is covered with The Dutchman's overcoat, and as we come in The Dutchman tiptoes over to her and pulls back the coat and what do we see but a baby with a noggin no bigger than a crab apple and a face as wrinkled as some old pappy guy's, and The Dutchman states that it is a boy, and a very healthy one, at that.

"Furthermore," The Dutchman says, "the mamma is doing as well as can be expected. She is as strong a doll as ever I see," he says, "and all we have to do now is send out a croaker when we go through town just to make sure there are no complications. But," The Dutchman says, "I guarantee the croaker will not have much to do."

Well, the old Dutchman is as proud of this baby as if it is his own, and I do not wish to hurt his feelings, so I say the baby is a darberoo, and a great credit to him in every respect, and also to Miss Clarabelle Cobb, while Blondy Swanson just stands there looking at it as if he never sees a baby before in his life, and is greatly astonished.

It seems that Miss Clarabelle Cobb is a very strong doll, just as The Dutchman states, and in about an hour she shows signs of being wide awake, and Blondy Swanson sits down on the floor beside her, and she talks to him quite a while in a low voice, and while they are talking The Dutchman pulls up the floor in another corner of the barn, and digs around underneath a few minutes, and finally comes up with a gripsack covered with dirt, and he opens this gripsack and shows me it is filled with lovely, large coarse banknotes.

Later Blondy Swanson tells The Dutchman and me the story of Miss Clarabelle Cobb, and parts of this story are rather sad. It seems that after Miss Clarabelle Cobb goes back to her old home in Akron, Ohio, she winds up marrying a young guy by the name of Joseph Hatcher, who is a bookkeeper by trade, and has a pretty good job in Akron, so Miss Clarabelle Cobb and this Joseph Hatcher are as happy as anything together for quite a spell.

Then about a year before the night I am telling about, Joseph Hatcher is sent by his firm to these parts where we find Miss Clarabelle Cobb, to do the bookkeeping in a factory there, and one night a few months afterwards, when Joseph Hatcher is staying after hours in the factory office working on his books, a mob of wrong gees breaks into the joint, and sticks him up, and blows open the safe, taking away a large sum of money and leaving Joseph Hatcher tied up like a turkey.

When Joseph Hatcher is discovered in this predicament the next morning, what happens but the gendarmes put the sleeve on him, and place him in the pokey, saying the chances are Joseph Hatcher is in and in with safe blowers, and that he tips them off the dough is in the safe, and it seems that the guy who is especially fond of this idea is a guy by the name of Ambersham, who is manager of the factory, and a very hard-hearted guy, at that.

And now, although this is eight or nine months back, there is Joseph Hatcher still in the pokey awaiting trial, and it is 7 to 5 anywhere in town that the judge throws

the book at him when he finally goes to bat, because it
seems from what Miss Clarabelle Cobb tells Blondy Swanson that nearly everybody figures Joseph Hatcher is guilty.

But of course Miss Clarabelle Cobb does not put in with
popular opinion about her ever-loving Joe, and she spends
the next few months trying to spring him from the pokey,
but she has no potatoes, and no way of getting any potatoes, so things go from bad to worse with Miss Clarabelle
Cobb.

Finally, she finds herself with no place to live in town,
and she happens to run into this old barn, which is on an
abandoned property owned by a doctor in town by the
name of Kelton, and it seems that he is a kind-hearted guy,
and he gives her permission to use it any way she wishes.
So Miss Clarabelle moves into the barn, and the chances
are there is many a time when she wishes she is back in
Mr. Georgie White's Scandals.

Now The Dutchman listens to this story with great interest, especially the part about Joseph Hatcher being left
tied up in the factory office, and finally The Dutchman
states as follows:

"Why, my goodness," The Dutchman says, "there is no
doubt but what this is the very same young guy we are
compelled to truss up the night we get this gripsack. As I
recollect it, he wishes to battle for his employer's dough,
and I personally tap him over the coco with a blackjack.

"But," he says, "he is by no means the guy who tips us
off about the dough being there. As I remember it now,
it is nobody but the guy whose name you mention in Miss
Clarabelle Cobb's story. It is this guy Ambersham, the
manager of the joint, and come to think of it, he is supposed to get his bit of this dough for his trouble, and it is
only fair that I carry out this agreement as the executor of
the estate of my late comrades, although," The Dutchman
says, "I do not approve of his conduct toward this Joseph

Hatcher. But," he says, "the first thing for us to do is to get a doctor out here to Miss Clarabelle Cobb, and I judge the doctor for us to get is this Doc Kelton she speaks of."

So The Dutchman takes the gripsack and we get into the old can and head back the way we come, although before we go I see Blondy Swanson bend down over Miss Clarabelle Cobb, and while I do not wish this to go any farther, I will take a paralyzed oath I see him plant a small kiss on the baby's noggin, and I hear Miss Clarabelle Cobb speak as follows:

"I will name him for you, Blondy," she says. "By the way, Blondy, what is your right name?"

"Olaf," Blondy says.

It is now along in the early morning and not many citizens are stirring as we go through town again, with Blondy in the front seat again holding the gripsack on his lap so The Dutchman can drive, but finally we find a guy in an all-night lunch counter who knows where Doc Kelton lives, and this guy stands on the running board of the old can and guides us to a house in a side street, and after pounding on the door quite a spell, we roust the Doc out and Blondy goes inside to talk with him.

He is in there quite a spell, but when he comes out he says everything is okay, and that Doc Kelton will go at once to look after Miss Clarabelle Cobb, and take her to a hospital, and Blondy states that he leaves a couple of C's with the Doc to make sure Miss Clarabelle Cobb gets the best of care.

"Well," The Dutchman says, "we can afford a couple of C's out of what we have in this gripsack, but," he says, "I am still wondering if it is not my duty to look up this Ambersham, and give him his bit."

"Dutchman," Blondy says, "I fear I have some bad news for you. The gripsack is gone. This Doc Kelton strikes me as a right guy in every respect, especially," Blondy says, "as he states to me that he always half suspects there is a wrong rap in on Miss Clarabelle Cobb's ever-loving Joe, and that if it is not for this guy Ambersham agitating all the time other citizens may suspect the same thing, and it will not be so tough for Joe.

"So," Blondy says, "I tell Doc Kelton the whole story, about Ambersham and all, and I take the liberty of leaving the gripsack with him to be returned to the rightful owners, and Doc Kelton says if he does not have Miss Clarabelle Cobb's Joe out of the sneezer, and this Ambersham on the run out of town in twenty-four hours, I can call him a liar. But," Blondy says, "let us now proceed on our way, because I only have Doc Kelton's word that he will give us twelve hours' leeway before he does anything except attend to Miss Clarabelle Cobb, as I figure you need this much time to get out of sight, Dutchman."

Well, The Dutchman does not say anything about all this news for a while, and seems to be thinking the situation over, and while he is thinking he is giving his old can a little more gas than he intends, and she is fairly popping along what seems to be the main drag of the town when a gendarme on a motorcycle comes up alongside us, and motions The Dutchman to pull over to the curb.

He is a nice-looking young gendarme, but he seems somewhat hostile as he gets off his motorcycle, and walks up to us very slow, and asks us where the fire is.

Naturally, we do not say anything in reply, which is the only thing to say to a gendarme under these circumstances, so he speaks as follows:

"What are you guys carrying in this old skillet, anyway?" he says. "Stand up, and let me look you guys over."

And then as we stand up, he peeks into the front and back of the car, and under our feet, and all he finds is a bottle which once holds some of Good Time Charley's rock candy and rye whisky without the rock candy, but which is now very empty, and he holds this bottle up, and sniffs at the nozzle, and asks what is formerly in this bottle, and I tell him the truth when I tell him it is once full of medicine, and The Dutchman and Blondy Swanson nod their heads in support of my statement. But the gendarme takes another sniff, and then he says like this:

"Oh," he says, very sarcastic, "wise guys, eh? Three wise guys, eh? Trying to kid somebody, eh? Medicine, eh?" he says. "Well, if it is not Christmas Day I will take you in and hold you just on suspicion. But I will be Santa Claus to you, and let you go ahead, wise guys."

And then after we get a few blocks away, The Dutchman speaks as follows:

"Yes," he says, "that is what we are, to be sure. We are wise guys. If we are not wise guys, we will still have the gripsack in this car for the copper to find. And if the copper finds the gripsack, he will wish to take us to the jail house for investigation, and if he wishes to take us there I fear he will not be alive at this time, and we will be in plenty of heat around and about, and personally," The Dutchman says, "I am sick and tired of heat."

And with this The Dutchman puts a large Betsy back in a holster under his left arm, and turns on the gas, and as the old can begins leaving the lights of the town behind, I ask Blondy if he happens to notice the name of this town.

"Yes," Blondy says, "I notice it on a signboard we just pass. It is Bethlehem, Pa."

The Lemon Drop Kid

I AM GOING to take you back a matter of four or five years ago to an August afternoon and the race track at Saratoga, which is a spot in New York state very pleasant to behold, and also to a young guy by the name of The Lemon Drop Kid, who is called The Lemon Drop Kid because he always has a little sack of lemon drops in the side pocket of his coat, and is always munching at same, a lemon drop being a breed of candy that is relished by many, although personally I prefer peppermints.

On this day I am talking about, The Lemon Drop Kid is looking about for business, and not doing so good for himself, at that, as The Lemon Drop Kid's business is telling the tale, and he is finding it very difficult indeed to discover citizens who are willing to listen to him tell the tale.

And of course if a guy whose business is telling the tale cannot find anybody to listen to him, he is greatly handicapped, for the tale such a guy tells is always about how he knows something is doing in a certain race, the idea of the tale being that it may cause the citizen who is listening to it to make a wager on this certain race, and if the race comes out the way the guy who is telling the tale says it will come out, naturally the citizen is bound to be very grateful to the guy, and maybe reward him liberally.

Furthermore, the citizen is bound to listen to more tales, and a guy whose business is telling the tale, such as The Lemon Drop Kid, always has tales to tell until the cows come home, and generally they are long tales, and sometimes they are very interesting and entertaining, according to who is telling them, and it is well known to one and all that nobody can tell the tale any better than The Lemon Drop Kid.

But old Cap Duhaine and his sleuths at the Saratoga track are greatly opposed to guys going around telling the tale, and claim that such guys are nothing but touts, and they are especially opposed to The Lemon Drop Kid, because they say he tells the tale so well that he weakens public confidence in horse racing. So they are casing The Lemon Drop Kid pretty close to see that he does not get some citizen's ear and start telling him the tale, and finally The Lemon Drop Kid is greatly disgusted and walks up the lawn toward the head of the stretch.

And while he is walking, he is eating lemon drops out of his pocket, and thinking about how much better off he will be if he puts in the last ten years of his life at some legitimate dodge, instead of hopscotching from one end of the country to the other telling the tale, although just offhand The Lemon Drop Kid cannot think of any legitimate dodge at which he will see as much of life as he sees around the race tracks since he gets out of the orphan asylum in Jersey City where he is raised.

At the time this story starts out, The Lemon Drop Kid

is maybe twenty-four years old, and he is a quiet little guy with a low voice, which comes of keeping it confidential when he is telling the tale, and he is nearly always alone. In fact, The Lemon Drop Kid is never known to have a pal as long as he is around telling the tale, although he is by no means an unfriendly guy, and is always speaking to everybody, even when he is in the money.

But it is now a long time since The Lemon Drop Kid is in the money, or seems to have any chance of being in the money, and the landlady of the boarding house in Saratoga where he is residing is becoming quite hostile, and making derogatory cracks about him, and also about most of her other boarders, too, so The Lemon Drop Kid is unable to really enjoy his meals there, especially as they are very bad meals to start with.

Well, The Lemon Drop Kid goes off by himself up the lawn and stands there looking out across the track, munching a lemon drop from time to time, and thinking what a harsh old world it is, to be sure, and how much better off it will be if there are no sleuths whatever around and about.

It is a day when not many citizens are present at the track, and the only one near The Lemon Drop Kid seems to be an old guy in a wheel chair, with a steamer rug over his knees, and a big, sleepy-looking stove lid who appears to be in charge of the chair.

This old guy has a big white mouser, and big white bristly eyebrows, and he is a very fierce-looking old guy, indeed, and anybody can tell at once that he is nothing but a curmudgeon, and by no means worthy of attention. But he is a familiar spectacle at the race track at Saratoga, as he comes out nearly every day in a limousine the size of a hearse, and is rolled out of the limousine in his wheel chair on a little runway by the stove lid, and pushed up to this spot where he is sitting now, so he can view the sport of kings without being bothered by the crowds.

It is well known to one and all that his name is Rarus P. Griggsby, and that he has plenty of potatoes, which he makes in Wall Street, and that he is closer than the next second with his potatoes, and furthermore, it is also well known that he hates everybody in the world, including himself, so nobody goes anywhere near him if they can help it.

The Lemon Drop Kid does not realize he is standing so close to Rarus P. Griggsby, until he hears the old guy growling at the stove lid, and then The Lemon Drop Kid looks at Rarus P. Griggsby very sympathetic and speaks to him in his low voice as follows:

"Gout?" he says.

Now of course The Lemon Drop Kid knows who Rarus P. Griggsby is, and under ordinary circumstances The Lemon Drop Kid will not think of speaking to such a character, but afterwards he explains that he is feeling so despondent that he addresses Rarus P. Griggsby just to show he does not care what happens. And under ordinary circumstances, the chances are Rarus P. Griggsby will start hollering for the gendarmes if a stranger has the gall to speak to him, but there is so much sympathy in The Lemon Drop Kid's voice and eyes, that Rarus P. Griggsby seems to be taken by surprise, and he answers like this:

"Arthritis," Rarus P. Griggsby says. "In my knees," he says. "I am not able to walk a step in three years."

"Why," The Lemon Drop Kid says, "I am greatly distressed to hear this. I know just how you feel, because I am troubled from infancy with this same disease."

Now of course this is strictly the old ackamarackus, as The Lemon Drop Kid cannot even spell arthritis, let alone have it, but he makes the above statement just by way of conversation, and furthermore he goes on to state as follows:

"In fact," The Lemon Drop Kid says, "I suffer so I can scarcely think, but one day I find a little remedy that fixes me up as right as rain, and I now have no trouble whatsoever."

And with this, he takes a lemon drop out of his pocket and pops it into his mouth, and then he hands one to Rarus P. Griggsby in a most hospitable manner, and the old guy holds the lemon drop between his thumb and forefinger and looks at it as if he expects it to explode right in his pan, while the stove lid gazes at The Lemon Drop Kid with a threatening expression.

"Well," Rarus P. Griggsby says, "personally I consider all cures fakes. I have a standing offer of five thousand dollars to anybody that can cure me of my pain, and nobody even comes close so far. Doctors are also fakes," he says. "I have seven of them, and they take out my tonsils, and all my teeth, and my appendix, and they keep me from eating anything I enjoy, and I only get worse. The waters here in Saratoga seem to help me some, but," he says, "they do not get me out of this wheel chair, and I am sick and tired of it all."

Then, as if he comes to a quick decision, he pops the lemon drop into his mouth, and begins munching it very slow, and after a while he says it tastes just like a lemon drop to him, and of course it is a lemon drop all along, but The Lemon Drop Kid says this taste is only to disguise the medicine in it.

Now, by and by, The Lemon Drop Kid commences telling Rarus P. Griggsby the tale, and afterwards The Lemon Drop Kid says he has no idea Rarus P. Griggsby will listen to the tale, and that he only starts telling it to him in a spirit of good clean fun, just to see how he will take it, and he is greatly surprised to note that Rarus P. Griggsby is all attention.

Personally, I find nothing unusual in this situation, because I often see citizens around the race tracks as prominent as Rarus P. Griggsby, listening to the tale from guys who do not have as much as a seat in their pants, especially if the tale has any larceny in it, because it is only human nature to be deeply interested in larceny.

And the tale The Lemon Drop Kid tells Rarus P. Griggsby is that he is a brother of Sonny Saunders, the jock, and that Sonny tells him to be sure and be at the track this day to bet on a certain horse in the fifth race, because it is nothing but a boat race, and everything in it is as stiff as a plank, except this certain horse.

Now of course this is all a terrible lie, and The Lemon Drop Kid is taking a great liberty with Sonny Saunders' name, especially as Sonny does not have any brothers, anyway, and even if Sonny knows about a boat race the chances are he will never tell The Lemon Drop Kid, but then very few guys whose business is telling the tale ever stop to figure they may be committing perjury.

So The Lemon Drop Kid goes on to state that when he arrives at the track he has fifty bobs pinned to his wishbone to bet on this certain horse, but unfortunately he gets a tip on a real good thing in the very first race, and bets his fifty bobs right then and there, figuring to provide himself with a larger taw to bet on the certain horse in the fifth, but the real good thing receives practically a criminal ride from a jock who does not know one end of a horse from the other, and is beat a very dirty snoot, and there The Lemon Drop Kid is with the fifth race coming up, and an absolute cinch in it, the way his tale goes, but with no dough left to bet on it.

Well, personally I do not consider this tale as artistic as some The Lemon Drop Kid tells, and in fact The

Lemon Drop Kid himself never rates it among his master-pieces, but old Rarus P. Griggsby listens to the tale quite intently without saying a word, and all the time he is munching the lemon drop and smacking his lips under his big white mouser, as if he greatly enjoys this delicacy, but when The Lemon Drop Kid concludes the tale, and is standing there gazing out across the track with a very sad expression on his face, Rarus P. Griggsby speaks as follows:

"I never bet on horse races," Rarus P. Griggsby says. "They are too uncertain. But this proposition you present sounds like finding money, and I love to find money. I will wager one hundred dollars on your assurance that this certain horse cannot miss."

And with this, he outs with a leather so old that The Lemon Drop Kid half expects a cockroach to leap out at him, and produces a C note which he hands to The Lemon Drop Kid, and as he does so, Rarus P. Griggsby inquires:

"What is the name of this certain horse?"

Well, of course this is a fair question, but it happens that The Lemon Drop Kid is so busy all afternoon think-ing of the injustice of the sleuths that he never even bothers to look up this particular race beforehand, and afterwards he is quite generally criticized for slovenliness in this matter, for if a guy is around telling the tale about a race, he is entitled to pick out a horse that has at least some kind of a chance.

But of course The Lemon Drop Kid is not expecting the opportunity of telling the tale to arise, so the question finds him unprepared, as offhand he cannot think of the name of a horse in the race, as he never consults the scratches, and he does not wish to mention the name of some plug that may be scratched out, and lose the chance to make the C note. So as he seizes the C note from Rarus P. Griggsby and turns to dash for the book-makers over in front of the grandstand, all The Lemon Drop Kid can think of to say at this moment is the following:

"Watch No. 2," he says.

And the reason he says No. 2, is he figures there is bound to be a No. 2 in the race, while he cannot be so sure about a No. 7 or a No. 9 until he looks them over, because you understand that all The Lemon Drop Kid states in telling the tale to Rarus P. Griggsby about know-ing of something doing in this race is very false.

And of course The Lemon Drop Kid has no idea of betting the C note on anything whatever in the race. In the first place, he does not know of anything to bet on, and in the second place he needs the C note, but he is somewhat relieved when he inquires of the first bookie he comes to, and learns that No. 2 is an old walrus by the name of The Democrat, and anybody knows that The Democrat has no chance of winning even in a field of mud turtles.

So The Lemon Drop Kid puts the C note in his pants pocket, and walks around and about until the horses are going to the post, and you must not think there is any-thing dishonest in his not betting this money with a bookmaker, as The Lemon Drop Kid is only taking the bet himself which is by no means unusual, and in fact it is so common that only guys like Cap Duhaine and his sleuths think much about it.

Finally The Lemon Drop Kid goes back to Rarus P. Griggsby, for it will be considered most ungenteel for a guy whose business is telling the tale to be absent when it comes time to explain why the tale does not stand up, and about this time the horses are turning for home, and a few seconds later they go busting past the spot where Rarus P. Griggsby is sitting in his wheel chair, and what is in front to the wire by a Salt Lake City block but The Democrat with No. 2 on his blanket.

Well, old Rarus P. Griggsby starts yelling and waving his hands, and making so much racket that he is soon the center of attention, and when it comes out that he bets a C note on the winner, nobody blames him for cutting up these didoes, for the horse is a 20 to 1 shot, but all this time The Lemon Drop Kid only stands there looking very, very sad and shaking his head, until finally Rarus P. Griggsby notices his strange attitude.

"Why are you not cheering over our winning this nice bet?" he says. "Of course I expect to declare you in," he says. "In fact I am quite grateful to you."

"But," The Lemon Drop Kid says, "we do not win. Our horse runs a jolly second."

"What do you mean, *second*?" Rarus P. Griggsby says. "Do you not tell me to watch No. 2, and does not No. 2 win?"

"Yes," The Lemon Drop Kid says, "what you state is quite true, but what I mean when I say watch No. 2 is that No. 2 is the only horse I am afraid of in the race, and it seems my fear is well founded."

Now at this, old Rarus P. Griggsby sits looking at The Lemon Drop Kid for as long as you can count up to ten, if you count slow, and his mouser and eyebrows are all twitching at once, and anybody can see that he is very much perturbed, and then all of a sudden he lets out a yell and to the great amazement of one and all he leaps right out of his wheel chair and makes a lunge at The Lemon Drop Kid.

Well, there is no doubt that Rarus P. Griggsby has murder in his heart, and nobody blames The Lemon Drop Kid when he turns and starts running away at great speed, and in fact he has such speed that finally his feet are throwing back little stones off the gravel paths of the race track with such velocity that a couple of spectators who get hit by these stones think they are shot.

For a few yards, old Rarus P. Griggsby is right at The Lemon Drop Kid's heels, and furthermore Rarus P. Griggsby is yelling and swearing in a most revolting manner. Then some of Cap Duhaine's sleuths come running up and they take after The Lemon Drop Kid, too, and he has to have plenty of early foot to beat them to the race track gates, and while Rarus P. Griggsby does not figure much in the running after the first few jumps, The Lemon Drop Kid seems to remember hearing him cry out as follows:

"Stop, there! Please stop!" Rarus P. Griggsby cries. "I wish to see you."

But of course The Lemon Drop Kid is by no means a chump, and he does not even slacken up, let alone stop, until he is well beyond the gates, and the sleuths are turning back, and what is more, The Lemon Drop Kid takes the road leading out of Saratoga instead of going back to the city, because he figures that Saratoga may not be so congenial to him for a while.

In fact, The Lemon Drop Kid finds himself half regretting that he ever tells the tale to Rarus P. Griggsby, as The Lemon Drop Kid likes Saratoga in August, but of course such a thing as happens to him in calling a winner the way he does is just an unfortunate accident, and is not apt to happen again in a lifetime.

Well, The Lemon Drop Kid keeps on walking away from Saratoga for quite some time, and finally he is all tuckered out and wishes to take the load off his feet. So when he comes to a small town by the name of Kibbsville, he sits down on the porch of what seems to be a general store and gas station, and while he is sitting there thinking of how nice and quiet and restful this town seems to be, with pleasant shade trees, and white houses all around and about, he sees standing in the doorway of a very little white house across the street from the store, in a gingham dress, the most beautiful young doll that ever lives, and I know this is true, because The Lemon Drop Kid tells me so afterwards.

This doll has brown hair hanging down her back, and her smile is so wonderful that when an old pappy guy with a goatee comes out of the store to sell a guy in a flivver some gas, The Lemon Drop Kid hauls off and asks him if he can use a clerk.

Well, it seems that the old guy can, at that, because it seems that a former clerk, a guy by the name of Pilloe, recently lays down and dies on the old guy from age and malnutrition, and so this is how The Lemon Drop Kid comes to be planted in Kibbsville, and clerking in Martin Potter's store for the next couple of years, at ten bobs per week.

And furthermore, this is how The Lemon Drop Kid meets up with Miss Alicia Deering, who is nobody but the beautiful little doll that The Lemon Drop Kid sees standing in the doorway of the little house across the street.

She lives in this house with her papa, her mamma being dead a long time, and her papa is really nothing but an old bum who dearly loves his applejack, and who is generally around with a good heat on. His first name is Jonas, and he is a house painter by trade but he seldom feels like doing any painting, as he claims he never really recovers from a terrible backache he gets when he is in the Spanish-American War with the First New York, so Miss Alicia Deering supports him by dealing them off her arm in the Commercial Hotel.

But although The Lemon Drop Kid now works for a very great old skinflint who even squawks about The Lemon Drop Kid's habit of filling his side pocket now and then with lemon drops out of a jar on the shelf in the store,

The Lemon Drop Kid is very happy, for the truth of the matter is he loves Miss Alicia Deering, and it is the first time in his life he ever loves anybody, or anything. And furthermore, it is the first time in his life The Lemon Drop Kid is living quietly, and in peace, and not losing sleep trying to think of ways of cheating somebody.

In fact, The Lemon Drop Kid now looks back on his old life with great repugnance, for he can see that it is by no means the proper life for any guy, and sometimes he has half a mind to write to his former associates who may still be around telling the tale, and request them to mend their ways, only The Lemon Drop Kid does not wish these old associates to know where he is.

He never as much as peeks at a racing sheet nowadays, and he spends all his spare time with Miss Alicia Deering, which is not so much time, at that, as old Martin Potter does not care to see his employees loafing between the hours of 6. A.M. and 10 P.M., and neither does the Commercial Hotel. But one day in the spring, when the apple blossoms are blooming in these parts, and the air is chock-a-block with perfume, and the grass is getting nice and green, The Lemon Drop Kid speaks of his love to Miss Alicia Deering, stating that it is such a love that he can scarcely eat.

Well, Miss Alicia Deering states that she reciprocates this love one hundred per cent, and then The Lemon Drop Kid suggests they get married up immediately, and she says she is in favor of the idea, only she can never think of leaving her papa, who has no one else in all this world but her, and while this is a little more extra weight than The Lemon Drop Kid figures on picking up, he says his love is so terrific he can even stand for her papa, too.

So they are married, and go to live in the little house across the street from Martin Potter's store with Miss Alicia Deering's papa.

When he marries Miss Alicia Deering, The Lemon Drop Kid has a bank roll of one hundred and eighteen dollars, including the C note he takes off of Rarus P. Griggsby, and eighteen bobs that he saves out of his salary from Martin Potter in a year, and three nights after the marriage, Miss Alicia Deering's papa sniffs out where The Lemon Drop Kid plants his roll and sneezes same. Then he goes on a big applejack toot, and spends all the dough.

But in spite of everything, including old man Deering, The Lemon Drop Kid and Miss Alicia Deering are very, very happy in the little house for about a year, especially when it seems that Miss Alicia Deering is going to have a baby, although this incident compels her to stop dealing them off the arm at the Commercial Hotel, and cuts down their resources.

Now one day, Miss Alicia Deering comes down with a great illness, and it is such an illness as causes old Doc Abernathy, the local croaker, to wag his head, and to state that it is beyond him, and that the only chance for her is to send her to a hospital in New York City where the experts can get a crack at her. But by this time, what with all his overhead, The Lemon Drop Kid is as clean as a jaybird, and he has no idea where he can get his dukes on any money in these parts, and it will cost a couple of C's, for low, to do what Doc Abernathy suggests.

Finally, The Lemon Drop Kid asks old Martin Potter if he can see his way clear to making him an advance on his salary, which still remains ten bobs per week, but Martin Potter laughs, and says he not only cannot see his way clear to doing such a thing, but that if conditions do not improve he is going to cut The Lemon Drop Kid off altogether. Furthermore, about this time the guy who owns the little house drops around and reminds The Lemon Drop Kid that he is now in arrears for two months' rent, amounting in all to twelve bobs, and if The Lemon Drop Kid is not able to meet this obligation shortly, he will have to vacate.

So one way and another The Lemon Drop Kid is in quite a quandary, and Miss Alicia Deering is getting worse by the minute, and finally The Lemon Drop Kid hoofs and hitch-hikes a matter of maybe a hundred and fifty miles to New York City, with the idea of going out to Belmont Park, where the giddy-aps are now running, figuring he may be able to make some kind of a scratch around there, but he no sooner lights on Broadway than he runs into a guy he knows by the name of Short Boy, and this Short Boy pulls him into a doorway, and says to him like this:

"Listen, Lemon Drop," Short Boy says, "I do not know what it is you do to old Rarus P. Griggsby, and I do not wish to know, but it must be something terrible, indeed, as he has every elbow around the race tracks laying for you for the past couple of years. You know Rarus P. Griggsby has great weight around these tracks, and you must commit murder the way he is after you. Why," Short Boy says, "only last week over in Maryland, Whitey Jordan, the track copper, asks me if ever I hear of you, and I tell him I understand you are in Australia. Keep away from the tracks," Short Boy says, "or you will wind up in the clink."

So The Lemon Drop Kid hoofs and hitch-hikes back to Kibbsville, as he does not wish to become involved in any trouble at this time, and the night he gets back home is the same night a masked guy with a big six pistol in his duke steps into the lobby of the Commercial Hotel and sticks up the night clerk and half a dozen citizens who are sitting around in the lobby, including old Jonas Deering, and robs the damper of over sixty bobs, and it is also the same night that Miss Alicia Deering's baby is born dead,

and old Doc Abernathy afterwards claims that it is all because the experts cannot get a crack at Miss Alicia Deering
a matter of about twelve hours earlier.

And it is along in the morning after this night, around
four bells, that Miss Alicia Deering finally opens her eyes,
and sees The Lemon Drop Kid sitting beside her bed in
the little house, crying very hard, and it is the first time
The Lemon Drop Kid is leveling with his crying since the
time one of the attendants in the orphans' asylum in Jersey
City gives him a good belting years before.

Then Miss Alicia Deering motions to The Lemon Drop
Kid to bend down so she can whisper to him, and what
Miss Alicia Deering whispers, soft and low, is the fol-
lowing:

"Do not cry, Kid," she whispers. "Be a good boy after
I am gone, Kid, and never forget I love you, and take
good care of poor papa."

And then Miss Alicia Deering closes her eyes for good
and all, and The Lemon Drop Kid sits there beside her,
watching her face until some time later he hears a noise at
the front door of the little house, and he opens the door
to find old Sheriff Higginbotham waiting there, and after
they stand looking at each other a while, the sheriff speaks
as follows:

"Well, son," Sheriff Higginbotham says, "I am sorry,
but I guess you will have to come along with me. We find
the vinegar barrel spigot wrapped in tin foil that you use
for a gun in the back yard here where you throw it last
night."

"All right," The Lemon Drop Kid says. "All right,
Sheriff. But how do you come to think of me in the first
place?"

"Well," Sheriff Higginbotham says, "I do not suppose
you recall doing it, and the only guy in the hotel lobby
that notices it is nobody but your papa-in-law, Jonas Deer-

ing, but," he says, "while you are holding your home-made pistol with one hand last night, you reach into the side pocket of your coat with the other hand and take out a lemon drop and pop it into your mouth."

I run into The Lemon Drop Kid out on the lawn at Hialeah in Miami last winter, and I am sorry to see that the twoer he does in Auburn leaves plenty of lines in his face, and a lot of gray in his hair.

But of course I do not refer to this, nor do I mention that he is the subject of considerable criticism from many citizens for turning over to Miss Alicia Deering's papa a purse of three C's that we raise to pay a mouthpiece for his defense.

Furthermore, I do not tell The Lemon Drop Kid that he is also criticized in some quarters for his action while in the sneezer at Auburn in sending the old guy the few bobs he is able to gather in by making and selling knick-knacks of one kind and another to visitors, until finally Jonas Deering saves him any more bother by up and passing away of too much applejack.

The way I look at it, every guy knows his own business best, so I only duke The Lemon Drop Kid, and say I am glad to see him, and we are standing there carving up a few old scores, when all of a sudden there is a great commotion and out of the crowd around us on the lawn comes an old guy with a big white mouser, and bristly white eyebrows, and as he grabs The Lemon Drop Kid by the arm, I am somewhat surprised to see that it is nobody but old Rarus P. Griggsby, without his wheel chair, and to hear him speak as follows:

"Well, well, well, well, well!" Rarus P. Griggsby says to The Lemon Drop Kid. "At last I find you," he says. "Where are you hiding all these years? Do you not know I have detectives looking for you high and low because I wish to pay you the reward I offer for anybody curing

me of my arthritis? Yes," Rarus P. Griggsby says, "the
medicine you give me at Saratoga which tastes like a
lemon drop, works fine, although," he says, "my seven
doctors all try to tell me it is nothing but their efforts
finally getting in their work, while the city of Saratoga is
attempting to cut in and claim credit for its waters.

"But," Rarus P. Griggsby says, "I know it is your medicine, and if it is not your medicine, it is your scallawaggery
that makes me so hot that I forget my arthritis, and never
remember it since, so it is all one and the same thing. Anyway, you now have forty-nine hundred dollars coming
from me, for of course I must hold out the hundred out of
which you swindle me," he says.

Well, The Lemon Drop Kid stands looking at Rarus P.
Griggsby and listening to him, and finally The Lemon
Drop Kid begins to laugh in his low voice, ha-ha-ha-ha-ha,
but somehow there does not seem to be any laughter in
the laugh, and I cannot bear to hear it, so I move away
leaving Rarus P. Griggsby and The Lemon Drop Kid
there together.

I look back only once, and I see The Lemon Drop Kid
stop laughing long enough to take a lemon drop out of the
side pocket of his coat and pop it into his mouth, and then
he goes on laughing, ha-ha-ha-ha-ha.

🌱 🌱 🌱

Sense of Humor

ONE NIGHT I am standing in front of Mindy's restaurant on Broadway, thinking of practically nothing whatever, when all of a sudden I feel a very terrible pain in my left foot.

In fact, this pain is so very terrible that it causes me to leap up and down like a bullfrog, and to let out loud cries of agony, and to speak some very profane language, which is by no means my custom, although of course I recognize the pain as coming from a hot foot, because I often experience this pain before.

Furthermore, I know Joe the Joker must be in the neighborhood, as Joe the Joker has the most wonderful sense of humor of anybody in this town, and is always around giving people the hot foot, and gives it to me more times than I can remember. In fact, I hear Joe the Joker invents the hot foot, and it finally becomes a very popular idea all over the country.

The way you give a hot foot is to sneak up behind some

guy who is standing around thinking of not much, and stick a paper match in his shoe between the sole and the upper along about where his little toe ought to be, and then light the match. By and by the guy will feel a terrible pain in his foot, and will start stamping around, and hollering, and carrying on generally, and it is always a most comical sight and a wonderful laugh to one and all to see him suffer.

No one in the world can give a hot foot as good as Joe the Joker, because it takes a guy who can sneak up very quiet on the guy who is to get the hot foot, and Joe can sneak up so quiet many guys on Broadway are willing to lay you odds that he can give a mouse a hot foot if you can find a mouse that wears shoes. Furthermore, Joe the Joker can take plenty of care of himself in case the guy who gets the hot foot feels like taking the matter up, which sometimes happens, especially with guys who get their shoes made to order at forty bobs per copy and do not care to have holes burned in these shoes.

But Joe does not care what kind of shoes the guys are wearing when he feels like giving out hot foots, and furthermore, he does not care who the guys are, although many citizens think he makes a mistake the time he gives a hot foot to Frankie Ferocious. In fact, many citizens are greatly horrified by this action, and go around saying no good will come of it.

This Frankie Ferocious comes from over in Brooklyn, where he is considered a rising citizen in many respects, and by no means a guy to give hot foots to, especially as Frankie Ferocious has no sense of humor whatever. In fact, he is always very solemn, and nobody ever sees him laugh, and he certainly does not laugh when Joe the Joker gives him a hot foot one day on Broadway when Frankie Ferocious is standing talking over a business matter with some guys from the Bronx.

He only scowls at Joe, and says something in Italian, and while I do not understand Italian, it sounds so unpleasant that I guarantee I will leave town inside of the next two hours if he says it to me.

Of course Frankie Ferocious' name is not really Ferocious, but something in Italian like Feroccio, and I hear he originally comes from Sicily, although he lives in Brooklyn for quite some years, and from a modest beginning he builds himself up until he is a very large operator in merchandise of one kind and another, especially alcohol. He is a big guy of maybe thirty-odd, and he has hair blacker than a yard up a chimney, and black eyes, and black eyebrows, and a slow way of looking at people.

Nobody knows a whole lot about Frankie Ferocious, because he never has much to say, and he takes his time saying it, but everybody gives him plenty of room when he comes around, as there are rumors that Frankie never likes to be crowded. As far as I am concerned, I do not care for any part of Frankie Ferocious, because his slow way of looking at people always makes me nervous, and I am always sorry Joe the Joker gives him a hot foot, because I figure Frankie Ferocious is bound to consider it a most disrespectful action, and hold it against everybody that lives on the Island of Manhattan.

But Joe the Joker only laughs when anybody tells him he is out of line in giving Frankie the hot foot, and says it is not his fault if Frankie has no sense of humor. Furthermore, Joe says he will not only give Frankie another hot foot if he gets a chance, but that he will give hot foots to the Prince of Wales or Mussolini, if he catches them in the right spot, although Regret, the horse player, states, that Joe can have twenty to one any time that he will not give Mussolini any hot foots and get away with it.

Anyway, just as I suspect, there is Joe the Joker watching me when I feel the hot foot, and he is laughing very heartily, and furthermore, a large number of other citizens are also laughing heartily, because Joe the Joker never sees any fun in giving people the hot foot unless others are present to enjoy the joke.

Well, naturally when I see who it is gives me the hot foot I join in the laughter, and go over and shake hands with Joe, and when I shake hands with him there is more laughter, because it seems Joe has a hunk of Limburger cheese in his duke, and what I shake hands with is this Limburger. Furthermore, it is some of Mindy's Limburger cheese, and everybody knows Mindy's Limburger is very squashy, and also very loud.

Of course I laugh at this, too, although to tell the truth I will laugh much more heartily if Joe the Joker drops dead in front of me, because I do not like to be made the subject of laughter on Broadway. But my laugh is really quite hearty when Joe takes the rest of the cheese that is not on my fingers and smears it on the steering wheels of some automobiles parked in front of Mindy's, because I get to thinking of what the drivers will say when they start steering their cars.

Then I get to talking to Joe the Joker, and I ask him how things are up in Harlem, where Joe and his younger brother, Freddy, and several other guys have a small organization operating in beer, and Joe says things are as good as can be expected considering business conditions. Then I ask him how Rosa is getting along, this Rosa being Joe the Joker's ever-loving wife, and a personal friend of mine, as I know her when she is Rosa Midnight and is singing in the old Hot Box before Joe hauls off and marries her.

Well, at this question Joe the Joker starts laughing, and I can see that something appeals to his sense of humor, and finally he speaks as follows:

"Why," he says, "do you not hear the news about Rosa? She takes the wind on me a couple of months ago for my friend Frankie Ferocious, and is living in an apartment over in Brooklyn, right near his house, although," Joe says, "of course you understand I am telling you this only to answer your question, and not to holler copper on Rosa."

Then he lets out another large ha-ha, and in fact Joe the Joker keeps laughing until I am afraid he will injure himself internally. Personally, I do not see anything comical in a guy's ever-loving wife taking the wind on him for a guy like Frankie Ferocious, so when Joe the Joker quiets down a bit I ask him what is funny about the proposition.

"Why," Joe says, "I have to laugh every time I think of how the big greaseball is going to feel when he finds out how expensive Rosa is. I do not know how many things Frankie Ferocious has running for him in Brookyn," Joe says, "but he better try to move himself in on the mint if he wishes to keep Rosa going."

Then he laughs again, and I consider it wonderful the way Joe is able to keep his sense of humor even in such a situation as this, although up to this time I always think Joe is very daffy indeed about Rosa, who is a little doll, weighing maybe ninety pounds with her hat on and quite cute.

Now I judge from what Joe the Joker tells me that Frankie Ferocious knows Rosa before Joe marries her and is always pitching to her when she is singing in the Hot Box, and even after she is Joe's ever-loving wife, Frankie occasionally calls her up, especially when he commences to be a rising citizen of Brooklyn, although of course Joe does not learn about these calls until later. And about the time Frankie Ferocious commences to be a rising citizen of Brooklyn, things begin breaking a little tough for Joe the Joker, what with the depression and all, and he has to economize on Rosa in spots, and if there is one thing Rosa cannot stand it is being economized on.

Along about now, Joe the Joker gives Frankie Ferocious the hot foot, and just as many citizens state at the time, it is a

mistake, for Frankie starts calling Rosa up more than somewhat, and speaking of what a nice place Brooklyn is to live
in—which it is, at that—and between these boosts for Brooklyn and Joe the Joker's economy, Rosa hauls off and takes
the subway to Borough Hall, leaving Joe a note telling him
that if he does not like it he knows what he can do.

"Well, Joe," I say, after listening to his story, "I always
hate to hear of these little domestic difficulties among my
friends, but maybe this is all for the best. Still, I feel sorry
for you, if it will do you any good," I say.

"Do not feel sorry for me," Joe says. "If you wish to feel
sorry for anybody, feel sorry for Frankie Ferocious, and,"
he says, "if you can spare a little more sorrow, give it to
Rosa."

And Joe the Joker laughs very hearty again and starts telling me about a little scatter that he has up in Harlem where
he keeps a chair fixed up with electric wires so he can give
anybody that sits down in it a nice jolt, which sounds very
humorous to me, at that, especially when Joe tells me how
they turn on too much juice one night and almost kill Commodore Jake.

Finally Joe says he has to get back to Harlem, but first he
goes to the telephone in the corner cigar store and calls up
Mindy's and imitates a doll's voice, and tells Mindy he is
Peggy Joyce, or somebody, and orders fifty dozen sandwiches sent up at once to an apartment in West Seventy-
second Street for a birthday party, although of course there
is no such number as he gives, and nobody there will wish
fifty dozen sandwiches if there is such a number.

Then Joe gets in his car and starts off, and while he is
waiting for the traffic lights at Fiftieth Street, I see citizens
on the sidewalks making sudden leaps, and looking around
very fierce, and I know Joe the Joker is plugging them with
pellets made out of tin foil, which he fires from a rubber
band hooked between his thumb and forefinger.

Joe the Joker is very expert with this proposition, and it is very funny to see the citizens jump, although once or twice in his life Joe makes a miscue and knocks out somebody's eye. But it is all in fun, and shows you what a wonderful sense of humor Joe has.

Well, a few days later I see by the papers where a couple of Harlem guys Joe the Joker is mobbed up with are found done up in sacks over in Brooklyn, very dead indeed, and the coppers say it is because they are trying to move in on certain business enterprises that belong to nobody but Frankie Ferocious. But of course the coppers do not say Frankie Ferocious puts these guys in the sacks, because in the first place Frankie will report them to Headquarters if the coppers say such a thing about him, and in the second place putting guys in sacks is strictly a St. Louis idea and to have a guy put in a sack properly you have to send to St. Louis for experts in this matter.

Now, putting a guy in a sack is not as easy as it sounds, and in fact it takes quite a lot of practice and experience. To put a guy in a sack properly, you first have to put him to sleep, because naturally no guy is going to walk into a sack wide awake unless he is a plumb sucker. Some people claim the best way to put a guy to sleep is to give him a sleeping powder of some kind in a drink, but the real experts just tap the guy on the noggin with a blackjack, which saves the expense of buying the drink.

Anyway, after the guy is asleep, you double him up like a pocketknife, and tie a cord or a wire around his neck and under his knees. Then you put him in a gunny sack, and leave him some place, and by and by when the guy wakes up and finds himself in the sack, naturally he wants to get out and the first thing he does is to try to straighten out his knees. This pulls the cord around his neck up so tight that after a while the guy is all out of breath.

So then when somebody comes along and opens the sack

they find the guy dead, and nobody is responsible for this unfortunate situation, because after all the guy really commits suicide, because if he does not try to straighten out his knees he may live to a ripe old age, if he recovers from the tap on the noggin.

Well, a couple of days later I see by the papers where three Brooklyn citizens are scragged as they are walking peaceably along Clinton Street, the scragging being done by some parties in an automobile who seem to have a machine gun, and the papers state that the citizens are friends of Frankie Ferocious, and that it is rumored the parties with the machine gun are from Harlem.

I judge by this that there is some trouble in Brooklyn, especially as about a week after the citizens are scragged in Clinton Street, another Harlem guy is found done up in a sack like a Virginia ham near Prospect Park, and now who is it but Joe the Joker's brother, Freddy, and I know Joe is going to be greatly displeased by this.

By and by it gets so nobody in Brooklyn will open as much as a sack of potatoes without first calling in the gendarmes, for fear a pair of No. 8 shoes will jump out at them.

Now one night I see Joe the Joker, and this time he is all alone, and I wish to say I am willing to leave him all alone, because something tells me he is hotter than a stove. But he grabs me as I am going past, so naturally I stop to talk to him, and the first thing I say is how sorry I am about his brother.

"Well," Joe the Joker says, "Freddy is always a kind of a sap. Rosa calls him up and asks him to come over to Brooklyn to see her. She wishes to talk to Freddy about getting me to give her a divorce," Joe says, "so she can marry Frankie Ferocious, I suppose. Anyway," he says, "Freddy tells Commodore Jake why he is going to see her. Freddy always likes Rosa, and thinks maybe he can patch it up between us. So," Joe says, "he winds up in a sack. They get him after he leaves her apartment. I do not claim Rosa will ask him to come over if she has any idea he will be sacked," Joe says, "but," he says, "she is responsible. She is a bad-luck doll."

Then he starts to laugh, and at first I am greatly horrified, thinking it is because something about Freddy being sacked strikes his sense of humor, when he says to me like this:

"Say," he says, "I am going to play a wonderful joke on Frankie Ferocious."

"Well, Joe," I say, "you are not asking me for advice, but I am going to give you some free gratis, and for nothing. Do not play any jokes on Frankie Ferocious, as I hear he has no more sense of humor than a nanny goat. I hear Frankie Ferocious will not laugh if you have Al Jolson, Eddie Cantor, Ed Wynn and Joe Cook telling him jokes all at once. In fact," I say, "I hear he is a tough audience."

"Oh," Joe the Joker says, "he must have some sense of humor somewhere to stand for Rosa. I hear he is daffy about her. In fact, I understand she is the only person in the world he really likes, and trusts. But I must play a joke on him. I am going to have myself delivered to Frankie Ferocious in a sack."

Well, of course I have to laugh at this myself, and Joe the Joker laughs with me. Personally, I am laughing just at the idea of anybody having themselves delivered to Frankie Ferocious in a sack, and especially Joe the Joker, but of course I have no idea Joe really means what he says.

"Listen," Joe says, finally. "A guy from St. Louis who is a friend of mine is doing most of the sacking for Frankie Ferocious. His name is Ropes McGonnigle. In fact," Joe says, "he is a very dear old pal of mine, and he has a wonderful sense of humor like me. Ropes McGonnigle has nothing whatever to do with sacking Freddy," Joe says, "and he is very indignant about it since he finds out Freddy is my brother, so he is anxious to help me play a joke on Frankie.

"Only last night," Joe says, "Frankie Ferocious sends for Ropes and tells him he will appreciate it as a special favor if Ropes will bring me to him in a sack. I suppose," Joe says, "that Frankie Ferocious hears from Rosa what Freddy is bound to tell her about my ideas on divorce. I have very strict ideas on divorce," Joe says, "especially where Rosa is concerned. I will see her in what's-this before I ever do her and Frankie Ferocious such a favor as giving her a divorce.

"Anyway," Joe the Joker says, "Ropes tells me about Frankie Ferocious propositioning him, so I send Ropes back to Frankie Ferocious to tell him he knows I am to be in Brooklyn to-morrow night, and furthermore, Ropes tells Frankie that he will have me in a sack in no time. And so he will," Joe says.

"Well," I say, "personally, I see no percentage in being delivered to Frankie Ferocious in a sack, because as near as I can make out from what I read in the papers, there is no future for a guy in a sack that goes to Frankie Ferocious. What I cannot figure out," I say, "is where the joke on Frankie comes in."

"Why," Joe the Joker says, "the joke is, I will not be asleep in the sack, and my hands will not be tied, and in each of my hands I will have a John Roscoe, so when the sack is delivered to Frankie Ferocious and I pop out blasting away, can you not imagine his astonishment?"

Well, I can imagine this, all right. In fact, when I get to thinking of the look of surprise that is bound to come to Frankie Ferocious' face when Joe the Joker comes out of the sack I have to laugh, and Joe the Joker laughs right along with me.

"Of course," Joe says, "Ropes McGonnigle will be there to start blasting with me, in case Frankie Ferocious happens to have any company."

Then Joe the Joker goes on up the street, leaving me still

laughing from thinking of how amazed Frankie Ferocious will be when Joe bounces out of the sack and starts throwing slugs around and about. I do not hear of Joe from that time to this, but I hear the rest of the story from very reliable parties.

It seems that Ropes McGonnigle does not deliver the sack himself, after all, but sends it by an expressman to Frankie Ferocious' home. Frankie Ferocious receives many sacks such as this in his time, because it seems that it is a sort of passion with him to personally view the contents of the sacks and check up on them before they are distributed about the city, and of course Ropes McGonnigle knows about this passion from doing so much sacking for Frankie.

When the expressman takes the sack into Frankie's house, Frankie personally lugs it down into his basement, and there he outs with a big John Roscoe and fires six shots into the sack, because it seems Ropes McGonnigle tips him off to Joe the Joker's plan to pop out of the sack and start blasting.

I hear Frankie Ferocious has a very strange expression on his pan and is laughing the only laugh anybody ever hears from him when the gendarmes break in and put the arm on him for murder, because it seems that when Ropes McGonnigle tells Frankie of Joe the Joker's plan, Frankie tells Ropes what he is going to do with his own hands before opening the sack. Naturally, Ropes speaks to Joe the Joker of Frankie's idea about filling the sack full of slugs, and Joe's sense of humor comes right out again.

So, bound and gagged, but otherwise as right as rain in the sack that is delivered to Frankie Ferocious, is by no means Joe the Joker, but Rosa.

A Nice Price

ONE HOT MORNING in June, I am standing in front of the Mohican Hotel in the city of New London, Conn., and the reason I am in such a surprising spot is something that makes a long story quite a bit longer.

It goes back to a couple of nights before when I am walking along Broadway and I run into Sam the Gonoph, the ticket speculator, who seems to have a very sour expression on his puss, although, even when Sam the Gonoph is looking good-natured his puss is nothing much to see.

Now Sam the Gonoph is an old friend of mine, and in fact I sometimes join up with him and his crew to hustle duckets to one thing and another when he is short-handed, so I give him a big hello, and he stops and the following conversation ensues:

"How is it going with you, Sam?" I say to Sam the Gonoph, although of course I do not really care two pins how it is going with him. "You look as if you are all sored up at somebody."

"No," Sam says, "I am not sored up at anybody. I am never sored up at anybody in my life, except maybe Society Max, and of course everybody knows I have a perfect right to be sored up at Society Max, because look at what he does to me."

Well, what Sam the Gonoph says is very true, because what Society Max does to Sam is to steal Sam's fiancée off of him a couple of years before this, and marry her before Sam has time to think. This fiancée is a doll by the name of Sonia, who resides up in the Bronx, and Sam the Gonoph is engaged to her since the year of the Dempsey-Firpo fight, and is contemplating marrying her almost any time, when Society Max bobs up.

Many citizens afterwards claim that Max does Sam the Gonoph a rare favor, because Sonia is commencing to fat up in spots, but it breaks Sam's heart just the same, especially when he learns that Sonia's papa gives the happy young couple twenty big G's in old-fashioned folding money that nobody ever knows the papa has, and Sam figures that Max must get an inside tip on this dough and that he takes an unfair advantage of the situation.

"But," Sam the Gonoph says, "I am not looking sored up at this time because of Society Max, although of course it is well-known to one and all that I am under oath to knock his ears down the first time I catch up with him. As a matter of fact, I do not as much as think of Society Max for a year or more, although I hear he deserts poor Sonia out in Cincinnati after spending her dough and leading her a dog's life, including a few offhand pastings, not that I am claiming Sonia may not need a pasting now and then.

"What I am looking sored up about," Sam says, "is because I must get up into Connecticut tomorrow to a spot that is called New London to dispose of a line of merchandise."

"Why, Sam," I say, "what can be doing in such a place?"

"Oh," Sam says, "a large boat race is coming up between the Harvards and the Yales. It comes up at New London every year, and is quite an interesting event from what I read in the papers about it, but the reason I am sored up about going tomorrow is because I wish to spend the week-end on my farm in New Jersey to see how my onions are doing. Since I buy this farm in New Jersey, I can scarcely wait to get over there on week-ends to watch my onions grow.

"But," Sam the Gonoph says, "this is an extra large boat race this year, and I am in possession of many choice duckets, and am sure to make plenty of black ink for myself, and business before pleasure is what I always say. By the way," Sam says, "do you ever see a boat race?"

Well, I say that the only boat races I ever see are those that come off around the race tracks, such a race being a race that is all fixed up in advance, and some of them are pretty raw, if you ask me, and I am by no means in favor of things of this kind unless I am in, but Sam the Gonoph says these races are by no manner of means the same thing as the boat races he is talking about.

"I never personally witness one myself," Sam says, "but the way I understand it is a number of the Harvards and the Yales, without any clothes on, get in row boats and row, and row, and row until their tongues hang out, and they are all half dead. Why they tucker themselves out in this fashion I do not know and," Sam says, "I am too old to start trying to find out why these college guys do a lot of things to themselves.

"But," Sam says, "boat racing is a wonderful sport, and I always have a nice trade at New London, Conn., and if you wish to accompany me and Benny South Street and Liver-lips and maybe collect a few bobs for yourself, you are as welcome as the flowers in May."

So there I am in front of the Mohican Hotel in New Lon-

don, Conn., with Sam the Gonoph and Benny South Street
and old Liverlips, who are Sam the Gonoph's best hustlers,
and all around and about is a very interesting sight, to be
sure, as large numbers of the Harvards and the Yales are
passing in and out of the hotel and walking up and down
and back and forth, and making very merry, one way and
another.

Well, after we are hustling our duckets for a couple of
hours and it is coming on noon, Benny South Street goes
into the hotel lobby to buy some cigarettes, and by and by
he comes out looking somewhat excited, and states as
follows:

"Say," Benny says, "there's a guy inside with his hands
full of money offering to lay 3 to 1 that the Yales win the
boat race. He says he has fifteen G's cash with him to wager
at the price stated."

"Are there any takers?" Sam the Gonoph asks.

"No, not many," Benny says, "From all I hear, the Yales
figure. In fact, all the handicappers I speak with have them
on top, so the Harvards do not care for any part of the guy's
play. But," Benny says, "there he is offering 3 to 1."

"Three to one?" Sam the Gonoph says, as if he is mentioning these terms to himself. "Three to one, eh? It is a
nice price."

"It is a lovely price," old Liverlips puts in.

Well, Sam the Gonoph stands there as if he is thinking,
and Benny South Street seems to be thinking, too, and even
old Liverlips seems to be thinking, and by and by I even
find myself thinking, and finally Sam the Gonoph says like
this:

"I do not know anything about boat races," Sam says,
"and the Yales may figure as you say, but nothing between
human beings is 1 to 3. In fact," Sam the Gonoph says, "I
long ago come to the conclusion that all life is 6 to 5 against.
And anyway," he says, "how can anybody let such odds as

these get away from them? I think I will take a small nibble at this proposition. What about you, Benny?"

"I will also nibble," Benny South Street says. "I will never forgive myself in this world if I let this inviting offer go and it turns out the Harvards win."

Well, we all go into the hotel lobby, and there is a big, gray-haired guy in a white cap and white pants standing in the center of a bunch of other guys, and he has money in both hands. I hear somebody say he is one of the real old-time Yales, and he is speaking in a loud voice as follows:

"Why," he says, "what is the matter, Harvards, are you cowards, or are you just broke? If you are broke, I will take your markers and let you pay me on the installment plan. But," he says, "bet me. That is all, just bet me."

Personally, I have a notion to let on I am one of the Harvards and slip the guy a nice marker, but I am afraid he may request some identification and I do not have anything on me to prove I am a college guy, so I stand back and watch Sam the Gonoph shove his way through the crowd with a couple of C notes in his hand, and Benny South Street is right behind him.

"I will take a small portion of the Harvards at the market," Sam the Gonoph says, as he offers the gray-haired guy his dough.

"Thank you, my friend," the guy says, "but I do not think we are acquainted," he says. "Who do you wish to hold the stakes?"

"You hold them yourself, Mr. Campbell," Sam the Gonoph says. "I know you, although you do not know me, and I will gladly trust you with my dough. Furthermore, my friend here who also wishes a portion of the Harvards, will trust you."

So the gray-haired guy says that both Sam the Gonoph and Benny South Street are on at 3 to 1, and thanks again to them, at that, and when we get outside, Sam explains that

he recognizes the guy as nobody but Mr. Hammond Campbell, who is a very important party in every respect and
who has more dough than Uncle Sam has bad debts. In fact,
Sam the Gonoph seems to feel that he is greatly honored in
getting to bet with Mr. Hammond Campbell, although from
the way Mr. Campbell takes their dough, I figure he thinks
that the pleasure is all his.

Well, we go on hustling our duckets but neither Sam the
Gonoph nor Benny South Street seem to have much heart
in their work, and every now and then I see one or the other
slip into the hotel lobby, and it comes out that they are still
nibbling at the 3 to 1, and finally I slip in myself and take a
little teensy nibble for twenty bobs myself, because the way
I look at it, anything that is good enough for Sam the
Gonoph is good enough for me.

Now Sam the Gonoph always carries quite a little ready
money on his body, and nobody will deny that Sam will
send it along if he likes a proposition, and by and by he is
down for a G on the Harvards, and Benny South Street has
four C's going for him, and there is my double saw, and even
old Liverlips weakens and goes for a pound note, and ordinarily Liverlips will not bet a pound that he is alive.

Furthermore, Mr. Hammond Campbell says we are about
the only guys in town that do bet him and that we ought to
get degrees off the Harvards for our loyalty to them, but of
course what we are really loyal to is the 3 to 1. Finally, Mr.
Campbell says he has to go to lunch, but that if we feel like
betting him any more we can find him on board his yacht,
the Hibiscus, out in the river, and maybe he will boost the
price up to 3½ to 1.

So I go into the hotel and get a little lunch myself, and
when I am coming out a nice-looking young doll who is
walking along in front of me accidentally drops her poke
from under her arm, and keeps right on walking. Naturally,
I pick it up, but several parties who are standing around in

the lobby see me do it, so I call to the young doll and when she turns around I hand her the poke, and she is very grateful to me, to be sure. In fact, she thanks me several times, though once will do, and then all of a sudden she says to me like this:

"Pardon me," the young doll says, "but are you not one of the gentlemen I see wagering with my papa that the Harvards will win the boat race?"

"Yes," I say, "and what is more, we may keep on wagering him. In fact," I say, "a friend of mine by the name of Sam the Gonoph is just now contemplating wiring home for another G to accept your papa's generous offer of 3½ to 1."

"Oh," the young doll says, "do not do it. You are only throwing your money away. The Harvards have no chance whatever of winning the boat race. My papa is never wrong on boat races. I only wish he is today."

And with this she sits down in a chair in the lobby and begins crying boo-hoo until her mascara is running down her cheeks, and naturally I am greatly embarrassed by this situation, as I am afraid somebody may come along and think maybe she is my step-child and that I am just after chastising her.

"You see," the young doll says, "a boy I like a very, very great deal belongs to the Harvards' crew and when I tell him a couple of weeks ago that my papa says the Yales are bound to win, he grows very angry and says what does my papa know about it, and who is my papa but an old money-bags, anyway, and to the dickens with my papa. Then when I tell him my papa always knows about these things, Quentin grows still angrier, and we quarrel and he says all right, if the Harvards lose he will never, never, never see me again as long as he lives. And Quentin is a very obstinate and unreasonable boy, and life is very sad for me."

Well, who comes along about now but Sam the Gonoph

and naturally he is somewhat surprised by the scene that is presented to his eyes, so I explain to him, and Sam is greatly touched and very sympathetic, for one thing about Sam is he is very tender-hearted when it comes to dolls who are in trouble.

"Well," Sam says, "I will certainly be greatly pleased to see the Harvards win the boat race myself, and in fact," he says, "I am just making a few cautious inquiries around here and there to see if there is any chance of stiffening a couple of the Yales, so we can have a little help in the race.

"But," Sam says, "one great trouble with these college propositions is they are always leveling, though I cannot see why it is necessary. Anyway," he says, "it looks as if we cannot hope to do any business with the Yales, but you dry your eyes, little miss, and maybe old Sam can think up something."

At this the young doll stops her bawling and I am very glad of it, as there is nothing I loathe and despise so much as a doll bawling, and she looks up at Sam with a wet smile and says to him like this:

"Oh, do you really think you can help the Harvards win the boat race?"

Well, naturally Sam the Gonoph is not in a position to make any promises on this point, but he is such a guy as will tell a doll in distress anything whatever if he thinks it will give her a little pleasure for a minute, so he replies as follows:

"Why, who knows?" Sam says. "Who knows, to be sure? But anyway do not bawl any more, and old Sam will give this matter further consideration."

And with this Sam pats the young doll on the back so hard he pats all the breath out of her and she cannot bawl any more even if she wishes to, and she gets up and goes away looking very happy, but before she goes she says:

"Well, I hear somebody say that from the way you gentlemen are betting on the Harvards you must know something and," she says, "I am very glad I have the courage to talk to you. It will be a wonderful favor to Quentin and me if you help the Harvards win, even though it costs my papa money. Love is more than gold," she says.

Personally, I consider it very wrong for Sam the Gonoph to be holding out hope to a young doll that he is unable to guarantee, but Sam says he does not really promise anything and that he always figures if he can bring a little joy into any life, no matter how, he is doing a wonderful deed, and that anyway we will never see the young doll again, and furthermore, what of it?

Well, I cannot think what of it just offhand, and anyway I am glad to be rid of the young doll, so we go back to disposing of the duckets we have left.

Now the large boat race between the Harvards and the Yales takes place in the early evening, and when it comes on time for the race one and all seem to be headed in the direction of the river, including all the young guys with the stir haircuts, and many beautiful young dolls wearing blue and red flowers, and old guys in sports pants and flat straw hats, and old dolls who walk as if their feet hurt them, and the chances are they do, at that.

Well, nothing will do Sam the Gonoph but we must see the boat race, too, so we go down to the railroad station to take the very train for which we are hustling duckets all day, but by the time we get there the race train is pulling out, so Benny South Street says the next best thing for us to do is to go down to the dock and hire a boat to take us out on the river.

But when we get to the dock, it seems that all the boats around are hired and are already out on the river, but there is an old pappy guy with a chin whisker sitting in a rickety-looking little motor boat at the dock, and this old guy says he will take us out where we can get a good peek at the race for a buck apiece.

Personally, I do not care for the looks of the boat, and neither does Benny South Street nor old Liverlips, but Sam the Gonoph is so anxious to see the race that finally we all get into the boat and the old guy heads her out into the river, which seems to be filled with all kinds of boats decorated with flags and one thing and another, and with guys and dolls walking back and forth on these boats.

Anybody must admit that it is quite a sight, and I am commencing to be glad I am present, especially when Benny South Street tells me that these guys and dolls on the boats are very fine people and worth plenty of money. Furthermore, Benny South Street points out many big white boats that he says are private yachts, and he tells me that what it costs to keep up these private yachts is a sin and a shame when you start to figure out the number of people in the world who are looking for breakfast money. But then Benny South Street is always talking of things of this kind, and sometimes I think maybe he is a dynamiter at heart.

We go putt-putting along under a big bridge and into a sort of lane of boats, and Benny South Street says we are now at the finish line of the large boat race and that the Harvards and the Yales row down this lane from away up the river, and that it is here that they have their tongues hanging out and are nearly all half dead.

Well, it seems that we are in the way, because guys start yelling at us from different boats and shaking their fists at us, and it is a good thing for some of them that they are not close enough for us to get a pop at them, but the old pappy guy keeps the motor boat putt-putting and sliding in and out among the boats until we come to a spot that he says is about a hundred yards above the finish and a great spot to see the best part of the race.

We are slipping alongside of a big white boat that Benny South Street says is a private yacht and that has a little set of stair steps running down one side almost into the water, when all of a sudden Sam the Gonoph notices his feet are wet, and he looks down and sees that the motor boat is half full of water and furthermore that the boat is commencing to sink.

Now this is quite a predicament, and naturally Sam the Gonoph lets out a slight beef and wishes to know what kind of accommodations we are paying for, anyway, and then the old pappy guy notices the water and the sinking, and he seems somewhat put out about the matter, especially as the water is getting up around his chin whiskers.

So he steers the boat up against the stair steps on the yacht and all of us, including the old pappy guy, climb out onto the stairs just as the motor boat gives a last snort and sinks from sight. The last I see of the motor boat is the hind end sticking up in the air a second before it disappears, and I remember the name that is painted on the hind end. The name is Baby Mine.

Well, Sam the Gonoph leads the way up the stairs to the deck of the yacht, and who meets us at the head of the stairs but Mr. Hammond Campbell in person, and who is right behind him but the young doll I am talking with in the hotel lobby, and at first Mr. Campbell thinks that we come out to his yacht to pick up a little of his 3½ to 1, and he is greatly disappointed when he learns that such is by no means our purpose and that we are merely the victims of disaster.

As for the young doll, whose name turns out to be Clarice, she gazes at Sam the Gonoph and me with her eyes full of questions, but we do not get a chance to talk to her as things begin occurring at once.

There are quite a number of guys and dolls on the yacht, and it is a very gay scene to be sure, as they walk around laughing and chatting, when all of a sudden I see Sam the Gonoph staring at a guy and doll who are leaning over the rail talking very earnestly and paying no attention to what is going on around and about them.

The guy is a tall, dark-complected young guy with a little mustache, and he is wearing white flannel pants and a blue coat with brass buttons, and white shoes, and he is a very foreign-looking guy, to be sure. The doll is not such a young doll, being maybe around middle age, giving her a few points the best of it, but she is a fine-looking doll, at that, especially if you like dolls with gray hair, which personally I am not so much in favor of.

I am close enough to Sam the Gonoph to hear him breathing heavily as he stares at this guy and doll, and finally the dark-complected young guy looks up and sees Sam and at the same instant Sam starts for him, and as Sam starts the young guy turns and takes to running in the other direction from Sam along the deck, but before he takes to running I can see that it is nobody but Society Max.

Naturally, I am somewhat surprised at seeing Society Max at a boat race between the Harvards and the Yales, because I never figure him such a guy as will be interested in matters of this kind, although I remember that Society Max is once a life guard at Coney Island, and in fact it is at Coney Island that Sonia gets her first peek at his shape and is lost forever to Sam the Gonoph, so I get to thinking that maybe Society Max is fond of all aquatic events.

Now of course the spectacle of Sam the Gonoph pursuing Society Max along the deck is quite surprising to one and all, except Benny South Street and old Liverlips and myself, who are aware of the reason, and Mr. Hammond Campbell wishes to know what kind of game they are playing, especially after they round the deck twice, with Society Max showing much foot, but none of us feel called on to explain. Finally the other guys and dolls on the yacht enter into the spirit of the chase, even though they do not know what it is all about, and they shout encouragement to both Sam the Gonoph and Society Max, although Max is really the favorite.

There is no doubt but what Society Max is easily best in a sprint, especially as Sam the Gonoph's pants legs are wet from the sinking motor boat and he is carrying extra weight, but Sam is a wonderful doer over a route, and on the third trip around the deck, anybody can see that he is cutting down Max's lead.

Well, every time they pass the gray-haired doll that Society Max is talking to when we come on the yacht she asks what is the matter, Max, and where are you going, Max, and other questions that seem trivial at such a time, but Max never has an opportunity to answer, as he has to save all his breath to keep ahead of Sam the Gonoph, and in fact Sam the Gonoph stops talking, too, and just keeps plugging along with a very determined expression on his puss.

Well, now all the whistles on the boats in the river around us start blowing, and it seems this is because the large boat race between the Harvards and the Yales is now approaching the finish, and one and all on our yacht rush to the side of the yacht to see it, forgetting about everything else, and the side they rush to is the same side the stair steps are on.

But I am too much interested in Sam the Gonoph's pursuit of Society Max to pay any attention to the boat race, and as they come around the deck the fifth or sixth time, I can see that Sam will have Max in the next few jumps, when all of a sudden Society Max runs right down the stairs and dives off into the river, and he does it so fast that nobody seems to notice him except Sam the Gonoph and me and the gray-haired doll, and I am the only one that notices her fall in a big faint on the deck as Max dives.

Naturally, this is not a time to be bothering with fainting dolls, so Sam the Gonoph and me run to the side of the yacht and watch the water to see where Society Max comes up, but he does not appear at once, and I remember hearing he is a wonderful diver when he is a life guard, so I figure he is going to keep under water until he is pretty sure he is too far away for Sam the Gonoph to hit him with anything, such as maybe a slug from a Betsy.

Of course Sam the Gonoph does not happen to have a Betsy on him, but Society Max can scarcely be expected to know this, because the chances are he remembers that Sam often has such an article in his pants pocket when he is around New York, so I suppose Society Max plays it as safe as possible.

Anyway, we do not see hide or hair of him, and in the meantime the excitement over the large boat race between the Harvards and the Yales is now so terrific that I forget Society Max and try to get a peek at it.

But all I remember is seeing the young doll, Clarice, kissing Sam the Gonoph smack-dab on his homely puss, and jumping up and down in considerable glee, and stating that she knows all along that Sam will figure out some way for the Harvards to win, although she does not know yet how he does it, and hearing Mr. Hammond Campbell using language even worse than Sam the Gonoph employs when he is pursuing Society Max, and saying he never sees such a this-and-that boat race in all his born days.

Then I get to thinking about the gray-haired doll, and I go over and pick her up and she is still about two-thirds out and is saying to herself, as follows:

"Max, oh, my dear, dear Max."

Well, by and by Mr. Hammond Campbell takes Sam
the Gonoph into a room on the yacht and pays him what
is coming to all of us on the race, and then he takes to
asking about Society Max, and when Sam the Gonoph
explains how Max is a terrible fink and what he does to
Sonia and all, Mr. Hammond Campbell hands Sam five
large G's extra, and states to him as follows:

"This," he says, "is for preventing my sister, Emma,
from making a fool of herself. She picks this Max up
somewhere in Europe and he puts himself away with her
as a Russian nobleman, and she is going to marry him next
week, although from what you tell me it will be bigamy
on his part. By the way," Mr. Hammond Campbell says,
"not that it makes any difference, but I wonder whatever
becomes of the guy?"

I am wondering this somewhat myself, not that I really
care what becomes of Society Max, but I do not find out
until later in the evening when I am at the Western Union
office in New London, Conn., sending a telegram for Sam
the Gonoph to the guy who runs his farm in New Jersey
telling the guy to be sure and watch the onions, and I
hear a newspaper scribe talking about the large boat race.

"Yes," the newspaper scribe says, "the Yales are leading
by a boat length up to the last hundred yards and going
easy, and they seem to be an absolute cinch to win, when
No. 6 man in their boat hits something in the water and
breaks his oar, throwing the rest of the crew out of kilter
long enough for the Harvards to slip past and win. It is
the most terrible upset of the dope in history," he says.

"Now," the scribe says, "of course a broken oar is not
unheard of in a boat race, but what No. 6 says he hits is
a guy's head which pops out of the water all of a sudden
right alongside the Yales' boat, and which disappears again
as the oar hits it.

"Personally," the scribe says, "I will say No. 6 is seeing

things but for the fact that a Coast Guard boat which is laying away down the river below the finish just reports that it picks up a guy out of the river who seems to be alive and all right except he has a lump on his noggin a foot high."

I do not see Sam the Gonoph again until it comes on fall, when I run into him in Mindy's restaurant on Broadway, and Sam says to me like this:

"Say," he says, "do you remember what a hit I make with the little doll because she thinks I have something to do with the Harvards winning the large boat race? Well," Sam the Gonoph says, "I just get a note from her asking me if I can do anything about a football game that the Harvards have coming up with the Dartmouths next month."

Undertaker Song

Now THIS STORY I am going to tell you is about the game of
football, a very healthy pastime for the young, and a great
character builder from all I hear, but to get around to this
game of football I am compelled to bring in some most
obnoxious characters, beginning with a guy by the name
of Joey Perhaps, and all I can conscientiously say about
Joey is you can have him.

It is a matter of maybe four years since I see this Joey
Perhaps until I notice him on a train going to Boston, Mass.,
one Friday afternoon. He is sitting across from me in the
dining-car, where I am enjoying a small portion of baked
beans and brown bread, and he looks over to me once,
but he does not rap to me.

There is no doubt but what Joey Perhaps is bad company, because the last I hear of him he is hollering copper
on a guy by the name of Jack Ortega, and as a result of
Joey Perhaps hollering copper, this Jack Ortega is taken
to the city of Ossining, N. Y., and placed in an electric

chair, and given a very, very, very severe shock in the seat of his pants.

It is something about plugging a most legitimate business guy in the city of Rochester, N. Y., when Joey Perhaps and Jack Ortega are engaged together in a little enterprise to shake the guy down, but the details of this transaction are dull, sordid, and quite uninteresting, except that Joey Perhaps turns state's evidence and announces that Jack Ortega fires the shot which cools the legitimate guy off, for which service he is rewarded with only a small stretch.

I must say for Joey Perhaps that he looks good, and he is very well dressed, but then Joey is always particular about clothes, and he is quite a handy guy with the dolls in his day and, to tell the truth, many citizens along Broadway are by no means displeased when Joey is placed in the state institution, because they are generally pretty uneasy about their dolls when he is around.

Naturally, I am wondering why Joey Perhaps is on this train going to Boston, Mass., but for all I know maybe he is wondering the same thing about me, although personally I am making no secret about it. The idea is I am en route to Boston, Mass., to see a contest of skill and science that is to take place there this very Friday night between a party by the name of Lefty Ledoux and another party by the name of Mickey McCoy, who are very prominent middleweights.

Now ordinarily I will not go around the corner to see a contest of skill and science between Lefty Ledoux and Mickey McCoy, or anybody else, as far as that is concerned, unless they are using blackjacks and promise to hurt each other, but I am the guest on this trip of a party by the name of Meyer Marmalade, and I will go anywhere to see anything if I am a guest.

This Meyer Marmalade is really a most superior character, who is called Meyer Marmalade because nobody can ever think of his last name, which is something like Marmaladowski, and he is known far and wide for the way he likes to make bets on any sporting proposition, such as baseball, or horse races, or ice hockey, or contests of skill and science, and especially contests of skill and science.

So he wishes to be present at this contest in Boston, Mass., between Lefty Ledoux and Mickey McCoy to have a nice wager on McCoy, as he has reliable information that McCoy's manager, a party by the name of Koons, has both judges and the referee in the satchel.

If there is one thing Meyer Marmalade dearly loves, it is to have a bet on a contest of skill and science of this nature, and so he is going to Boston, Mass. But Meyer Marmalade is such a guy as loathes and despises traveling all alone, so when he offers to pay my expenses if I will go along to keep him company, naturally I am pleased to accept, as I have nothing on of importance at the moment and, in fact, I do not have anything on of importance for the past ten years.

I warn Meyer Marmalade in advance that if he is looking to take anything off of anybody in Boston, Mass., he may as well remain at home, because everybody knows that statistics show that the percentage of anything being taken off of the citizens of Boston, Mass., is less per capita than anywhere else in the United States, especially when it comes to contests of skill and science, but Meyer Marmalade says this is the first time they ever had two judges and a referee running against the statistics, and he is very confident.

Well, by and by I go from the dining-car back to my seat in another car, where Meyer Marmalade is sitting reading a detective magazine, and I speak of seeing Joey Perhaps to him. But Meyer Marmalade does not seem greatly interested, although he says to me like this:

"Joey Perhaps, eh?" he says. "A wrong gee. A dead

wrong gee. He must just get out. I run into the late Jack Ortega's brother, young Ollie, in Mindy's restaurant last week," Meyer Marmalade says, "and when we happen to get to talking of wrong gees, naturally Joey Perhaps' name comes up, and Ollie remarks he understands Joey Perhaps is about due out, and that he will be pleased to see him some day. Personally," Meyer Marmalade says, "I do not care for any part of Joey Perhaps at any price."

Now our car is loaded with guys and dolls who are going to Boston, Mass., to witness a large football game between the Harvards and the Yales at Cambridge, Mass., the next day, and the reason I know this is because they are talking of nothing else.

So this is where the football starts getting into this story.

One old guy that I figure must be a Harvard from the way he talks seems to have a party all his own, and he is getting so much attention from one and all in the party that I figure he must be a guy of some importance, because they laugh heartily at his remarks, and although I listen very carefully to everything he says he does not sound so very humorous to me.

He is a heavy-set guy with a bald head and a deep voice, and anybody can see that he is such a guy as is accustomed to plenty of authority. I am wondering out loud to Meyer Marmalade who the guy can be, and Meyer Marmalade states as follows:

"Why," he says, "he is nobody but Mr. Phillips Randolph, who makes the automobiles. He is the sixth richest guy in this country," Meyer says, "or maybe it is the seventh. Anyway, he is pretty well up with the front runners. I spot his monicker on his suitcase, and then I ask the porter, to make sure. It is a great honor for us to be traveling with Mr. Phillips Randolph," Meyer says, "because of him being such a public benefactor and having so much dough, especially having so much dough."

Well, naturally everybody knows who Mr. Phillips Randolph is, and I am surprised that I do not recognize his face myself from seeing it so often in the newspapers alongside the latest model automobile his factory turns out, and I am as much pleasured up as Meyer Marmalade over being in the same car with Mr. Phillips Randolph.

He seems to be a good-natured old guy, at that, and he is having a grand time, what with talking, and laughing, and taking a dram now and then out of a bottle, and when old Crip McGonnigle comes gimping through the car selling his football souvenirs, such as red and blue feathers, and little badges and pennants, and one thing and another, as Crip is doing around the large football games since Hickory Slim is a two-year-old, Mr. Phillips Randolph stops him and buys all of Crip's red feathers, which have a little white H on them to show they are for the Harvards.

Then Mr. Phillips Randolph distributes the feathers around among his party, and the guys and dolls stick them in their hats, or pin them on their coats, but he has quite a number of feathers left over, and about this time who comes through the car but Joey Perhaps, and Mr. Phillips Randolph steps out in the aisle and stops Joey and politely offers him a red feather, and speaks as follows:

"Will you honor us by wearing our colors?"

Well, of course Mr. Phillips Randolph is only full of good spirits, and means no harm whatever, and the guys and dolls in his party laugh heartily as if they consider his action very funny, but maybe because they laugh, and maybe because he is just naturally a hostile guy, Joey Perhaps knocks Mr. Phillips Randolph's hand down, and says like this:

"Get out of my way," Joey says. "Are you trying to make a sucker out of somebody?"

Personally, I always claim that Joey Perhaps has a right to reject the red feather, because for all I know he may prefer a blue feather, which means the Yales, but what I say is he does not need to be so impolite to an old guy such as Mr. Phillips Randolph, although of course Joey has no way of knowing at this time about Mr. Phillips Randolph having so much dough.

Anyway, Mr. Phillips Randolph stands staring at Joey as if he is greatly startled, and the chances are he is, at that, for the chances are nobody ever speaks to him in such a manner in all his life, and Joey Perhaps also stands there a minute staring back at Mr. Phillips Randolph, and finally Joey speaks as follows:

"Take a good peek," Joey Perhaps says. "Maybe you will remember me if you ever see me again."

"Yes," Mr. Phillips Randolph says, very quiet. "Maybe I will. They say I have a good memory for faces. I beg your pardon for stopping you, sir. It is all in fun, but I am sorry," he says.

Then Joey Perhaps goes on, and he does not seem to notice Meyer Marmalade and me sitting there in the car, and Mr. Phillips Randolph sits down, and his face is redder than somewhat, and all the joy is gone out of him, and out of his party, too. Personally, I am very sorry Joey Perhaps comes along, because I figure Mr. Phillips Randolph will give me one of his spare feathers, and I will consider it a wonderful keepsake.

But now there is not much more talking, and no laughing whatever in Mr. Phillips Randolph's party, and he just sits there as if he is thinking, and for all I know he may be thinking that there ought to be a law against a guy speaking so disrespectfully to a guy with all his dough as Joey Perhaps speaks to him.

Well, the contest of skill and science between Lefty Ledoux and Mickey McCoy turns out to be something of a disappointment, and, in fact, it is a stinkeroo, because there is little skill and no science whatever in it, and by the fourth round the customers are scuffling their feet, and saying throw these bums out, and making other derogatory remarks, and furthermore it seems that this Koons does not have either one of the judges, or even as much as the referee, in the satchel, and Ledoux gets the duke by unanimous vote of the officials.

So Meyer Marmalade is out a couple of C's, which is all he can wager at the ringside, because it seems that nobody in Boston, Mass., cares a cuss about who wins the contest, and Meyer is much disgusted with life, and so am I, and we go back to the Copley Plaza Hotel, where we are stopping, and sit down in the lobby to meditate on the injustice of everything.

Well, the lobby is a scene of gayety, as it seems there are a number of football dinners and dances going on in the hotel, and guys and dolls in evening clothes are all around and about, and the dolls are so young and beautiful that I get to thinking that this is not such a bad old world, after all, and even Meyer Marmalade begins taking notice.

All of a sudden, a very, very beautiful young doll who is about 40 per cent in and 60 per cent out of an evening gown walks right up to us sitting there, and holds out her hand to me, and speaks as follows:

"Do you remember me?"

Naturally, I do not remember her, but naturally I am not going to admit it, because it is never my policy to discourage any doll who wishes to strike up an acquaintance with me, which is what I figure this doll is trying to do; then I see that she is nobody but Doria Logan, one of the prettiest dolls that ever hits Broadway, and about the same time Meyer Marmalade also recognizes her.

Doria changes no little since last I see her, which is quite some time back, but there is no doubt the change is for the better, because she is once a very rattle-headed young doll, and now she seems older, and quieter, and even prettier than ever. Naturally, Meyer Marmalade and I are glad to see her looking so well, and we ask her how are tricks, and what is the good word, and all this and that, and finally Doria Logan states to us as follows:

"I am in great trouble," Doria says. "I am in terrible trouble, and you are the first ones I see that I can talk to about it."

Well, at this, Meyer Marmalade begins to tuck in somewhat, because he figures it is the old lug coming up, and Meyer Marmalade is not such a guy as will go for the lug from a doll unless he gets something more than a story. But I can see Doria Logan is in great earnest.

"Do you remember Joey Perhaps?" she says.

"A wrong gee," Meyer Marmalade says. "A dead wrong gee."

"I not only remember Joey Perhaps," I say, "but I see him on the train today."

"Yes," Doria says, "he is here in town. He hunts me up only a few hours ago. He is here to do me great harm. He is here to finish ruining my life."

"A wrong gee," Meyer Marmalade puts in again. "Always a 100 per cent wrong gee."

Then Doria Logan gets us to go with her to a quiet corner of the lobby, and she tells us a strange story, as follows, and also to wit:

It seems that she is once tangled up with Joey Perhaps, which is something I never know before, and neither does Meyer Marmalade, and, in fact, the news shocks us quite some. It is back in the days when she is just about sixteen and is in the chorus of Earl Carroll's Vanities, and I remember well what a standout she is for looks, to be sure.

Naturally, at sixteen, Doria is quite a chump doll, and does not know which way is south, or what time it is, which is the way all dolls at sixteen are bound to be, and she has no idea what a wrong gee Joey Perhaps is, as he is goodlooking and young, and seems very romantic, and is always speaking of love and one thing and another.

Well, the upshot of it all is the upshot of thousands of other cases since chump dolls commence coming to Broadway, and the first thing she knows, Doria Logan finds herself mixed up with a very bad character, and does not know what to do about it.

By and by, Joey Perhaps commences mistreating her no little, and finally he tries to use her in some nefarious schemes of his, and of course everybody along Broadway knows that most of Joey's schemes are especially nefarious, because Joey is on the shake almost since infancy.

Well, one day Doria says to herself that if this is love, she has all she can stand, and she hauls off and runs away from Joey Perhaps. She goes back to her people, who live in the city of Cambridge, Mass., which is the same place where the Harvards have their college, and she goes there because she does not know of any other place to go.

It seems that Doria's people are poor, and Doria goes to a business school and learns to be a stenographer, and she is working for a guy in the real estate dodge by the name of Poopnoodle, and doing all right for herself, and in the meantime she hears that Joey Perhaps gets sent away, so she figures her troubles are all over as far as he is concerned.

Now Doria Logan goes along quietly through life, working for Mr. Poopnoodle, and never thinking of love, or anything of a similar nature, when she meets up with a young guy who is one of the Harvards, and who is maybe twenty-one years old, and is quite a football player, and where Doria meets up with this guy is in a drug store over a banana split.

Well, the young Harvard takes quite a fancy to Doria and, in fact, he is practically on fire about her, but by this time Doria is going on twenty, and is no longer a chump doll, and she has no wish to get tangled up in love again.

In fact, whenever she thinks of Joey Perhaps, Doria takes to hating guys in general, but somehow she cannot seem to get up a real good hate on the young Harvard, because, to hear her tell it, he is handsome, and noble, and has wonderful ideals.

Now as time goes on, Doria finds she is growing pale, and is losing her appetite, and cannot sleep, and this worries her no little, as she is always a first-class feeder, and finally she comes to the conclusion that what ails her is that she is in love with the young Harvard, and can scarcely live without him, so she admits as much to him one night when the moon is shining on the Charles River, and everything is a dead cold setup for love.

Well, naturally, after a little offhand guzzling, which is quite permissible under the circumstances, the young guy wishes her to name the happy day, and Doria has half a notion to make it the following Monday, this being a Sunday night, but then she gets to thinking about her past with Joey Perhaps, and all, and she figures it will be bilking the young Harvard to marry him unless she has a small talk with him first about Joey, because she is well aware that many young guys may have some objection to wedding a doll with a skeleton in her closet, and especially a skeleton such as Joey Perhaps.

But she is so happy she does not wish to run the chance of spoiling everything by these narrations right away, so she keeps her trap closed about Joey, although she promises to marry the young Harvard when he gets out of college, which will be the following year, if he still insists, because Doria figures that by then she will be able to break the news to him about Joey very gradually, and gently, and especially gently.

Anyway, Doria says she is bound and determined to tell him before the wedding, even if he takes the wind on her as a consequence, and personally I claim this is very considerate of Doria, because many dolls never tell before the wedding, or even after. So Doria and the young Harvard are engaged, and great happiness prevails, when, all of a sudden, in pops Joey Perhaps.

It seems that Joey learns of Doria's engagement as soon as he gets out of the state institution, and he hastens to Boston, Mass., with an inside coat pocket packed with letters that Doria writes him long ago, and also a lot of pictures they have taken together, as young guys and dolls are bound to do, and while there is nothing much out of line about these letters and pictures, put them all together they spell a terrible pain in the neck to Doria at this particular time.

"A wrong gee," Meyer Marmalade says. "But," he says, "he is only going back to his old shakedown dodge, so all you have to do is to buy him off."

Well, at this, Doria Logan laughs one of these little short dry laughs that go "hah," and says like this:

"Of course he is looking to get bought off, but," she says, "where will I get any money to buy him off? I do not have a dime of my own, and Joey is talking large figures, because he knows my fiancé's papa has plenty. He wishes me to go to my fiancé and make him get the money off his papa, or he threatens to personally deliver the letters and pictures to my fiancé's papa.

"You can see the predicament I am in," Doria says, "and you can see what my fiancé's papa will think of me if he learns I am once mixed up with a blackmailer such as Joey Perhaps.

"Besides," Doria says, "it is something besides money with Joey Perhaps, and I am not so sure he will not double-cross me even if I can pay him his price. Joey Perhaps is very angry at me. I think," she says, "if he can spoil my happiness, it will mean more to him than money."

Well, Doria states that all she can think of when she is

talking to Joey Perhaps is to stall for time, and she tells Joey that, no matter what, she cannot see her fiancé until after the large football game between the Harvards and the Yales as he has to do a little football playing for the Harvards, and Joey asks her if she is going to see the game, and naturally she is.

And then Joey says he thinks he will look up a ticket speculator, and buy a ticket and attend the game himself, as he is very fond of football, and where will she be sitting, as he hopes and trusts he will be able to see something of her during the game, and this statement alarms Doria Logan no little, for who is she going with but her fiancé's papa, and a party of his friends, and she feels that there is no telling what Joey Perhaps may be up to.

She explains to Joey that she does not know exactly where she will be sitting, except that it will be on the Harvard's side of the field, but Joey is anxious for more details than this.

"In fact," Doria says, "he is most insistent, and he stands at my elbow while I call up Mr. Randolph at this very hotel, and he tells me the exact location of our seats. Then Joey says he will endeavor to get a seat as close to me as possible, and he goes away."

"What Mr. Randolph?" Meyer says. "Which Mr. Randolph?" he says. "You do not mean Mr. Phillips Randolph, by any chance, do you?"

"Why, to be sure," Doria says. "Do you know him?"

Naturally, from now on Meyer Marmalade gazes at Doria Logan with deep respect, and so do I, although by now she is crying a little, and I am by no means in favor of crying dolls. But while she is crying, Meyer Marmalade seems to be doing some more thinking, and finally he speaks as follows:

"Kindly see if you can recall these locations you speak of."

So here is where the football game comes in once more.

Only I regret to state that personally I do not witness this game, and the reason I do not witness it is because nobody wakes me up the next day in time for me to witness it, and the way I look at it, this is all for the best, as I am scarcely a football enthusiast.

So from now on the story belongs to Meyer Marmalade, and I will tell it to you as Meyer tells it to me.

It is a most exciting game (Meyer says). The place is full of people, and there are bands playing, and much cheering, and more lovely dolls than you can shake a stick at, although I do not believe there are any lovelier present than Doria Logan.

It is a good thing she remembers the seat locations, otherwise I will never find her, but there she is surrounded by some very nice-looking people, including Mr. Phillips Randolph, and there I am two rows back of Mr. Phillips Randolph, and the ticket spec I get my seat off of says he cannot understand why everybody wishes to sit near Mr. Phillips Randolph to-day when there are other seats just as good, and maybe better, on the Harvards' side.

So I judge he has other calls similar to mine for this location, and a sweet price he gets for it, too, and I judge that maybe at least one call is from Joey Perhaps, as I see Joey a couple of rows on back up of where I am sitting, but off to my left on an aisle, while I am almost in a direct line with Mr. Phillips Randolph.

To show you that Joey is such a guy as attracts attention, Mr. Phillips Randolph stands up a few minutes before the game starts, peering around and about to see who is present that he knows, and all of a sudden his eyes fall on Joey Perhaps, and then Mr. Phillips Randolph proves he has a good memory for faces, to be sure, for he states as follows:

"Why," he says, "there is the chap who rebuffs me so

churlishly on the train when I offer him our colors. Yes," he says, "I am sure it is the same chap."

Well, what happens in the football game is much pulling and hauling this way and that, and to and fro, between the Harvards and the Yales without a tally right down to the last five minutes of play, and then all of a sudden the Yales shove the football down to within about three-eighths of an inch of the Harvards' goal line.

At this moment quite some excitement prevails. Then the next thing anybody knows, the Yales outshove the Harvards, and now the game is over, and Mr. Phillips Randolph gets up out of his seat, and I hear Mr. Phillips Randolph say like this:

"Well," he says, "the score is not so bad as it might be, and it is a wonderful game, and," he says, "we seem to make one convert to our cause, anyway, for see who is wearing our colors."

And with this he points to Joey Perhaps, who is still sitting down, with people stepping around him and over him, and he is still smiling a little smile, and Mr. Phillips Randolph seems greatly pleased to see that Joey Perhaps has a big, broad crimson ribbon where he once wears his white silk muffler.

But the chances are Mr. Phillips Randolph will be greatly surprised if he knows that the crimson ribbon across Joey's bosom comes of Ollie Ortega planting a short knife in Joey's throat, or do I forget to mention before that Ollie Ortega is among those present?

I send for Ollie after I leave you last night, figuring he may love to see a nice football game. He arrives by plane this morning, and I am not wrong in my figuring. Ollie thinks the game is swell.

Well, personally, I will never forget this game, it is so exciting. Just after the tally comes off, all of a sudden, from the Yales in the stand across the field from the

Harvards, comes a long-drawn-out wail that sounds so mournful it makes me feel very sad, to be sure. It starts off something like Oh-oh-oh-oh-oh, with all the Yales Oh-oh-oh-oh-oh-ing at once, and I ask a guy next to me what it is all about.

"Why," the guy says, "it is the Yales' 'Undertaker Song.' They always sing it when they have the other guy licked. I am an old Yale myself, and I will now personally sing this song for you."

And with this the guy throws back his head, and opens his mouth wide and lets out a yowl like a wolf calling to its mate.

Well, I stop the guy, and tell him it is a very lovely song, to be sure, and quite appropriate all the way around, and then I hasten away from the football game without getting a chance to say good-by to Doria, although afterwards I mail her the package of letters and pictures that Ollie gets out of Joey Perhaps' inside coat pocket during the confusion that prevails when the Yales make their tally, and I hope and trust that she will think the crimson streaks across the package are just a little touch of color in honor of the Harvards.

But the greatest thing about the football game (Meyer Marmalade says) is I win two C's off of one of the Harvards sitting near me, so I am now practically even on my tip.

Breach of Promise

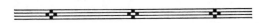

ONE DAY a certain party by the name of Judge Goldfobber, who is a lawyer by trade, sends word to me that he wishes me to call on him at his office in lower Broadway, and while ordinarily I do not care for any part of lawyers, it happens that Judge Goldfobber is a friend of mine, so I go to see him.

Of course Judge Goldfobber is not a judge, and never is a judge, and he is 100 to 1 in my line against ever being a judge, but he is called Judge because it pleases him, and everybody always wishes to please Judge Goldfobber, as he is one of the surest-footed lawyers in this town, and beats more tough beefs for different citizens than seems possible. He is a wonderful hand for keeping citizens from getting into the sneezer, and better than Houdini when it comes to getting them out of the sneezer after they are in.

Personally, I never have any use for the professional services of Judge Goldfobber, as I am a law-abiding citizen at all times, and am greatly opposed to guys who violate

the law, but I know the Judge from around and about for
many years. I know him from around and about the night
clubs, and other deadfalls, for Judge Goldfobber is such a
guy as loves to mingle with the public in these spots, as he
picks up much law business there, and sometimes a nice doll.

Well, when I call on Judge Goldfobber, he takes me into
his private office and wishes to know if I can think of a
couple of deserving guys who are out of employment, and
who will like a job of work, and if so, Judge Goldfobber
says, he can offer them a first-class position.

"Of course," Judge Goldfobber says, "it is not steady
employment, and in fact it is nothing but piece-work, but
the parties must be extremely reliable parties, who can be
depended on in a pinch. This is out-of-town work that requires tact, and," he says, "some nerve."

Well, I am about to tell Judge Goldfobber that I am no
employment agent, and go on about my business, because I
can tell from the way he says the parties must be parties who
can be depended on in a pinch, that a pinch is apt to come up
on the job any minute, and I do not care to steer any friends
of mine against a pinch.

But as I get up to go, I look out of Judge Goldfobber's
window, and I can see Brooklyn in the distance beyond the
river, and seeing Brooklyn I get to thinking of certain parties
over there that I figure must be suffering terribly from the
unemployment situation. I get to thinking of Harry the
Horse, and Spanish John and Little Isadore, and the reason
I figure they must be suffering from the unemployment situation is because if nobody is working and making any
money, there is nobody for them to rob, and if there is nobody for them to rob, Harry the Horse and Spanish John
and Little Isadore are just naturally bound to be feeling the
depression keenly.

Anyway, I finally mention the names of these parties to
Judge Goldfobber, and furthermore I speak well of their

reliability in a pinch, and of their nerve, although I cannot conscientiously recommend their tact, and Judge Goldfobber is greatly delighted, as he often hears of Harry the Horse, and Spanish John and Little Isadore.

He asks me for their addresses, but of course nobody knows exactly where Harry the Horse and Spanish John and Little Isadore live, because they do not live anywhere in particular. However, I tell him about a certain spot in Clinton Street where he may be able to get track of them, and then I leave Judge Goldfobber for fear he may wish me to take word to these parties, and if there is anybody in this whole world I will not care to take word to, or to have any truck with in any manner, shape, or form, it is Harry the Horse, and Spanish John and Little Isadore.

Well, I do not hear anything more of the matter for several weeks, but one evening when I am in Mindy's restaurant on Broadway enjoying a little cold borscht, which is a most refreshing matter in hot weather such as is going on at the time, who bobs up but Harry the Horse, and Spanish John and Little Isadore, and I am so surprised to see them that some of my cold borscht goes down the wrong way, and I almost choke to death.

However, they seem quite friendly, and in fact Harry the Horse pounds me on the back to keep me from choking, and while he pounds so hard that he almost caves in my spine, I consider it a most courteous action, and when I am able to talk again, I say to him as follows:

"Well, Harry," I say, "it is a privilege and a pleasure to see you again, and I hope and trust you will all join me in some cold borscht, which you will find very nice, indeed."

"No," Harry says, "we do not care for any cold borscht. We are looking for Judge Goldfobber. Do you see Judge Goldfobber round and about lately?"

Well, the idea of Harry the Horse and Spanish John and Little Isadore looking for Judge Goldfobber sounds somewhat alarming to me, and I figure maybe the job Judge Goldfobber gives them turns out bad and they wish to take Judge Goldfobber apart, but the next minute Harry says to me like this:

"By the way," he says, "we wish to thank you for the job of work you throw our way. Maybe some day we will be able to do as much for you. It is a most interesting job," Harry says, "and while you are snuffing your cold borscht I will give you the details, so you will understand why we wish to see Judge Goldfobber."

It turns out (Harry the Horse says) that the job is not for Judge Goldfobber personally, but for a client of his, and who is this client but Mr. Jabez Tuesday, the rich millionaire, who owns the Tuesday string of one-arm joints where many citizens go for food and wait on themselves. Judge Goldfobber comes to see us in Brooklyn in person, and sends me to see Mr. Jabez Tuesday with a letter of introduction, so Mr. Jabez Tuesday can explain what he wishes me to do, because Judge Goldfobber is too smart a guy to be explaining such matters to me himself.

In fact, for all I know maybe Judge Goldfobber is not aware of what Mr. Jabez Tuesday wishes me to do, although I am willing to lay a little 6 to 5 that Judge Goldfobber does not think Mr. Jabez Tuesday wishes to hire me as a cashier in any of his one-arm joints.

Anyway, I go to see Mr. Tuesday at a Fifth Avenue hotel where he makes his home, and where he has a very swell layout of rooms, and I am by no means impressed with Mr. Tuesday, as he hems and haws quite a bit before he tells me the nature of the employment he has in mind for me. He is a little guy, somewhat dried out, with a bald head, and a small mouser on his upper lip, and he wears specs, and seems somewhat nervous.

Well, it takes him some time to get down to cases, and tell me what is eating him, and what he wishes to do, and then it all sounds very simple, indeed, and in fact it sounds so simple that I think Mr. Jabez Tuesday is a little daffy when he tells me he will give me ten G's for the job.

What Mr. Tuesday wishes me to do is to get some letters that he personally writes to a doll by the name of Miss Amelia Bodkin, who lives in a house just outside Tarrytown, because it seems that Mr. Tuesday makes certain cracks in these letters that he is now sorry for, such as speaking of love and marriage and one thing and another to Miss Amelia Bodkin, and he is afraid she is going to sue him for breach of promise.

"Such an idea will be very embarrassing to me," Mr. Jabez Tuesday says, "as I am about to marry a party who is a member of one of the most high-toned families in this country. It is true," Mr. Tuesday says, "that the Scarwater family does not have as much money now as formerly, but there is no doubt about its being very, very high-toned, and my fiancée, Miss Valerie Scarwater, is one of the high-tonedest of them all. In fact," he says, "she is so high-toned that the chances are she will be very huffy about anybody suing me for breach of promise, and cancel everything."

Well, I ask Mr. Tuesday what a breach of promise is, and he explains to me that it is when somebody promises to do something and fails to do this something, although of course we have a different name for a proposition of this nature in Brooklyn, and deal with it accordingly.

"This is a very easy job for a person of your standing," Mr. Tuesday says. "Miss Amelia Bodkin lives all alone in her house the other side of Tarrytown, except for a couple of servants, and they are old and harmless. Now the idea is," he says, "you are not to go to her house as if you are looking for the letters, but as if you are after something else, such as her silverware, which is quite antique, and very valuable.

"She keeps the letters in a big inlaid box in her room,"

Mr. Tuesday says, "and if you just pick up this box and carry it away along with the silverware, no one will ever suspect that you are after the letters, but that you take the box thinking it contains valuables. You bring the letters to me and get your ten G's," Mr. Tuesday says, "and," he says, "you can keep the silverware, too. Be sure you get a Paul Revere teapot with the silverware," he says. "It is worth plenty."

"Well," I say to Mr. Tuesday, "every guy knows his own business best, and I do not wish to knock myself out of a nice soft job, but," I say, "it seems to me the simplest way of carrying on this transaction is to buy the letters off this doll, and be done with it. Personally," I say, "I do not believe there is a doll in the world who is not willing to sell a whole post-office full of letters for ten G's, especially in these times, and throw in a set of Shakespeare with them."

"No, no," Mr. Tuesday says. "Such a course will not do with Miss Amelia Bodkin at all. You see," he says, "Miss Bodkin and I are very, very friendly for a matter of maybe fifteen or sixteen years. In fact, we are very friendly, indeed. She does not have any idea at this time that I wish to break off this friendship with her. Now," he says, "if I try to buy the letters from her, she may become suspicious. The idea," Mr. Tuesday says, "is for me to get the letters first, and then explain to her about breaking off the friendship, and make suitable arrangements with her afterwards.

"Do not get Miss Amelia Bodkin wrong," Mr. Tuesday says. "She is an excellent person, but," he says, "you know the saying, 'Hell hath no fury like a woman scorned.' And maybe Miss Amelia Bodkin may figure I am scorning her if she finds out I am going to marry Miss Valerie Scarwater, and furthermore," he says, "if she still has the letters she may fall into the hands of unscrupulous lawyers, and demand a very large sum, indeed. But," Mr. Tuesday says, "this does not worry me half as much as the idea that Miss Valerie Scarwater may learn about the letters and get a wrong impression of my friendship with Miss Amelia Bodkin."

Well, I round up Spanish John and Little Isadore the next afternoon, and I find Little Isadore playing klob with a guy by the name of Educated Edmund, who is called Educated Edmund because he once goes to Erasmus High School and is considered a very fine scholar, indeed, so I invite Educated Edmund to go along with us. The idea is, I know Educated Edmund makes a fair living playing klob with Little Isadore, and I figure as long as I am depriving Educated Edmund of a living for awhile, it is only courteous to toss something else his way. Furthermore, I figure as long as letters are involved in this proposition it may be a good thing to have Educated Edmund handy in case any reading becomes necessary, because Spanish John and Little Isadore do not read at all, and I read only large print.

We borrow a car off a friend of mine in Clinton Street, and with me driving we start for Tarrytown, which is a spot up the Hudson River, and it is a very enjoyable ride for one and all on account of the scenery. It is the first time Educated Edmund and Spanish John and Little Isadore ever see the scenery along the Hudson although they all reside on the banks of this beautiful river for several years at Ossining. Personally, I am never in Ossining, although once I make Auburn, and once Comstock, but the scenery in these localities is nothing to speak of.

We hit Tarrytown about dark, and follow the main drag through this burg, as Mr. Tuesday tells me, until finally we come to the spot I am looking for, which is a little white cottage on a slope of ground above the river, not far off the highway. This little white cottage has quite a piece of ground around it, and a low stone wall, with a driveway from the highway to the house, and when I spot the gate to the driveway I make a quick turn, and what happens but I run the car slap-dab into a stone gatepost, and the car folds up like an accordion.

You see, the idea is we are figuring to make this a fast stick-up job without any foolishness about it, maybe leaving any parties we come across tied up good and tight while we make a getaway, as I am greatly opposed to house-breaking, or sneak jobs, as I do not consider them dignified. Further-more, they take too much time, so I am going to run the car right up to the front door when this stone post gets in my way.

The next thing I know, I open my eyes to find myself in a strange bed, and also in a strange bedroom, and while I wake up in many a strange bed in my time, I never wake up in such a strange bedroom as this. It is all very soft and dainty, and the only jarring note in my surroundings is Spanish John sitting beside the bed looking at me.

Naturally I wish to know what is what, and Spanish John says I am knocked snoring in the collision with the gatepost, although none of the others are hurt, and that while I am stretched in the driveway with the blood running out of a bad gash in my noggin, who pops out of the house but a doll and an old guy who seems to be a butler, or some such, and the doll insists on them lugging me into the house, and placing me in this bedroom.

Then she washes the blood off of me, Spanish John says, and wraps my head up and personally goes to Tarrytown to get a croaker to see if my wounds are fatal, or what, while Educated Edmund and Little Isadore are trying to patch up the car. So, Spanish John says, he is sitting there to watch me until she comes back, although of course I know what he is really sitting there for is to get first search at me in case I do not recover.

Well, while I am thinking all this over, and wondering what is to be done, in pops a doll of maybe forty odd, who is built from the ground up, but who has a nice, kind-looking pan, with a large smile, and behind her is a guy I can see at once is a croaker, especially as he is packing a little black bag, and has a gray goatee. I never see a nicer-looking doll if you care for middling-old dolls, although personally I like them young, and when she sees me with my eyes open, she speaks as follows:

"Oh," she says, "I am glad you are not dead, you poor chap. But," she says, "here is Doctor Diffingwell, and he will see how badly you are injured. My name is Miss Amelia Bodkin, and this is my house, and this is my own bedroom, and I am very, very sorry you are hurt."

Well, naturally I consider this a most embarrassing situation, because here I am out to clip Miss Amelia Bodkin of her letters and her silverware, including her Paul Revere teapot, and there she is taking care of me in first-class style, and saying she is sorry for me.

But there seems to be nothing for me to say at this time, so I hold still while the croaker looks me over, and after he peeks at my noggin, and gives me a good feel up and down, he states as follows:

"This is a very bad cut," he says. "I will have to stitch it up, and then he must be very quiet for a few days, otherwise," he says, "complications may set in. It is best to move him to a hospital at once."

But Miss Amelia Bodkin will not listen to such an idea as moving me to a hospital. Miss Amelia Bodkin says I must rest right where I am, and she will take care of me, because she says I am injured on her premises by her gatepost, and it is only fair that she does something for me. In fact, from the way Miss Amelia Bodkin takes on about me being moved, I figure maybe it is the old sex appeal, although afterwards I find out it is only because she is lonesome, and nursing me will give her something to do.

Well, naturally I am not opposing her idea, because the way I look at it, I will be able to handle the situation about the letters, and also the silverware, very nicely as an inside job, so I try to act even worse off than I am, although of course anybody who knows about the time I carry eight slugs in my body from Broadway and Fiftieth Street to Brooklyn will laugh very heartily at the idea of a cut on the noggin keeping me in bed.

After the croaker gets through sewing me up, and goes away, I tell Spanish John to take Educated Edmund and Little Isadore and go on back to New York, but to keep in touch with me by telephone, so I can tell them when to come back, and then I go to sleep, because I seem to be very tired. When I wake up later in the night, I seem to have a fever, and am really somewhat sick, and Miss Amelia Bodkin is sitting beside my bed swabbing my noggin with a cool cloth, which feels very pleasant, indeed.

I am better in the morning, and am able to knock over a little breakfast which she brings to me on a tray, and I am commencing to see where being an invalid is not so bad, at that, especially when there are no coppers at your bedside every time you open your eyes asking who does it to you.

I can see Miss Amelia Bodkin gets quite a bang out of having somebody to take care of, although of course if she knows who she is taking care of at this time, the chances are she will be running up the road calling for the gendarmes. It is not until after breakfast that I can get her to go and grab herself a little sleep, and while she is away sleeping the old guy who seems to be the butler is in and out of my room every now and then to see how I am getting along.

He is a gabby old guy, and pretty soon he is telling me all about Miss Amelia Bodkin, and what he tells me is that she is the old-time sweetheart of a guy in New York who is at the head of a big business, and very rich, and of course I know this guy is Mr. Jabez Tuesday, although the old guy who seems to be the butler never mentions his name.

"They are together many years," he says to me. "He is very poor when they meet, and she has a little money, and establishes him in business, and by her management of this business, and of him, she makes it a very large business, indeed. I know, because I am with them almost from the start," the old guy says. "She is very smart in business, and also very kind, and nice, if anybody asks you.

"Now," the old guy says, "I am never able to figure out why they do not get married, because there is no doubt she loves him, and he loves her, but Miss Amelia Bodkin once tells me that it is because they are too poor at the start, and too busy later on to think of such things as getting married, and so· they drift along the way they are, until all of a sudden he is rich. Then," the old guy says, "I can see he is getting away from her, although she never sees it herself, and I am not surprised when a few years ago he convinces her it is best for her to retire from active work, and move out to this spot.

"He comes out here fairly often at first," the old guy says, "but gradually he stretches the time between his visits, and now we do not see him once in a coon's age. Well," the old guy says, "it is just such a case as often comes up in life. In fact, I personally know of some others. But Miss Amelia Bodkin still thinks he loves her, and that only business keeps him away so much, so you can see she either is not as smart as she looks, or is kidding herself. Well," the old guy says, "I will now bring you a little orange-juice, although I do not mind saying you do not look to me like a guy who drinks orange-juice as a steady proposition."

Now I am taking many a gander around the bedroom to see if I can case the box of letters that Mr. Jabez Tuesday speaks of, but there is no box such as he describes in sight. Then in the evening, when Miss Amelia Bodkin is in the room, and I seem to be dozing, she pulls out a drawer in the bureau, and hauls out a big inlaid box, and sits down at a table under a reading-lamp, and opens this box and begins reading some old letters. And as she sits there reading those letters, with me watching her through my eyelashes, sometimes she smiles, but once I see little tears rolling down her cheeks.

All of a sudden she looks at me, and catches me with my eyes wide open, and I can see her face turn red, and then she laughs, and speaks to me, as follows:

"Old love letters," she says, tapping the box. "From my old sweetheart," she says. "I read some of them every night of my life. Am I not foolish and sentimental to do such a thing?"

Well, I tell Miss Amelia Bodkin she is sentimental, all right, but I do not tell her just how foolish she is to be letting me in on where she plants these letters, although of course I am greatly pleased to have this information. I tell Miss Amelia Bodkin that personally I never write a love letter, and never get a love letter, and in fact, while I hear of these propositions, I never even see a love letter before, and this is all as true as you are a foot high. Then Miss Amelia Bodkin laughs a little, and says to me as follows:

"Why," she says, "you are a very unusual chap, indeed, not to know what a love letter is like. Why," she says, "I think I will read you a few of the most wonderful love letters in this world. It will do no harm," she says, "because you do not know the writer, and you must lie there and think of me, not old and ugly, as you see me now, but as young, and maybe a little bit pretty."

So Miss Amelia Bodkin opens a letter and reads it to me, and her voice is soft and low as she reads, but she scarcely ever looks at the letter as she is reading, so I can see she knows it pretty much by heart. Furthermore, I can see that she thinks this letter is quite a masterpiece, but while I am no judge of love letters, because this is the first one I ever hear, I wish to say I consider it nothing but great nonsense.

"Sweetheart mine," this love letter says, "I am still thinking of you as I see you yesterday standing in front of the house with the sunlight turning your dark brown hair to wonderful bronze. Darling," it says, "I love the color of your hair. I am so glad you are not a blonde. I hate blondes, they are so emptyheaded, and mean, and deceitful. Also they are bad-tempered," the letter says. "I will never trust a blonde any farther than I can throw a bull by the tail. I never see a blonde in my life who is not a plumb washout," it says. "Most of them are nothing but peroxide, anyway. Business is improving," it says. "Sausage is going up. I love you now and always, my baby doll."

Well, there are others worse than this, and all of them speak of her as sweetheart, or baby, or darlingest one, and also as loveykins, and precious, and angel, and I do not know what all else, and several of them speak of how things will be after they marry, and as I judge these are Mr. Jabez Tuesday's letters, all right, I can see where they are full of dynamite for a guy who is figuring on taking a run-out powder on a doll. In fact, I say something to this general effect to Miss Amelia Bodkin, just for something to say.

"Why," she says, "what do you mean?"

"Well," I say, "documents such as these are known to bring large prices under certain conditions."

Now Miss Amelia Bodkin looks at me a moment, as if

wondering what is in my mind, and then she shakes her head as if she gives it up, and laughs and speaks as follows:

"Well," she says, "one thing is certain, my letters will never bring a price, no matter how large, under any conditions, even if anybody ever wants them. Why," she says, "these are my greatest treasure. They are my memories of my happiest days. Why," she says, "I will not part with these letters for a million dollars."

Naturally I can see from this remark that Mr. Jabez Tuesday makes a very economical deal with me at ten G's for the letters, but of course I do not mention this to Miss Amelia Bodkin as I watch her put her love letters back in the inlaid box, and put the box back in the drawer of the bureau. I thank her for letting me hear the letters, and then I tell her good-night, and I go to sleep, and the next day I telephone to a certain number in Clinton Street and leave word for Educated Edmund, and Spanish John and Little Isadore to come and get me, as I am tired of being an invalid.

Now the next day is Saturday, and the day that comes after is bound to be Sunday, and they come to see me on Saturday, and promise to come back for me Sunday, as the car is now unraveled and running all right, although my friend in Clinton Street is beefing no little about the way his fenders are bent. But before they arrive Sunday morning, who is there ahead of them bright and early but Mr. Jabez Tuesday in a big town car.

Furthermore, as he walks into the house, all dressed up in a cutaway coat, and a high hat, he grabs Miss Amelia Bodkin in his arms, and kisses her ker-plump right on the smush, which information I afterwards receive from the old guy who seems to be the butler. From upstairs I can personally hear Miss Amelia Bodkin crying more than somewhat, and then I hear Mr. Jabez Tuesday speak in a loud, hearty voice as follows:

"Now, now, now, 'Mely," Mr. Tuesday says. "Do not be crying, especially on my new white vest. Cheer up," Mr. Tuesday says, "and listen to the arrangements I make for our wedding to-morrow, and our honeymoon in Montreal. Yes, indeed, 'Mely," Mr. Tuesday says, "you are the only one for me, because you understand me from A to Izzard. Give me another big kiss, 'Mely, and let us sit down and talk things over."

Well, I judge from the sound that he gets his kiss, and it is a very large kiss, indeed, with the cutout open, and then I hear them chewing the rag at great length in the living-room downstairs. Finally I hear Mr. Jabez Tuesday speak as follows:

"You know, 'Mely," he says, "you and I are just plain ordinary folks without any lugs, and," he says, "this is why we fit each other so well. I am sick and tired of people who pretend to be high-toned and mighty, when they do not have a white quarter to their name. They have no manners whatever. Why, only last night," Mr. Jabez Tuesday says, "I am calling on a high-toned family in New York by the name of Scarwater, and out of a clear sky I am grossly insulted by the daughter of the house, and practically turned out in the street. I never receive such treatment in my life," he says. " 'Mely," he says, "give me another kiss, and see if you feel a bump here on my head."

Of course, Mr. Jabez Tuesday is somewhat surprised to see me present later on, but he never lets on he knows me, and naturally I do not give Mr. Jabez any tumble whatever at the moment, and by and by Educated Edmund and Spanish John and Little Isadore come for me in the car, and I thank Miss Amelia Bodkin for her kindness to me, and leave her standing on the lawn with Mr. Jabez Tuesday waving us good-by.

And Miss Amelia Bodkin looks so happy as she snuggles

up close to Mr. Jabez Tuesday that I am glad I take the chance, which is always better than an even-money chance these days, that Miss Valerie Scarwater is a blonde and send Educated Edmund to her to read her Mr. Tuesday's letter in which he speaks of blondes. But of course I am sorry that this and other letters that I tell Educated Edmund to read to her heats her up so far as to make her forget she is a lady and causes her to slug Mr. Jabez Tuesday on the bean with an 18-karat vanity case, as she tells him to get out of her life.

So (Harry the Horse says) there is nothing more to the story, except we are now looking for Judge Goldfobber to get him to take up a legal matter for us with Mr. Jabez Tuesday. It is true Mr. Tuesday pays us the ten G's, but he never lets us take the silverware he speaks of, not even the Paul Revere teapot, which he says is so valuable, and in fact when we drop around to Miss Amelia Bodkin's house to pick up these articles one night not long ago, the old guy who seems to be the butler lets off a double-barreled shotgun at us, and acts very nasty in general.

So (Harry says) we are going to see if we can get Judge Goldfobber to sue Mr. Jabez Tuesday for breach of promise.

✿   ✿   ✿

A Piece of Pie

On Boylston Street, in the city of Boston, Mass., there is a joint where you can get as nice a broiled lobster as anybody ever slaps a lip over, and who is in there one evening partaking of this tidbit but a character by the name of Horse Thief and me.

This Horse Thief is called Horsey for short, and he is not called by this name because he ever steals a horse but because it is the consensus of public opinion from coast to coast that he may steal one if the opportunity presents.

Personally, I consider Horsey a very fine character, because any time he is holding anything he is willing to share his good fortune with one and all, and at this time in Boston he is holding plenty. It is the time we make the race meeting at Suffolk Down, and Horsey gets to going very good, indeed, and in fact he is now a character of means, and is my host against the broiled lobster.

Well, at a table next to us are four or five characters who all seem to be well-dressed, and stout-set, and red-faced, and prosperous-looking, and who all speak with the true Boston accent, which consists of many ah's and very few r's. Characters such as these are familiar to anybody who is ever in Boston very much, and they are bound to be politicians, retired cops, or contractors, because Boston is really quite infested with characters of this nature.

I am paying no attention to them, because they are drinking local ale, and talking loud, and long ago I learn that when a Boston character is engaged in aleing himself up, it is a good idea to let him alone, because the best you can get out of him is maybe a boff on the beezer. But Horsey is in there on the old Ear-ie, and very much interested in their conversation, and finally I listen myself just to hear what is attracting his attention, when one of the characters speaks as follows:

"Well," he says, "I am willing to bet ten thousand dollars that he can outeat anybody in the United States any time."

Now at this, Horsey gets right up and steps over to the table and bows and smiles in a friendly way on one and all, and says:

"Gentlemen," he says, "pardon the intrusion, and excuse me for billing in, but," he says, "do I understand you are speaking of a great eater who resides in your fair city?"

Well, these Boston characters all gaze at Horsey in such a hostile manner that I am expecting any one of them to get up and request him to let them miss him, but he keeps on bowing and smiling, and they can see that he is a gentleman, and finally one of them says:

"Yes," he says, "we are speaking of a character by the name of Joel Duffle. He is without doubt the greatest eater alive. He just wins a unique wager. He bets a character from Bangor, Me., that he can eat a whole window display of oysters in this very restaurant, and he not only eats all the oysters but he then wishes to wager that he can also eat the shells, but," he says, "it seems that the character from Bangor, Me., unfortunately taps out on the first proposition and has nothing with which to bet on the second."

"Very interesting," Horsey says. "Very interesting, if true, but," he says, "unless my ears deceive me, I hear one of you state that he is willing to wager ten thousand dollars on this eater of yours against anybody in the United States."

"Your ears are perfect," another of the Boston characters says. "I state it, although," he says, "I admit it is a sort of figure of speech. But I state it all right," he says, "and never let it be said that a Conway ever pigs it on a betting proposition."

"Well," Horsey says, "I do not have a tenner on me at the moment, but," he says, "I have here a thousand dollars to put up as a forfeit that I can produce a character who will outeat your party for ten thousand, and as much more as you care to put up."

And with this, Horsey outs with a bundle of coarse notes and tosses it on the table, and right away one of the Boston characters, whose name turns out to be Carroll, slaps his hand on the money and says:

"Bet."

Well, now this is prompt action to be sure, and if there is one thing I admire more than anything else, it is action, and I can see that these are characters of true sporting instincts and I commence wondering where I can raise a few dibs to take a piece of Horsey's proposition, because of course I know that he has nobody in mind to do the eating for his side but Nicely-Nicely Jones.

And knowing Nicely-Nicely Jones, I am prepared to wager all the money I can possibly raise that he can outeat anything that walks on two legs. In fact, I will take a chance on Nicely-Nicely against anything on four legs, except maybe an elephant, and at that he may give the elephant a photo finish.

I do not say that Nicely-Nicely is the greatest eater in all history, but what I do say is he belongs up there as a contender. In fact, Professor D, who is a professor in a college out West before he turns to playing the horses for a livelihood, and who makes a study of history in his time, says he will not be surprised but what Nicely-Nicely figures one-two.

Professor D says we must always remember that Nicely-Nicely eats under the handicaps of modern civilization, which require that an eater use a knife and fork, or anyway a knife, while in the old days eating with the hands was a popular custom and much faster. Professor D says he has no doubt that under the old rules Nicely-Nicely will hang up a record that will endure through the ages, but of course maybe Professor D overlays Nicely-Nicely somewhat.

Well, now that the match is agreed upon, naturally Horsey and the Boston characters begin discussing where it is to take place, and one of the Boston characters suggests a neutral ground, such as New London, Conn., or Providence, R.I., but Horsey holds out for New York, and it seems that Boston characters are always ready to visit New York, so he does not meet with any great opposition on this point.

They all agree on a date four weeks later so as to give the principals plenty of time to get ready, although Horsey and I know that this is really unnecessary as far as Nicely-Nicely is concerned, because one thing about him is he is always in condition to eat.

This Nicely-Nicely Jones is a character who is maybe five feet eight inches tall, and about five feet nine inches wide, and when he is in good shape he will weigh upward of two hundred and eighty-three pounds. He is a horse player by trade, and eating is really just a hobby, but he is undoubtedly a wonderful eater even when he is not hungry.

Well, as soon as Horsey and I return to New York, we hasten to Mindy's restaurant on Broadway and relate the bet Horsey makes in Boston, and right away so many citizens, including Mindy himself, wish to take a piece of the proposition that it is oversubscribed by a large sum in no time.

Then Mindy remarks that he does not see Nicely-Nicely Jones for a month of Sundays, and then everybody present remembers that they do not see Nicely-Nicely around lately, either, and this leads to a discussion of where Nicely-Nicely can be, although up to this moment if nobody sees Nicely-Nicely but once in the next ten years it will be considered sufficient.

Well, Willie the Worrier, who is a bookmaker by trade, is among those present, and he remembers that the last time he looks for Nicely-Nicely hoping to collect a marker of some years' standing, Nicely-Nicely is living at the Rest Hotel in West Forty-ninth Street, and nothing will do Horsey but I must go with him over to the Rest to make inquiry for Nicely-Nicely, and there we learn that he leaves a forwarding address away up on Morningside Heights in care of somebody by the name of Slocum.

So Horsey calls a short, and away we go to this address, which turns out to be a five-story walk-up apartment, and a card downstairs shows that Slocum lives on the top floor. It takes Horsey and me ten minutes to walk up the five flights as we are by no means accustomed to exercise of this nature, and when we finally reach a door marked Slocum, we are plumb tuckered out, and have to sit down on the top step and rest a while.

Then I ring the bell at this door marked Slocum, and who appears but a tall young Judy with black hair who is without doubt beautiful, but who is so skinny we have to look twice to see her, and when I ask her if she can give me any information about a party named Nicely-Nicely Jones, she says to me like this:

"I guess you mean Quentin," she says. "Yes," she says, "Quentin is here. Come in, gentlemen."

So we step into an apartment, and as we do so a thin, sickly looking character gets up out of a chair by the window, and in a weak voice says good evening. It is a good evening, at that, so Horsey and I say good evening right back at him, very polite, and then we stand there waiting for Nicely-Nicely to appear, when the beautiful skinny young Judy says:

"Well," she says, "this is Mr. Quentin Jones."

Then Horsey and I take another swivel at the thin character, and we can see that it is nobody but Nicely-Nicely, at that, but the way he changes since we last observe him is practically shocking to us both, because he is undoubtedly all shrunk up. In fact, he looks as if he is about half what he is in his prime, and his face is pale and thin, and his eyes are away back in his head, and while we both shake hands with him it is some time before either of us is able to speak. Then Horsey finally says:

"Nicely," he says, "can we have a few words with you in private on a very important proposition?"

Well, at this, and before Nicely-Nicely can answer aye, yes, or no, the beautiful skinny young Judy goes out of the room and slams a door behind her, and Nicely-Nicely says:

"My fiancée, Miss Hilda Slocum," he says. "She is a wonderful character. We are to be married as soon as I lose twenty pounds more. It will take a couple of weeks longer," he says.

"My goodness gracious, Nicely," Horsey says. "What do you mean lose twenty pounds more? You are practically emaciated now. Are you just out of a sick bed, or what?"

"Why," Nicely-Nicely says, "certainly I am not out of

a sick bed. I am never healthier in my life. I am on a diet. I lose eighty-three pounds in two months, and am now down to two hundred. I feel great," he says. "It is all because of my fiancée, Miss Hilda Slocum. She rescues me from gluttony and obesity, or anyway," Nicely-Nicely says, "this is what Miss Hilda Slocum calls it. My, I feel good. I love Miss Hilda Slocum very much," Nicely-Nicely says. "It is a case of love at first sight on both sides the day we meet in the subway. I am wedged in one of the turnstile gates, and she kindly pushes on me from behind until I wiggle through. I can see she has a kind heart, so I date her up for a movie that night and propose to her while the newsreel is on. But," Nicely-Nicely says, "Hilda tells me at once that she will never marry a fat slob. She says I must put myself in her hands and she will reduce me by scientific methods and then she will become my ever-loving wife, but not before.

"So," Nicely-Nicely says, "I come to live here with Miss Hilda Slocum and her mother, so she can supervise my diet. Her mother is thinner than Hilda. And I surely feel great," Nicely-Nicely says. "Look," he says.

And with this, he pulls out the waistband of his pants, and shows enough spare space to hide War Admiral in, but the effort seems to be a strain on him, and he has to sit down in his chair again.

"My goodness gracious," Horsey says. "What do you eat, Nicely?"

"Well," Nicely-Nicely says, "I eat anything that does not contain starch, but," he says, "of course everything worth eating contains starch, so I really do not eat much of anything whatever. My fiancée, Miss Hilda Slocum, arranges my diet. She is an expert dietician and runs a widely known department in a diet magazine by the name of *Let's Keep House*."

Then Horsey tells Nicely-Nicely of how he is matched to eat against this Joel Duffle, of Boston, for a nice side bet, and how he has a forfeit of a thousand dollars already posted for appearance, and how many of Nicely-Nicely's admirers along Broadway are looking to win themselves out of all their troubles by betting on him, and at first Nicely-Nicely listens with great interest, and his eyes are shining like six bits, but then he becomes very sad, and says:

"It is no use, gentlemen," he says. "My fiancée, Miss Hilda Slocum, will never hear of me going off my diet even for a little while. Only yesterday I try to talk her into letting me have a little pumpernickel instead of toasted whole wheat bread, and she says if I even think of such a thing again, she will break our engagement. Horsey," he says, "do you ever eat toasted whole wheat bread for a month hand running? Toasted?" he says.

"No," Horsey says. "What I eat is nice, white French bread, and corn muffins, and hot biscuits with gravy on them."

"Stop," Nicely-Nicely says. "You are eating yourself into an early grave, and, furthermore," he says, "you are breaking my heart. But," he says, "the more I think of my following depending on me in this emergency, the sadder it makes me feel to think I am unable to oblige them. However," he says, "let us call Miss Hilda Slocum in on an outside chance and see what her reactions to your proposition are."

So we call Miss Hilda Slocum in, and Horsey explains our predicament in putting so much faith in Nicely-Nicely only to find him dieting, and Miss Hilda Slocum's reactions are to order Horsey and me out of the joint with instructions never to darken her door again, and when we are a block away we can still hear her voice speaking very firmly to Nicely-Nicely.

Well, personally, I figure this ends the matter, for I can see that Miss Hilda Slocum is a most determined character, indeed, and the chances are it does end it, at that, if Horsey does not happen to get a wonderful break.

He is at Belmont Park one afternoon, and he has a real good thing in a jump race, and when a brisk young character in a hard straw hat and eyeglasses comes along and asks him what he likes, Horsey mentions this good thing, figuring he will move himself in for a few dibs if the good thing connects.

Well, it connects all right, and the brisk young character is very grateful to Horsey for his information, and is giving him plenty of much-obliges, and nothing else, and Horsey is about to mention that they do not accept much-obliges at his hotel, when the brisk young character mentions that he is nobody but Mr. McBurgle and that he is the editor of the *Let's Keep House* magazine, and for Horsey to drop in and see him any time he is around his way.

Naturally, Horsey remembers what Nicely-Nicely says about Miss Hilda Slocum working for this *Let's Keep House* magazine, and he relates the story of the eating contest to Mr. McBurgle and asks him if he will kindly use his influence with Miss Hilda Slocum to get her to release Nicely-Nicely from his diet long enough for the contest. Then Horsey gives Mr. McBurgle a tip on another winner, and Mr. McBurgle must use plenty of influence on Miss Hilda Slocum at once, as the next day she calls Horsey up at his hotel before he is out of bed, and speaks to him as follows:

"Of course," Miss Hilda Slocum says, "I will never change my attitude about Quentin, but," she says, "I can appreciate that he feels very bad about you gentlemen relying on him and having to disappoint you. He feels that he lets you down, which is by no means true, but it weighs upon his mind. It is interfering with his diet.

"Now," Miss Hilda Slocum says, "I do not approve of your contest, because," she says, "it is placing a premium on gluttony, but I have a friend by the name of Miss Violette Shumberger who may answer your purpose. She is my dearest friend from childhood, but it is only because I love her dearly that this friendship endures. She is extremely fond of eating," Miss Hilda Slocum says. "In spite of my pleadings, and my warnings, and my own example, she persists in food. It is disgusting to me but I finally learn that it is no use arguing with her.

"She remains my dearest friend," Miss Hilda Slocum says, "though she continues her practice of eating, and I am informed that she is phenomenal in this respect. In fact," she says, "Nicely-Nicely tells me to say to you that if Miss Violette Shumberger can perform the eating exploits I relate to him from hearsay she is a lily. Good-bye," Miss Hilda Slocum says. "You cannot have Nicely-Nicely."

Well, nobody cares much about this idea of a stand-in for Nicely-Nicely in such a situation, and especially a Judy that no one ever hears of before, and many citizens are in favor of pulling out of the contest altogether. But Horsey has his thousand-dollar forfeit to think of, and as no one can suggest anyone else, he finally arranges a personal meet with the Judy suggested by Miss Hilda Slocum.

He comes into Mindy's one evening with a female character who is so fat it is necessary to push three tables together to give her room for her lap, and it seems that this character is Miss Violette Shumberger. She weighs maybe two hundred and fifty pounds, but she is by no means an old Judy, and by no means bad-looking. She has a face the size of a town clock and enough chins for a fire escape, but she has a nice smile and pretty teeth, and a laugh that is so hearty it knocks the whipped cream off an order of strawberry shortcake on a table fifty feet away and arouses the indignation of a customer by the name of Goldstein who is about to consume same.

Well, Horsey's idea in bringing her into Mindy's is to get some kind of line on her eating form, and she is clocked by many experts when she starts putting on the hot meat, and it is agreed by one and all that she is by no means a selling-plater. In fact, by the time she gets through, even Mindy admits she has plenty of class, and the upshot of it all is Miss Violette Shumberger is chosen to eat against Joel Duffle.

Maybe you hear something of this great eating contest that comes off in New York one night in the early summer of 1937. Of course eating contests are by no means anything new, and in fact they are quite an old-fashioned pastime in some sections of this country, such as the South and East, but this is the first big public contest of the kind in years, and it creates no little comment along Broadway.

In fact, there is some mention of it in the blats, and it is not a frivolous proposition in any respect, and more dough is wagered on it than any other eating contest in history, with Joel Duffle a 6 to 5 favorite over Miss Violette Shumberger all the way through.

This Joel Duffle comes to New York several days before the contest with the character by the name of Conway, and requests a meet with Miss Violette Shumberger to agree on the final details and who shows up with Miss Violette Shumberger as her coach and adviser but Nicely-Nicely Jones. He is even thinner and more peaked-looking than when Horsey and I see him last, but he says he feels great, and that he is within six pounds of his marriage to Miss Hilda Slocum.

Well, it seems that his presence is really due to Miss Hilda Slocum herself, because she says that after getting her dearest friend Miss Violette Shumberger into this jack-pot, it is only fair to do all she can to help her win it, and the only way she can think of is to let Nicely-Nicely give Violette the benefit of his experience and advice.

But afterward we learn that what really happens is that this editor, Mr. McBurgle, gets greatly interested in the contest, and when he discovers that in spite of his influence, Miss Hilda Slocum declines to permit Nicely-Nicely to personally compete, but puts in a pinch eater, he is quite indignant and insists on her letting Nicely-Nicely school Violette.

Furthermore we afterward learn that when Nicely-Nicely returns to the apartment on Morningside Heights after giving Violette a lesson, Miss Hilda Slocum always smells his breath to see if he indulges in any food during his absence.

Well, this Joel Duffle is a tall character with stooped shoulders, and a sad expression, and he does not look as if he can eat his way out of a tea shop, but as soon as he commences to discuss the details of the contest, anybody can see that he knows what time it is in situations such as this. In fact, Nicely-Nicely says he can tell at once from the way Joel Duffle talks that he is a dangerous opponent, and he says while Miss Violette Shumberger impresses him as an improving eater, he is only sorry she does not have more seasoning.

This Joel Duffle suggests that the contest consist of twelve courses of strictly American food, each side to be allowed to pick six dishes, doing the picking in rotation, and specifying the weight and quantity of the course selected to any amount the contestant making the pick desires, and each course is to be divided for eating exactly in half, and after Miss Violette Shumberger and Nicely-Nicely whisper together a while, they say the terms are quite satisfactory.

Then Horsey tosses a coin for the first pick, and Joel Duffle says heads, and it is heads, and he chooses, as the first course, two quarts of ripe olives, twelve bunches of celery, and four pounds of shelled nuts, all this to be split fifty-fifty between them. Miss Violette Shumberger names twelve dozen cherry-stone clams as the second course, and Joel Duffle says two gallons of Philadelphia pepper-pot soup as the third.

Well, Miss Violette Shumberger and Nicely-Nicely whisper together again, and Violette puts in two five-pound striped bass, the heads and tails not to count in the eating, and Joel Duffle names a twenty-two pound roast turkey. Each vegetable is rated as one course, and Miss Violette Shumberger asks for twelve pounds of mashed potatoes with brown gravy. Joel Duffle says two dozen ears of corn on the cob, and Violette replies with two quarts of lima beans. Joel Duffle calls for twelve bunches of asparagus cooked in butter, and Violette mentions ten pounds of stewed new peas.

This gets them down to the salad, and it is Joel Duffle's play, so he says six pounds of mixed green salad with vinegar and oil dressing, and now Miss Violette Shumberger has the final selection, which is the dessert. She says it is a pumpkin pie, two feet across, and not less than three inches deep.

It is agreed that they must eat with knife, fork or spoon, but speed is not to count, and there is to be no time limit, except they cannot pause more than two consecutive minutes at any stage, except in case of hiccups. They can drink anything, and as much as they please, but liquids are not to count in the scoring. The decision is to be strictly on the amount of food consumed, and the judges are to take account of anything left on the plates after a course, but not of loose chewings on bosom or vest up to an ounce. The losing side is to pay for the food, and in case of a tie they are to eat it off immediately on ham and eggs only.

Well, the scene of this contest is the second-floor dining-room of Mindy's restaurant, which is closed to the general public for the occasion, and only parties immediately concerned in the contest are admitted. The contestants are seated on either side of a big table in the center of the room, and each contestant has three waiters.

No talking and no rooting from the spectators is permitted, but of course in any eating contest the principals may speak to each other if they wish, though smart eaters never wish to do this, as talking only wastes energy, and about all they ever say to each other is please pass the mustard.

About fifty characters from Boston are present to witness the contest, and the same number of citizens of New York are admitted, and among them is this editor, Mr. McBurgle, and he is around asking Horsey if he thinks Miss Violette Shumberger is as good a thing as the jumper at the race track.

Nicely-Nicely arrives on the scene quite early, and his appearance is really most distressing to his old friends and admirers, as by this time he is shy so much weight that he is a pitiful scene, to be sure, but he tells Horsey and me that he thinks Miss Violette Shumberger has a good chance.

"Of course," he says, "she is green. She does not know how to pace herself in competition. But," he says, "she has a wonderful style. I love to watch her eat. She likes the same things I do in the days when I am eating. She is a wonderful character, too. Do you ever notice her smile?" Nicely-Nicely says.

"But," he says, "she is the dearest friend of my fiancée, Miss Hilda Slocum, so let us not speak of this. I try to get Hilda to come to see the contest, but she says it is repulsive. Well, anyway," Nicely-Nicely says, "I manage to borrow a few dibs, and am wagering on Miss Violette Shumberger. By the way," he says, "if you happen to think of it, notice her smile."

Well, Nicely-Nicely takes a chair about ten feet behind Miss Violette Shumberger, which is as close as the judges will allow him, and he is warned by them that no coaching from the corners will be permitted, but of course Nicely-Nicely knows this rule as well as they do, and furthermore by this time his exertions seem to have left him without any more energy.

There are three judges, and they are all from neutral territory. One of these judges is a party from Baltimore, Md., by the name of Packard, who runs a restaurant, and another is a party from Providence, R.I., by the name of Croppers, who is a sausage manufacturer. The third judge is an old Judy by the name of Mrs. Rhubarb, who comes from Philadelphia, and once keeps an actors' boarding-house, and is considered an excellent judge of eaters.

Well, Mindy is the official starter, and at 8:30 P.M. sharp, when there is still much betting among the spectators, he outs with his watch, and says like this:

"Are you ready, Boston? Are you ready, New York?"

Miss Violette Shumberger and Joel Duffle both nod their heads, and Mindy says commence, and the contest is on, with Joel Duffle getting the jump at once on the celery and olives and nuts.

It is apparent that this Joel Duffle is one of these rough-and-tumble eaters that you can hear quite a distance off, especially on clams and soups. He is also an eyebrow eater, an eater whose eyebrows go up as high as the part in his hair as he eats, and this type of eater is undoubtedly very efficient.

In fact, the way Joel Duffle goes through the groceries down to the turkey causes the Broadway spectators some uneasiness, and they are whispering to each other that they only wish the old Nicely-Nicely is in there. But personally, I like the way Miss Violette Shumberger eats without undue excitement, and with great zest. She cannot keep close to Joel Duffle in the matter of speed in the early stages of the contest, as she seems to enjoy chewing her food, but I observe that as it goes along she pulls up on him, and I figure this is not because she is stepping up her pace, but because he is slowing down.

When the turkey finally comes on, and is split in two halves right down the middle, Miss Violette Shumberger looks greatly disappointed, and she speaks for the first time as follows:

"Why," she says, "where is the stuffing?"

Well, it seems that nobody mentions any stuffing for the turkey to the chef, so he does not make any stuffing, and Miss Violette Shumberger's disappointment is so plain to be seen that the confidence of the Boston characters is somewhat shaken. They can see that a Judy who can pack away as much fodder as Miss Violette Shumberger has to date, and then beef for stuffing, is really quite an eater.

In fact, Joel Duffle looks quite startled when he observes Miss Violette Shumberger's disappointment, and he gazes at her with great respect as she disposes of her share of the turkey, and the mashed potatoes, and one thing and another in such a manner that she moves up on the pumpkin pie on dead even terms with him. In fact, there is little to choose between them at this point, although the judge from Baltimore is calling the attention of the other judges to a turkey leg that he claims Miss Violette Shumberger does not clean as neatly as Joel Duffle does his, but the other judges dismiss this as a technicality.

Then the waiters bring on the pumpkin pie, and it is without doubt quite a large pie, and in fact it is about the size of a manhole cover, and I can see that Joel Duffle is observing this pie with a strange expression on his face, although to tell the truth I do not care for the expression on Miss Violette Shumberger's face, either.

Well, the pie is cut in two dead center, and one half is placed before Miss Violette Shumberger, and the other half before Joel Duffle, and he does not take more than two bites before I see him loosen his waistband and take a big swig of water, and thinks I to myself, he is now down to a slow walk, and the pie will decide the whole heat, and I am only wishing I am able to wager a little more dough on Miss Violette Shumberger. But about this moment, and before she as much as touches her pie, all of a sudden Violette turns her head and motions to Nicely-Nicely to approach her, and as he approaches, she whispers in his ear.

Now at this, the Boston character by the name of Conway jumps up and claims a foul and several other Boston characters join him in this claim, and so does Joel Duffle, although afterwards even the Boston characters admit that Joel Duffle is no gentleman to make such a claim against a lady.

Well, there is some confusion over this, and the judges hold a conference, and they rule that there is certainly no foul in the actual eating that they can see, because Miss Violette Shumberger does not touch her pie so far.

But they say that whether it is a foul otherwise all depends on whether Miss Violette Shumberger is requesting advice on the contest from Nicely-Nicely and the judge from Providence, R.I., wishes to know if Nicely-Nicely will kindly relate what passes between him and Violette so they may make a decision.

"Why," Nicely-Nicely says, "all she asks me is can I get her another piece of pie when she finishes the one in front of her."

Now at this, Joel Duffle throws down his knife, and pushes back his plate with all but two bites of his pie left on it, and says to the Boston characters like this:

"Gentlemen," he says, "I am licked. I cannot eat another mouthful. You must admit I put up a game battle, but," he says, "it is useless for me to go on against this Judy who is asking for more pie before she even starts on what is before her. I am almost dying as it is, and I do not wish to destroy myself in a hopeless effort. Gentlemen," he says, "she is not human."

Well, of course this amounts to throwing in the old napkin and Nicely-Nicely stands up on his chair, and says:

"Three cheers for Miss Violette Shumberger!"

Then Nicely-Nicely gives the first cheer in person, but the effort overtaxes his strength, and he falls off the chair in a faint just as Joel Duffle collapses under the table, and the doctors at the Clinic Hospital are greatly baffled to receive, from the same address at the same time, one patient who is suffering from undernourishment, and another patient who is unconscious from over-eating.

Well, in the meantime, after the excitement subsides, and wagers are settled, we take Miss Violette Shumberger to the main floor in Mindy's for a midnight snack, and when she speaks of her wonderful triumph, she is disposed to give much credit to Nicely-Nicely Jones.

"You see," Violette says, "what I really whisper to him is that I am a goner. I whisper to him that I cannot possibly take one bite of the pie if my life depends on it, and if he has any bets down to try and hedge them off as quickly as possible.

"I fear," she says, "that Nicely-Nicely will be greatly disappointed in my showing, but I have a confession to make to him when he gets out of the hospital. I forget about the contest," Violette says, "and eat my regular dinner of pig's knuckles and sauerkraut an hour before the contest starts and," she says, "I have no doubt this tends to affect my form somewhat. So," she says, "I owe everything to Nicely-Nicely's quick thinking."

It is several weeks after the great eating contest that I run into Miss Hilda Slocum on Broadway and it seems to me that she looks much better nourished than the last time I see her, and when I mention this she says:

"Yes," she says, "I cease dieting. I learn my lesson," she says. "I learn that male characters do not appreciate anybody who tries to ward off surplus tissue. What male characters wish is substance. Why," she says, "only a week ago my editor, Mr. McBurgle, tells me he will love to take me dancing if only I get something on me for him to take hold of. I am very fond of dancing," she says.

"But," I say, "what of Nicely-Nicely Jones? I do not see him around lately."

"Why," Miss Hilda Slocum says, "do you not hear what this cad does? Why, as soon as he is strong enough to leave the hospital, he elopes with my dearest friend, Miss Violette Shumberger, leaving me a note saying something about two souls with but a single thought. They are down in Florida running a barbecue stand, and," she says, "the chances are, eating like seven mules."

"Miss Slocum," I say, "can I interest you in a portion of Mindy's chicken fricassee?"

"With dumplings?" Miss Hilda Slocum says. "Yes," she says, "you can. Afterwards I have a date to go dancing with Mr. McBurgle. I am crazy about dancing," she says.

☘ ☘ ☘

The Lacework Kid

Now, of course, the war makes itself felt along Broadway no little and quite some and in fact it is a most disturbing element at times as it brings many strangers to the city who crowd Mindy's restaurant to the doors and often compel the old-time regular customers to stand in line waiting for tables, which is a very great hardship, indeed.

It does no good to complain to Mindy about this situation as he is making so much money he is practically insolent and he only asks you if you do not know there is a war going on, and besides Mindy is generally waiting for a table himself.

Well, one evening I am fortunate enough to out-cute everyone else for a chair that is the only vacant chair at a little table for two and the other chair is occupied by a soldier, and who is this soldier but a guy by the name of The Lacework Kid who is eating as if Hitler is coming up Broadway.

Now The Lacework Kid, who is generally called Lace for short, is a personality who is maybe thirty years old but looks younger and is a card player by trade. Furthermore he is considered one of the best that ever riffles a deck. In fact, he comes by his monicker because someone once remarks that his work with the cards is as delicate as lace, although personally I consider this an understatement.

He comes from the city of Providence which is in Rhode Island, and of course it is well known to one and all that for generations Providence produces wonderful card players, and in his childhood The Lacework Kid has the advantage of studying under the best minds there, and afterwards improves his education in this respect by much travel.

Before the war he is a great hand for riding the tubs and makes regular trips back and forth across the Atlantic Ocean because a guy in his line can always find more customers on the boats than anywhere else and can also do very good for himself by winning the pools on the ship's daily run if he can make the proper connections to get the information on the run in advance.

I only wish you can see The Lacework Kid before the war when he is at the height of his career. He is maybe five feet nine and very slender and has brown eyes and wavy brown hair and a face like a choirboy and a gentle voice.

He wears the best clothes money can buy and they are always of soft quiet materials and his linen is always white and his shoes black. He wears no jewelry showing, but he carries a little gold watch in his pants pocket that stands him a G-er in Paris and a gold cigarette box that sets him back a gob in the same place.

He has long slim white hands like a society broad and in fact there is no doubt that his hands are the secret of The Lacework Kid's success at his trade of card playing as they are fast and flexible and have youth in them, and youth is one thing a good card player must have, because age stiffens fingers up more than somewhat. But of course age is a drawback in everything in this wicked old world.

It is really a beautiful sight to watch The Lacework Kid handle a deck of cards because he makes the pasteboards just float together when he is shuffling and causes them to fall as light as flecks of foam when he is dealing. His specialty is a game called bridge when he is riding the tubs and he is seldom without customers because in the first place he does not look like a guy who can play bridge very well and in the second place he does not appear to be such a personality as the signs in the smoking rooms on the boats refer to when they say "Beware of Card Sharks." In fact The Lacework Kid generally tries to get a chair right under one of these signs to show that it cannot possibly mean him.

I see The Lacework Kid a few years before this night in Mindy's when he just gets in on a German liner and he has a guy by the name of Schultz with him and is entertaining this Schultz royally because it seems Schultz is the smoking room steward on the liner and is The Lacework Kid's connection in winning the pools and in introducing bridge customers to him and putting him away with them as a rich young American zillionaire and as the trip nets Lace two thou on the pools alone he feels quite grateful to Schultz.

But of course this is before there is any war and later when I see him the unpleasantness is on and no liners are running and Lace tells me his trade is the greatest economic casualty of the whole war, and he is wondering if there is any use trying to ride the submarines back and forth looking for customers.

And now here he is again as large as life and in fact slightly larger as I can see he puts on a little weight and he looks very good in his uniform and has a red ribbon on his chest, so I say to him like this:

"Lace," I say, "it is indeed a pleasure to run into you and I can see by your uniform that you are in the war business and by your ribbon that you distinguish yourself in some manner. Perhaps you are decorated for dealing the general a nice hand off the bottom?"

Well, at this, The Lacework Kid gives me a most severe look and says:

"It is a Good Conduct Medal. I get it for being a fine soldier. I may get an even better award for an experience I will now relate to you."

I will omit the details of my early career in the Army (The Lacework Kid says) except to tell you that my comrades know me only as Sergeant Fortescue Melville Michael O'Shay, my mamma getting the first two names out of a novel she is reading at the time I am born, and my papa's papa bringing the last two over from Ireland.

Furthermore, they know nothing of my background and while there are occasions when I am greatly tempted to make assessments against them out of my great store of knowledge when they are playing such trifling games as blackjack, I resist the urge and confine myself strictly to the matter in hand, which is the war.

I am the waist gunner in a Flying Fortress on a raid over Germany one pleasant afternoon when our ship is so severely jostled by antiaircraft shells that we are compelled to bail out and no sooner do I land than up comes three German soldiers with rifles in their dukes.

They point these rifles at me in a most disquieting manner and while I only know a word or two of the German language I can see that I am their prisoner and the next thing I know I am in a prison camp where I find my comrades and also several hundred other gees who seem to be British and one thing and another.

It is not a large camp and in fact I learn that it is just a sort of temporary detention spot for prisoners who are rounded up in this particular section of the country and that they are usually transferred to a larger gaff after a while.

It is located in a hilly country not far from the Swiss border and you can see high mountains in the distance that I am told are the Alps.

But even with the view it is by no means a desirable place. The life in this camp is most monotonous and the cuisine is worse, which is a terrible disappointment to me as I am rather fond of German cooking, and particularly adore the apple strudel of this race, and the chow they give us makes me more violently anti-Nazi than ever and also gives me indigestion. To tell the truth, I spend most of my time trying to figure a way to escape though they tell me that if I am patient I will sooner or later be exchanged for a German prisoner.

There is a company of maybe a hundred German soldiers guarding the camp and I am only there a few hours before I learn that the officer who is in charge of the joint is a captain by the name of Kunz, and that he is also sometimes called The Butcher because it seems that in the early days of the war he is in command of an outfit in Poland and thinks nothing of killing people right and left for no reason whatever except he enjoys seeing them die.

But it seems he finally gets himself in bad with his boss and is sent to this little out-of-the-way prison camp as a lesson to him and he runs the place like the tough warden of a stir back home though he does not show up much in person around the camp and in fact I never see him myself until the time I am going to tell you about.

One afternoon a German sergeant comes into the prison yard where I am taking a little exercise and beckons me off to one side and I am somewhat suprised to observe that the sergeant is nobody but Schultz the steward, who speaks to me in a low voice as follows:

"Hello, Lace," he says. "How is everything?"

"Schultz," I say, "everything stinks."

"Lace," he says, "what do you know about something American that is called gin rummy?"

"Gin rummy?" I say. "Why I know it is supposed to be a card game but as a matter of fact it is nothing but a diversion for idiots."

"Are you a gin rummy man?" Schultz says. "I mean do you play the game?"

"Schultz," I say, "nearly everybody in the United States of America plays gin rummy. The little children in the street play it. Old broads play it. I understand there is a trained ape in the Bronx Zoo that plays it very nicely and I am not surprised, because," I say, "I can teach any dumb animal to play gin rummy if I can get it to hold ten cards."

"Well," Schultz says, "what I am getting at is do you play it as well as you play bridge and in the same way? What I must know is are you a mechanic at gin? I mean if necessary?"

Well naturally I am slightly vexed by this question as I consider it an insult to my integrity as well as a reflection upon my card playing to even hint that I do anything in cards except outplay my opponent through my superior skill. To tell the truth, I feel it is just the same as asking Joe Louis if he uses the difference in his gloves when he is meeting a chump.

"Schultz," I say, "you are undoubtedly a scoundrel to always be thinking in terms of larceny. I never swindle anybody at anything despite any rumors to the contrary that you may hear. And I never hear of any swindles in gin rummy except planting a guy who is supposed to have a piece of your opponent's play alongside him to tip off his cards to you.

"But," I say, "I consider this a low form of thievery. However, Schultz," I say, "I will be guilty of false modesty if I do not admit to you that like all gin players I think

I am the best. In fact, I know of but one who can beat me consistently at gin and that is Kidneyfoot, the waiter in Mindy's, but then he teaches me the game and naturally figures to top me slightly."

Well, then this Schultz unfolds a very strange tale to me. He says that when Captain Kunz is in the United States for some years before the war as an attaché of the German embassy in Washington, he learns the game of gin rummy and it becomes a great passion with him.

It seems from what Schultz says that after Kunz returns to Germany, he misses his gin rummy no little as the game is practically unknown in his country where card players generally favor pinochle or maybe klabriasch. It seems that Kunz tries to teach some of his countrymen how to play gin but has little success and anyway the war comes on and promoting an American game will be deemed unpatriotic, so he has to cease his efforts in this direction.

But he cannot stop thinking of gin, so he finally invents a sort of solitaire gin and plays it constantly all by himself, but it is most unsatisfactory and when he hears of American prisoners arriving in his camp, he sends for Schultz and asks him to canvass us and see if there are any gin-rummy players in the crowd. And in looking us over, Schultz spots me.

"Now," Schultz says, "I build you up to the captain as the champion gin player of the United States, and he finally tells me the other night that he wishes to play you if it can be done in secret, as of course it will be very bad for morale if it gets out that the commandant of a prison camp engages in card games with a prisoner. The captain is rich and likes to play for high stakes, too," Schultz says.

"Look, Schultz," I say, "I do not have any moolouw with me here. All my potatoes are planted in a jug in England and I do not suppose the captain will accept notes of hand payable there."

"Listen," Schultz says, dropping his voice to a whisper, "I tell all my fellow soldiers here about your gin playing and how you are so clever you can make a jack jump out of a deck and sing Chattanooga Choo-Choo if necessary, and we all agree to pool our resources to provide you with a taw. We can raise maybe fifty thousand marks. But," Schultz says, "you must not breathe a word of this to your comrades. The captain must think they are the ones who are backing you. You will receive twenty-five per cent of your winnings, and I will personally guarantee your end."

Naturally, I figure Schultz is giving me the old rol-de-dol-dol for some reason because it does not make sense that an officer in the German army will wish to play an American prisoner gin rummy, but then I remember that gin players will do anything to play gin and I figure that maybe the captain is like the old faro bank player who is warned as he is going into a gambling house to beware of the bank game there because it is crooked and who says:

"Yes, I know it is, but what am I going to do? It is the only game in town."

Well, of course this is an ancient story to you and you will kindly forgive me for springing it at this time, but I am trying to explain the psychology of this captain as I see it. Anyway, I tell Schultz to go ahead and arrange the game and in the meantime I get a deck of cards and practice to refresh my memory.

Now, one night Schultz shows up at my quarters and tells me to come with him and he says it in such a stern voice and acts so mysterious that everyone figures I am being taken out to be shot and to tell you the truth I am not so sure myself that this is not the case. But when we get away from the other prisoners, Schultz is quite nice to me.

He takes me outside the gates of the prison camp and we walk along a road about a mile when we come to a

small house set back from the road in a grove of trees and
Schultz stops in front of this house and speaks to me as
follows:

"Lace," he says, "in the course of your playing with
the captain kindly do not refer to our people as krauts,
pretzels, beerheads, Heinies, Boches, sausages, wienies or
by the titles of any other members of the vegetable or animal kingdom, and do not tell him what you Americans
are going to do to us. It will only make for an unfriendly
atmosphere, and his replies may distract you from your
gin. He understands English, so please be discreet in every
respect."

Then he hands me a roll of German marks a steeplechase
horse will be unable to hurdle and leads the way into the
house, and by this time I figure out what the scamus is. I
figure that Schultz pegs me for a bleater, and the captain
is going to try to get some information out of me and, in
fact, I am looking for a touch of the old third degree from
the Gestapo.

But on entering the house, which seems to be very
plainly furnished, the only person present is a big guy in
uniform with a lot of gongs on his chest, which is a way
of saying medals, and whose head is shaved like Eric von
Stroheim's in a Nazi picture. He is sitting at a table in front
of a burning fireplace fooling with a deck of cards.

Schultz introduces me to him, but the guy only nods and
motions me to sit down at the table opposite him and tosses
the deck of cards to me. I examine the backs carefully to
see if they are marked, but they seem strictly kosher in
every way, and then I say to Captain Kunz like this:

"Captain," I say, "let us understand one thing. I am a
noncommissioned officer, and you outrank me from hell to
breakfast time, but in this game you must not take advantage of your rank in any way, shape, manner or form, to
intimidate me. We will play New York rules, with gins

and undercuts to count twenty each and blitzes double."

Kunz nods and motions me to cut the cards for the deal, and he wins it and away we go. We play three games at once and as soon as both of us are on all three games, we start another frame of three, with Schultz keeping score, and it is not long before we have as many as three frames or nine games going at once, which makes a very fast contest, indeed. We are playing for a hundred marks a game or three hundred marks across, which Schultz tells me is about a hundred and twenty dollars in my money, the way the Germans figure their marks.

I will not attempt to describe gin rummy in detail as you can call up any insane asylum and get any patient on the phone and learn all about it in no time, as all lunatics are bound to be gin players, and in fact the chances are it is gin rummy that makes them lunatics. Furthermore, I will not bore you with my philosophy of the game, but I say it is ninety-five per cent luck and five per cent play, and the five per cent is the good card player's strength in the pinches, if there are any pinches.

The cards in gin rummy run hot and cold the same as the dice in a crap game. It is by no means necessary to go to Harvard to learn to play gin and in fact a moron is apt to play it better than Einstein. If you get the tickets in gin, you are a genius, and if you do not get them, you are a bum. When they do not come, you can only sit and suffer, and the aggravation of waiting on cards that never arrive will give you stomach ulcers in no time.

Well, I can see at once that Captain Kunz plays as good a game of gin as anybody can play and he also has good regulation dialogue, such as "This is the worst hand I ever see in my life," and "I only need one little card from the draw to get down," and so forth and so on, but he delivers his dialogue in German and then Schultz translates it for me as it seems the captain does not care to address me direct in English, which I consider very snobbish of him.

About the only word he says I can understand is *frischer*
when he picks up a bad hand and wishes to know if I am
agreeable to a fresh deal, which is a courtesy a gin player
sometimes extends if he also has a bad hand, though personally I am opposed to *frischers*. In fact, when I get a
bad hand, I play the Pittsburgh Muddle system on Kunz,
which is to pick up every card he discards whether I need
it or not and then throw it back at him when my hand
improves, the idea being to confuse your opponent and
make him hold cards that gum up his hand.

Well, I get my rushes right away and win the first frame
and am going so strong on the second that Kunz gets up
and peels his coat down to a pair of pink suspenders and
ten minutes later he drops the suspenders off his shoulders
and opens his waist band. In the meantime, Schultz kibitzes
the captain on one hand and me on the next, and of course
a kibitzer is entitled to present his views on a play after it
is over, and Schultz is undoubtedly a real kibitzer and becomes quite excited at times in his comment.

However, once he is very bitter in his criticism of a play
that costs the captain a game, and Kunz turns on him like
a wolf and bawls him out and scares Schultz silly. But
later the captain apologizes because as a gin player he is
bound to respect the right of a kibitzer.

I keep waiting for Kunz to slip in questions to me about
our Air Forces and one thing and another, but he never
makes a remark that is not in connection with the game
and finally I can see that my suspicions are unfounded and
that he is nothing but a gin player after all.

Well, daylight is coming through the windows of the
house when the captain says we must knock off playing,
and Schultz must hurry me back to camp, and I am somewhat startled to realize that I am four hundred marks loser,
which I whip out and pay immediately. Furthermore,

Schultz is terribly depressed by this situation and all the way back to the camp he keeps telling me how I disappoint him in not winning and asking me what becomes of my mechanics, and finally I get sore and speak to him as follows:

"Schultz," I say, "the guy is not only better than a raw hand at gin but he also outlucks me. And I tell you I do not know of any mechanics in gin rummy and if you do not care to trust to my superior skill to finally prevail, you can call it all off now."

Then Schultz cools down a little and says maybe I will do better next time, but I judge his disappointment is communicated to the other German soldiers as they seem very crusty with me all day though my greatest trouble is standing off the questions of my own gang about my absence.

Well, Schultz is around after me again that night to take me to the house in the grove, and in fact every night for a month hand-running I play the captain and it is not long before I am beating him like breaking sticks. And every night the captain pays off like a slot machine and every day I turn my dough over to Schultz and he pays me twenty-five per cent and then distributes the balance among the guys in his syndicate.

Naturally, I stand first-class with all the Jerries who are in on the play and they also become more pleasant toward my comrades, and finally I tell these comrades what is going on and while they are greatly amused I can see that they are also greatly relieved, because it seems they are troubled by my nightly absences from the camp and are glad to learn that it is only for the purpose of playing gin with the enemy.

At the end of the month and basing my estimate on around ten thousand marks I have stashed away, I figure I am forty thousand marks winner on Kunz. Then one night I beat him for a thousand marks and he does not

whip it out as usual but says something in German to
Schultz, and Schultz tells me the captain says he forgets
his wallet somewhere, and I say all right, but that it is only
fair for him to give me a scratch for the dough.

Schultz translates this to the captain, who looks very
angry and seems to be highly insulted, but finally he outs
with a notebook and scribbles an I.O.U., because, of course,
at this stage of my life I am not trusting anyone and especially a Nazi.

He settles the next night before we start playing, but he
takes a good bath this time and gives me the finger again,
and while he comes alive the following night, this continues to happen again and again, and something tells me
that Kunz is troubled with the shorts. When I mention this
suspicion to Schultz, he seems a trifle uneasy and finally he
says:

"Well, Lace," he says, "I fear you are right. I fear our
good captain is in over his head. To tell the truth, your
game is commencing to bore me and the other soldiers of
the Fatherland no little because the captain borrows money
from us every day, which is a terrible thing for a high
officer to do to the soldiers of his command and, while you
win it back for us promptly, we now fear he will never
replace the principal."

"Why, Schultz," I say, "do you not tell me that the
captain is richer than six feet down in Mississippi mud?"

"Yes," Schultz says, "and he keeps talking of his proper-
ties in Berlin, but we are nonetheless uneasy. And the worst
thing about it is that your twenty-five per cent is eating
up all the funds in circulation. It is a vicious circle. Lace,"
Schultz says, "can you spare me a couple of thou? I must
send something to my frau and I will repay you when the
boats get to running again."

"Schultz," I say, "your story smacks of corn because I
do not believe you have a wife and, if you do have one,

you will never be sending her money. But," I say, "I will advance you a thousand marks for old times' sake on your marker."

So I weed him the thousand and accept his Kathleen Mavourneen, which is a promise to pay that may be for years and may be forever, and the reason I do this is because I am by no means certain that Schultz may not incite his fellow soldiers to gang up and deprive me of my hard-earned twenty-five per cent by force, if he can find out where I have it carefully buried. To tell the truth, I do not repose great confidence in Schultz.

Well, that night I beat Kunz for twelve hundred marks, and he pays me five hundred on account, and as Schultz and I are getting ready to leave, he says something in German to Schultz, and when we are on our way back to camp, Schultz tells me he has to return to the house and see the captain, and then I really commence to worry because I fear the two may get their heads together and plot against my well-being.

But as far as Captain Kunz is concerned, my worry is groundless as along toward noon of this same day, we hear a rumor that he commits suicide by shooting himself smack-dab through the head and this causes so much excitement that our guards forget to lock us in that night or even to watch us carefully, and all of us Americans and some of the British walk out of the gates and scatter over the countryside, and most of us reach safety in Switzerland, and I afterwards hear there is quite a scandal in German circles about the matter.

But before we go, I have a slight chat with Schultz and say to him like this:

"Schultz," I say, "tell me all."

"Well," Schultz says, "I know that when the captain asks me to return to the house after taking you back to camp, he wishes to borrow the money I get from you to play you again tonight, because when I tell him yesterday I am personally broke and cannot advance him any more, he is the one who suggests I approach you for a touch and in fact he threatens to make trouble for me over certain matters that transpire in Poland if I fail to do so.

"So," Schultz says, "when I reach the house, I first peer through a window into the living room and see the captain still sitting at the table with the deck of cards you use spread out before him as if he is examining them, and all of a sudden, I am seized with a terrible fury at the thought that he is waiting there to take my money to gamble it away frivolously, and an impulse that I cannot restrain causes me to out with my pistol and give it to him through the window and also through the onion.

"And," Schultz says, "I will always remember how the blood drips down off the table and splatters over the nine of diamonds that is lying on the floor under your chair and how it comes to my mind that the nine of diamonds is considered a very unlucky card indeed and how fortune-tellers say it is a sign of death. It is a great coincidence," Schultz says, "considering the number of times you catch the captain with big counts in his hands when he is waiting for that very nine."

"Ah," I say, "I figure you have something to do with his demise."

"But," Schultz says, "as far as anyone but you and me know, it is suicide because I also have the presence of mind to fire one shot from his pistol which is the same make as mine, and leave it in his hand. It is suicide because of despondency, which his superior officers say is probably because he learns of his impending purge."

"Schultz," I say, "you are bound to come to a bad end, but now goodby."

"Goodby," Schultz says. "Oh, yes," he says. "Maybe I ought to state that I am also prompted to my act by the fear that the captain will finally find the nine of diamonds on the floor, that you forget to retrieve when you leave him this morning."

"What do you mean, Schultz?" I say.

"Goodby," Schultz says.

And this is all there is to the story (The Lacework Kid says).

"Well, Lace," I say, "it is all very exciting, and it must be nice to be back on Broadway as free as the birds and with all that moolouw you collect as your twenty-five per cent in your pants pockets."

"Oh," Lace says, "I do not return with a white quarter. You see I use all my end to bribe Schultz and the rest of the German soldiers to leave the doors and gates unlocked that night and to be looking the other way when we depart."

Then The Lacework Kid leaves, and I am sitting there finishing my boiled yellow pike, which is a very tasty dish, indeed, and thinking about the captain's blood dripping on the nine of diamonds, when who comes up but old Kidneyfoot the waiter, who is called by this name because he walks as if he has kidneys in both feet and who points to Lace going out the door and says to me like this:

"Well," Kidneyfoot says, "there goes a great artist. He is one of the finest card players I ever see except in gin rummy. It is strange how this simple game baffles all good card players. In fact," Kidneyfoot says, "The Lacework Kid is a rank sucker at gin until I instruct him in one small maneuver that gives you a great advantage, which is to drop any one card to the floor accidentally on purpose."

🌱 🌱 🌱